Readers love the
Sinners Series by RHYS FORD

Sinner's Gin

"This is a sexy, fast-paced, hurt/comfort, murder mystery with… scorching hot sexy times!"

eviews

Whiskey and W

"It's one thing ⎯⎯ ⎰ level of talent to w ⎯⎯⎯ ⎰s delivers."

⎯rter, *USA Today*

Tequila Mock⎰ ⎰

"The author has done it again with a complex intriguing story line that explodes from the beginning and never slows down…"

—Guilty Indulgence Romance Reviews

Sloe Ride

"*Sloe Ride* is rife with mystery and intrigue. If you're looking for unconventional characters and action, Rhys Ford's books would be a perfect match for you."

—Fresh Fiction

Absinthe of Malice

"It made me laugh, it made me angry, it made me irritated and at times, I was gutted. But in the end… it made me smile and be grateful I got to go on this journey with the guys."

—The Novel Approach

By Rhys Ford

Published by DREAMSPINNER PRESS
www.dreamspinnerpress.com

RHYS FORD

SIN AND TONIC

Published by
DREAMSPINNER PRESS

5032 Capital Circle SW, Suite 2, PMB# 279,
Tallahassee, FL 32305-7886 USA
www.dreamspinnerpress.com

This is a work of fiction. Names, characters, places, and incidents either are the product of author imagination or are used fictitiously, and any resemblance to actual persons, living or dead, business establishments, events, or locales is entirely coincidental.

Sin and Tonic
© 2018, 2020 Rhys Ford

Cover Art
© 2018, 2020 Reece Notley
reece@vitaenoir.com
Cover content is for illustrative purposes only and any person depicted on the cover is a model.

Digital ISBN: 978-1-64080-623-8
Mass Market Paperback ISBN: 978-1-64108-065-1
Trade Paperback ISBN: 978-1-64080-624-5
Library of Congress Control Number: 2017919626
Mass Market Paperback published February 2020
v. 1.0

Printed in the United States of America
∞
This paper meets the requirements of
ANSI/NISO Z39.48-1992 (Permanence of Paper).

This book is dedicated to every band I've ever listened to. From Hyde to Metallica, from Big Bang to Stevie Ray Vaughan, from Aerosmith to the Four Horsemen to Testament to Ministry to AC/DC and Dong Bang Shin Ki… you all have kept me company throughout this series and will continue to keep me grounded as I go forward. Please know every crappy gig was worth it because you've brought joy—and some tears—to countless lives.

Lisa — Connor is now yours. Please keep him safe.

Mary — Dude, you've already got Cole and Jae. You've gotta share.

E — I could really use that bobbing pool. This one killed me.

And for everyone who's picked up a Sinners book and continued on their journey with me, thank you. Seriously, thank you. You, like the bands I love, bring me so much damned joy. And in the immortal words of a band from Down Under, I salute you.

ACKNOWLEDGMENTS

THIS IS my… God, I don't know what number I'm on… book, but as always, there is the Five. There will always be the Five. Smooches and love to Tamm, Lea, Jenn, and Penny. Because you know, the Five.

A special hug and thanks to my other sisters, Ree, Ren, Lisa, and Mary. And I also want to shout out to the San Diego Crewe of Steve, Maite, Andy, and Felix. God, it's been a long ride.

Miki and Kane and the rest of the Sinners cast wouldn't be here without Dreamspinner, so much love and gratitude to Elizabeth, Lynn, Grace and her editing crew, Naomi, Jaime, and everyone else who delves into my sticky messes of novels. Thank you.

To everyone else, I encourage you to try new bands… listen to them… stretch yourself out and revel in the voices and sounds we have around us. You never know where you might find your own brand of Gin.

That is, up until a few seconds ago when Miki discovered, to his amazement, pain was a greater monster than any death ever could be.

Today, pain came in the form of a forty-year-old Vietnamese woman with long, silver-streaked black hair and a face life gouged out with a hard awl. The lines on her face so deeply etched into her skin, a heavy rain would pour rivers from her jowls. Her pallor was stark, the slate gray of the sky over an icy Bay, but her cheeks ran florid with angry lesions, red constellations of flaking skin and puckering scabs. Her tongue darted across her lips, a gecko-quick daub over cracked fissures. One corner of her mouth was puffed up, or at least it appeared to be. It was difficult to tell from where Miki and Kane were standing, their view filtered through a curtain of palm fronds and mist from a nearby sprinkler. The green-yellow fans couldn't obscure her bright clothing, a too tight, too short wrap of spandex and large eye-bleeding flowers on a sea of pink.

Miki knew Kane well enough to know that his cop was assessing the woman, judging her appearance, and every once in a while, sneaking a glance in Miki's direction as if to check to see if he was holding up. His cop was a massive block of Celtic warrior, a slab of granite carved from a mountain who taught Kane how to be a man. He didn't know how the woman could miss the blue-eyed, black haired Celtic warrior barely hidden behind a row of ornamental foliage, but then, Miki supposed, it could've just been him. His eyes always searched the shadows for Kane—hell, he searched the light for him too—there was something about his Irish cop that both calmed him down and fired him up.

Miki ached for Kane like he ached for music.

Unfortunately, he'd stopped aching for music, but his desire for Kane stayed steady and strong.

"How good are you at reading lips?" Miki strained to see around the cement planter, disliking the hitch in his hip when he shifted his weight from one foot to another. "I can't… I can see her talking but I can't figure out what she's saying. We should have had Edie open her phone line or something so I could listen in."

Kane's midnight gaze flicked over Miki's face, an amused grin teasing at the corner of his mouth. As he turned his attention back to the women standing near one of the garden's tall cement signs, his sexy, whiskey-amber voice purred with hints of rolling emerald hills and ancient myths, "And here you say you don't think like a cop. That was a very cop thing to say, Mick. If it weren't against the law."

"Well, if I've picked up anything cop-like, I got it from your father." Miki sneered. "Considering he's the only real cop I know."

"I'll be reminding you of those very words later on tonight when I have you in bed and I've got a pair of handcuffs nearby."

"Is that supposed to scare me?" Miki jabbed Kane in the ribs. "For some of us, we just call it Tuesday."

The words were out of his mouth before Miki could stop them—before he could actually *hear* them—and the stab of pain in Kane's expression dug out what little guilt he had in his soul. Joking about sex was something the band did on the road, something the group fell into, a sideshow banter about the hard life they lived slogging music and their equipment across the blacktop and the stage. It said something about how far he'd come—the teasing of Kane—and how little he picked at the scabs in his psyche or contemplated the scars on his soul.

"I didn't mean—" Kane started to say but closed his mouth when Miki shook his head. "I didn't think. I just—"

Everyone close to Miki knew his body had been a plaything for men with little regard for him other than to be their toy. But Kane—his righteous, slightly off-white knight—had seen Miki at his lowest, at his least human. Kane had not only seen Miki's nightmares captured by a flash of the camera and a spot of film, but still dealt with the aftermath of those memories.

"You don't have to watch your words with me, K," Miki reassured his lover. "Damie says shit all the time and I don't jump down his throat. It's just words. And if ever you actually wanted to use a pair of handcuffs, you'd tell me so I'd have a chance to tell you *fuck off and die* or *sure, just don't lose the key*. Because if there's one thing that I am *not* ever going to live through, it's calling up one of your sibs to unlock my wrist from our bed."

"The siblings I can handle," Kane growled. "It's the parents—Brigid—that I'm scared of. She'd skin me alive."

And just because he knew Kane would shudder at the thought, Miki said softly, "Dude, you don't think your dad's used his cuffs on your mom? She's got eight kids. Probably wants to change things up every once in a while, you know?"

"Thank you for that. There isn't enough bleach in San Francisco to get that thought out of my head." Kane made a noise that sounded like Miki's dog swallowing a fly, and Miki smirked with satisfaction when Kane's shoulders actually shook. "Now, if ever I do lose a handcuff key and you're involved, I'm just going to leave you there. And no, I can't tell what they're saying. Next time we do something like this, I want to make Edie wear a wire. As illegal as it is, I'm wishing we'd done *something*."

Miki snorted. "How the fuck many women do you think are going to come out of the gutter and say they knew my mother? Only reason I'm giving this one the time of day is because Edie said she sounded legit."

If Crossroads Gin was Miki's salvation, then Edie, their manager, was the mother of all things. She was a sharp-faced woman with a cutting manner only softened by her affection for the young men she herded and cared for. He'd not liked her when he first met Edie across a long conference table in a room at their record studio's main building. She'd been aggressive, brash, and stood toe-to-toe with Damien, arguing about percentages and copyrights until the lead guitarist's British accent was so thick with fury, Miki expected the fog to roll in and the coffee in his mug to turn to tea. Just as Damien was about to walk out of the door, Edie's manner gentled and her tone shifted.

"Now do you understand why you need me?" she'd said to the shocked band members. "You just lost an argument with the person who is willing to go to the mat for you. Imagine how far you'll get when you go head-to-head with somebody who wants to bleed you dry? Now, sit your ass down on the chair, Mitchell, and we can get down to making sure you hold on to every penny the four of you earn, and I am only going to charge you five percent to do it."

Through Sinner's Gin's rise and then death, Edie was Miki's rock. She'd been with him as he struggled to walk and battled every lawyer Damien's family threw at him, bloodsucking leeches hoping to turn a quick buck on Damien's corpse. When Damien returned, alive despite a lie his family concocted to bilk his estate, Edie donned her armor once again, ensuring their assets—and lives—were secure. It had been a no-brainer to ask her to manage the new band, but when she came to the final show of its Resurrection Tour, she'd brought with her a revelation—news of a ghost Miki never knew haunted him—and a woman who said she knew Miki's mother.

When they agreed to meet the woman at the Yerba Buena Gardens, Edie cautioned him to remain at home. Her arguments were sound, but Miki needed to see the face of the one person who'd come forward about the woman who'd carried him but hadn't kept him.

"Hey, look." His cop jerked his chin toward the women. "She's handing Edie something."

From what Miki could see, it was one of those padded envelopes he often got ordering things online, its oddly unique but familiar brown-yellow surface wrinkled and grimy. It looked old, beat-up around the edges, and torn at the top instead of cut open, but Edie handled it as if it were treasure, carefully taking it from the woman's hands and glancing into its depths.

Kane was moving before Miki realized his cop was no longer next to him. His lover's hands were on him, moving him. Miki's shoulders were turned then the sky tilted, slivers of blue dotted with clouds turning into a kaleidoscope through the leaves above them. The pops were loud, echoing booms Miki knew all too well. The screaming began nearly the moment Miki's knee gave and he struck the ground, Kane's heavy body stretched out over him.

It was a hellish agony when Miki struggled to get out from under his lover's prostrate body. Kane's forearms were up, covering Miki's face, smearing dirt and debris into his mouth, but Miki couldn't see, couldn't tell if Kane had been hit. His world became a single moment, turning only when he felt Kane's chest rise against his belly, and then the voice that murmured sweet, filthy things into his ears during sex told him to stay down.

Everything happened so fast—the gunfire, the shouting, and then the squeal of brakes coming from the road. Miki heard sobbing, but he was too concerned about running his hands over Kane's sides, feeling for any bit of wetness or, worse, injury he couldn't heal with a kiss. His panic must have shown on his face because Kane brushed his mouth over Miki's lips, then rolled off him.

"Are you hit?" Kane barked, startling the shock from Miki's belly. "Tell me you're okay."

"I'm fine. Edie—" But Kane stood before Miki could say another word.

"Stay here," Kane ordered as he scrambled toward where the women met. "*Call 911.*"

And then he was gone, taking his warmth and comfort with him.

Kane's long legs easily ate up the distance between the planter and where Edie lay on the ground. Her pristine, sunflower-bright power suit now bore bloodied poppies across her side and arms. A few feet away, the woman he'd watched through the palms was sprawled against the cement monolith with its maps and directions splattered with her blood. Her eyes were open, her jaw slack, and the bullet wounds on her stomach made a polka-dot mess of her clothing, but it was the shattered remains of her forehead that shocked Miki into moving.

Kane was two hundred pounds of muscle and bone, but he moved like a shark through still water, cutting through the stream of people running away from the road and into the surrounding buildings.

"*Edie*!" Miki wasn't as fast as Kane, but he was going to be damned if he didn't get to Edie's side.

There were already sirens in the air, drowning out the crowd's murmuring shock and startled cries. Miki caught his foot on the pylon or maybe one of the stones used to decorate the mulch surrounding the trees and the palms, but he ignored the hit of pain in his hip, scaling the wide staircase to do what he could.

It was hard to kneel, but it was even harder to hold Edie's hand as her life poured out of her. Something dug into his knee, finding the one too-tender spot he never seemed to be able to heal. He shoved the envelope aside, jerking his head up when Kane hissed at him.

"Don't touch that. It's evidence." His lover's eyes were hard, stony bits of blue marbled with an arrogant authority with no tolerance for argument. "If you're going to be here, press down on her wounds. Ambulances are going to be here soon. Stay with her. I've got to see if anybody else was hurt. There's a couple people down by the sidewalk."

"This is *Edie*," Miki spat. He didn't know where the rage came from or, rather, maybe he did. She was a connection to his past, a life he built with her and then cobbled back together when it fell apart. "Don't you fucking walk away from her. I *need* you. *She* needs you."

The smile he got from Kane was resigned and bittersweet, and Miki had to blink away his tears to see it. Kane's fingers brushed Miki's jaw, then ran through his wind-tangled hair, pulling away before Miki could lean into his lover's touch.

"I know you'll take care of her, babe." Kane's whisper dug down deep into Miki's love for him, hooking into every thread of every moment they'd shared. "She'll be all right, but I have to go. This is what I do. I'm a cop, Mick, I *have* to go."

IT WAS never a good thing when Captain Book called one of his inspectors into his office. Even worse when Casey, their lieutenant, was waiting with him. Book was a congenial man, someone who worked to be approachable, the kind of captain a police officer felt comfortable talking to, even when washing their hands and standing side by side in the bathroom. Kane liked and respected the man nearly as much as he respected his own father, so when his partner, Kel, tapped Kane on the shoulder and jerked his head toward the captain's office, Kane would never have thought in a million years he would be standing in the middle of the greatest ass chewing in his life as soon as he walked through the door.

"What were you thinking, Morgan?" The beefy man's snarl was ferocious, years of riding a desk hardly putting a dent in the street-tough cop who'd been dragged up from one of the worst neighborhoods in Los Angeles. "The DA tells me he thinks you were there for a sting of some kind and that rock star you sleep with is ass-deep in it. Tell me you weren't there doing something sketchy."

"No hard feelings, Morgan," Casey assured him, patting him on the shoulder. "Internal Affairs isn't looking at you, and I sure as hell don't want you at a desk, but the DA is pushing it. I might not have a choice if they go up the chain of command."

"I *am* the damned chain of command." Book slapped at his desk, nearly upending a wire basket of pens. He caught it before it spilled, righting it with a scowl on his face. "If the DA wants a fight, I'll be more than happy to give it to that bastard. He's not going to take one of my cops off the streets because he needs to show he's tough on anyone wearing a badge. Just explain to me, Kane, what you were doing there, and make sure that none of it includes an undercover operation I knew nothing about."

"It wasn't a sting or anything undercover," Kane replied. "Do you think I would take St. John with me on something like that? His manager was meeting with a woman, one who said she had information about St. John's mother. She'd been in contact with his management company, and they'd arranged to meet at the gardens. St. John wanted to be there, but his manager cautioned him to remain behind until she had more information."

"So why didn't he stay home? If she told him she didn't want him there, why was he there?" Casey asked. "He was setting himself up for a confrontation, or worse, her attacking him."

"Because the surefire way to get Miki St. John to do something is to tell him he shouldn't," he informed his superior officers, unable to keep a grin off his face, but he sobered up quickly when Book shot him a hard look. "It was supposed to be a simple meet. She was coming with the packet that was recovered on the scene and anecdotal evidence of her connection to St. John's mother. At the most, we expected her to shake down the manager for money, precisely the reason St. John shouldn't have been there."

"Stop calling him St. John. We all know who he is. It's one thing to be formal when you're giving a report, but it's another thing entirely when you're talking about the guy you go home to every night," his captain interjected. "The manager? That's the survivor, right?"

"Yes, sir. She took a shot to the ribs, which deflected into her abdomen. She's in surgery right now, but I was assured by the hospital she will be okay. I'm hoping that once she regains consciousness, I'll be able to question her about—"

"You're not going anywhere near her, Morgan," Casey cut him off. "One, you're too close to the case. Two, we still haven't decided if you are going to be placed on administrative leave."

"I've decided." Book leaned back in his chair, nestling his shoulders into its padded leather cushion. "Morgan isn't going to ride a desk, not if I have anything to say about it. We are already overloaded and down three inspectors this week. There's a dead woman in the morgue with sketchy identification and nothing on her but a manila envelope of photos and a couple of letters. You were on the scene, tell me what happened. Was the shooter random and they were caught in the cross-fire spray, or was the manager targeted? Did it look like the woman signaled to someone?"

"No, she was fully engaged with Edie, the manager. The victim wasn't looking at the road; her left side was facing the street and I could see her face." Kane distanced himself from the turbulent emotions he'd been suppressing since he first heard the gunfire and shoved Miki to the ground, praying nothing struck the man he loved. Thinking back on what he saw, he parsed out the woman's expressions and body language. "She was aggressive, a little pushy, and if I had to guess, she was trying to get something out of Edie, either money or maybe she wanted to talk to Miki. I didn't get a chance to talk to either of them and, well, listening in on the conversation could have potentially been sticky. The meet happened quickly. I only got notification about it about half an hour before it happened."

"Did St. John know?" Book asked. "Does he know the woman's name?"

"He might. I don't know if Edie shared it with him. Up until she knocked on our front door, he was adamant about not having a damned thing to do with getting into contact with the woman. I think Edie pressed it because she said she had things to give to him, things from his mother." Kane looked down at his hands, surprised to see speckles of blood along his knuckles. "They might've talked before, but he didn't want—no, he refused—to even consider meeting with her."

"Then why did he?" Casey straightened, getting up from his perch on the credenza against the office's long wall. "Why did he change his mind? And why did you go with him?"

"Because Edie said please. And after everything he's been through with her, Miki will do anything if it is something she feels strongly about. He was found in the middle of the street—on St. John—covered in bruises, wearing a dirty diaper, and some asshole had put a tattoo on his arm. He wasn't even three years old and someone tossed him out like he was trash." Kane squared his shoulders, looked his lieutenant straight in the eye. "To answer your question, I went because I love him, and I'm never going to send him out to face his monsters without me standing right next to him. As long as I have breath in my body, I'm going to be there."

CHAPTER TWO

Quinn: Rafe, ever consider marriage?
Rafe: Like to each other?
Quinn: Sort of. I mean, everyone seems
to be getting married, but I don't
know if it's for me. Or for you. It
seems... weird.
Rafe: Works for your mom and dad. Works
for a lot of people. Guess it comes
down to if you need to be married.
Quinn: Do you?
Rafe: I wouldn't say no if you were ask-
ing. I happen to like doing weird
with you. It's kind of our thing.
—Lazy afternoon on the couch, Harley
on Rafe's feet

THE BAYSIDE warehouse was still standing when
Kane rolled up. A single light was on, a sliver of gold

peeking through the slit in the curtains hung across the front windows. It was hard to believe it had only been a few years since Miki's godforsaken terrier broke into his woodworking studio, stole a valuable piece of koa, and brought the irascible, sexy singer into Kane's life. Climbing down from his Hummer, Kane wondered what lay in wait for him behind the warehouse's front door. He was tired, fatigued to his marrow, but he knew he was probably going into one of the few times he and Miki would fight.

"Maybe Mick will be rational," Kane muttered, willing his hand to turn the doorknob. He never thought of his brain as sarcastic, but the echoing laughter bouncing off the inside of his skull somehow didn't surprise him. "Might as well get this over with."

The living room was empty.

And so was the kitchen at the far end of the warehouse.

It was an open sight line, the long space only divided by a kitchen peninsula the interior designer enthusiastically saw doubling as a casual eating area. The long dining room table set between the nest of sectionals in the living space rarely saw a meal on it. Instead it was home to a collection of guitar parts, sheet music, and a couple of ratty tennis balls Kane occasionally found in his sneakers.

He wasn't sure what the warehouse originally had been other than a brick structure with cement floors and sweeping arches, but now it was home. With half its space on the lower floor dedicated to the main living areas and the formal dining room now converted to the master bedroom he shared with Miki, it was comfortable, a retreat from the day-to-day business of dealing with mankind's casual evil.

At least it was comfortable when Miki was around.

"Well, he's probably upstairs on the roof." Kane put away his weapon, locking up the gun he carried on his hip. Dude, Miki's dog, was nowhere to be found on the main floor, but since the front door hadn't been locked—something he talked to Miki about until he was blue in the face—he didn't think his lover had gone roaming through the city. "Question is, do I take a beer with me? Or a bottle of whiskey for both of us to share?"

Kane took a bottle of Hibiki 21 with him.

The rooftop deck with its open wooden pergola and thick canopy covered the mounds of pillows forming Miki's sanctuary. It had started off small, like most things in Miki's life, then grew to form a shelter away from the bustle of living going on downstairs. Kane put the covering up so San Francisco's unpredictable weather was kept off his lover's space, and another large deck had been built by the access door, a home for a grill, wet bar, and enough seating for two baseball teams—or one Irish cop family. He'd been able to talk Miki into letting him install an outhouse of sorts, just a toilet and a sink, so no one had to go downstairs to use the bathroom, but when it was all said and done, the rooftop with its incredible view of San Francisco Bay and Chinatown was Miki's domain.

In the couple of years Kane had called the warehouse home, he still hadn't gotten used to its opulent view of the city. Tucked into a steep drop-off with Russian Hill on one side and a vibrant Asian community on the other, the structure's roof was the perfect perch for an evening of night gazing. Behind them and to the right, Chinatown rarely slept. It murmured even late at night, its flashes of neon and savory aromas creeping over the rooftop's short protective wall, but it was the view of the water and its embellishments of light that took Kane's breath away.

He loved the city he was raised in as much as he loved the green-hilled countryside owned by the Morgans and Finnegans back in Ireland. Coming up to the roof was like seeing an old family friend his parents told him to take with a grain of salt, a familiar but intriguing personality he would never get tired of.

Much like his Mick.

But also like his Mick, the city held threads of darkness he could never seem to heal, and where in Miki he could encourage the exploration of his pain in the hopes of the singer finding some peace, San Francisco demanded he abrade its evil from its streets, taking the worst of its shadows and hopefully leaving room for its brightest lights.

The woman with Edie—a dead woman with another woman's name on her lips—shouldn't have died today. He'd been prepared for all sorts of things where she was concerned: extortion, blackmail, even catfishing, not death. Not murder. Even as he mentally girded himself for battle, he knew he was carrying that woman with him and would continue to shoulder her until he found out who extinguished her light.

"Let's just hope the love of my life and the scourge of my existence feels the same way," Kane muttered, hefting the whiskey. "Not like he didn't know I was a cop before he signed up for this ride."

Dude let out a halfhearted woof when Kane opened the rooftop door, but other than a bit of a thump of a tail against a paisley pillow, the small sand-colored terrier didn't move. Miki, however, was a different story.

The fairy lights strung under the pergola's beams sparkled a soft firefly-like glow over Miki's tall, sprawled body. His hazel eyes were nearly obsidian under the shadow of his shaggy brown mane, but Kane could see the suspicion and anger lingering in their depths. He expected a snarl, or at least a sarcastic rejoinder, but Miki remained silent, watching Kane as he approached.

It was always difficult to reconcile himself with the fact he was in love with—was the love of—the magnificent, complicated feral creature that was Miki St. John. The lead singer of a tragic and now resurrected band had been a constant and ignored presence in the Morgan household, especially since his youngest sister wallpapered her room with Sinner's Gin posters, so Kane knew he'd seen the man's beautiful face more than a few times before their first meeting. It'd taken him a bit to connect the man who couldn't control his thieving dog with the rock star plastered on his sibling's walls, but by the time he had, Kane was pretty certain he'd already gotten hung up on the guy.

He'd never known that rock star. Instead, he knew the musician and the man with a haunting past and sad eyes. Kane was there to catch Miki when his childhood abusers were found murdered and held him up when Damien, the man he called brother, returned from the dead. They'd been through a lot in the short time they'd been together, and now it looked as if they needed to go through a little bit more.

"I brought the whiskey." Kane held up the Hibiki's distinctive bottle. "I'm ready for my ass chewing. But just to warn you, I might chew back."

Moving the dog proved to be more problematic than Kane expected, and he had to get around Miki's acoustic guitar. The singer wasn't doing much to help him, just watching with his hooded eyes and feline-flat expression. Kane wasn't sure what was worse, Miki's hot anger or his cold rage. The cushions let out a puff of air as he settled into them. Then Dude decided Kane's legs were his personal heater, and he snuggled his slightly grimy furry body against Kane's thigh.

"So on a scale of one to volcano, how pissed off are you?" Kane asked, unstoppering the whiskey. He took a sip of it, enjoying the sting in his throat and the numbness of the back of his tongue, then swallowed. Holding the bottle out, he suppressed a relieved smile when Miki took it from him. "Are we arguing tonight or are we talking? And before we get started, where's your brother and my cousin?"

"D and Sionn took a drive over to Half Moon Bay. Something about a grunion run, which is bullshit because it's not time for that. Pretty sure they just want to fuck on the beach." The swig Miki took was longer than Kane's, and when his tongue darted out to lick the drops on his lower lip, Kane longed to chase it back into Miki's mouth. He would've if he didn't fear getting bitten. "We're not going to argue. Not going to lie to you, I was planning on coming home and tossing your shit out onto the driveway 'cause I was that pissed, but Dad—Donal—talked me down.

"I guess I forget you're a cop sometimes. Don't know how 'cause you might as well tattoo a badge on top of your forehead, but I do," he remarked in a voice so soft Kane nearly couldn't hear him. "I think I was more scared and hurt. Because it was Edie lying there and there wasn't anything I could do. I fucking hate being helpless. And I just guess… I needed you to do something, I don't know what, but *something*. That's not like me. I don't *need* people to do things for me, but today I did. And you couldn't. So I've got to get over that. Something like that happens and you've got to be a cop first, and Kane second. I forgot that, but Dad helped me see that."

"So we're okay, then?" There was a bit of satisfaction at hearing Miki call Donal *Dad*. Kane wasn't going to mention it because he knew discussing some things was best done in the middle of the night while it was dark and they were in bed next to each other. Miki needed the dark to talk, an odd quirk Kane hadn't quite figured out but was willing to accept. "If I had a choice, I would have stayed there with you, but I had faith you would take care of Edie while I saw to everyone else. I came back as soon as I could."

"I know." The tiny sparkles above them played with the sensual angles of Miki's face. "When are they going to give me back the package? The cop that took my statement said they might not hand it over because there's no proof that it's mine."

"It was in Edie's possession and, well, in this case that nine tenths of the law rule makes it hers. Book said that if they can't get it released from evidence, they will document what's inside and share with us. Providing everyone involved isn't an asshole and lets us. I checked in on her before I came home, and the nurse in charge said she was sleeping peacefully. She might be a bit groggy tomorrow." He moved Miki's guitar, sitting it gently into a stand near a post. "Did Edie tell you the woman's name? I haven't caught up on the reports to see if it's in there. Planned on doing it tomorrow morning."

His lover was a bit tense, his shoulders taut and challenging, but Kane could read the expression on

Miki's face. He needed to be held, and despite the low-grade grumbling, Miki fit into the curve of Kane's arm, then settled against his side. Laying his head on Kane's shoulder, Miki stared into the sky, his long lashes throwing shadows over his cheeks, and not for the first time, Kane wondered about the secrets Edie'd had in her hand when she'd been shot.

"She said it was Sandy Chai-something. Um, I wasn't paying a lot of attention." Miki's mouth twisted, then he bit his lower lip. Reaching over, he scratched at Dude's upturned belly and the dog stretched, burying his nose into the pillows. "I really didn't want to know—about *her*—my mother. The only reason I went was because I didn't want Edie to go alone. And she wasn't going to let this go. I guess it would help if they knew who I really was, legally, you know? The lawyers *made* me. The state of California gave me an ID number, but I didn't exist, not really. I didn't have a birth certificate or anything that proved I even existed. They don't know if I was born here or where I came from. I mean, look at me. There's a pretty good chance I'm not even American.

"I've just fought so fucking hard to survive, and I can't look at someone erasing who I am. If they take away me being Miki St. John, then what do I have left?" Miki's voice hitched, and he swallowed. "My mother wasn't real until today, and now a woman who says she'd been friends with her is dead and I still don't know anything more about her than I did when I woke up this morning. All I've got is more questions, and a woman who I like a lot and who's gone to bat for me more times than I can count is in a hospital because she felt like I needed to know who gave me up."

"You have a birth certificate and a passport," Kane pointed out, stroking Miki's side. Hitching up Miki's shirt, Kane found the skin beneath warm to his touch. Miki shivered a bit at the touch of cold but let Kane continue his caress. "I don't think they can take away who you are, and if anyone tries, you know we'll fight them."

"Thing is, K," Miki whispered, "I'm sick to death of fighting them. I'm sick to death of fighting me. I'm tired inside. Some days I just want to stay in bed and never go back outside. The only thing keeping me from doing that is that you wouldn't be there with me."

DOCTOR HORAN was a familiar, friendly face Kane usually saw over a dead body. Today was no exception. He just wished there weren't so many dead bodies and they would catch up every once in a while at the biannual cops' picnic. The slender, stalwart blonde was one of the best medical examiners he'd ever worked with, and over the years he'd learned exactly how to get on her good side at nine o'clock in the morning.

Armed with a venti skinny vanilla latte, a chocolate croissant, and a pound of peanut M&M's for later that afternoon, he strolled into the morgue prepared to beg, borrow, and steal any time she might have to spare to jumpstart his case, his partner and best friend, Kel Sanchez, ambling along beside him.

The morgue was, as always, a cold, hard place to walk into. At first glance, the place was starkly professional and edged with clean lines, resembling more of a futuristic R&D think tank than the first place a corpse stopped on its journey toward its final rest. The dead were all that mattered here, and none of the staff, as far as Kane knew, cut corners when chasing down answers to questions most people hated to ask. There was a bit of the macabre humor often found on crime scenes dotting the walls and desks, little mementos reminding the living that death came for them all. He smiled at the plastic skull vase filled with pink daisies but sobered when he thought of the number of times he'd gone through the double doors at the end of the hall.

He'd started his day early, rolling out of bed before the sun thought about kissing the city's horizon, and even the dog hadn't been willing to go outside to go to the bathroom by the time Kane had his first cup of coffee. He'd left Dude asleep on the still warm bed and kissed what he'd hoped was the top of Miki's head under the mound of blankets tucked against the far wall.

Kane was going to probably end his day the same way, moving aside a sleeping dog and digging Miki out of the blankets so he could kiss him good night.

"No woman is going to want M&M's this early in the morning, Morgan." Kel flirted with a teasing smile at one of the residents walking by. The woman rolled her eyes, obviously used to Kel's ways, but her snort was more amusement than disgust. "Is that how you smooth things over with Miki? Candy? And it's not even good candy. If you'd been serious, you would have gotten Godiva's."

"We're in San Francisco, asshole," Kane shot back. "It's Ghirardelli's here, remember? And just you watch, *boyo*, I know what I'm about."

"You just think you can serve up anything you want in that *look-at-me-Lucky-Charms* accent of yours and you can get away with stealing the moon." Kel sipped at his coffee, then blew at the tiny opening in the lid. "Damn, this shit is hot. I'm telling you, I called ahead. They're stacked knees to armpits in dead bodies. There's no way in hell we're jumping the line."

"A package of M&M's says you're wrong," Kane replied, rattling the bag. "I don't want anything other than verification of ID. I've got a name, but I don't want to go off half-cocked in this. Not with Book holding back the DA's office for me. He just handed me the case to piss them off, but we step wrong in this and he's going to have our heads. We get ID verified, and then we'll start asking questions."

"I've got one question." Kel nudged him with his elbow. "Is the case we're working on that woman's murder or are we going to go looking for St. John's mother? Because my gut tells me we might be starting off with the first but we're going to end up with the second."

"I don't know if he wants her found," Kane admitted, shouldering the morgue's door open and holding it so Kel could go by. "But if she turns up—dead or alive—that's going to be for him to deal with. I just got to make sure he doesn't fall apart while doing it."

It turned out Kane didn't have to beg. The pleasant-faced doctor stood over the woman's body while an assistant took photos. Horan looked up when the inspectors entered, her eyes lighting up behind her face shield at the sight of either the coffee or the M&M's. Pulling off her gloves, she strode over to the cordoned-off area where morgue visitors were allowed to stand. After tucking her gloves into her pocket and putting her face shield on a rolling stainless steel table, she took the coffee from Kane's outstretched hand and murmured a soft litany of thanks.

"If those M&M's and whatever is in that bag are for me, you can put them on the table next to you. And if they aren't, whatever you want isn't ever going to happen," she teased. "You don't walk into my lab with a bag like that if they're not mine. That's just not right."

"They're yours. The other's a *pain au chocolat*. I brought them hoping I could get you to look at the woman you've got on the slab right now." Kane set the bags down. "Bribes are still yours."

"I don't call them bribes, I refer to them as gifts I sometimes share with my staff as a thank you from the SFPD for jobs well done." She eyed the M&M's. "Except for those. The yellow bag is mine. As to your gun-shot victim, she's connected to another case that came in—or may be connected—I'll leave it to your side of the wall to figure it out."

Putting the coffee down, Horan picked up a tablet, then keyed in her password to unlock the screen. Kane could see the report she pulled up was only half filled, but enough was there for him to get started on digging through the woman's life.

"I had her name as Sandy Chaiprasit, but I was hoping we could confirm that with a driver's license or something in her personal effects. They took her purse into evidence and I haven't had a chance to check it out yet," Kane said, leaning against the counter, being careful not to dislodge any of the equipment behind him. "Or at least that's the name she gave Edie Price, Miki's manager."

"Price was the other victim, yes?" Horan asked. "Is she doing okay?"

"Yeah, she is out of recovery and in a private room," Kel replied. "They're hoping to watch her for a few days, and then she can be released. I don't know if she's planning to stay in the city or not. Morgan here might have more information there."

"I don't know yet. I don't think anyone's talked about it, but I'd rather she stay in the city so we have access to her as we work on the case. She lives down in Los Angeles, so it's not that she's far, but traveling with a gunshot wound isn't a good idea." Kane brought his mind back to something Horan said earlier. "You mentioned you think she's connected to another case. How?"

"Not necessarily how, but what." She tapped on the screen a few times, opening up attachments to her unfinished report. Turning the tablet around, she zoomed in on what Kane thought was a woman's thigh. "Do you see this? Same symbol was on a middle-aged Chinese man who was killed in an alleged robbery night before last. His was on his chest, but the same marking. Neither are well done, more like the kind of tattoo someone had done in prison or someone's garage. Definitely not professional ink quality, and patchy.

"I would say, if I had to guess, they were done not by machine but by hand, possibly with a single needle and ballpoint pen ink." Horan pulled up another page, putting the woman's tattoo next to another rendering of the symbol, this one on a stretch of darker, hairier skin. "They've finally started to fill in the gang database with known markings. This one came up, but there wasn't any information around it, it just referred me to the Chinatown Gang Task Force."

"Holy *shit*," Kel murmured what was going through Kane's mind. "Do you see that shit, Morgan?"

"Do you recognize it?" she asked, turning the screen so Kane could get a better look.

"Oh yeah, I know it." Hell, he did more than *recognize* it. Kane'd kissed it, bitten it, and washed soap from the muscled curve of the upper arm it sat on. He knew the taste of the symbol, or at least the one he'd

CHAPTER THREE

Damien: Shit, that was... shit.

Rafe: I'd tell you to fuck off but that would mean you'd have to put some effort into something, and since you couldn't seem to work your fingers on your guitar, I don't think you'd be able to stroke your own dick off, Mitchell.

Forest: Guys—

Damien: At least I was in tune!

Rafe: Yeah, if only tone-deaf Mongolian throat-singing penguins bought the fucking album.

Forest: Hey, guys... come on—

Damien: Listen you wanking—

Miki, glancing up from his notebook: Swear to fucking God, if I have to shove my fists into your mouths to

shut you up, I'm okay with that. Try-
ing to think here, fuckers.

Damien and Rafe fall quiet, shuffling
about while making apologetic nois-
es at each other.

Forest: (disgusted) Why the hell doesn't
anyone listen when I tell them to
knock it off?

Rafe, muttering under his breath: Man,
I love you but you're kind of going
to end up driving kids to school in
between arena shows. You're not re-
ally all that scary, even if your hus-
band drives a tank at work.

—1:00 a.m. Saturday recording

DAMIEN MITCHELL was both Miki's savior and personal devil.

He never regretted following Damie that rainy night a long time ago. They'd been so young, so damn skinny, and so fucking hungry to take a bite of the world. It was funny, he could remember everything about the moment he heard a British-tinted voice call up to him from the alleyway below. Miki could still feel the uneven scrape of the fire escape's peeling paint on the palms of his hands and the back of his neck where he leaned against its side. He'd been eating noodles—he thought he remembered—beef chow fun dry style, and the back-kitchen cook had shoved a few pieces of fried *gau gee* into his bowl that night, drizzling the crispy dumplings with a bit of shoyu and Coleman's mustard.

He remembered the *gau gee* because he'd eaten it first, savoring the stinging saltiness of the shoyu-mustard mixture and the green-onion-rich pork inside.

There'd been a heavy rush that night, and his hands were wrinkled from hours of washing dishes and scraping food into bins. He'd been too young to waiter but old enough to bus tables, a distinction he was happy for because he was shitty with people yet could still score some of the tips at the end of the night. He'd run away from Shing and Vega only a few months before, living in hollowed-out foundations of old buildings or a rooftop he could reach climbing up a fire ladder.

He'd been listening to his music player, the first thing he bought when the restaurant's owner handed him his pay envelope, cash instead of a check because he had no identification and he'd been willing to work for less than minimum wage. Food came with the gig, something Miki had been very thankful for, because what little money he made, he needed to save. He didn't feel safe in Chinatown, but there was nowhere else for him to go. He avoided Shing as much as he could, skirting the area he knew the family frequented, and Vega was nowhere to be found, not that Miki had been looking for him. Others had pushed their fingers and other things into him, but Vega and Shing actually had owned him—or at least that's what it'd felt like.

Miki was calculating how much it would take him to get out of the city when Janis Joplin cycled up into his playlist. He *loved* her voice, adored her writing, and he'd found every scrap of song she'd ever sang to load onto the battered device he'd gotten from a thrift store. Singing along with the woman he'd connected with, Miki hadn't heard Damien's approach, nor did he hear him stop beneath the fire escape Miki often used as a place to eat his late-night dinner.

But he sure as hell heard Damien when he cut through Janis's song with a loud shout calling him out to play.

Miki answered that call. Keeping the job at the Chinese food place was a no-brainer, and so was moving into Damien's roach-infested studio a few blocks away and then stealing a couple of bug bombs from the storeroom so he didn't have to worry about sleeping with his mouth open. It took him about three weeks to believe Damie was serious about starting a band and wanting him as a lead singer, but as soon as his brain latched on to the idea, Miki hadn't looked back.

Now, after everything they'd gone through and sitting pretty in a gorgeous refurbished warehouse with a full fridge and soft beds, Miki watched Damien attempt to add a third pickup to an old beater guitar they'd found at a going-out-of-business music store and wondered if he shouldn't have questioned his sanity the moment Damien Mitchell asked him to be a part of his band.

Because the damned jerk never listened to a single thing Miki said... or at least not until the situation bit him in the ass and there was nothing else to try.

"That's not going to work," he said for the third time. "There isn't enough room and what good is it? It's going to sound like shit."

"It can be done," Damien muttered around the screwdriver he had clenched in his teeth. "I just haven't done it myself before. Do me a favor, unwrap those strings."

"No, because you're not going to get this to work. You already have a three pickup with the Gibson, and you hate it because you hang your pick on the middle pickup." Miki reached for the packages anyway, digging through the stack until he found a set of Ernie

Ball's. "Why are you going to make one yourself when it's just going to piss you off and you won't play it?"

"I'll play it because I made it," Damien reasoned. "Haven't you ever done something just because you really wanted to do it?"

"Yeah, that's how I ended up with you," Miki replied, stretching out over the beanbag he'd dragged into the studio's workroom.

"You sure that wasn't just you looking for someplace to hide?" His brother in all but blood pinned Miki with a look as sharp as the end of the guitar string Miki'd just poked into his thumb. "Kind of like what you're doing right now, about Edie and your mom."

There was the one thing Miki hated about Damien Mitchell. It was the ability to punch through the walls Miki built up over the years, the thick, full-of-glass-shards fences he layered around himself. He knew he kept people at arm's length. That wasn't a surprise. Until Damien came along, he'd bled out emotionally every time he interacted with someone, a part of him constantly seeking someone to help him stop the pain, stop the terrors that lived in his soul and mind. The world *hurt*. Since as long as he could remember, it stabbed at him, carving him into little pieces for stronger and meaner people he couldn't fight to consume.

Damie was the first brick in his wall, an anchor for Miki to build on, but that also meant he had an easy in. And if there was one thing Damien was never afraid to do, it was to pick Miki apart and scrape off the scabs he'd been ignoring.

"Edie's going to be fine, remember? She's already fighting with them to go back to LA. I tried to get her to stay here, but she said she would rather live with a pack of dogs by the river than share a place with the two of us. It's like she's been on the road with us or something." Miki sucked on his pierced thumb pad, making a face at the taste of blood. He was sick of tasting his own blood, but life seemed to always serve him up a spoonful now and then. His knee hurt a little bit, more from the cold than overexertion, although the physical therapy he'd done two days ago stretched him out to the point of aching, and scrambling over the cement planters to get to Edie hadn't helped. "I don't know what this has to do with my mother. I told you, they're not going to hand over the package to me until… actually, we don't know when. Kane said he'd ask about it today, but Edie might have to ask for it."

"Doesn't she have to prove that it's hers?" Damien asked, returning to digging at the guitar. "Or because it was handed to her, that makes it hers?"

"I guess that's how they're going to look at it, or at least Kane hopes."

Damien's eyes flicked up for a second, settling on Miki as he said, "Is that what you want? Do you want to know what's inside that envelope? Or do you just want to bury it back up again?"

"Fuck you," he spat. Miki was… *angry*, and he couldn't find the beginning of it, the point where it started. "I wasn't burying *anything*. She wasn't even on my radar, now all of a sudden some woman I never knew existed is in the middle of my life, and there's another one that's dead that I can't do anything about. How the hell is that hiding?"

"What are you going to do if they hand you that package? Are you going to look at it or are you going to shove it into one of the steamer trunks you've put all the Sinners stuff in?" It was another jab, a small slice but one so accurately aimed, it felt like Miki's guts were pouring out when Damien turned back to the guitar. "I know you. I love you, but you pack everything away. Shit, you pack Kane away—"

"You fucking take that back." The beanbag shifted underneath him as Miki struggled to sit up. "I do *not* hide Kane."

"Really? Because I asked you if you are ever going to write him a love song and you told me you're not ready to share him," Damien responded, putting down the screwdriver. His blue eyes were alert and as sharp as always, but the sympathy in his brother's face was almost too much for Miki. "What I'm saying is you keep waiting for the other shoe to drop, for somebody to hurt you. Shit, Sinjun, you're pissed as fuck because I wasn't here to deal with Dave and Johnny's deaths. And I'm not saying it's wrong to feel that, but—"

"I know. I *fucking* know it's stupid." Their road trip as a band had opened up old wounds for everyone, but Miki felt like he'd spent the time digging pieces of metal out from under his skin with a plastic spoon. He felt savaged by his emotions, the whispering thoughts he couldn't chase away. They were like gnats, swarming into his nose and mouth, and they turned to a powdery bitterness on his tongue when he tried to stamp them out. "I just can't... I can't sort shit out in my head. It's getting harder to write anymore, and...."

Damien set the torn-apart guitar to the side and tossed the screwdriver into the band's toolbox. Crossing the small room, Damie nudged Miki's leg with the back of his hand. "Move over, Sinjun."

He moved.

The beanbag was big enough for both of them, but it was a little bit tight. It wasn't the first time he'd shared a closed-in space with Damien, and it probably wouldn't be the last, but for some reason, this time Miki couldn't breathe. He sat on the bubble of some hard mix of emotions, and Damien was a thumbtack headed straight for him. Miki had never feared Damien, that was never anything he even remotely associated with his brother, but as Damien lowered himself into the microbead-stuffed oversize velvet pillow, Miki's stomach clenched and he tasted metal in his spit.

"You are shaking, Sinjun." Damien looped an arm around him, and Miki let himself be pulled in. "What's going on in that busy head of yours? Are you and Kane okay? Are *we* okay?"

There were tears in Miki's eyes before there were words in his mouth. It was getting harder every day to keep himself from crying in front of other people, and he'd taken to avoiding anyone—everyone—during the day. He'd woken up feeling all right, a little bit more stable than he had over the past few weeks, but Damien's prodding punctured his control and suddenly the rocks were back in his throat.

This was Damien. One guy Miki could count on through thick and thin since the first day they'd met, but there he was, fighting the urge to get up and leave, to put as much distance between him and Damien as possible. Anything to stop him thinking about the heaviness in his chest and the numbness in the back of his brain.

Damien deserved better than that. *He* deserved better than that. Once Damien returned, Miki promised himself he wouldn't run away from life anymore, and he'd seen how burying himself in a nothingness was slowly killing him. Kane pulled him out of the shadows, out of that existence, but he hadn't truly appreciated the life he'd begun to live until he had his brother back.

So much changed when Damien walked through the Morgans' kitchen door and back into Miki's life. And then everything spiraled down before Miki could hold on to the happiness he'd found. He'd come off the tour hating being onstage, unable to feel the music in everyday things, and hating the touch of everyone on him. It took him a few weeks to shake off the maelstrom of darkness hanging over him, but now it was back, raging around in his head and sending him spinning.

"I don't know what's wrong with me, D. I watched a woman I didn't know die in front of me, and I felt *nothing*. Then Edie—Jesus fucking Christ, Damien— the fucker had to hit Edie before I felt anything. And then I got scared about everything. I couldn't let Kane do his job, I didn't want to let him go, and there were people screaming for help, but I didn't want to let him go. I knew better. I *know* better." He took a breath, wishing the cold in the air would freeze away the sharpness stabbing through him. "But I still am angry about everything. About you leaving me. About Kane leaving me. And I get so frightened inside about… I got scared yesterday because Donal told me to hold on for a little bit on the phone, and I knew in my gut he was just going to hang up on me—"

"Donal would never turn his back on you. He's your *dad*," Damien insisted.

He was wrapped into Damien a moment later. Neither one of them were large men, certainly not the size of the Morgan and Finnegan bloodline they'd both fallen in love with, but they weren't short either. Still, Damien was strong after years of slinging heavy guitars and even heavier stage equipment around. Miki could have bitten him to hold his best friend off, but even as the thought occurred to him, Damien held him tight. It had been too long since they'd spent an afternoon leaning on each another, but the memories of long conversations about dreams and lyrics simmered in Damien's hug.

"I know he is. Like my brain knows it, but...." Miki paused, searching for a way to explain how he felt when he heard cheesy music in his ear and then the panic of never hearing Donal's voice again. "I'm drowning, Damien. That's what it feels like, and no matter what I do, no matter who I reach out for, it doesn't ever go away. It got worse when Edie told me this Sandy woman knew my mom, because up until then, she wasn't real. She wasn't an actual fucking person before, but now, all of a sudden, she's *real* and... *she* didn't want me, so what makes me think no one else does?"

"WELL, THIS looks like a shithole," Kel muttered as the elevator doors fought to open. "How come the morgue looks all sleek and shiny and this place looks like its last life was a war bunker? Are we sure we are in the right place?"

"I'm following where Casey told us to go." Kane looked one more time at the directions he'd been given. "He said it was easier to go in this way than through the front, but... it's a bit sketchy."

"Makes me kind of want to draw my gun just in case we get attacked by rats." Kel shuffled, careful not to brush against the elevator's dingy walls. "Swear to God, Morgan, you take us to some of the shittiest places."

His partner wasn't wrong. The Asian Gang Task Force was located in a building that probably should've been marked as unsuitable, but beggars couldn't be choosers in Chinatown. Although they were cops in every sense of the word, the task force was relegated to a rental space behind a fortune cookie factory, a movie trope even Kane had a hard time believing. Yet, there they were, two Homicide inspectors traveling down a rickety lift that smelled more of vanilla and flour than cop-house coffee.

They'd been in the building before, a while back. Not the particular area they were going to, but a side entrance cut off from the larger floor plan. It was a warren of add-ons and corridors, difficult to navigate especially if you didn't know where you were going. The building itself had seen some hard times, but now it was caught up in a gentrification wave that promised to send already high rents to astronomical levels, despite the fact that it had housed more than its fair share of criminal activity.

Kane remembered walking through one of the off-alley doors to work that case. It had been nearly a year, and they'd been working a raid on a gambling den, which turned up a couple of dead bodies in a back room that looked like it hadn't been cleaned since the Great Earthquake. They'd come through hot on the heels of a SWAT team that included his older brother, Connor, and stumbled on a prostitution ring with little regard for its employees surviving more than a few months. It'd been an ugly case, one that had for some reason reminded him of Miki at the oddest times.

So it was ironic to be headed back into what had been a pit of hell, carrying a bit of Miki's problems on his back.

The elevator let out into a hallway still bearing the marks of the raid. Boot prints on doors that were barely hanging on their hinges and a couple of bullet holes in the ceiling tiles. Kel pointed to them as they walked under the water-stained squares, chuckling.

"That's what you get when you take a rookie on a raid." Kel stepped over a mound of garbage left near an overflowing trash bin. "See, this is why cops get a bad rep. You get assholes like Gang Task Force who don't care about where they live. It's like a sewer rat is their mascot and they're fucking proud of it."

"Maybe it's supposed to look like shit," Kane suggested. "Could be they don't want to announce a police presence."

"Just you being here announces a police presence. Have you looked at yourself in a mirror, Morgan?" Kel shot back. "You *ooze* cop. I'm surprised you don't bleed blue. Pretty sure your first words were: 'Stop! Police! Pass me the donut!'"

"That goes to show how much you know." Kane counted the doors, remembering the instructions the lieutenant had given him to find the task force's main room. "There's eight kids in my family. Asking someone to pass you a donut is like begging them to eat it for you. If you want something, you have to grab it. And if somebody got there first, you have to fight for it. Unless you're Quinn."

"Why Quinn?" Kel frowned. "He's like… number three. It's usually the babies who don't have to fight over scraps because Mom's always going to step in."

"Because my baby brother, as passive and peaceful as he is, will fuck your shit up if you take something that's his. And that includes a donut." Kane cocked his head. "Actually, especially a donut."

The door they wanted was heavy and made of metal, a firebreak in the wall. At the far end of the hall was an open staircase leading out to another alley, sunlight pouring down through the access way. It was odd, considering Casey told him to come down the elevator, but their lieutenant could be quirky at times.

"Here it is. Guy we are looking for is named Chang—" Kane swung open the door and all hell broke loose.

The shift from graffitied hallway to a lunch room was startling, but not as much of a surprise as the looks on the cops' faces when Kane and Kel walked through a door marked emergency exit. Klaxons broke over them, and after a flurry of almost drawn weapons, Kane and Kel found themselves saddled with a baby-faced undercover cop named Thomas O'Brien who could have easily boarded a school bus without anyone blinking an eye. After their credentials checked out and a quick call to Casey, who thought the whole thing was hilarious, O'Brien promised to take them to the lead inspector in charge, hustling them out of a bullpen full of young officers and down yet another hall.

"Casey's got a sense of humor on him. Just told you, he used to work this detail. Not at this spot but on the crew. Keeps up with Chang, the senior guy on deck. Asshole knew we were taking over the space officially, but he sent you down that way anyway?" The detective barely looked old enough to buy candy by himself, but the badge hanging from a lanyard around his neck assured them he was a cop. O'Brien's penny-red hair, blue eyes, and freckles were at odds with his tanned Asian features, but his easy Californian rolling tones marked him as a native and probably one of the many poi dog kids born to the city's racial diversity. "Come on down this way. Chang said to give you anything you needed, but I'm going to be honest with you, we don't got much."

"Jesus, you can't trust them to lock the back door and this kid's going to help us?" Kel muttered behind Kane's back. "He looks like he was beaten up for his lunch money just last week."

"Week before last," O'Brien threw over his shoulder. "And that door should've been locked. Or at least from that side. Mostly we run analysis here, and strategic ops. Most of the undercover work is run out of the main building, but they consider us overflow. We're just petty crimes. Anything that jumps up the ladder goes to you guys, and you aren't ones for sharing any of the glory."

"I wouldn't exactly call it glory," Kane said, shaking his head. "We're all on the same team. Badges of the same color. Bleed the same red."

O'Brien gave him a funny look, then chuckled. "God, they weren't kidding. You Morgans really are chipped off the old man, aren't you. Does he make you call him Captain at home?"

"I call him Da," Kane replied, his shoulders straightening. "*You* can call him *sir*."

"Yeah, kid." Kel smirked as he edged by O'Brien when the younger cop stopped in his tracks. "They really are chips off the old block. It'll probably be a good idea for you to remember that when you meet one of them and make a joke about their father, because you never know who's going to end up being your boss."

They found Chang sitting alone in a command center of sorts, tapping away at a computer with dual monitors while K-Pop played in the background. He was older and resembled a hound dog with his black hair combed away from his face and silver streaks at his temples. An attempt at a mustache sat below his thick nose, but it was sparse, and he stroked at it as he stared at the screen, his fingers working the mouse to scroll through a series of reports. The windowless rectangular room was nearly as cold as the morgue they'd visited, but the resemblance ended there.

Where Horan's domain was spotless and order-ly, Chang's was a pile of papers and odd debris Kane couldn't figure out what to do with. One of the desks was piled high with what looked like wooden toys, but a malformed horse on wheels lay cracked open, its body empty but fitted with a plastic egg case. Most of the items looked like everyday things tourists would buy from kiosks and shops right off the sidewalks outside, but each was tagged, small precise letters written in black pen, referencing case numbers and street names.

Chang caught sight of them coming in and stood, holding his hand out for Kane to shake. He came up to Kel's shoulder but was broad, a fireplug of a man with powerful legs and beefy arms. His glance at O'Brien was on the edge of frustration, but that disappeared be-neath a wide smile.

"Casey pulled a prank on you, huh?" His grip was a vise, but quick, releasing Kane's hand before he could do serious damage. "Actually, it was probably on me. A couple of my rookies duck out that door to go smoke in the alleyway. Probably think I don't know, but I do. Damn fire code means I can't lock that door down, but I sure as hell can make them scrub down that hallway outside. O'Brien, make sure that door is secured, and if anyone gives you shit, you come see me. Or better yet, you tell *them* to come see me."

After the young officer left, Chang pulled out a couple of chairs for them to sit, then wheeled his own. "You guys want coffee? All I got down here's tea, but I can send somebody out for you."

"No, I think we're good." Kane shook his head, ignoring Kel's murmuring protest. "You have a DB in the morgue that might be connected to the shooting I attended yesterday. Horan sent us down with a couple of photos of a tattoo on my vic. Our lieutenant figured it was just easier to come by than go through all of the bureaucracy and red tape just to get a report. Especially since Casey used to work this detail. Sorry about the back door."

"It's okay. He and I used to be partners. I'm used to him being an asshole," Chang said, holding out his hand. "Give me what you have, and I'll see what I've got loaded up into Big Blue here. We just brought the system online about a year ago and are slowly adding in as much reference material as we can get. It's spotty, but we're making progress. I don't know who they've got on the slab, but if you give me the case file, I can look it up to get a cross-check."

"What we've got is kind of old, almost thirty years ago. Medical examiner said the tattoo was homegrown or prison ink. All three match, for the most part. Definitely not solid or professional work, but the same symbol. As far as the meaning goes, could be Asiatic, or culturally influenced, but without a reference point, we couldn't dig anything up. So we thought we'd start with you and see what your guys had." Kel opened the case file, then dug through what was inside to extract photos Horan had printed out for them. He glanced at Kane, then pushed on. "The male vic was pulled from an attempted robbery your crew was brought in on. The second photo is from our vic, a middle-aged Thai female fatally shot at Yerba Buena early yesterday morning."

"And the third?" Chang held up a photo, different from the two they'd gotten from Horan, and Kane's stomach twisted below his heart. "Where's this one from?"

"That is tattooed on my…" Kane never knew what to call Miki. Boyfriend seemed too childish but partner seemed too strange, especially since he already had a partner, a Hispanic smartass named Kel Sanchez. "My significant other, Miki St. John. They found him when he was about three, and that tattoo was already on his arm. A few months ago, he was attacked in Las Vegas by a man with the same marking. The attacker was struck by a car and killed, but his body never made it to the Nevada examiners' office.

"Someone jacked the van carrying him and took his body. Up until Vegas, Miki had never seen or heard of anyone having this symbol on them. At the time he was found, no one would admit to knowing what it stood for or if it was connected to anyone. Now dead people are dropping out of the trees with this on them." Kane leaned forward in his chair to pull out the deceased woman's photo, sliding it across the table toward Chang. "The woman's name was Sandy Chaiprasit, and she was meeting with Miki's manager when she was killed. So all of this is connected to something or someone, we just don't know who or how."

If anything, Chang's face sagged even further, and he rubbed at his forehead, studying the photos. Sighing, he finally said, "Yeah, they're connected. That's an old tattoo. We're talking back in the eighties. We still see it on some of the older guys, the ones doing small runs. The marks belong to Danny Wong, the most evil son of a bitch that ran Chinatown before he was shut down by the DEA. About a month ago, they let him out on sympathy leave, said he was dying of cancer. Instead of checking into hospice, he went underground, and they haven't got a clue on his whereabouts. Now we've got dead bodies popping up in the Bay and old ugly grudges rising up again. So one bit of advice: if your boyfriend has anything to do with this, get him someplace safe and keep him there until we can lock this asshole down."

men who were in the right place at the wrong time for their enemies.

"Homicides I know, and I've had some crossover with a couple of the Gang Task Forces, but not enough to be an expert on them," Kane remarked, shuffling through the mounds of old files stacked in front of them. They'd caved to the offer of coffee, especially since the growing stack of paperwork promised to be a headache and a half to go through and Kane wanted a buzz to keep him going. One of the task force guys brought over a couple of mugs and a full carafe, wishing them luck then bum-rushing the door before he could be roped into helping. "I've heard the name Wong, but not as someone who's got a grip on Chinatown today."

"No, he doesn't have any influence on the gangs running the streets now. It's harder for Asian gangs to keep a hold on outside activity once they've been locked down. Loyalties shift along family lines, and it's all about who you connect with outside of the city as much as it is how much you control it. Wong was put away for a long time, and much of what he gained slipped through his fingers." Chang handed Kel a couple of packets of sugar for his coffee, then offered up a spoon to stir with. "His nephew took over the territory a few years back, but he and the old man are very different mind-sets to deal with. Adam Lee is smarter, sharper. It's hard to catch him at anything because he's slick and covers his tracks. Wong was like a sledgehammer, cross him and he pounded you down into the ground. That's what slipped him up."

"How so?" Kel put the spoon down on a paper towel already marbled with coffee and tea stains. "I worked a gang detail for about half a year, but a different district, more Latino. Lots of family ties there amongst the gangs. It was almost Hatfield and McCoy in some places."

"You get some of that here, but sometimes you've got cousin against cousin too. Could be because smaller families and tighter clans, throwbacks from the old country they came from, and a lot of their money goes back overseas." Chang made a face. "But those connections also bring over what they consider product: drugs and pretty girls they can get to work for cheap. Most of the girls we find refuse to talk and don't care if they get deported back to where they came from. They know they'll be on the next plane coming back and there's nothing we can do about it. Lee makes sure there's a good distance between him and what's going down on the streets, plausible deniability all the way around. His uncle Wong liked to roll in it. He liked playing with the girls, hurting them. In the end, a couple of those close to him were willing to flip just to protect themselves, but only after he went in. Before that, nobody saw or heard anything. I'm pretty sure there's a couple of guys out there who'd still do anything the old man asked them to do. We just don't know who they are."

"Do you think Chaiprasit was one that flipped? It looks like Wong was popped about two years after Miki was found on the street. St. John Street is on the far end of Chinatown, so he could have wandered off, but no one in the area recognized him when they showed his photo around. Or at least that's what Miki was told. There's a park there now, but I don't know what it looked like back then. Could be the park was there and his mother took him to play in it, but Wong took her out, leaving him behind." Kane looked up from a report of a twenty-five-year-old drug bust. "You said that Wong took a walk after getting released. Do you think some of his people were loyal enough to start taking potshots at anyone who crossed him back then?"

"From what I heard about Wong, I wouldn't be surprised. Same with the theory about leaving the kid behind," Chang replied. "But I don't know why he would send somebody after St. John now. He's what? Not even thirty? I can't see why Wong would target him. He's not a game piece on the board."

"No, but his mother might've been. Hell, for all we know she's still alive and working on some of the action. We don't have a name for her yet. But she could be in your files here." Kane tapped at a stack of papers. "It's not like Miki hasn't been photographed one and a half million times. Someone could have seen Wong's mark on him and put two and two together about who he is. We just don't have any clue how Miki is connected."

"Somebody would've had to know," Kel suggested softly. "He was young, and that tattoo was pretty well healed by the time they found him, so it was done to him when he was a baby. Someone's going to remember a baby being inked up with Wong's mark. That's going to stick in somebody's head."

"Our first priority has to be finding Chaiprasit's killer. It's looking like she's connected to something bigger than just a drive-by, but until we do some digging, we are not going to know who pulled the trigger." Somewhere in the reports under Kane's hands lay Miki's mother's name, possibly her photo as well. He wasn't there to chase down his lover's ghosts, but the itch was there, especially since an attempt had already been made on Miki in Vegas. "I guess the first thing we need to do is find out which of Wong's guys—and women—are still alive and loyal to him."

"And if one of those women is St. John's mother? Then what?" Kel poked at a bubble Kane hadn't wanted to burst, but that's what made him a good partner. He was fearless in his inquiries and good to have in a fight. Still, he brought up a lot of questions Kane didn't have answers to. "I don't think we should ignore chasing her down just because it looks a little sticky with you digging around for her name. Like I said, someone is going to remember who inked up a little kid, and if she let Wong do that to her son, it was probably to prove her loyalty. We could very well find her at the end of this really shitty rainbow, and that's something we need to take into account."

"Most of these guys have aged out of the business," Chang interjected. "I don't know how many of them are still active, but it could be quite a few. Cancer's taking Wong down, but a lot of people these days live very healthy lifestyles. It wouldn't surprise me if some of Wong's old associates are still up for a kill or two."

"All he'd need is one guy willing to still do a job or two for him. We just need to find out who that'd be." Kel's pen flew across the pages as he took notes, scribbling down names to look into, then roughing out a flowchart connecting groups with lines. "St. John is definitely a target, no two ways about it. He was attacked once and on scene for a hit. It's not going to take long before somebody tries again. We need to find out who is driving this and why."

"Wong wasn't one to share the spotlight, especially not with the women, but he definitely had a few favorites," Chang said with a shrug. "He ran prostitutes, usually out of a business front. He would put a woman in charge of the girls he had working for him. St. John's mother could've been one of those in charge. Chaiprasit had to have been close to her to have the woman's personal effects on her. I could see Wong wanting to mark someone's kid as a power play, so every time she looked at the kid, she would know who owned them. Problem is, there's a lot of names to dig through, and you'd have to spend a lot of time figuring out who's still alive. Then you'd have to divide them between loyal and not. I just don't have those resources."

"No," Kel said, shaking his head. "That'll be on us. We just had to coordinate with you to make sure we don't step on any toes. This definitely sits in Homicide, but we need to be able to tap into you if we run into issues. It's not a playground we know."

"If his mother was loyal to Wong, it wouldn't make sense that he's a target. Unless it's somebody hitting people who were loyal to Wong, maybe trying to cut his legs out from under him so he doesn't build back up. That reads weak for me because Wong's dying, but he could want to go out with a bang. Maybe climb back up and end on a high note." Kane liked that reasoning even less, but he had to look at all of the possibilities. "Do we know who was instrumental in taking Wong down? Because that's the first place I'd want to look if I was going to settle grudges. At least it'll give us some place to start."

"That kind of thing actually sits in the DEA's office. I've got files here, but the case was punted over. DEA was running an undercover operation through Wong, and SFPD became a supporting actor in the whole thing. One of the biggest charges Wong had to fight was drugs and racketeering, so he was a pretty big feather to stick in somebody's cap. It was like an alphabet soup fight, according to the reports here. There's so many acronyms on these pages, I kind of want to buy a vowel." Chang rocked back in his chair, his eyes settling on Kane. "Those guys are hard to talk to. They like to defend their rice bowl. They don't like sharing information or resources, and don't get me started on handing out credit for busts. Unless you got an in over there, you're not going to get anyone to talk."

"Luckily for me, I have an in." Kane grinned over at his partner. "And he even owes me a favor or two."

WHEN DAMIEN convinced Miki to go in on a pair of warehouses on the fringes of Chinatown and above the Piers, Miki thought he'd lost his mind. Both structures were in seriously bad shape and gutted from a fire. They languished while Sinner's Gin was on tour, and were a project they promised themselves they would get around to fixing up once they had enough time and space to breathe. A semitruck plowing into their limousine gave Miki all the time he needed and all the sorrow he could ever imagine to fill the empty space. Edie talked him into turning his side of the property over to an interior designer while he struggled through rehab, his extensive injuries nearly crippling him after the accident. He'd come home to a house he'd never known, a refurbished, sleek style of living he never truly grew accustomed to. Damien's warehouse was sold by his parents and refitted as a gallery with workspace for artisans. Kane rented one of those bays and eventually stumbled into Miki's life.

When Damien walked back up out of the pits of hell or, rather, the insane asylum he'd been kept in, he sued for ownership of the warehouse and won, then set about reconfiguring the space so he and Sionn could live next door. The remodel was taking forever, and while Miki liked having his brother close by, there were times when he longed for the peace and quiet he had before his life was invaded by the people he now loved.

"I'm not talking about you, Dude." He glanced down at the rough-coated terrier trotting next to him. The leash connecting Miki's hand to the dog's collar was superfluous, but the law—and Kane—were sticklers for the rules. Dude never left his side on their walks. He was a constant in Miki's life, a silent furry sentinel he'd grown to love, the first creature he would admit to loving after losing his band. "*You* don't make noise in my head. I mean, I love all of them, but sometimes they just pick at me until I want to choke to death."

He didn't want to admit there was a lot to pick at. Miki didn't need someone to point out all of the bumps and ripples in his psyche. He knew he was fucked in the head. He didn't need anyone who shared a spot in his heart to tell him he didn't think right, process things the same way other people did, and most of all, he didn't need anyone to tell him there were monsters in his darkness. He already knew all of that. Miki just didn't have any intention of waking them up to evict them because, as he'd learned from the past, shaking his boo-wooglies out into the light just pissed them off, and they would eat their fill of him before slinking back into the shadows.

"I just want some *bao*. If you're lucky, they'll have some of the beef shanks out and we can grab one. Just don't eat the bone on Kane's dirty clothes. You are going to get both of us killed." Miki trotted across the narrow side street to reach one of Chinatown's main avenues. "And whatever you do, don't try to hump the statue in their shrine. It's embarrassing. Makes it look like I haven't taught you any manners. Okay, I *haven't* taught you any manners, but… *still*."

Despite his past, Miki adored Chinatown. It was someplace he felt safe and, oddly, normal. It was loud and brash with extravagant treasures shuffled in among miles of trashy, kitschy, fascinating things, and when he walked the district's crowded streets, he always felt like he was walking through home. He knew bits and pieces of the languages he heard, and the scents wafting out of various storefronts were achingly familiar. Little bits of happiness were tucked in here and there, everything from the slightly sweet, yeasty aroma of freshly steamed buns to the crackling earthiness of roasting ducks lightened any heaviness he carried. Damien once accused him of loving food more than he loved people, and at the time, with the exception of the guitarist himself, Miki would've agreed. But things were different now.

Still, he did love food, especially when he wasn't the one who had to cook it.

"I should try to cook dinner." Dude panted, giving him a silly grin, but Miki wasn't taking it as approval. Dude smiled at everything. "There is a fried rice thing I saw. It looked really easy. I can maybe pick up some *char siu* to put into it. 'Course it would be a hell of a lot easier to just order in, but I could do it. I would just have to try to cook it when no one's around so if I burn the fuck out of it, I could toss it before anyone finds out. Shit, is it Wednesday?"

The parking lot next to the Hongwanji was packed with stalls arranged into neat little rows overflowing with produce and other wares. The days had slipped away from him, and Miki found himself in the middle of one of the busiest public markets Chinatown had to offer. Most of the food was geared for locals, but a few stalwart tourists waded through the crowd. A couple of food trucks were parked on the street, one just opening its canopy while another was already slinging out boba milk teas and slushies. He recognized a cook he knew from a restaurant down the street working a steam table with barbecue meats and fried noodles. Sitting at the end of the parking lot, Fred's hadn't built up a line yet, but Miki knew from experience that if he didn't get what he wanted now, it would be an hour wait in line once the surrounding businesses emptied out for lunch.

"Haven't seen you around," Fred grumbled at Miki as he approached. "Thought you were getting too big to eat what I make."

"You and I both know you're just heating up what you brought with you," Miki sneered back. Leaning over the steam table, he shook the old man's hand. "It's good to see you. How are you doing? Your wife left you yet?"

"No, she's holding out for you. And since you're hooked up with that cop, she's not going to go." He guffawed, peeling his lips back into a nearly toothless grin. "I'll tell her you said hi."

Their relationship stretched back to the time when Miki washed dishes and Fred worked the wok line at Golden Panda Palace. Both had been paid under the table and often scrounged for leftovers off plates coming back from the front of the house. Miki did it because he was hungry and every penny counted, but Fred did it because he was cheap and hated to see food go to waste. His wife, Mabel, a round-cheeked older Chinese woman, worked as the main evening hostess during the weekends and spent much of her time trying to save Miki's soul. She'd left off once Fred shooed her away, but she continued to look the other way when he shoveled food into take-out containers and snuck out with them at the end of the night.

They were two of the people Miki took care of once Sinner's Gin began to make money. He owed the Wu family, and purchasing the Panda for them seemed like the least he could do. Fred fought him, but Mabel shut her husband down before he could finish his first argument. The food was still mediocre at best, but there were a few dishes Fred nailed every time.

And the best of them was char siu and crispy roasted pork.

"You want a bag of each?" Fred gestured with his cleaver at the mound of meat his helper was about to load into the steam table. "I have a bone for the dog if you want it."

"No, I want a pound of each. And some of the spicy fried green beans." Miki caught Fred's curious look. "I'm going to use the char siu to make fried rice."

"You better stop at the drugstore and buy Pepto. Or what is that thing they give to people so they vomit?" The old man snorted, then shoved his rolled-up cotton beanie to the back of his head. "You'd be better off buying food instead. I can make you up a bunch of boxes. You can take home and pretend you made it. It would be—"

The pop-pop-pop startled Miki, and he turned toward the sound, the world slowing down around him. He was caught in a gelatin shift of time, Fred continuing to berate Miki's past attempts at making a meal while streams of people began to scatter away from the stall's corner of the parking lot. Out of the corner of his eye, Miki saw Fred's expression change, morphing from confusion straight into anger.

Something stung his arm. Something sharp and hard, but he couldn't quite process what hit him, not until he saw the trickle of blood smeared over his elbow. Dude's booming bark shattered the protective shell around Miki's consciousness; then time returned to its normal flow. The world hit him hard, its sounds blaring loudly, making him wince with the sudden jolt of volume. This time—God, Miki was tired of counting the times—the shouts around him were a mélange of Mandarin, Cantonese, and English, but the one voice he heard above the cacophony was his terrier growling as he tried to pull Miki away from the side of the road.

He saw the shooter—no missing him, despite the chaos. He was older, slung down low in the seat of an old wide-bodied car Damien could probably instantly identify if he'd been there. The man had shaved his head recently enough there was a white ring around the back of his skull where his hair should have grown, but his eyebrows were thick dark splotches over his narrowed eyes. He'd slowed down to a near stop to get his shots off, but when the screaming began, he put his car into gear to pull away—but not before making eye contact with Miki.

The hatred Miki saw was a bitterness strong enough for him to taste, and then a moment later, the man was gone, his land shark of a car swallowed up by Chinatown's ever-moving traffic.

"Call the cops," Fred ordered the cowering teenager hiding next to the steam table. "And an ambulance. Mieko—*Miki*—sit down. You've been shot! Move the dog. *Sit down.*"

"I saw him," Miki mumbled, hissing when the pain finally struck. Clamping his hand over the wound, he peered around, looking for other victims, but it was hard to tell what was going on around him. Dude hugged his side, sticking to Miki's calf, and he reached down with his other hand to scratch the dog's shoulders, hoping to calm the agitated terrier. "I don't know who he is. I don't know why—"

"I know who he is." Fred's voice was shaky, crackling as he pulled Miki's hand away, as he pressed a kitchen towel against the wound. The older man's fingers trembled, and he looked up, fear blanching his cheeks and lips. "That was Rodney Chin, but he hasn't caused trouble in years. Not since he came back out of prison. Something is going on, Miki, but I don't know why you are in the middle of it."

CHAPTER FIVE

Miki: This looks like a tree took a shit in a cup.

Forest: It's tea. Just... take a sip. It's supposed to help calm you down. Ease away anxiety.

Miki: Dude, there isn't enough tree shit in this world to help me calm down, but I'll give it a try.

Forest: I'd appreciate it. Especially now since I won't ever be able to brew tea without thinking I'm making a cup of tree shit.

—Staff table, Marshall's Amp coffee shop

"MICK, YOU should have let them take you to the hospital." Kane didn't like the stubborn look on Miki's face any more than he liked seeing the blood on his arm. "I know you think it isn't a big deal, but—"

"The ambulance guys wouldn't let me take Dude." Miki's jaw clenched, a signal he wasn't going to budge in this fight. "The dog doesn't go, I don't go."

Kane debated with himself for a brief moment on whether or not to push. A few feet away, his father, Donal, caught his attention with a shake of his head, warning Kane off. "Why do you have to be so…." He stopped himself before he dug a hole he couldn't get out of.

He'd rinsed his mouth out before finding Miki. The drive over to the station was a blur in his mind, but the sour taste of his sick lingered at the back of Kane's throat. Relief at seeing his father in the bullpen took off some of the edge, but Kane's nerves were stretched too thin and his spit felt viscous, sticking to his teeth and hard to swallow. He'd known fear before he'd met Miki St. John, but he hadn't realized what terror tasted like until he'd fallen in love.

The sounds of the police station were oddly soothing for Kane. The rattle of handcuffs and gun belts combined with the smell of hand-oiled leather and slightly burnt coffee was practically the backdrop of his childhood. The time he spent in San Francisco as a young boy was among a sea of blue and badges. The chatter was familiar, the kind of low rumble, crowd noise someone would find in any cop house, regardless of where it was. It was almost cliché how there was always a splash of inappropriate, boisterous laughter and the mock outrage of someone being pulled in after being caught red-handed. It was a million and one conversations amid ringing phones, complaining perps, and overeager rookies, but to Kane's ears, it was as much his home as the warehouse he shared with the sensual, pretty man sprawled on a borrowed inspector's chair.

It was difficult to alter his perspective to see the police station as Miki did. It was hard to hear the camaraderie of a shared shift as a steel-toed boot of authority on his neck. If ever there was a divide between them, it was the badge Kane wore, and not the brother who'd crawled back up from the pits of hell. He'd resented Damien a little bit; then the tour the band took opened Kane's eyes. Damien protected as much as he pushed, forming a barrier between the fragile-souled artist Kane knew and the charismatic, sexy singer fronting Crossroads Gin. They'd reached an understanding of sorts—he and Damien—about Miki, a silent pact that they would do anything to keep him happy and whole. Staring at Miki's closed-off expression, Kane realized he hadn't been holding up his end of the bargain, and now he was going to have to dance fast and hard to catch up.

"Why don't you finish what you were going to say?" Miki cocked his head, a bit of street rat peeking out. "Why do I have to be so *what*?"

The last thing he needed was to have a fight in the far corner of an intake area while waiting for the inspector who'd taken Miki's statement. It was already bad enough Donal beat him to the police station, but he was thankful for the support, especially since it looked like Miki was in one of his moods. To be fair, getting shot—even just winged—would make anyone pissy.

"I don't think I'm going to. What I'd like to do is kiss the hell out of you right now, but this isn't the time or place for that. Let me see if they'll cut you loose." Glancing around, Kane couldn't find the inspector in charge but knew the man was around someplace. "Then you and I have to talk about keeping you safe until we get to the bottom of this."

"I'll be looking for yer man, K," Donal offered. "Chances are, I'll be able to shake him out of the trees before ye could. And I want to be in on that talk the two of ye have. Don't give me that look, Miki boy. Yer getting locked down even if I'm the one tossing ye into a cage to do it."

His father slapped him on the shoulder as he went by, a stinging reminder he was an adult and had to deal with the things life threw his way. Things like a rock star boyfriend with a serious chip on his shoulder and a hatred for authority. Watching Donal cut a path through the uniforms hovering nearby, Kane wondered if he would ever be as unflappable as the man who'd raised him.

Then again, there probably was a very good reason Donal's study was usually stocked with at least four full whiskey bottles and had a thick wooden door that shut out most of the family's noise.

Kane dragged a chair over, straddling it to talk to Miki. Dude whined at the intrusion of Kane's foot, then rested his muzzle on his shoe. Leaning over, he scratched the dog's ears, and then his heart clenched over the speckles of dried blood he found on the tips. Picking off the crusty spots gave Kane something to focus on, anything to take his mind off the gauze dressing wrapped around Miki's arm and the heart-stopping phone call he'd taken in the middle of the task force's control center.

"You've got to see Da's right in this," Kane murmured beneath the bustle around them. He didn't want to push, but the panic in his thoughts drove him to reach some kind of compromise with the man he loved. "I'm not saying that you were wrong for taking a walk today. You should be safe in your own neighborhood, on your own streets, but what I found out today leads me to believe we need to keep you inside for a while."

Kane *hated* the dead silence Miki could achieve. Hot molten-steel thoughts churned behind Miki's cunning hazel eyes, but unspoken, so Kane couldn't counter them with any reasonable argument. It was impossible to fight with the stone, his grandmother used to say, and if ever she'd met Miki, she would probably have agreed with Kane he was less a single stone and more an entire cliff.

"Talk to me, Mick. I just want to keep you safe. I've got a few names to chase down—"

"Fred Wu said he recognized the guy who shot me. Some old gangbanger named Rodney Chin. Donal's not talking. So I guess I am going to have to ask you." Miki's attention drifted to the rest of the room, a dead gaze taking in the goings-on of a busy police station. "Fred *knew* this guy. Said he used to work for some asshole who got taken down. Was my mother connected to that asshole? Is that why I have to watch my back, because that woman came sniffing around me? Is that why Edie got shot? Because of me?"

Any doubt Miki spent more than a few of his formative years on the street was wiped away. The prickliness slathered over Miki's artistic soul was gone, replaced by a hard-edged armor battered from more than a decade of abuse. Rage was barely controlled in his lover's taut, muscular body, his thighs tense beneath his jeans, and his long fingers were curled into trembling fists he'd pushed into the chair's vinyl seat. Dude's eyes were on Miki's face, his ears alert and his haunches primed, his weight resting on his forelegs, ready to strike if Miki needed him. Someone passed by, his pants' fabric squeaking between his legs as he walked, and Dude's hackles rose, his teeth bared when his upper lip lifted.

Telling Miki to calm down would be like taking a lit match to a firecracker or tapping a nuclear bomb with a ball peen hammer. Kane had seen that explosive reaction only a few times since he'd hooked up with Miki, but those instances were more than enough of a warning. Lately, the tension never seemed to leave Miki's shoulders, and he slept less and less, sometimes waking up in the middle of the night to pace off the living room until he dropped from exhaustion. Edie's shooting hadn't helped, and today's events at the market would probably mean another bout of angry insomnia, something Kane was helpless to cure.

"There is no one to blame for Edie's shooting or Sandy Chaiprasit's death other than the man who pulled the trigger. You did not put either one of those women in front of those bullets any more than you put yourself in front of that gun today. I know you. And I love you, so I'm not blind to how you feel about being caged in." Kane inched forward until his knees touched Miki's and he laid his hands upon Miki's thighs. He felt warm beneath Kane's palms, but Kane's thumb rested on top of a splatter of dried blood near a frayed hole by Miki's reconstructed knee. "I understand. You know I do. I know the walls close in on you sometimes, and maybe you feel like you're back with Shing and—"

"Don't bring them into this," Miki urged. The raspy, honey-slick voice Kane sometimes heard croon over the radio turned harsh, and Dude shifted, putting himself between Kane's and Miki's legs. Reaching down, Miki stroked the dog's head, soothing the crinkle between his eyes. "I know what you're saying. I'm not stupid. I'm just... *mad*. I'm being led around by the nose by people who didn't care I existed, but now all of a sudden they've got to *kill* me? And why now? What changed over the last week that all of a sudden I'm the most important thing in the world they've got to wipe out?"

"See, *a ghra*," Kane murmured, taking Miki's hands in his and holding them, hoping his lover could feel how deeply he cared for him in his touch. "It's more than this last week. That guy in Vegas, he's connected to this too, and right now, all I've got to go on is a couple of names and a gut feeling that you might be neck-deep in some really nasty shit. I don't ever beg, Mick, but I'm begging you now. I need to know that you're safe while Kel and I work this case and nail whoever is behind those attacks. I can't work worrying if someone's going to kill you because you've gone out. So I'm asking you to please let me protect you until this is done."

"What does that mean? Protect me?" Miki's eyes narrowed, and his snarl resembled Dude's. "Are you going to pin me down and microchip me like we did the dog?"

"No, although that wouldn't be a bad idea." He saw his joke didn't go over as well as he'd hoped. Miki had no intention of lightening the mood between them.

"Fuck *you*," Miki spat, but his hands remained in Kane's.

"Actually, I was thinking Sionn could keep you and Damie safe." It was an ace of spades card Kane hadn't wanted to play, but sometimes life dealt a hand that could only be beat by cheating. "Because I don't want what happened to Edie to happen to Damie. He's already been taken from you once. You'd not survive him being taken from you again."

STANDING IN the living room with Donal cloaked in the partial shadows as the afternoon sun drifted down into the horizon, Kane could see how much his older brother, Connor, resembled their father. Their parents began their family early in their marriage, with Connor and Kane being born before they immigrated to San Francisco. Their ties to Ireland were strong, but there was never any question about where Donal's loyalty lay. His heart and soul belonged to the city he'd adopted as his own, and that love was something he'd shared with his children, along with a love for family and a generosity of spirit Kane always hoped to emulate.

He'd known he was going to be a cop since the day he'd placed his father's uniform cap on his head and fought with Connor over who would own their father's first name tag. Con won that fight for the tag, but Kane eventually got the cap. If anyone had asked him who would end up more like their father, Kane would've said Connor, but he was the one who ended up with the mercurial partner, while Con found the love of his life with Crossroads Gin's drummer, Forest, who was the exact opposite of their mother, Brigid.

"He's not going to like being penned in. Ye heard him right now arguing about having to take the dog to the bathroom in the alley. That's not going to get any better." Kane's father was a master at stating the obvious. For once, Donal looked a little perplexed when he studied his son. Up until that point in his life, Kane had always thought his father could peel away any layers he might have wrapped around himself and see directly into Kane's soul. "My question to ye is why are ye having him stay here instead of up at the house?"

"One word: Mom." He held up a finger—his index finger—then matched his father's grimace. "They may be getting along better than they ever have, but that's not something I want to ruin unless I really have to. From what little I've been able to read, Danny Wong and his people were mostly brute force. Once Sionn gets some guys on the property and we lock down the front gate at the cul-de-sac entrance, Miki will be okay. It's easily defensible and the band can come here and practice, so that will go a long way in keeping his mind off of things."

"Just knowing he can't go out that front gate without somebody on his tail is going to drive him crazy," Donal remarked. "He's too much like yer mother. This would drive her spare.

"I don't have to tell ye, son, this could go very wrong very fast if Miki doesn't cooperate. The last thing I want is to lose him. I love that boy," his father rumbled, leaning against the back of the couch and crossing his arms over his chest. "Now why don't ye catch me up about what's going on so I know what we're facing."

"I have a dead woman in the morgue named Sandy Chaiprasit. She is connected to a recently released prison inmate named Danny Wong. Wong used to control a major part of Chinatown's drug and prostitution rackets before the DEA took him down. He was given almost thirty years, but a few months ago, they released him on sympathy leave because he has terminal cancer." Kane shoved his hands into his pockets, listening for the back door to open. Grateful for Dude's reluctant bladder and Miki's need to bitch to Damien, he figured he had a few minutes before they had to take their conversation elsewhere. "Problem is, they lost track of him, and

Chang, who's the head of the Asian Gang Task Force for C-Town, thinks Wong is getting some of his people to settle outstanding grudges before he dies.

"I'm going to hit up a guy I know at the DEA to see if they will release the list of Wong's closest associates. Chang's records are sketchy because they're old, the SFPD wasn't in charge of the case, and they haven't been digitized. Or at least not a lot of them." His head ached at the thought of digging through the reports he'd piled into the back of his Hummer. "Chang gave us copies, but the information is only as good as what someone decided was worthy of putting in."

"And this Sandy woman knew Miki's mother?" Donal frowned, staring off into space as he thought. "So they were both probably working for Wong's. Question is, was his mother an associate or victim? And why go after our Mick?"

"That is something we might find out, but Book was very clear, my focus is solving Chaiprasit's murder. Now with the shooting, I'm going to be working with whoever I can tap to hunt down Rodney Chin, who was IDed on the scene. I'm hoping the lab can at least say there is a likelihood of the first shooting's bullets matching today's. If not, then I've either got another gun or another shooter."

"Eyewitness ID? Or cameras?" his father asked.

"Witness, but fairly reliable. One of the inspectors who works in the area says Wu is a solid guy. He's also known Miki since before he and Damien met. My gut says he's telling the truth about Chin. So I have one name—a solid line—to Wong, who is probably orchestrating all of this. Even if Chin goes down for the shooting, Wong will probably have at least a couple of other people willing to go dirty for him. He's the head of the snake in this. If I cut him off, then hopefully anyone left will be easier to contain." A bit of noise from outside drew Kane's attention, but he recognized it as the garbage truck collecting the cans from the front of the warehouse. "Da, I'm on the fence here. There's a good chance I'll find Miki's mother somewhere in this case. I don't know what was in the package Chaiprasit gave to Edie, so it might be a moot point because her name might be in there. The DA still hasn't ruled if the package is admissible, but they're also not willing to hand it over to Edie. Either way, I'd get my hands on it, but someone's not budging over there. It shouldn't be that hard. We do this kind of shit every day."

"Someone's either not pushed the right piece of paper across a desk or they're holding it up on purpose. I can push on that for ye, son." Donal unfolded his arms and looked toward the back door. "I think right now might be a good time to have a talk with our Mick. If the woman's information isn't in that package but ye stumble across it, yer going to be in a position to share it. The question is, after all of this, does he really want to know? It could be fair or foul with her, and that might be something he doesn't want to deal with."

"I know. That's been hanging on me since I realized there was a good possibility of her being in those files. Kel agrees. Actually, he was the one who pointed out that since Miki was tattooed with Wong's symbol, there is a good chance his mother is in pretty deep… or was." Kane wrinkled his nose, contemplating the tangled threads and connections running through the case. "There's also a good chance that she's still alive. And if there's one thing that I do need to prepare him for, it's that."

"I'll be needing to tell your mother that too." Donal sighed. "If she wanted to punch Forest's mother out, she's going to want to skin Miki's. I'm going to be spending the next few weeks hiding the kitchen knives."

"HE'S NOT going to go anywhere, Sinjun." Damien pulled on Miki's sleeve, keeping him by the back door. "Talk to me about what's going on. Sionn said you and I are on lockdown. Going to have to tell you, you gave me a right scare what with being shot and everything."

"Look, I just wanted to get something to eat and walk off the shit that was growing in my head." Miki leaned against the brick wall, staring across the broad alley at Damie's warehouse, not more than a few yards away. There'd been a lot of progress on building a woodworking shop for Kane between them, as well as a covered deck to connect their homes. With the renovations almost finished in the other warehouse, the last stages of construction on the workshop weren't far behind. "I'm sick of saying that I'm tired. I can't even wrap my head around what's going on with me, and then today was just… a clusterfuck. I'm just pissed off at everyone, even Kane."

"He's the one person you shouldn't be mad at." His brother whistled at Dude, calling the terrier away from the row of dumpsters lining the alley. Wood scraps and discarded drywall filled most of them, making the matte green metal containers look like giant vases bristling with avant-garde flowers. "Kane wants to keep you safe. *Sionn* wants to keep *us* safe. It's not like you won't have company in this. We'll get a lot done. Or we'll get nothing done and spend the entire time playing video games and getting fat on junk food."

Damien was looking for a smile. Miki could feel that, but he couldn't scrape up enough effort to put one on his face. The past few days overwhelmed him. Shit, he could say that about the past few years. His control was unraveling, spooling out around him and turning into dust whenever he tried to grab hold of anything, leaving him with powdery ashen fragments where he'd once had focused thoughts.

"What is Dude doing over there?" He couldn't see around the dumpsters, especially with all of the overflowing debris from the other warehouse's reconstruction. "Hey! Dude! *Come!*"

The dog—*his* dog—couldn't seem to leave one in particular alone. They were too far inside the city for any wild animals, not like Kane's parents' home—something Miki found out one day at the Morgans' house when he'd taken the terrier out for a bathroom break in the middle of the night and found himself in the middle of a possum party. But something definitely grabbed his attention, and Miki took a few steps toward the dumpster to look.

"Okay, he's not listening." Damien craned his neck, using the few inches he had over Miki to his advantage. "What the fu—"

It was the throaty click-click that got Miki into a full run. He couldn't see anything but the dog—*his* fucking dog—scratching at the dumpster's grimy wheel, but then Dude jumped back with a yelp. Miki came in hard and fast, his mind washed with a red sea of anger and frustration. And when he found a bearded man crouching behind the trash receptacle, his enormous hand wrapped around something black and long, Miki lost his mind.

Dude was moving, Miki was assured of that, but he didn't know anything beyond his dog crying and finding someone sitting practically on his back door. Or at least he didn't *think* past that. The man was getting up, rage forming in a cloud over his obscured face, and he swore when he spotted Miki, kicking out at Miki's feet. The thing in his hand flashed silver, a brilliant line of white against the darkness between the overloaded dumpsters, and Miki's mind—Miki's *fear*—grabbed at the worst thought he could have.

A gun.

He didn't know if it was because Dude spent his afternoon covered in Miki's blood or if it was because Damien—*oh my God Damien*—was only a few feet behind him, but Miki wasn't going to be *anyone's* victim anymore.

Whatever he grabbed from the dumpster had a sharp edge. It could have been wood or metal. He didn't care. It felt heavy and short enough for him to do serious damage in such a tight space. He let his anger fill him, an unfettered and wild beast who'd fed on Miki's patience for far too long. Unleashed, it savaged Miki's control, and his adrenaline surged with every pounding beat of his heart.

He tasted blood, but it wasn't his. Miki knew the taste of his own flesh, his own skin, and his own anguish. This was different. This was sweet and justified, honeyed with the knowledge the man and his weapon couldn't hurt Damien, couldn't hurt Dude, wouldn't be able to touch Miki. They would all be safe. No one could hurt anyone he loved ever again if he could just make this *one* man go away.

"*Sinjun*! For the love of God, stop!" Damie's voice punctured the crimson fog, his fingers digging into Miki's shoulders and pulling him away from the dumpsters.

Miki fought his brother off, fueled by his anger and Dude's alarmed barks. Kane was inside their warehouse. So was Donal. Sionn was somewhere around, and a hot white panic pierced Miki's brain. If the man was there, between their places, then something could've happened to Sionn. *Damien's Sionn.*

He couldn't let go of—Miki looked at what he had in his hand, startled slightly by the length of perforated metal dotted with pieces of crumbling drywall. Its dark gray surface was mottled with splatters of blood, and at his feet, an overweight man wearing a flannel shirt and jeans cradled his broken and deformed hand against his chest. He had cuts on his forehead, trickles of blood running into his sparse brown hair and thick beard. His eyes were wild with fright, and when he met Miki's gaze, he whimpered.

A broken piece of equipment lay on the wet cement a few inches from his knees.

"He's just a photographer, Sinjun," Damien murmured into his ear, his brother's arms wrapped tight around him, stilling Miki's blows. "He's not going to hurt you. He's not going to hurt me. That's just a camera, brother. Nothing more than a camera and not worth killing a man over."

CHAPTER SIX

A marble bowl was my coffin
Woke up to find my life dead
Thought I'd stopped my breathing
But it was our love that died instead
God I wish every other waking hour
I could spare a minute or two
Sometimes I think it should be me
Sleeping that final death, not you
—Marble Coffins

HIDING WAS the only thing left for Miki to do. After a swarm of stormtrooper-like cops descended on the cul-de-sac, Miki's life, already in the shithouse, was now rolling in dog poop. He couldn't keep track of who was asking him what, and after an hour or two, he also didn't know who was a lawyer or who'd come to arrest him. He couldn't turn around without bumping into a Morgan. They'd all swooped in, badges flashing and tempers flaring as they fought for Miki's freedom. One of the suits seemed familiar, a death puppet of a man in black with pale skin and swept-back ebony hair. The only spot of color on him was his red tie. Even his eyes were a milky gray, just enough blue to tint but not enough to actually hold a hue. After about half an hour, Miki realized the man worked for him, or at least worked for the band, and he'd come out of a room with Damien, ready to do battle.

He didn't know what had happened to the photographer. He also didn't care. Miki washed blood off his hands, staining the water red before it swirled down the drain, but it seemed to be from his own skin rather than splatter he'd drawn out of someone else. Heavy circles lay under his eyes when he stared at himself in the mirror. Hell, it seemed like his eyes were *bruised*, and no matter how hard Miki rubbed, he couldn't erase the shadows he saw within them.

The band's lawyer argued in whispers, barely audible even though Miki stood close by. He spoke to another suit, this one polished up, gleaming like he was about to step in front of a camera and do the news. Damien told him in a low voice the other man was a district attorney, but Miki only had eyes for Kane, who stared at him from across the room.

He didn't like what he saw in Kane's face any more than he liked what he saw on his own.

There was a resignation there, and a detachment Miki had never seen before. It was more than the cop mask Kane wore once in a while. This look had such a finality to it, it chilled Miki's guts with an icy clench. He barely stood there long enough to hear the Plasticine lawyer agree to drop the assault charges if the band didn't prosecute the photographer for trespassing and invasion of privacy. They chattered about paparazzi laws, and Miki's state of mind—already shaky considering the day's events—but the other lawyer gave a good show of hemming and hawing before capitulating to the death puppet's demands.

That was when Miki fled.

The rooftop was out. It was too open and much too comforting for his mood. He needed sterile, something closed in and without air, someplace he could scream and not be heard or cry and not be seen.

Luckily for him, he'd built a studio into the warehouse's docking bay.

Windowless and white-walled, the recording room was large but still not quite homey. They'd done their best with a few Persian rugs to muffle the floor beneath their feet so they didn't make any sound while they played, but other than a couple of beanbags and a couch too short for anybody to sleep on except for the dog, it was serviceable at best. He hoped that in time, it would become someplace they would hang out, warmed by shared experiences and inside jokes, but for now it was still cold enough a space for Miki to empty himself in.

He didn't know how long he sat there in the muted space, the lights set too low and the silence nearly deafening behind a wall of soundproof glass and thick metal door. It could've been ten minutes. It could have been three hours. He couldn't tell. Dude got up a couple of times to get a drink of water out of the bowl they kept filled next to the door, but most of the time, the dog lay at his feet on the couch, curled up into a ball Miki could scratch with his toes.

A tap on the glass surprised him, and he jerked up, laying a hand on Dude's shoulder. Dude's muzzle was damp, but his grin was wide, his tongue spooling out as he recognized the pretty-faced Irish man standing in the control room outside.

Quinn pressed his hand against the glass and gave Miki a gentle smile, then pointed at the doorknob. It was a question—a request—for permission to come in, permission to flay Miki's soul. Or that's what he would've thought if it had been anyone else besides the green-eyed Morgan.

The third Morgan son understood him probably more than anyone else in the world. To be fair, Quinn probably understood most people more than anyone else in the world did. Built more for swimming the channel than storming the castle, he was a fractured looking-glass bard among a—

Miki mimed opening the door, and a second later Quinn walked through it, closing the heavy panel behind him.

"What's a group of paladins called?" Miki asked as he joined him on the couch. "A windmill of paladins?"

"I think they would be called a congregation," Quinn replied, cocking his head. His expression went from thoughtful to puzzled, and he stared up at the ceiling, his eyes unfocused. "I like a clade of paladins only because that would mean they have a common ancestor and are its lineal descendants, so they would be a branch off of that philosophy or God." Lowering his gaze to settle on Miki, he asked, "Why?"

"Because I was thinking you were different than everybody else in your family, but I didn't have a good name for what you'd call a flock of Morgans."

The Irish in Quinn came out in his voice and in his smile. "That would be called a clan. We are a clan. And you are part of it."

"I could never be a Morgan," Miki refuted. "Did you see what I did to that guy? Kane says it's lucky he didn't lose an eye. None of you would've lost it like that. Don't tell me you would've."

"Have you met my mother?" His eyebrows went up, mocking Miki slightly. "Don't discount the Finnegan blood we have in our veins. You're not the only one with a stranglehold on their temper. I'm the same way. I can hold on for only so long and then… I see red. I don't blame you for what happened today. I don't think anybody does. The man was in your house, practically. On your feet. On your brother's feet. He *kicked* your dog. If someone did that to Harley, I'd have taken him apart. Even if I hadn't been shot at."

"God, it doesn't even seem like that was today." Miki sniffed, then rubbed at the burning in his eyes. "I haven't fed Dude yet. He's probably hungry."

Quinn looked down at the dog between them, who rolled over onto his back, stuck his legs in the air, and snored. "Don't think he's hurting for food. When was the last time *you* ate?"

Miki didn't have an answer for him, but his stomach didn't seem willing to entertain the thought of putting anything into it. He glanced at the door connecting the control room to the rest of the warehouse.

"How are you feeling? Physically. So far it sounds like your day has been like an action movie." Quinn was careful around Miki's knee, something he was very grateful for. "You look pretty good for somebody who has been shot. And in a fight."

"It was more of a burn than a shot. What's really hurting are my hands and my leg." Miki flexed his fingers, not liking the pull of tight skin across his palms.

"But you should really see the other guy. He got the worst of it. He tried to take sleazy shots of my dog."

The joke fell flat, but Miki wasn't expecting it to do much more than possibly turn Quinn off. However, the third Morgan son was made of much stronger material, and Miki was shocked when Quinn actually chuckled.

"I would've done the same thing if someone tried to take pictures of Harley. Especially since she's nude all the time." Quinn winked. "I don't want to judge, but she's kind of a slattern. She runs around naked all the time and leaves butt marks on everything I own. I mean, sure, she's an exhibitionist, but that doesn't give anybody the right to take photos. I'm sure Dude feels the same way."

Quinn always did surprise him, and Miki smiled despite himself. Sobering, he pricked at the bubble of humor between them. "Did you draw the short straw? Is that why you're here?"

"No. Damien wanted to come in, but I think he's too used to bullying you into changing how you feel instead of letting you get there yourself. And I like him, but if I didn't know better, I'd think he was related to Mom." Quinn shrugged. "Forest might have wandered in here eventually, but I actually locked the outside door. Sometimes you need someone to agree that life can be shitty, and he is not good at that. Forest is always looking for the brighter side of things. It's why he and Connor work together really well. They both have very sunny outlooks on life, even if they both pound on things for a living."

"You know, I never thought of Connor as an optimist until right now." Miki turned the idea over in his head and couldn't find a flaw in Quinn's argument. "I guess I always thought of Forest as glass half-full and Connor as half-empty."

"Oh no," Quinn said, shaking his head. "If it were like that, they wouldn't have gotten married in Vegas without Mom knowing. They're impetuous and only think of the consequences afterwards. One of us is going to have to propose to somebody else soon so Mom can have a wedding she can plan."

"Wait, you know about them being married?" Miki scrambled through his memories, trying to figure out if he'd been the one who'd let slip the secret. "How long have you known?"

"Since the weekend they came back from getting married. The day after they did it." Quinn shrugged. "Connor borrowed my car to drive over to Vegas because he wanted something cooler than the refrigerator box he drives. They left the license in my Audi."

"And you haven't told Brigid?"

"Oh, I can tell you didn't grow up with any siblings." The look Quinn gave him was pitying, as was the gentle pat he gave Miki's knee. "Never ever, *ever* share a secret. They're too good of a coin. You can either use them to get something—actually, you can use them more than once for that—or when you get into trouble yourself, if you have a really big secret, you can throw it out in front of you and they'll forget all about what you've done and focus on what *he's* done. Secrets like this are few and far between. You hold on to them and use them if you need leverage."

Despite the pressure in his chest about the day, Miki was fascinated by Quinn's confession. "Yeah, but there's a flaw there. What happens when your mom and dad find out anyway? Before you can spill the beans or whatever?"

"See, that's even better because what that does is shore up your loyalty. They think—the brothers, because it's usually Kane and Connor—that since you weren't the reason the parents found out, you're good at keeping their secrets." He grinned wickedly. "And if you do it right, if you *are* the one to tell Mom and Da about what's going on, they won't let slip that you were the one who told on him. It's a win-win."

"I'm not sure I could ever trust you with anything ever again," Miki said. "I mean… that's… what's that guy's name? That puppet master guy?"

"Machiavelli. But it's different between you and me. I would never use your secrets, Miki. Those aren't the type of things you share. There's a difference between leverage and betrayal of trust. I would never betray you. None of us in the family would ever betray each other. And that's how we think of you, as a part of the family." Quinn slid his hand under the dog's back end and moved him so his legs wouldn't dig into Miki's ankle. "It's why I came looking for you. Because you don't need anybody to talk to you, you need someone to listen to you. And even though Forest is very calming, sometimes you need family to hear you out because they understand wanting to rip out someone's throat."

"Yeah, Forest can be a little bit too Zen about things when I just want to tear something apart." He snorted and Dude opened one eye to look at him. Rubbing the dog's belly, Miki murmured, "I really could have killed that guy today. I *almost* killed him. If Damien hadn't been there—"

"If he hadn't been there—that guy—he wouldn't have been *almost* killed," Quinn argued back. After pulling his legs up, he hugged his shins and rested his chin on his knee, his unblinking cobalt gaze focused on

Miki's face. "Sorry. I promised to listen. That wasn't very good of me. Why don't you go on?"

It was hard to feel sorry for himself with Quinn in front of him, but Miki's dark thoughts were giving it a good go. Exhaling hard, he tried to find the beginning of his confusion, but everything was too tangled up in his head and he didn't know where to start. The dog was warm under his fingers, a reminder of life Miki needed very much at the moment. If he'd lost Dude… he didn't even want to entertain that thought, but it flew up anyway, slapping at him with a tortured reality.

"Dude was kind of the beginning of my life. I mean, before him… he decided to move in, I was going to kill myself." The rush of those familiar emotions hit him, a putrid stream of loathing and loss. Miki swallowed around the lump in his throat, willing it to be dislodged and washed away, but it remained, choking him. "I didn't have a plan or anything, I just… didn't want to live anymore. But then there was him and all of a sudden—well, not all of a sudden, but—eventually, I had someone who needed me.

"I've never had anyone who needed me before." He looked up, thankful to see Quinn's eyes were bright and clear. Miki wouldn't have been able to take pity or sorrow, but Quinn's attention he gladly embraced. "Dude needed me. He didn't ask, he just was there. Then your damned brother was there and, well… when God gives you a Morgan, you just don't throw him away."

"Do you feel guilty that you loved Kane and Dude even though you were mourning Damie?" As gently as Quinn asked, the question was a slap. He must've flinched because Quinn stroked the back of Miki's hand with his thumb. "I wonder about that sometimes."

"I feel more guilty about starting a new band," he confessed. "It feels good with Forest and Rafe, but sometimes it is kind of a shock not to see Johnny and Dave behind me. That's when I feel the most guilt. When we're playing and for a little bit I forget they are not there. But the playing is different, so I turn around to give them a hard time about changing things up, but… it's not them. I hate those times when I forget."

"I think it's okay to feel like that. I haven't lost anyone like you have. I know one day I will, but the closest I came to that was Rafe losing himself," Quinn said. "And I guess in a lot of ways, I got him back. Just not as dramatically as you got back Damie. He was never dead. Just lost."

"Getting Damie back was a gift, but it's kind of also a curse." Miki laughed, his bones still aching from sleeping on cheap mattresses in cramped hotel rooms. "He makes me live. Like, he doesn't let me do nothing. He's always pushing me to write or to play. I think that's why I love him and sometimes hate him. Kane loves me for who I am, but Damien loves me for who I can be. I guess it's why he feels like a brother. I didn't understand that until I saw how you guys worked. I mean, I called him my brother because it seemed like the word that fit. I just didn't realize how well it fit."

"I would kill for one of my brothers. And my sisters," Quinn amended quickly. "That's what today was for you. After this afternoon and the other day, I can see why you always get scared. Why you'd attack someone like that."

"I was more angry than scared," Miki admitted. The fear had been fleeting, a brief brush of quicksilver against the red rage filling him, but it had been there. He'd felt helpless and then powerful, wielding a piece of metal eventually dripping with blood. It was the carnage afterward that jolted him, and the deadness he felt inside while the photographer screamed. "Something cracked inside of me, Q. It wasn't because of this afternoon or me getting hurt. I was so done with life kicking me. I just wanted to kick it back. But I couldn't stop. I should have been able to, but I couldn't."

Quinn cocked his head, his long black hair falling away from his face. "Do you feel like this all the time?"

"Lately? Yeah." Miki looked down as Quinn's hands nearly swallowed his up and marveled at how similar they were to Kane's. "I am never *not* angry. And I should be happy, right? Because I have everything. I mean *everything*. I have Damie. I have a band that's solid and are good friends. And I've got Kane—fucking Kane—who made me feel things I never thought I could and loves me despite the fact that I'm an asshole. I just don't know what to do, because I think that if I don't fix what's broken inside of me, he's going to walk away because it's too hard—"

"My brother is never going to walk away," Quinn interrupted. "Did I already say that? He *loves* you and he's willing to stand with you, but I've got to be telling you, Miki, you've got to be willing to stand for yourself first. I'm thinking maybe it is time you find someone to help you get rid of that anger so you can find the happiness you drowned in it."

BY THE time Kane got the warehouse cleared of cops and family, it was nearly one in the morning. After a brief chat with Captain Book and Lieutenant Casey, he and Kel could start their shift around noon if they needed it, but Kane had high hopes he could hit up the DEA before lunchtime and begin to hunt down Rodney

Chin. He'd seen Miki only briefly, when his lover came out of the studio with Quinn and Dude not far behind. The dog had been fed, and then the band's lawyer snagged Miki and Damien for a quick discussion.

He'd been relieved to hear of the deal made with the DA, but uneasiness over the photographer lingered. The man's injuries were excessive, or at least the DA thought so. Kane wasn't so sure, but he also knew he was too close to the situation. He'd wanted to take the photographer apart. Not for the photos, but for scaring Miki.

That's how Kane knew he was too close to the situation to think straight. He didn't need his father to tell him the man had been close to beaten unconscious. If it had been anyone else administrating the attack, Kane would have pressed for his arrest. But it was Miki—*his* Mick—and Kane struggled with knowing what he should have done and with what he wanted to do.

"I want to wrap him in a blanket and put him away someplace safe until this is done," Kane muttered as he locked the front door. The dog trotted out of the kitchen, licking his lips with a look of contentment on his furry face. Since he'd been fed dinner over an hour before, Kane didn't want to know what he'd gotten into. "That best have been the bacon Sionn was going to sneak into your dish and not the garbage, dog. Because we do not need any more shit today."

Dude picked up the beef bone he'd been given earlier, jumped up on the couch with it, and began to gnaw on its end.

"You are the shittiest roommate I have ever had." Kane studied the terrier. "And that's saying a lot because I used to share a room with Connor. Well, I hope you get used to shitting in the alleyway for a little while because Sionn's going to have security guards crawling all over the outside of this place and I'm not going to be having Miki take you out to the grass out front for your constitutionals."

What was he going to do about Miki?

Their bedroom doors were closed, shutting out the crowd and noise that had been there not more than ten minutes before. They needed to talk, but what he needed more than anything else was to have Miki lying next to him and in his arms so he could reassure himself Miki was okay.

That was *exactly* what he needed.

Kane only hoped Miki needed it as well… if not more.

A light was on in the bedroom, probably the banker's lamp by Kane's side of the bed. He could see a bit of the glow creeping out from under the door, and after taking one last glance at the dog, he slipped into the bedroom, closing the door behind him.

Miki never failed to steal Kane's heart.

He'd been with pretty men and women before, and he'd had more than a few relationships that ended from an unwillingness to commit by his former partners than anything else. They hadn't liked his long hours or his sometimes weeks-on-end cases, and a couple who hadn't liked his closeness with his family. Those were the first ones Kane showed the door. The others simply fell off, not able to adapt to being part of a cop's life.

Miki didn't have that problem, despite his dislike for authority. He didn't care about the odd times Kane was gone, and once he'd said his *I love you* for the first time, Kane knew Miki was all in. He never had to question his lover's commitment or his devotion.

Staring at Miki sprawled out across the bed—*their* bed—Kane was struck by the familiar thump-thump of his heart filling with the love he had for the young man most people had written off.

He was beautiful in a way only untamed things were. There was a freedom of spirit beneath his creamy gold skin and a fierceness in his tumbled emerald-and-citrine eyes. He was careless with his striking looks, letting his brown hair grow shaggy around his sharp-featured face. Miki's mouth always drew Kane in, a perfect blend of sardonic consensuality with a full lower lip he loved to suckle on. The sounds he could draw out of that mouth were incredible, as was the responsiveness of Miki's body when Kane took his time to explore it.

Their love didn't come without the stain of sadness, a pervasive sticky paper wariness Miki wrapped himself in. As hard as he tried, Kane would never be able to unwrap it fully, stripping Miki of a protective layer he'd hidden behind for years. As grateful as Kane was to be let into Miki's heart, he longed for one simple thing—to hear Miki's unfettered laughter and see his face light up from an unguarded smile.

Nothing hurt more than the ripples of suspicion in Miki's gaze when he looked up from the book he was reading, although it whispered away into an appreciative rake over Kane's body. He did like the smile he was able to put on Miki's face, and he *liked* his lover's low purr of a growl when he stripped his jeans and shirt off, leaving them on the floor when he padded over to the king-size bed.

It felt hard to be sexy when the bed's memory foam topping dimpled under his hands and knees, but Kane was more interested in getting to Miki than in putting on a show. As large as the room was, Miki needed the bed shoved up against the wall, preferring to have that firmness behind him as he slept. Kane didn't mind so much, especially since Miki wasn't one to get up in the middle of the night, but there was a brief warning flare in Miki's wide eyes whenever Kane stalked him across the bed. Those were from ghosts Miki couldn't exorcise but Kane could definitely kiss away.

Or hug. Today it seemed like Miki needed more contact, to be held and spoken to, at least for a few minutes. So Kane did exactly that, pulling Miki into an embrace and dragging him into the pillows, losing Miki's book somewhere in the blankets.

"That's going to dig at me," Miki grumbled, then hissed when Kane dug the book out and tossed it onto the tufted bench at the foot of the bed. "Hey, you're going to break the spine."

"I'll get you a new one," he muttered, snagging Miki's earlobe with his teeth. "Why aren't you reading on one of the five hundred tablets we have in the house?"

"I like *books*." Miki nestled down, his bare chest slightly cold from being out of the covers. "I love the way they smell, kind of like creamy vanilla tea. There's just something about paper and the weight. I like how it feels in my hands because I can feel how much the words weigh. I don't get that with a reader. That just makes all of the books weigh the same, and they don't. Some of them are heavier because they have more to say. I want to feel that. So don't fuck up my book."

"Duly noted," Kane acknowledged. He slid his hands down, cupping Miki's ass and elated to find bare, smooth skin under Miki's cotton pants. "No underwear? I like no underwear nights."

"I was going to be naked, but I didn't know if somebody was going to walk in. There were just so many fucking people in our house."

"How are you doing? Today has been pretty rough." The *our* in *our house* warmed Kane's heart as much as Miki's fingers playing with his belly button. "Did you get to talk to Damie? I know he was worried about you."

"We did. A little bit." Miki's eyes went dark, shuttering away his emotion. "I scared him today. I scared me today, but now he looks at me and it's different. I… wonder if he's ever going to feel safe around me again."

"I don't think he was scared of you, *a ghra*." He was going to have to step carefully around the land mines Miki had surrounded himself with. Nothing resurrected the terrified child hidden inside his lover more than the possibility of losing the love of someone he cared for. "Damie's worried about you. We all are. Today was an anomaly—"

"No, it's not," Miki sliced in. "I'm going to go find someone to talk to about… today… *every* day."

Kane went still, suddenly aware of what Miki meant. He said words weighed something, and some words were definitely chunks of steel while others were feathers. The burden of Miki's words, of what he carried inside of him, was very real and open between them, more than it had ever been before.

"I talked to Quinn about it, and he said there are a couple of people he knows from the university who I'd like. He told me a lot of things about what happens and that I should find somebody I like to talk to. That person is more important than someone who's going to dish out medication to me." Miki shifted in Kane's arms, enough for him to look up. "I mean, I might need something to balance out the chemicals in my head, and I hate the idea of that. I *really* do. I hate thinking that I have to take something to feel okay. I'm scared I am going to lose even more of me, but if I don't do something, I feel like there's not going to be anything of me left."

"I've watched Quinn go through this over the years." Kane began to stroke at the spot between Miki's shoulder blades. "And I've seen you struggle through physical therapy and medication for your knee. If you want my opinion, I think finding someone to talk to is a good idea. Quinn needed somebody outside of the family to give him perspective without judgment. I think you would do well getting some of that too. The problem with everyone who loves you is we're all strong-willed and stubborn-headed. We all think we know what's best for you, but we don't know what we're talking about.

"Well, maybe Quinn does," Kane amended. "But the rest of us are flying by the seat of our pants, and there are traumas in your life we can't touch, can't fully understand. There are people out there who spend their lives understanding the kind of evil you had to live through. They may never have dealt with somebody quite like you, though. I think you are too much *you* to be lost in any medication or therapy, but I would love to see you smile again."

"Me too," Miki whispered, sliding his hands over Kane's chest. "Would you believe me if I told you that even though I've been shot across the arm and my hands hurt from the stupid thing I did today in the alleyway, I really want you to make me smile?"

"I would not only believe it," he murmured through a kiss on Miki's mouth, "I had every intention of doing so even before I came into our room."

CHAPTER SEVEN

Donal: Just take yer time.

Miki: How much do I put in? Do I fill it up all the way? How the hell do you know?

Donal: It's like music. Ye've got to feel yer way through. Find what works for ye. Eventually ye'll get yer groove.

Miki: What if I fuck it up?

Donal: Mick. Nothing to worry over. Remember what I taught you.

Miki: Yeah, don't take this wrong, but this is a fuckton harder than making music. It's fucking pancakes, Dad. And I'm screwing them up.

—Morgan kitchen, Easter Sunday morning

UNTIL KANE entered his life, Miki never viewed his body as anything for pleasure. It had been a receptacle of pain for as long as he could remember. The intrusions into it, each act a forceful and violent domination, ended when he took control of his life, joining Damien on a journey to the stars. Sex then became something performed on him by nameless, faceless men who drifted in and out of his life in five- to ten-minute intervals and felt more like commercial spots in between the television show of his life rather than something to transform his heart and mind.

That is, until Kane.

He'd been found with a shattered body and an even more broken heart, but his cop hadn't stepped away from the challenge Miki hadn't realized he'd thrown down. He'd tried shoving Kane back, refusing to let him in, but his blue-eyed Irish man refused to be cowed by the snarl of a tiny dragon. Kane wasn't a savior. No, but he was definitely a knight of some sort. His armor wasn't pristine. It was battered and gouged from the wars he fought on the streets. But the heart behind the steel was pure and strong, shining with a light bright enough to chase away even the darkest of Miki's shadows.

Today of all days, Miki needed his shadows driven off.

They always returned, circling him and looking for a way back in, sensitive to any weakness he might show, then slithering in through the cracks in Miki's guard. It had been an endless dance, something Miki had grown used to, until Kane taught him he didn't need to be dragged out on that floor and waltz with the shadows until his soul was bloodied.

Kane's hands calmed him. His mouth invigorated him. And when the air ran sweet with the scent of vanilla lube, the promise of Kane pushing inside of him made Miki believe he could almost fly.

"You are so gorgeous, *a ghra*," Kane whispered, his breath ghosting across Miki's bare belly. "Let me play with you. Let me *feel* you. I think you need this… need *us*… more than anything else right now."

Kane's fingers were always rough, even though his touch was gentle. He carried the world on his skin, everything from the streets he walked on, the gun he carried, and the flesh of the trees he carved and worked until he could pull the beauty out of it. They were hands that were powerful enough to render a man unconscious, but Miki had also seen them tenderly wipe away a child's tear. He loved the feel of Kane's hands on his skin… enjoyed the rasp of his callused palms and fingers down his sides, across his back, and up the insides of his thighs. And he shivered when Kane cupped him, taking the most vulnerable parts of Miki's body into his palm, then caressed his cock with a feathering touch.

Life taught Miki to be frightened when someone touched him there. With Kane, that reaction—that horrific fear—never came. Instead, he gentled with every stroke of Kane's fingers, the anticipation of his release building along every stretch of bone beneath his skin.

And he fought to give Kane back every ounce of pleasure he'd been given.

He let himself be moved around the bed, mostly so he could end up against Kane's side and within reach of the heavy sac and thick cock between his lover's legs.

His body ached today, small bruises and strained muscles, but they faded into the background, much like the streetlights' glow peeking in through the heavy curtains. He was more interested in wrapping his mouth around the thick head of Kane's cock, flexing his tongue against its underside, and dragging a primal groan from his lover's mouth. With a taste of salt to the back of his throat, a sticky bitter sweetness on his tongue, Miki knew Kane was growing close, so he pulled off his lover's length to blow a stream of cold air on the overheated velvety head.

"You are killing me, Mick," Kane grunted, the Irish as thick in his words as his dick was in Miki's mouth. "I can't—"

If there was one thing Miki was good at, it was taking Kane into him, and he did just that, tilting his head up and swallowing Kane down. It was always an odd sensation, and no matter how often he did it, there was a brief flutter of panic before Miki remembered how to breathe.

And then he would swallow, the muscles in his throat rippling around Kane's length, and without fail, Kane would dig his fingers into Miki's shoulders.

Kane had been right. Kane was always right. Miki *needed* this. He needed to be able to feel alive and wanted to wash away all the bitterness and filth in his mind and throat. The taste of Kane would take care of all of that, as the press of Kane's flesh into him would erase every ache in his body.

"Babe, if you don't stop… I'm not going to be any good for you," Kane ground out between his clenched teeth. He arched, his fingers in Miki's hair, gently tugging to pull Miki off him. "I want to be inside of you."

That was the best idea Miki had heard all day.

His knee was slightly swollen, but Miki was willing to take the pressure of his weight on it when he knelt in the middle of the bed. Kane had other ideas. Kane *often* had other ideas.

"Lie down on your belly," Kane rasped. "Lift your hips up so I can put a pillow underneath you."

It was a position Miki hadn't liked in the beginning of the relationship. It felt too dominating, too controlling. Then something shifted inside of him, and Kane's weight made him feel safe. He loved the feel of Kane's chest on his back and the press of their bodies into the bed. It was harder to reach underneath himself, but the friction against the mattress and Kane's skilled fingers usually did the job.

Stupidly enough, he loved when Kane bit the back of his neck. It drove him crazier than anything else Kane did to him with the exception of actually being inside of him. It was the little affections that turned their sex into something glorious, a shared intimacy where Miki felt free.

Of course, he also had the sneaking suspicion Kane liked him on his stomach because that way Miki couldn't bite Kane's nipples. It was a perverse pleasure he delighted in every so often just to remind Kane he wasn't always the one in control.

"Open for me, *a ghra*," Kane whispered, the whiskey purr of his voice accompanied by the snick of the lube bottle opening. Its scent was sweet, a little bit different from what they normally used, but Miki wasn't complaining. At least not until Kane's slick fingers slid down the crease of his ass and the cold lube sent an icy frost over his skin.

Kane simply laughed at Miki's hiss.

"That's fucking cold," Miki grumbled, pulling one of the pillows over to hug against his chest.

The cant of his hips made the small of his back hurt, the spot tender from where he'd struck the lunch kiosk during the shooting. Tiny abrasions on the palms of his hands, the little scores left from the parking lot's rough blacktop cut through the bruises he'd gotten from wielding the drywall frame. Kane must have seen him moving slowly, or maybe he just knew Miki's body so well he could tell where he was hurt. As the lube warmed, heated up from their skin, Kane kissed the ache along Miki's spine.

"Let me make you feel good, Mick." Kane's fingers dipped into him and twisted down, spreading the lubricant around. "Just lie there for a moment and breathe. Let me give you this."

The stretch of flesh around Kane's fingers was something Miki knew so well. He sometimes had dreams about being spread open, slid into, and having Kane's muscular arms wrapped around his chest, pulling him back against Kane's hard body. He'd woken up more than a few times panting and hard, reaching for the man who'd already left for work... already awake, wearing a badge and a gun, pushing back other people's darkness with the light he had burning inside of him.

It was always best when Miki discovered he wasn't in a dream, because not only would Kane be there when he was done, Miki would have the feel of him inside for hours afterward.

Those fingers—rough, thick fingers—explored him slowly while Kane's mouth left trails of kisses along Miki's shoulders and back. His lips always found Miki's scars, taking the time to kiss at the twisted curls of badly healed wounds and mottled patches of sheared-off skin. His sides were a landscape of brutality and pain, left over from abuse and the accident that ripped apart his life. But when Kane's mouth touched on the badly done splotches of ink on his upper arm, Miki's eyes stung with a sudden rush of tears.

He'd been kissed there before. Only by Kane, but tonight that touch seemed a bit profane. Not the kiss, but the tattoo. It was a part of his body that had been his but a mystery, something he thought he would never know the answer to. So he'd given it over to Kane, and now someone else was trying to lay claim to that spot.

"I can hear you thinking, Mick," Kane scolded playfully, then slid his hand down, his fingers sliding over the spot inside of Miki where stars were released into his blood. "I must not be doing this right, then."

"I can definitely stop thinking," Miki gasped, intending to say more, but Kane's fingers parted and he lost the ability to think. The tingles along his body were flashes of lightning on the horizon of a storm Kane was going to bring down upon them. "Okay, stopping thinking."

They'd been together long enough that there were rituals, funny little habits they each did during sex. It had been odd when they no longer used condoms, secure knowing they were safe with each other, but Miki kind of missed the brief pause and Kane's muttering as he fought with the foil packet. A little bit of nonsense and laughter when his lover needed more lube to ease his way into Miki's body because his fingers were usually slick and his coordination was off. So Miki twisted over onto his side and reached for the bottle, like he always did.

And looked up at his lover's beautiful face and sculpted body.

He'd never been religious. In fact, his first true brush with religion came from falling in with the

Morgans and their worship of a benevolent God who was sometimes at odds with their church. They were raised carrying the stones of their religion, burdens of morals and ethics they bore on their backs to strengthen themselves. It seemed to be in their blood to help those weaker than them, shouldering others' troubles as well as their own. He'd been to Mass and heard passionate speeches about love, forgiveness, and forbearance.

For all the lyrical sermons and thoughtful speeches, it was the church's art that caught Miki's attention with depictions of Heaven and its warriors holding him in rapture as the Morgans sat around him.

He'd always imagined angels as perfect, ethereal beings, but crossing over the threshold of the house of worship that held generations of prayers, Miki realized he already walked among angels—or at least what he considered their true form.

Because he had fallen in love with one of them.

The power in Kane's body wasn't simply the planes of muscles and tight tendons under his skin. As beautiful as his form was, it was the strength of his generous heart that made Miki's heart clench with emotion. He was gorgeous, imperfect with small battle wounds he earned as a child and more than a few scars he'd absorbed as an adult. His power lay in his ability to make his broad shoulders seem more like a place where Miki could seek comfort rather than feel threatened, and he possessed a quick, sardonic mind cunning enough to make Miki laugh.

Still, as Miki's gaze touched on the corded strength of Kane's thighs and muscled belly, then up to his flat chest and strong arms, he was more than willing to admit Kane was a gorgeous man.

"I like the way you're looking at me, love," Kane murmured, taking the bottle from Miki's hand. "Now let's see if I can get you to shout my name."

He lay back down, chuckling as he heard Kane swear at the bottle. It was another ritual. Something familiar they'd done more than a few times before, and he *liked* it. His life had been a whirlwind of changes and chaos. Kane brought with him a foundation and, oddly enough, opened up the sky for him as well.

"Anytime you're—" Miki's breath hitched involuntarily at the press of Kane's fingers on his asscheeks.

He was being parted, opened up enough for him to feel the push of Kane's hard length at his entrance. He bowed his head, unthinkingly tensing in preparation for the weirdness he would feel. Clutching the pillow to his chest, Miki sucked in a breath and held it as Kane guided himself in.

Miki had no words to really describe how it felt when his lover entered him. The feel of his slick flesh, eased by a sweet-smelling ointment but still there, was a nerve-tingling burn, a tight sensation of oversensitive skin stimulated nearly too much. The initial sear of flesh meeting flesh was over in a few seconds, either burned away by the fire it brought with it or simply washed off because his body couldn't process any more of its pleasure. The push of Kane into him awoke a need to be filled, to be pushed past what he could take and begin a race toward a summit he could only briefly touch.

Kane held on to Miki's hips, slowly seating himself. Miki clenched his fingers into the pillow, rocking himself back onto Kane's length and mewling, needing more—aching for more—even as Kane nestled up against him, his cock fully enveloped by Miki's body. Kane shifted behind him, the mattress moving slightly between Miki's parted legs. The soft foam cradled his knees, lessening the strain on him, and his hips absorbed most of the motion. But when Kane began to move, Miki went with him, rolling with each stroke and clutching at the pillows and sheets as waves of pleasure lapped at his senses.

"I've got you, Mick," Kane murmured, settling down over Miki's back.

Kane slid one arm under Miki's chest, lifting him up slightly. Kane's hand worked down between Miki's belly and the bed, his fingers closing over Miki's turgid dick. His thumbnail scored a line over Miki's cock head, digging a razor-sharp edge through Miki's pleasure.

Oh God, when they began to move. His world changed when Kane moved inside of him. It opened them up in ways that Miki had never imagined experiencing. As much as he lay exposed, his emotions raw and his heart splayed, Kane was right there with him. They fit into each other, giving as much as they took. With each stroke of Kane's powerful hips, he pushed a bit of himself into Miki's warmth, leaving behind the fullness of his touch.

He was reaching a point where everything physical melded with the turbulence of emotions building up inside of Miki's heart and mind, and when it struck, when he merged with the parts of him that made music with the flesh that brought it to life, Miki finally felt whole.

And Kane—stubborn, bossy, gorgeous Kane—was the only one who could hold him together long enough for Miki to feel real.

Kane's fingers were a delicious glide across Miki's cock, the slight burr of his skin tantalizing Miki's shaft. His strokes were short, hampered by the lack of space between them, but any more would have driven Miki too quickly over the edge. He wanted Kane to ride him for a very long time, to keep him stretched open until maybe the sun rose or the world fell away.

The slaps of Kane's hips on his ass were sharp retorts in the nearly empty room, a percussion roll forming a baseline beneath Miki's needy growls. Their thrusts soon turned wild, their skin damp with sweat and their muscles aching with the effort of keeping up the rhythm they'd chosen. Kane tightened his grip on Miki, stilling him, but Miki twisted around Kane, clenching and releasing himself and marveling at the primal grunts Kane made over him.

Miki felt the surge of Kane's shaft thickening inside of him, and his own cock was nearly too tight to be touched, almost too brittle against the waves of sensations rocking Miki's body. Kane found the spot inside of him, sliding against it time and time again, and Miki could only hold on, lost in the swirl of his nerves exploding and his body clenching with release. The scent of their joining was strong in his nose, the musk of their sex and sweat clinging to the inside of his mouth and filling his throat. The air tasted of Kane and the oddly familiar echo of himself, the hint of salt he'd only tasted after Kane's mouth had been on him and then they shared a kiss.

"Now, *a ghra*—oh God." Kane gave one final push, piercing through the last of Miki's resolve.

It was always the rush of liquid heat running through him Miki needed from Kane before he could let go. His cock shook in Kane's hand, splattering over his palm, and Miki shuddered, closing in on Kane so tight he wondered on some level if they weren't really one person, one heartbeat and one soul.

A spattering of kisses now across his shoulder, and then the sting of Kane's teeth on the back of his neck. That was the trigger for Miki to find his climax, and the bite helped anchor him in place when he flew apart. He lost sight of anything cerebral he might've clung to in that moment, because everything he was became flesh. The ecstasy found in Kane's touch, on Kane's cock, was breathtaking—literally a long surge of pleasure hard enough to steal the air from his lungs.

Kane's thrusts continued, slowing but still strong enough to rock Miki's body and tilt his hips into the soft pillow beneath him. His belly was wet with come, and Kane's fingers moved over his stomach, spreading the viscous liquid around. The last of it was playful. The reverberations were lessening even as Miki's body pulled in, reluctant to give Kane up. They lay there panting, moving only when Miki's grunts alarmed Kane enough to roll them over onto their sides, but he remained lodged inside of Miki, his softening cock pressed past the tender stretch of Miki's entrance.

"Damn, I've made a mess of you." Kane chuckled, running his sticky, wet thumb through the damp hair below Miki's belly button. His breathing was a bit forced, as if he'd been run hard, and Miki took a small pleasure in knowing he'd driven Kane to that point. "We're probably going to have to change the sheets if we want to sleep here tonight."

"Too tired," Miki grumbled. "I don't care if we stick to the bed. I don't want to move."

"Neither do I," he said, burying his face into Miki's hair. "I don't ever want to leave this bed again. Sadly, I'm going to have to."

Miki needed to say things, needed to promise his cop. He could see Kane's hands spread over his chest in the dim light of the room and then move down his belly. He captured one thumb in his fingers, pulling the hand up to his mouth so he could kiss Kane's palm. Miki tasted himself on his lover's skin and closed his eyes, wondering what he'd done to deserve the man he'd found.

"I'm sorry for today," he whispered into Kane's open hand, into the darkness creeping over them as night fell further down over the city and the streets doused their lights. "I was out of control today. That man—I shouldn't have lost it. I never meant to go that far—"

"He wasn't hurt as bad as he let on, but I'm going to have to agree with you, it was too far." Kane held him, rocking Miki in his arms. "Not just because of you hitting him a few times, but because—*and do not take this wrong*—because you never reach out to any of us for help. You are not alone, Mick. We are all here for you. *I* am here for you. That is how you get lost. Because you see no one around you when things go bleak. You wrap yourself up in the dark that you carry, and you don't let any of us in. I need you to let me love you, *a ghra*, and I need you to find me before you break so I can hold you until you heal. But most of all, I need you to remember I love you. Through thick and thin, Mick."

"It's hard sometimes," Miki whispered, the day finally catching up with him. Lethargy stole into his bones and he drifted, cradled in Kane's warmth. "I'm afraid to ask, I think. Because it would break my heart if you said no. And not no to things like when you had to help with the shooting. I don't know where my head was at then, but—I don't know what I'm saying—I guess I'm just always scared. And I'm kind of sick of it."

"You find someone to talk to, and I'll be here to listen as well," Kane promised. "Just like I'll be here in the morning to help you peel the sheets off of us. Because if there's one thing I'm very sure of, Miki my love, we're not moving from this bed again."

"You have to move," Miki mumbled, his eyes growing heavy. "Who else is going to let the dog in? It's either you, or I have to climb over you to get out, and I'll just knee your balls if you make me do that. And just so you know, I love you too. More than anyone else in the world. I never want to live without you, K. I might not say it, but that's how I feel. I want to be better for you. A better person. Someone who can hold your hand out in the open or... all of that."

"Do you love me enough to let the dog in?" Kane teased.

"Yes." Miki yawned, scrunching down into the pillows. "But I also know that you love me enough to do it for me. So let him in so we can go to sleep, and I will try my best not to fuck up tomorrow."

CHAPTER EIGHT

A bit of silver for a lady
Slice of gold for a guy
Giving out my soul in pieces
Got to give it all away 'fore I die
Need to leave this world better
Better than when I found it that first day
Dance my way on through to Heaven
Hoping Hell's devils and demons
Don't hunt me down to pay
—Working Off the Red

SAN FRANCISCO'S sky hadn't lightened past a dove gray, refusing to let the sun creep past the dirty mix of clouds overhead. A light drizzle chased the dawn, then settled in for the rest of the day, misting the city in steady, filmy sheets. The rain slickened the streets and sidewalks, dampening the flotsam left behind in the rush of the crowds. Chinatown was subdued, quiet as it slowly woke to begin its day. Already small dribbles of delivery trucks and hurrying restaurant workers were playing a hopscotch roulette through the late morning traffic.

Kel met Kane at the station, grumbling slightly at the early hour, but he gratefully took the large coffee Kane handed him as they headed inside. His partner stayed silent during the nearly half-hour meeting they had with Book and Casey, absorbing the extent of what had happened to Miki the day before and murmuring his relief at the DA's final decision to drop all charges for both parties. They'd all agreed the photographer had been in the wrong, but Kane was the first to admit Miki pushed the situation too far.

That was something Book definitely didn't agree with.

"Someone comes to my house…," their captain groused, stabbing at the air with his finger, "starts taking pictures of me? You bet your ass I'm going to have more than words with them. Can't say I wouldn't do the same thing. Maybe worse. I've got grandkids, and I'm not some kind of rock star, so maybe it's something he should be used to, but… a man should be able to step outside of his house without worrying about someone dogging his every step. Mind you, that's my personal opinion, but we do have laws against what that photographer was doing there."

Casey murmured his agreement, but Kane noticed his partner only nodded, then shifted the conversation to the case they were working on. Kel's thoughtful quietude lingered even as they stopped to grab a couple of burritos from a taco stand not far from the task force's remote offices.

The rain forced them to retreat to Kane's Hummer, but they'd shared many a meal sitting side by side in its leather seats. It was a lived-in vehicle with a dusting of dog hair in the back from Dude's company on long car rides and a stash of napkins and wrapped straws in the glove compartment just in case they were needed. Still, Kel was habitually meticulous, unwilling to make a mess as he unwrapped his burrito over a spread-out paper bag on his lap, checking periodically to make sure nothing had bled through onto his pants. Kane was opening one of the sandwich baggies packed with a generous helping of jalapeño-carrots when Kel finally spoke up.

"I need to ask you something, man." Kel placed his food on the Hummer's dash, carefully setting it away from the edge. "I've been trying to figure out a way to talk to you about this without it coming across as intrusive, but... I don't know... I think I just need to bring it up."

They were rarely serious off the job. Their partnership was built on humor as much as their shared dedication to justice. Kel's tone... his expression... was different this time, heavy and poignant. Kane shoved his food back into his bag and wiped his hands, turning in his seat. Kel was past serious, a somber mood settling over him even before he shifted to face Kane.

"You and I are... we're like brothers. Or at least, I feel that way, man." Kel smiled at Kane's murmured assent. "I mean, I obviously am the better-looking brother, but... I think I've got to ask you this and I need you to be honest with me, okay?"

"Yeah, dude," Kane replied, frowning. The rain thickened a bit, obscuring the view outside, and Kane's heart skipped a beat, his thoughts homing in on his friend's troubled expression. "Kel, you can talk to me about anything. Shit, we've bled on each other. You almost backed up over my dog. What's up?"

"God, don't ever tell Miki that happened," Kel hissed, shaking his head. "And actually, this is about Miki. I need to know if you're all right. You know I love your guy, right? I've got every single damned record his band ever made and a couple of bootleg cuts too. One of my favorite bands and personally, he's a complicated fuck but a decent guy. And I know he makes you happy. I see that, but… I've got to ask you… is he hitting you, Kane? Because if he is—"

"Are you kidding me? Look at him! I'm nearly double his size and he—" Kane cut his laugh off short when Kel's chin lifted up, his dark gaze firm but gentle. "Kel, that's… insane. I mean—it's *Miki*."

"I love you, man, and I'd understand if you're pissed off at me for talking about this. I know how I would feel. I'd be pissed off, and I'm hoping you can see why I have to bring this up," Kel pressed, and Kane sat back against the Hummer's door, shocked to his core. "Look at the situation. All of the signs of potential domestic abuse are there. You know it. I know it. We've seen this kind of thing before. His size doesn't matter. Neither does yours. I *need* to know you're okay. Because if you aren't… if he is hitting you… then we're going to need to do something. Get you out of there. Don't tell me you love him. I *know* you love him. But after yesterday, I've got to ask you this. If I didn't then I wouldn't be somebody you could call your brother."

His partner was *serious*. Sitting next to him in the middle of a dreary San Francisco day, his best friend was asking him if his lover *beat* him. Processing through the shock Kel's words left him in, Kane was about to vehemently deny the whole situation, *angrily so*, but reason took hold.

They'd seen the aftermath of abuse. Spent countless hours counseling both the poor and the rich, as well as everyone else in between. It didn't matter a couple's gender, finances, or size, there were *always* signs. Kane couldn't count the hours he'd spent trying to convince someone to walk away from a dangerous situation. There'd always been apologies and excuses, an underlying obsession or fear neither cop could get the victim to shake off. Denial was their biggest obstacle, words sometimes flung at them in spits of rage, and assurances there was no physical or emotional damage being done to them.

Kane also couldn't count the number of times they ended up returning to a scene to stand over a dead body wearing a familiar face and all-too-familiar bruises.

"Okay." Kane puffed out his cheeks, exhaling slowly. It felt like Kel had punched him in the stomach, pushing all of the air out of him, and Kane struggled to catch his breath. The idea of Miki striking him was so far away from reality, Kane could barely wrap his mind around the idea. Still, Kel had to question their relationship, especially considering all of the things he and Kane saw on the job. "I get how you would think this. I *do*. And yeah, it's a conversation I would want you to have with me if—"

"I've seen—*we've seen*—some really big guys with tiny partners whose faces are all fucked-up and they're insisting everything's fine. Yeah, I'm worried. And it's nothing against Miki. I just need to make sure. If you look at it, you can take a lot of boxes off of the checklist. He's got a bad temper, has access to some pretty serious drugs, and yesterday took a piece of metal to a guy with a camera, beating the crap out of him because he was behind your guys' house." Kel held up his hand, telling Kane to wait before speaking. "He's not a small guy. Sure, he's not a Morgan, and you guys are built to fend off Viking hordes, but even as fucked-up as his knee is, Miki's got a lot of muscle on and he grew up *mean*."

"Miki is far from mean," Kane interjected. "He's just… irascible."

"Kane, *nice* isn't that boy's default setting. Miki grew up hard, and I'll be the first one to tell you I don't know how he gets through his day without taking the fuck out of everybody in front of him. If it was me and all of that shit went down during my childhood, I'd be fucking skinning people instead of making music. He's stronger than I ever could be, and I've got to give him props for that," Kel said. "But I've also got to acknowledge he's not somebody I would want to cross."

"Every single time shit's gone down with him it's because he's defended himself." Even though he'd never been in danger around Miki, Kane knew what it sounded like—what he sounded like—and his words were flimsy, potentially ripe with excuses. "He's never *ever* raised a hand to me. I can't imagine him ever doing that, but yesterday was troublesome. My gut says he was really scared yesterday. I saw him afterwards and he was shaking. It took him a while to even focus on me, and he kept asking if Damie was okay and if Dude was all right."

"I've seen what he can do to defend himself. See, you and I, we grew up in a family. Hell, I've seen you guys beat the shit out of each other playing touch football. I've even seen you and Connor get into a shoving match, but there's a key difference between how you guys… and me… go into a fight. You and me? We go in to win, but Miki? He goes and makes sure the other guy doesn't get back up to hurt him. There's no gauging when to stop or if the other guy is ready to give up. We've been in some fights, and there's always that holding back, but not for your Miki. He goes in to end it. He goes in to make sure he's the only one left standing."

"He's not a brawler," Kane agreed. It felt odd defending Miki to Kel of *all* people. "Miki isn't violent. Not unless pushed too far. And we agreed he needs to take a step back and really look at how he's doing, how his anger is affecting him. Last night was… too much. He knows that."

"All that's good, but do you see why I'm asking if he's hurting you? Because you love him and you're a Morgan. There's a lot of pressure being you. I don't know if that pressure includes not saying something if Miki's hitting you." Kel shrugged at Kane's doubtful hiss. "I have to ask. We have egos. We're big bad cops with guns, and you have a badge that's got a heavy name on it. I don't think you would hide that from me, but—"

"I wouldn't," Kane said softly. They didn't touch, not normally. A couple of slaps across their shoulders or even a pat on the ass during a workout, but hugs were few and far between, and a casual squeeze of each other's hand was unheard of. Still, Kane reached across the Hummer and took Kel's hand, gently clenching it. "I love you very much. I think of you as a scrawny brother—which is saying a lot because we think Quinn is scrawny—"

"Dude, that's messed up. Q is not a skinny guy. His upper arms are like my thighs," Kel objected.

"Shut up for a bit. I'm trying to have a moment here with you." He grinned, spoiling the effect of the mock outrage he'd put into his words. Kane tightened his grip once more, then said, "If Miki were beating on me, I would tell you. And I wouldn't stay. As much as I love him, and God, the idea of a life without him makes my heart weep, but there's no living with that kind of relationship. I'm grateful you care about me enough to ask me this. I know it was hard because it's not something guys talk about or even... well, most cops would admit to... but I'm okay. And Miki will be okay as soon as he finds somebody qualified to talk to about all of the shit he's gone through."

"So are we good?" Kel asked, returning Kane's clench. "I don't want you to be pissed off at me, but... I had to ask."

Kane patted Kel's hand, then let go, shaking his head as he reached for his food. "I'm not pissed at you, man. We're more than good. You're just looking out for me, and I appreciate that. I really do."

"Good." His partner sighed in relief. "For a moment there I was kind of scared I wouldn't just lose you, I'd lose my backstage access and kickass tickets. 'Cause you might be my brother, but they're my favorite band."

IT TOOK Miki five times dialing the number Quinn gave him before he said hello when someone picked up. The woman on the other end—a tender-voiced, hard-as-steel-underneath psychologist named Penny—*listened* as he spoke. She only interrupted to disabuse him of calling her by her last name and once again when he apologized for disturbing her day. Even though Quinn had told him she was expecting Miki's call, he was still wary when she admitted as much.

"Doctor Morgan reached out to me yesterday," she said in an accent similar to Damien's, but Miki'd been around enough to know there was a bit of North London in her words. "He said you had an incident where you felt like you are out of control and that you might feel that it's time to speak to somebody about it."

He meant to laugh, but it came out strangled and forced. Dude jumped up on the couch at that point, snuggling against Miki's leg, and the brittle, frenetic thread running through his chest stopped jiggling. Stroking the dog's belly, he'd settled in and let go of the hardest thing he ever had to say.

"It isn't just what happened yesterday." Miki didn't know why he was so scared, but suddenly a cliff in his mind appeared and he was standing on the edge of it, looking down into a nothingness that held every single nightmare he'd ever dreamed up and a few he knew were thrown in for good measure. Closing his eyes, he focused on Kane and anchored himself in the love he felt for his cop. "I think I am… no… I *know* I'm lost. And I don't know how to fix it.…"

He found the source of his fear. It squatted on the glittering broken-glass remains of his life before Kane, before the accident, before Damien. The monster he'd stitched together from tattered dreams and extinguished hopes stared back at him with dead eyes, daring him to speak its name.

Even when he'd been at his smallest, Miki hadn't liked curling up and taking his blows in silence. He'd been too weak, too malleable, and much too powerless when the men who held his life in their hands peeled off strips of him every time they touched him. He'd worked too hard to wall the monster up with bricks he made of good memories and exhilarating experiences.

But it all had come crumbling down, leaving him with a monster eating him alive.

"You say you're scared." Penny's voice reached across the line, dangling a bright shiny lure for him to bite. "Do you want to share that with me now or wait until we can meet in person?"

He liked how she was honest with him, a sandpaper-grit growl wrapped in velvet concern. She didn't press but made it clear she would take whatever he gave her and sit and wait if he had nothing to hand out.

It was time to name the monster. Time to pull it out into the light and stare at it while it smoked and caught fire, promising to blister Miki's soul as it burned.

"I'm scared shitless that if I do this…," he whispered into the phone, staring down into his terrier's soft brown eyes. "When I fix what's broken inside of me—*if* I can fix what's broken inside of me—I'm not going to be me anymore. That if I fix me, I'm not going to be able to write music or lyrics because everything that I write about comes from that space where I'm nothing but pieces inside. Suppose when I try to make all the pain inside of me go away, I erase myself too?"

Her laugh was better than his, lighter, but not without its own darkness. Then she replied, "But suppose if you do heal some of the hurt you have, you discover even more of yourself there? Isn't that worth the risk?"

He hung up after making an appointment, texting Kane the time, date, and place so they could arrange for one of Sionn's security friends to take him over. His lover shot back a quick message, informing Miki *he* would be the one to play chauffeur and to remind Miki he was loved.

"He's such a fucking goof," Miki told the dog. Dude wiggled, trying to erase the sliver of space between them, then yawned, blinking up at the man he refused to leave alone. "You are too. I hope this works out, because if it doesn't, then I just fucked up my life more."

"I don't think you fucked up your life." Damien's voice startled Miki and he twisted quickly, pulling all the sore muscles in his body and sending a twinge shooting up his arm where he'd been shot. His brother took the stairs two at a time, then crossed over to the sectional and flopped down next to Miki. The cushions jumped, and Dude rolled a little bit but remained on his back, his eyes half-closed in sleep.

"Weren't you supposed to be out with Sionn? Looking at bottle suppliers or something for Finnegan's?" The scowl he gave Damien did nothing but give Miki a headache from pulling his eyebrows together, because his brother shrugged it off like a stray drop of water on a clear sunny day. "If I'd known you were home—"

"You would have put that phone call off. Not a good life decision there, brother," Damien pointed out. He leaned against Miki, sitting shoulder to shoulder but leaving enough room for the small dog between them. "I don't want to be someone that gloats—"

"You are *totally* someone who gloats," Miki shot back.

Damien ignored him. "But you've been needing to talk to somebody for a long time. I'm glad you did it. Or least started to. Was he nice?"

"He was a *she*." He eyed Damien. "What's that look mean?"

Settling back, Damien said, "I'm surprised you decided to talk to a woman, that's all."

Damien felt nice against him, warm and familiar. It was odd how Miki was used to his brother's scent and weight. Miki supposed it went both ways, because if there was one thing Damien did, it was being overly familiar with Miki, and he had every right to meddle in his life. Much like it appeared he was going to do right now.

And as much as Miki didn't want to poke at his healed-over scabs, he rose to Damien's bait. "Why are you surprised?"

"Well, you are kind of on this yellow brick road to find out who your mother is," he said carefully, drawing his words out slowly. "And, well, you have issues with mothers and female figures in general. I would've thought you'd want to talk to a guy. But, honestly, Sinjun? I think you speaking with a woman is possibly the best idea you've had this year so far. It'll be good for you."

He wanted to get angry, but it was difficult to be mad at Damien, especially since the ring of truth in his words was so powerful it would take a volcano to melt it, and that would be only after a couple of short, hairy-footed men carried it across hundreds of miles to get there. Disgruntled, he slouched down into the couch and winced when his back grumbled with pain.

"I don't know what to do about... the woman who said she was my mom," Miki whispered. "Kane said that he will probably run into who she is while trying to figure out who killed the woman who met Edie, but—"

"You don't really know if you *want* to find out?" Damien bumped his head against Miki's shoulder. "Are you scared about what you're going to find?"

"More like... suppose I find out she really meant to toss me out? Then what?"

"So what if she did?" Damien lifted his eyes up to meet Miki's gaze. "That changes nothing. Besides, you already have a mother. Her name is Brigid, and other than the fact that she's a redheaded Oompa Loompa, she's exactly who I imagined would be your mom. I mean, I get wanting to know where you're from, but that doesn't define where you've been and where you're going.

"You kicked life's ass way before you knew that woman even existed, and right now even though Kane may or may not find out who your mother was, you need to focus on getting your feet underneath you. The rest of it, Sinjun, is all just noise. You've got a family—including the stinky dog of yours—and we're not going to go away."

"I was *so* mad at you for going away," Miki confessed, his voice breaking. "I never knew I could hurt so much until I woke up and they told me you weren't…. God, D! It hurt so *fucking* much. And it never stopped hurting. And I was just angry because I was alone again and there was a part of me that was missing. And I love Kane. Fuck, I love him so much, but I lost my *only* family."

Damien straightened up, pulling him close. The kiss he brushed over Miki's lips was as gentle as his arms wrapping around Miki for a hug. Dude slithered out from between them, grumbling as he found a new place to lie down, but Miki couldn't see him through the tears in his eyes.

"I love you like I've loved no one else. I would die without you. And see, you're made of better stuff than I am because you kept going after I was gone." Damien pulled Miki toward him until they sat together, tangled around each other as they had done years before when life had been both harder and simpler. "I'm glad Kane found you. And I'm fucking happy as hell he loves you. If there is one thing I know about you, Sin, it's that you are the fiercest, most loyal feral asshole I've ever met, and I am proud as hell to call you my brother. And if you need me to hold you up—for as long as you need me—I'm here. I will always be here. Just like Kane, the band, and the rest of your crazy family."

CHAPTER NINE

Red light, torn jeans
Filthy sheets by the hour
Aching feet, dirty greens
All of the work, none of the power
A skip along a white line
A snip of ice in my vein
Opens up the sky for a bit
Helps me forget all of my pain
—Reality Mirrored

"I WISH I had better news for you, but I don't." Chang twisted his mouth to the side, shrugging remorsefully as he handed Kel a stack of folders. "I thought I would dig through the cases that brought down Danny Wong, thinking it would give me a few names, but these things are more pixilated than Japanese porn."

"At least the pixels thing you can figure out what's going on behind it. Black bars are hard to see around." Kel shuffled through some papers, handing a couple over to Kane. "Man, they took everything out of this. Are we even sure this one went down in San Francisco?"

Kane was still a little bit tender from the conversation they'd had in the Hummer. The world hadn't been jerked out from underneath him often. He could probably count the times it had been on one hand if he tried: realizing he'd fallen in love with Miki St. John, standing in the hospital waiting for news about Quinn, then later on, his mother. And now, oddly enough, a Medusa head of words wrapped around something as beautiful as a friendship but with a bite sharp enough to hurt.

The shock of the discussion still resonated inside of him. It was a piano string wrapped around something he thought was solid—his relationship with Miki—and it had been tested with the yank of that edged metal line. It bloodied Kel's hands to yank and twist, but if Kane and Miki hadn't been stone, the severing of that dangerous, poisonous specter would've been done to save Kane's life.

He respected Kel's courage. It had been a risk, a frightening leap of faith and trust that Kane didn't know if he would have it inside of him to do, but there was Kel, willing to put a solid, close partnership on the line and poke at a wound Kane might not want to pick at.

"Hey, Morgan." Chang raised his voice. "Are you paying attention?"

"Yeah, we don't do the last name thing often," Kel said, chuckling. "Sure, it's protocol, but when you've got five of them within shouting distance of each other, calling out *Morgan* and hoping to get the right one is next to impossible."

"Well, there's about to be one more," Kane pointed out. "Ian is about to get his badge pinned on him. He's hoping to get someplace out of district so he won't have to run into any of us."

"It's got to be hard to be coming up behind a bunch of you," Chang commiserated. "My brother is over in Oakland under Narcotics. Every once in a while we end up crossing paths, and all I hear is about how great he is. If I wasn't already our mom's favorite, I would kill him and take his place." He grinned at Kel's confused look. "We're twins."

"What are we going to do about this lack of information?" Kel waved a handful of papers. "Are we going to have to cash in on that favor you have at the DEA, K? Because there is shit here. I mean, we've got a couple of first names, but nothing else. I'm going to guess that the Sandy here in this report is our vic, but that would be making an assumption. Have we gotten any information on the shooter? Rodney Chin, right?"

"I've got feelers out for him, but so far nothing's hit back," Chang said with a grimace. "In Chinatown, it's hard to find somebody who doesn't want to be found. You are also asking me to straddle a very thin line. Most of the people who would know about Chin are older, the same people we now get as informants because they've aged out of gang activity. You're talking someone who was active thirty years ago. People aren't going to know his name and face unless they are the same age, so they are less willing to hand them over to the cops."

"They'll turn in somebody's kid but not the guy who drank a beer with them in high school?" Kel clarified. Grunting at Chang's nod, he continued, "Then if we want to get more information, we are going to have to go to the DEA and beg. This would be a hell of a lot easier if everything was shared and on the computer."

"I definitely have somebody there," Kane replied. "Just give me a second and I'll see if he can meet us someplace. I don't think I want to do this officially until I know we can get something tangible. I don't want to walk into their office and stand around only to get told they have nothing for us."

"I'm sorry I can't give you more," Chang said. "I'm still going to have my guys asking after Chin. We're working with the station to bring him in. As soon as I get anything, I'll let you know. We all agree he needs to get off the street, especially if he is working for a loose cannon like Wong. The guys I have now that I'm trying to run herd on are at least sane. I don't have to worry about them shooting up a place on Grant or doing drag races down near the Embarcadero. They're sharp, keep their eye on the ball, and are very much aware they have a short lifespan. A lot of them go in, make a million, and then I never see them again. I did get a name of sorts. That guy, Adam Lee, who has a bit of a hold on the same area that Wong used to run. Lee's mother is Wong's sister, and at one time she'd been under federal protection, but she defaulted out."

"Why would you do that? Actually, you know why she went in?" Kane asked.

"No, but I'm guessing it has something to do with Wong because I got a lot of veiled references to the two of them fighting over how the family criminal business was being run. Susan Wong-Lee wanted her brother to golden parachute and he wasn't up for it." Chang shrugged, gathering up the materials he'd copied for the inspectors to take with them. "I don't know if she turned informant on them, because these reports are shit. But I can guess that something went down. Lee— the father—was a minor player in a few things, but his son Adam seems to be a heavy hitter. From what I could pick out, she came back because the father wouldn't let his son go with her."

"Could she be the one directing Chin?" Kel took the folders away into a messenger bag. "Was she loyal to her brother to that extent? Maybe giving the old guy a last hurrah?"

"No, I don't think so." Chang laughed. "One of the charges that she got amnesty for was his attempted murder. Her focus seems to be mostly on making sure Adam keeps his place in the hierarchy, maybe even growing some of his territory. I can't see her—what little I know about her—risking that just because her brother got out of jail and he wants to relive his glory days before kicking the bucket."

"Well, at least it gives us some place to start." Kane shook Chang's hand, then stepped back to give Kel room to get out. "Thanks a lot for all of your help. We really appreciate it."

"Just get Wong and his people off my streets," Chang grumbled, slapping Kel on the shoulder as he went by. "That kind of crazy really throws the routine off. I would rather take a coldhearted son of a bitch I can play a chess game with than some asshole who Wile E. Coyote's through my district. The sooner I go back to busting gambling rings and old grandmothers' high-stakes mah-jongg games, the better."

FINNEGAN'S WAS the cornerstone of the Morgans' migration to the city of San Francisco. Established by Brigid's family, it served as a waystation where most Morgan offspring waited tables and dealt with drunks for nearly two generations. Located on the pier side past the Embarcadero, the pub was an updated Irish tavern with broad windows overlooking the Bay, a resented sticking point with Sionn's grandmother. It was brighter than most pubs, with banks of recessed lights and pale walls. Still, it put up a traditional pub food menu and now served beers brewed under Sionn's direction. It was where Damien Mitchell found the love of his life, Sionn, who then led him to the Morgans' kitchen, where he found his long-lost brother, Miki.

The scent of fish and chips, the light perfume of seagull poop, and heavily waxed wood always brought out a sense of home in Kane. He'd bussed the tavern's tables for more afternoons and early evenings than he could count, and as a child must have rolled up at least a thousand sets of silverware into white napkins every day. He drank coffee at the corner banquette reserved for family and crew way past closing hours and puked up his first few shots of vodka over Connor's shoes when he was ten, bawling as his older brother reassured him it was okay while mopping it up before they were caught.

It was definitely tourist season, and the newest influx of Irish cousins was working the bar. The most recent one, Cassie, shot Kane and Kel a grin as she pulled a Guinness from the tap, twisting her head to flick her mane of red hair from her face. Cassie was like him and his siblings, a child of a Morgan and a Finnegan. She had the look of Brigid about her, with Quinn's startling green eyes, but her broad mouth was definitely Finnegan.

"Give me a minute and I will have the boy clean off the family table for you," she shouted at them over the bar. Letting the pint's head settle, she held the glass steady as she placed it on the counter. Her accent was thicker than Donal's, the hard burr of the country they'd all come from. "Connor is in the loo. Said something about having to move someone along outside, so God only knows what he put his hands on. Give me a minute and I'll bring you a pint."

"Coffee for us, Cass," Kane said, ignoring Kel's agonized groan. "We are on the clock. Something to nibble on wouldn't be amiss. What is coming out of the kitchen?"

"I've got chicken wings brined in kimchi juice then deep-fried twice, and grilled king oyster mushrooms. There's also some bacon-wrapped Brussels sprouts as well as the regular stuff." Cassie gave him a resigned lift of her slender shoulders, but the slightly disgusted look on her face told a different story. "I don't know what's wrong with just serving fish and chips. The rest of it just seems silly. If steak pie was good enough for Gran, it should be good enough for anybody. Told Sionn as much. Gran would turn over in her grave if she knew what was being served on her tables."

"She started turning over in her grave the moment Sionn let Damie play in front of the pub. As for the food, I lay that at his door too. He's always trying new stuff at other places and then convincing Sionn to carry it here," Kane muttered. "But, you have to remember, most of the people who come to those doors aren't Irish. Why don't you give us the wings and the mushrooms? Coffee for me and—"

"Iced tea for me," Kel said, a wicked smile curving across his mouth. He grunted when Kane kicked him in the shin, shooting his partner an angry, outraged glare when he bent over to rub at the spot. "I'm only being nice."

"No, you're flirting. And, just like my sisters, my cousin is off-limits," he warned.

"As if I had any chance with Kiki," his partner grumbled. "And if I so much as looked at your baby sister—who is still a minor, I might remind you—I would not only be drinking my food through a straw, that's probably also the same way I would have to shit. So, no, I am not a stupid man. No flirting."

"K!" Connor's voice boomed across of the pub, turning heads toward him. He covered the space between them in a few strides, pulling women's attention with him. Grabbing Kane, he gave him a quick hug. "When we're done here, I need to talk to you about something. Personal. Nothing serious."

His older brother always seemed larger than what Kane remembered, but his was a familiar embrace, the clench of arms around Kane's back and the fresh green scent of his cologne briefly ghosting through Kane's nose. They'd grown up in each other's pockets, nearly twins in looks except Connor had always been bigger, always been more. Both brothers had followed in their father's footsteps, from rolling in the dirt across Irish fields to wearing a badge on San Francisco's streets. They spoke their parents' native tongue, a Gaelic that clung to their words still, and rode their other siblings rough, keeping them in line as older brothers should. Standing shoulder to shoulder, Kane and Connor held the line until the baby Morgans could hold their own. He was close to Quinn, their quixotic, slightly younger brother, but he had a special bond with Connor, one forged of carving out the rules of their small clan and establishing dominance over the six children who followed them.

It was worrisome that Connor wanted to talk to him about something, but sometimes his older brother made plans he needed help with or promises he gave to their mother and wasn't quite able to fulfill.

"Glad you can meet with us." Kane patted his brother's bulging shoulder. "Go grab a seat and take Kel with you. I think I see Alex by the door. I'll go drag him to the back."

He let Alex wade through the crowd to get to him. There was just a little bit of a hitch to Special Agent Alexander Brandt's stride, and not all of it from the tourists he was having to get past or the messenger bag he had slung across his back. He moved like a man still learning his way around pain, although as far as Kane knew, Alex was well on his way to full recovery. He'd obviously caught Alex on a day off, unless the DEA's dress code now included black jeans and a snug-fitting short sleeve shirt. At six two, with a muscular build, neatly styled black hair, and expressive brown eyes, Alex was attractive and in a lot of ways reminded Kane of Kel. They'd both made inspector at the same time, but the DEA was a lure for the stalwart cop and Brandt exchanged one badge for another. Keeping in touch had been easy, and during Alex's recent hospital stay, Kane had gladly spent a few hours here and there keeping the man company. Calling in a favor with Alex wasn't necessarily a hardship. Kane never wanted to strain the relationship, but they'd reached a point where only someone with enough leverage could help them.

Alex Brandt was definitely that someone.

Their hug was quick, a brief stop hindered by the tide of people, but Kane put his heart into the slight clinch, cautious of Alex's healing wounds. A flash of black along his friend's arm edged out from under Alex's sleeve and Kane drew back, his fingers around Alex's thick bicep so he couldn't pull away. Alex chuckled when Kane shoved the fabric out of the way, deepening his laugh at Kane's whistle when he saw the whole outline.

"You got a tattoo?" Kane made a big deal of examining the large piece of unfinished artwork scrawled over his friend's upper shoulder and arm. Mostly outline, it promised to be a strong piece if done right. "What is that? A phoenix?"

"Yes. Or at least it will be once it's done. Gus Scott down at 415 Ink drew it up for me." Alex rubbed at the piece of art on his skin. It looked bumpy, rough in places from healing over the inked lines. "I wanted it to…. There is art that I saw at Dimah's place that… this is going to sound kind of stupid, but it spoke to me and I wanted to wear something like it. So I asked Gus to come up with pretty much a Russian phoenix. It's going to be black and red for the most part, but there'll be some oranges and yellows."

"Man, that is going to hurt something fierce." Kane led Alex to the secluded back area set aside for the family and staff. "I never thought I'd get anything that big. It was bad enough hearing Connor cry like a baby when he got his piece done."

"Fuck off, K," Connor growled at him. "There are tales I can tell about you if you want to play that game, *boyo*."

"You two make me glad I don't have brothers." Kel reached across the table to shake Alex's hand. "Good to see you again, man. Kane says you might be able to help us out of the red tape maze we seem to be caught in."

"I'll do my best," Alex said, setting the messenger bag on the table. "I dug into the back cases as much as I could before coming down here. There's not a lot, but probably a lot more than SFPD has. I spoke to my boss and he's okay with me sharing the information, considering our department is all about cross-agency cooperation these days. Although he did say he would like to avoid a SWAT task force storming through any of our takedowns."

"I take it he had some issues with that day I ran into Kane and his friend Miro," Connor drawled, the Irish in his voice bright with laughter. "Next time, maybe that boy should leave the heavy lifting to the SFPD."

"Alex is here to help us, Con. Try not to piss him off." Kane smiled a *thank you* to their cousin who'd brought over a round of coffee and appetizers on a bar tray. As Alex sat, his eyes flitted over her, a cold professional assessment in his gaze rather than a flirtation. "We appreciate your help. Anything to give us some background is good. Especially since we're pretty much operating on fumes. What did you bring us?"

"Let the man get settled first," Connor interjected, passing a coffee cup over to the agent. "Or at least let's get some brew and food into him."

"Thanks. Actually, what I have is pretty sparse, but you are welcome to it. I'd like to see what you brought and maybe we can stitch something together." The DEA agent took a sip of coffee, whistling appreciatively at its taste. Saluting Kane with his mug, he reached for the folder Kel offered. "I assume all of you have already read this part. Why don't you skim through what's in the portfolios and we can brainstorm."

Much of what Alex brought with him Kane already knew, but there were lists of names, some of them female, that gave him pause. He found Rodney Chin listed as one of Wong's lieutenants, as well as Sandy Chaiprasit under a column marked known associates. An asterisk next to her name referenced a footnote, denoting her occupation as a hostess/prostitute for one of Wong's businesses. There were other women listed as well, and Kane's blood stilled when he realized one of them could have been Miki's mother.

"So Wong primarily ran drugs, gambling, and prostitution?" Kel's question jarred Kane from his thoughts. "You guys pulled him down for distribution and tax evasion, right?"

"Yes," Alex agreed. "No matter how hard they pushed, the department couldn't get anyone in the area to testify against Wong before the DEA took him down. So they slid a couple of undercover agents into his organization. They were able to get enough on him for the drug charges, but back then sex trafficking wasn't as much of a priority as it is now."

"It's a sad day when a kilo of heroin is more important than a woman's life," Connor murmured. "It says here that the DEA suspected a couple of the SFPD were on Wong's payroll. Do they know who it was? If those officers are still working at the department, IA would probably like that information."

"Only rumors, from what I read, but that doesn't mean conversations didn't happen behind closed doors." Alex picked up a bacon-wrapped Brussels sprout and examined it. After popping it into his mouth, he chewed carefully, then murmured his approval, swallowing. "I've asked to see if I can get the agents' names released to you, because they might know who Wong was closest to. Their names are still classified because there are still players on the field that are active. But the agency might be willing to share that information, so you can at least talk to them. Most of his lieutenants were in their thirties and forties back then, so a lot of these guys who ran with Wong are dead or, let's face it, too old to do much."

"I've got a lover with a gunshot wound." Kane looked up from a stack of prostitution arrests. "You don't have to be young to do a drive-by. Hell, you don't even have to have good aim. Just a gun and a car that can move faster than someone can run."

"Fair enough," Alex commented. "Everything that I've read here corroborates with what the agency currently has on Wong and his nephew. Adam Lee, Wong's sister's kid, runs the area now, and from what little I got sniffing around, he doesn't care for his uncle very much. There are some rumblings about a bit of a gang war, but Wong doesn't have the support that he used to have."

"That doesn't mean he can't throw a monkey wrench into Lee's operation," Kel offered. "Did Kane tell you we are trying to back-door information on St. John's mother? She looks like she could have been one of Wong's."

"We're not back-dooring anything. There's enough here for me to hammer at the DA to release Chaiprasit's belongings so I can enter them into evidence for the case. Some asshole down there has been blocking our requests since this whole thing started. If her name is in that envelope somewhere and also on this list, that will at least verify that she was Wong's." Kane pushed at Kel's shoulder. "Miki's got that damn tattoo on his arm. Someone put it there when he was a baby. Tell me that wasn't a deliberate show of power. Chaiprasit confirmed that Miki's mother is dead—which we kind of already assumed—so it's odd that Wong is going after him. Other than the tattoo, there's nothing connecting Miki to Wong."

"Wong did put that tattoo on people close to him, so maybe there is a tighter connection than we know. He did it so they couldn't hide who they worked for, which usually ended up badly for them if they crossed one of Wong's competitors. It was his way of ensuring everyone around him knew who he owned." Alex shot Kane a look over the rim of his mug, wariness flaring in his brown eyes. Setting his coffee down, he shook his head. "I will be the first one to tell you, that's kind of a sticky web to get into. There were a lot of things going on thirty years ago that definitely wouldn't happen on an operation today."

"I'm not sure I follow." Kane cocked his head, leaning back in his chair. "The focus of the investigation is to find our victim's murderer. She was carrying mementos she'd stored for years. It's more than likely his mother's name is in there. We just have to get the DA's office to release it, so really, the information is out there already."

"Here's the part where it gets sticky," Alex said, picking up another Brussels sprout. "The agents who went undercover in the investigation against Wong were in deep. One way Wong showed his appreciation for a job well done was to give a subordinate a woman."

"What do you mean?" Connor leaned on the table. "Like a night with a prostitute?"

"No," Alex said, shaking his head. "Someone to own. She would be his. Anything he wanted to do to her, Wong was good with. The boss said he knew of at least two agents who'd been rewarded that way. They'd been instructed to… well, let's just say they had to stay in character so Wong wouldn't suspect them of anything. I don't know what happened to those women, but it wasn't a good life, and Wong viewed a pregnant prostitute as a renewable resource. I'm going to take a very short leap and guess your Miki was one of those kids."

A numbness spread over Kane's body. What Alex was implying sank in slowly. Catching his breath, he tapped at the pile of reports under his fingertips. "Nearly all of Wong's associates and subordinates were— *are*—Asian, but…."

"Your Miki is mixed," Connor rumbled. "And if Wong gave those agents women, that means—"

"It's possible that Miki's father is one of those DEA agents, but that's just speculation. There were other guys in Wong's organization who were just as likely to have gotten his mother pregnant, so I wouldn't mention it to him until we know for sure," Alex finished. "But in my opinion, there is no one Wong would want to hurt more than the man who took him down and destroyed his empire."

CHAPTER TEN

KANE, TRYING *to get soap bubbles out of Miki's hair: So let me get this straight, the dog reeked so you decided to give him a bath. In my parents' downstairs bathroom. Before they got home from church.*

Miki, disgruntled: *Yeah. Asshole found a pile of crap in the bushes. Someone took their diseased rhino out for a walk and it took a shit right where Dude could find it. Now it's all over the tub, the dog's somewhere in the house, still half-covered in rhino poop, and I swear to God, he looks like cotton candy. The damned shampoo turned him pink.*

Kane: *It's a house of redheaded women. They've got stuff to keep their hair red, especially in the summer when*

> *the sun bleaches it out. You don't use*
> *it on the dog.*
>
> Miki: *Well, I did. Now my dog looks like*
> *a goddamned carnation and I smell*
> *like rhino. And I swear to God if you*
> *laugh at me, you better sleep with*
> *one eye open, K.*
>
> Kane: *Well, a ghra, it's kind of hard not*
> *to laugh, because unless we can*
> *somehow strip this out of your hair,*
> *your dog's not the only one who's*
> *pink.*

"WHY DON'T you tell me how you felt about Kane finding those photos?" asked the older woman sitting across from him on the other end of the couch. "The ones in the box under the bed at Shing's restaurant."

Miki choked, wincing as if she'd knifed him with her words, their edges sharpened with his old pain and dipped into a poison Shing and Vega brewed up out of his own blood and tears. He should have expected the verbal shiv. She'd tagged him more than a few times before but, as always, he was fooled by her comfortably aged, sweet face and sugary smile. They were a lie he fell for every time, lulled into a false sense of security she welcomed him into her office, a space set up more like an aging hippie's retreat rather than the lair of a shrewd, cunning brain scraper with the ability to lay waste to his equilibrium at the drop of a hat.

Nothing made Miki more uncomfortable than a sunny room filled with bookshelves, a comfortable sectional with plump, rainbow-striped pillows, and a cup of steaming, hot, fragrant coffee sitting on a side table, ready for him to drink. There'd been other fears in his life. The sound of ripping steel dominated most of his nightmares for the past few years, and before that, intrusive fingers and red-hot pain slicing through his young body waited for him every time he tried to fall asleep. Those terrors still haunted him. They weren't going away any time soon, but now he had a new hell to walk through.

And the demon who stood waiting for him at its gate was named Penny, a therapist with a blunt-force-trauma personality and a tongue sharp enough to cut a lemon into wedges, much like the one sitting on the saucer next to her teacup.

She'd promised him nothing other than an ear for his troubles and a mirror to peer at his broken soul but delivered so much more. Dressed in a pair of loose jeans and a wine-colored tunic embroidered with dancing dragons, with her graying brown hair cropped short, Penny looked the farthest thing from a doctor Miki ever thought possible. He knew better. The certificates on the lobby's walls all bore her name, and countless awards—mostly abstract glass things affixed to wooden bases—were packed into a bank of shelves like toy soldiers lined up to march into any war Penny chose to take on.

Today he was her battle, and her first thrust was a good one, plunging her spear into his belly button, then ripping him up to his throat, bleeding him out before his coffee even had a chance to cool off.

"Jesus—you just go for the fucking throat," Miki finally stammered out.

"I find it helps jumpstart you into talking." She gave him a smug smile over the rim of her mug. "Also, get comfortable. You don't start to relax until you take your shoes off and pull your legs up, which you've already done, but you always need a little bit of a push to get started. Oh, and since I now know you hate tea, that's Vietnamese coffee in your cup. It's instant but Fala swears by it."

"Fuck, you sure you don't have a twin?" Miki held his hand up to his chest. "She's about so fucking tall with curly red hair and walks on snake-fang heels. 'Cause you remind me of her right now."

"Kane's mother?" Penny cocked her head. "Brigid, right? You've mentioned her. Do you want to talk about her instead? Because—"

"No." He crossed his legs, working his shoulders back into the couch's thick stuffing. "Not Brigid. Not yet."

There wasn't enough room in his thoughts to mull over Brigid, not with the white noise buzzing between his ears. The punch of Penny's words resonated in him still, a sharp thrum, not unlike his ears after a concert. He struggled to find where to start, hating the wall he'd built up to protect himself but at the same time thankful for its thickness. It kept out everything—everyone—coming at him, defending the broken-off bits of his heart and soul he'd gathered up along the way.

Penny leaned forward, cradling her cup in her hands. "Do you want to talk about those photos? We don't have to, but I think it's a beginning for you. That was the first time someone you loved witnessed what was done to you. It seems like a good place to talk about sharing how you feel and, maybe, a bit of healing you've already done."

That damned wall was in front of him. His head hurt from ramming into it, and his heart ached from being dragged against its rough surface. Staring out of the window helped.

Some.

Every word he pulled out of his darkness, each curl of reflection, was a battle, and Miki didn't think he had it in him to chip away at the concrete he'd encased himself in.

It was easier to get wrapped up in the ribbons of clouds strung over the faint cerulean sky than tear apart his emotions. The third-floor office was close enough to Chinatown's main streets that he could see a line of red lanterns dancing in the light breeze, the black cord holding them up swaying between the tightly packed buildings. There wasn't a whisper of street noise coming through the closed windows, and when a sea bird of some sort flew by, it screamed silently as its wide wings carried it past the room's three windows, a real-world triptych playing out one of the endless scenes caught in its frames.

The photos. The flashes of light. The stabbing pains. How he'd screamed himself hoarse, begging and tearful, but he was as mute to his ears as the bird outside. There wasn't enough hot water to wash off the filth of their hands, of their mouths, and he remembered thinking it couldn't go on forever. It—they—had to stop sometime. What they were doing—their forceful intrusions—had to stop.

There had to be an end. Then one day, it would never start up again and he would be free to fly.

Except it hadn't ended. Everything they'd done to him. Every disgusting and perverted act Vega, Shing, and whomever else they'd dragged in to play with him was captured on bits of film. The violation of his body and soul lay open and raw for other sick men to see, images of his tearstained face and bruised body traded like playing cards.

And Kane had seen them. Handled them. There was no looking away from his memories, and his cop carried Miki's filth with him—every day—and still loved him.

He just couldn't love himself.

"Breathe." Miki sucked in a mouthful of air, steadying his nerves much like he did before he stepped out onto a stage. He swallowed hard, reaching for his coffee to wash down the sour, curdled taste rising up from his throat. "I can do this."

To Penny's credit, she didn't say anything. He liked that about her. Her patience and willingness to wait for him to find a purchase on the slippery ground he constantly trod went a long way. Especially since his mind couldn't settle and it felt like his heart was going to pound its way out of his rib cage.

"I was…" Miki tasted the soup of emotions simmering in his center, dipping his way through the bitter and acrid flavors stewing on the hot flame of his repressed anger. "Scared. I think I was scared first. Because—shit, this is hard—it hurt. It's as stupid as fuck, but looking into Kane's face—into his eyes—and knowing he saw me like that, it fucking hurt.

"I mean, I know it was his job. He was riding the badge when he pulled that box out, and he's really fucking good at shutting shit down when he's got to be a cop, but he knew. He saw." He exhaled, a fetid, rank breath fouled by the memories he'd locked away a long time ago. "I didn't get a chance to talk to him about it. Not like I don't think I ever would have. I don't know. I didn't have…"

Miki lost himself in the cloudy veil, his attention caught on the lure of blood red shadows moving along the wind-tossed lanterns' curve, playing hide-and-go-seek with the sun on the cherry-painted paper spheres. A tiny brown sparrow picked at something it brought up to the opposite building's roofline, its talons holding down the white scrap so it wouldn't blow away as it ate.

"I didn't have a chance to tell him." Another breath, a pull of cold air scented with coffee and a hint of the citrusy perfume Penny wore. His rage rose up, threatening to drown him, and Miki forced himself to push past the surging tide, standing firm against its momentum. "It was taken from me. Like what Vega and Shing did to me. And don't get me wrong. I'm not mad at Kane. I just… wish I'd been the one who told him what happened to me. I guess. I don't know. We don't really talk about it. I mean, some, but it's not like I can—fuck, I don't want to talk to him about what they did. I just want it to go away. I fucking wish—"

He hit the wall hard. The impact left him breathless and aching. His chest tightened and Miki closed his eyes, plunging into the darkness he'd lived in for so long. He couldn't talk with all the sunlight and colors. He couldn't scrape back the rot and mold on his soul, surrounded by cheery pillows and a sympathetic woman sitting next to him, her hands resting on his knees.

They'd agreed beforehand to her putting her hands on him, a radical departure from the boundaries set by her practice but something they'd talked about to break through his repulsion of being touched. It was something they'd worked out down to the places he felt comfortable and the situations he would allow it, giving Miki all of the control should Penny feel he needed to be grounded.

She'd done it only a few times before, always guided by something instinctual between them, and each time Miki was glad for the weight on his knees, happy for the slight warmth to drive away the cold he seemed to always carry in his chest.

Her touch anchored him in ways Miki couldn't explain. It wasn't desirous, not in the way he loved the feel of Kane's fingers on the back of his neck or the comfortable weight of Damie's arm slung over his shoulders. It was nothing like the enveloping hugs Donal caught him up in or the press of Dude's warm body on his aching leg in the middle of the night. Penny's hands violated his space, forcing into the protective membrane he clung to, parting its thick skin, but as unwelcome and hateful as her contact was, Miki understood he needed it. The warmth of her palms through his jeans anchored him, stopped him from drowning, and most of all, she reminded him to keep moving forward, past the noxious debris he was kicking up from the past and into the now he lived in.

"Would you ever have told him?" she prodded gently.

Tears burned his eyes, but Miki refused to give in to them. Not now. Not yet.

"I don't know," he choked out. Opening his eyes, he was caught in Penny's soft brown gaze. "I told Damie a little bit, but we were kids then. He knows. I mean, he knows what happened. I woke him up back then. Because I'd have nightmares and—shit—I can't tell you how many times I hit him, because he couldn't wake me up."

"And he stuck by you, didn't he?"

"Yeah." Miki cracked a smile he didn't quite feel. "Even came back from the dead for me. I guess I'm scared if I talk about it—Vega and Shing—with Kane, it'll make it real again. Which is crazy, because it's not like I don't have problems. Hell, I hate getting hugged. And the Morgans, they fucking hug for everything. It's freaking weird. I can't get used to it. Swear to God, they hug each other when one of them comes back from the store. Like they fought a battle to get some eggs."

"You deflect again then?" she pointed out in a gentle reproach. "Poking fun at what makes you uncomfortable?"

He pondered his words, then nodded. "Yeah, I guess I do. Habit? Maybe? I don't know."

"Could be just how your mind works. It makes things less scary sometimes."

"I'm not—" Miki caught himself. There was no denying the thick fight-or-flight thread holding his sanity together. Penny saw it nearly as soon as he'd walked through her office door. Admitting to the monster curdling his insides was why he was sitting on the damned couch letting a perfectly good cup of coffee go cold, because he didn't think he could pick it up without trembling. Another damned breath, then he said, "Yeah, it does."

"Fuck." Tilting his head back dragged his attention to the ceiling and its odd pattern of recessed lights, but the dotted, creamy surface gave him something to focus on, something to distract him from the scabs he was about to pull up. "I'm scared all the damned time. I feel cornered, especially now, and I just want to be free of all this shit. I want to be able to lie in bed on Saturdays with half of Kane's body pinning me down because he's a goddamned mattress hog, and I have to get up to let the dog out but I can't. I just want to play music. I don't even care if we never make another record again. I just want to play. And write. And—shit, go to their fucking dinners on Sundays and sit on the couch so I can make fun of Kane's whole damned family because—"

The tears finally hit, as did the stew of emotions he'd stirred up. It was too much to handle, too strong of a wave for his feeble control to hold off, and Miki simply let go, allowing himself to weep. A tissue box appeared in his lap and he looked down, grateful for its presence. Scrubbing at his nose with a soft white square, he sat and let himself ride his sorrow while Penny looked on.

"I never wanted to fall in love. Hell, I couldn't even imagine anyone wanted to fall in love with me. It just wasn't a thing. It was never going to be real," he whispered, talking more to the sage-green box cradled against his stomach than the woman with her hands on his knees. "I'd lost Damie. Lost Dave and Johnny. That was it, you know? My shot at family. There wasn't going to be anyone else. I didn't want to *be* anymore, and if it wasn't for Dude—well, he kind of gave me a reason to get up in the mornings. Because I knew he'd need something. Food or maybe to go out. He waited for me most of the time. Go walking with me when I went for groceries or takeout.

"Then he brought me Kane. Stupid fucking dog went and stole a damned piece of wood—expensive fucking wood—and dragged it home because it's what he did. He'd bring me shit and leave it in the garage, like if he could just find the right thing, I'd be happy." Miki snorted. "Guess he found the right thing, because one day, there was Kane. All pissed off and Irish in my face because the dog stole his shit."

"When did you know you'd fallen in love?" Penny cocked her head, wrinkling her nose when Miki chuckled at her. "I'm serious. Because from where you started, I think it would have taken you a bit to discover that about yourself."

"A long time." She wasn't wrong. Loving Kane snuck up on him. They'd fought and butted heads, but Miki'd found himself missing the cop who'd appeared in his life. Much like the scruffy canine who'd moved into his house, Kane crept into Miki's heart and took up residence before Miki even realized it. "It was when I needed him with me. When all of the shit was going down—before Damie came back—he was there. I thought maybe Kane's the kind of guy who fixes stuff. Like maybe I'd lost my mind and just wanted someone to deal with everything so I didn't have to. It's what Damie did, you know? Take care of the crap because he's bossy.

"But it was more than that. It was me needing him. All the time. For stupid crap like keeping me warm in the morning or making me laugh when I was scared." Miki balled up the sodden tissue in his hand, then took another one. Sniffing, he worked to separate the thin layers of paper. "I liked when he touched me. I didn't worry he'd go too far or that he'd hurt me, and I should have because he's fucking huge. He could do some damage if he wanted to. All of them—the Morgans—can. But Kane's... so damned gentle with me. He makes me feel safe. And I don't have to pretend with him."

"Pretend what?"

"People always seem to want something from me, and I never know what. It's like I'm broken inside. Like I don't fit in the hole made for me. I can't figure people out and I never know what to say, but Kane doesn't care. Sure, I fuck shit up between us all the time, and sometimes he does too, but we work it out." Miki let go a real laugh, a short burst of bubbling humor breaking free of the receding shadows. "He's there. Steady. Constant. He's my rock. My fucking cop. Sometimes he's there too much because he's that guy who's got to fix things, and I have to shove him back once in a while so I have room to breathe, but that's okay. We're okay.

"He makes me happy inside. So him holding on to all of the shit I've been through. Seeing those pictures," Miki whispered, shaking off the residual anger in his chest. "I'm not angry he saw them, but I wish I'd been able to tell him. You know? Because he'd have believed me without needing that proof, but I still feel dirty inside. Like everything Vega did to me—what Shing did—made me like them. Like they rubbed their filth on me and I can't ever clean it off. So yeah, maybe I'm angry at that too. Maybe that's why I don't talk to the people I care about. I don't want them to see that. Maybe I'm scared they won't love me anymore."

"Do you really think that? After everything you've been through with your band and Kane's family?" Penny left her words there, hanging in front of him like bait for him to take.

"No. I don't. Not now. Not if I look at it rationally." Miki obliged and swallowed, squeezing his weary brain to bleed the truths it held. "The guys—the band—they're my brothers. My family, as ugly as we get sometimes, they're my band. And Donal, he's my Dad. Shit, even Brigid is something to me. I just can't figure out what yet. But they've been there. Solid. Behind me. I'm just so fucking scared of doing something wrong, even when I fuck shit up and they tell me it's okay. I don't want to lose them. I don't want to ask them to help me wash this crap off of me, even though I know it's slowly choking me to death. Because if I don't clean it off, they're going to get tired of dealing with me not handling it."

"I don't think that's true. They love you and you've taken a lot of steps forward, trying to heal over a lot of old wounds. You know you're not responsible for what those men did to you, and even when you lash out, you've learned how to care for your relationships. That's big, Miki." Her hands pressed down again, a light pressure to gain his attention and Miki glanced up, her face blurred behind the sting of his tears. "I asked about the photos because it was a defining moment for you and Kane. He saw the worst of your life and remained by your side, loving you at every turn. I want you to think on this when you go home today. Kane opened up that box, saw your demons and still loves you, right?"

"Yeah." Miki nodded, wiping at the thick saltiness on his lashes. "He's an idiot, but yeah."

"He put that box down at some point, Miki. Kane carried it out of that room, catalogued it for his case, then put it away. And continued to love you. Still loves you." Penny leaned back, leaving the memory of her hands on his knees. "So answer me this, why are you still living in that box? And what is it going to take for you to close it and leave it behind?"

CHAPTER ELEVEN

Metal on my fingers
Whiskey on my mind
Singing a tune to my baby
Wasting none of my time
Flip the record on that turntable
Pull the rug from the middle of the floor
Gonna spend the night with my baby
Send my blues out through that door
—Keeping Back The Blues

"IT'LL BE about another half an hour, Mr. St. John. Traffic's a bit tight today." The burly bald security guy Sionn assigned to him glanced over his shoulder at Miki sitting in the back seat of the glossy black sedan. "I should have you home soon enough."

Miki couldn't remember the man's name. He couldn't remember any of their names, and the thought of having to dredge them up from his body memory stressed him out. He'd already called one of them Dave, only to be told there wasn't a Dave on the security detail, and he'd spent the rest of the day huddled in his bedroom, wrapped around the guitar in the hopes of finding stray notes to play. Much like the team's names, his mind wasn't giving up anything other than white noise, much less the genesis of a song.

He'd argued for a visit to Edie, refusing to budge when Sionn suggested he hold off for another day. As expansive as the warehouse was, its walls were slowly moving inward, stiffening the air and throttling Miki's mind. He hated having Damien's lover as a gatekeeper. The normally affable Sionn had morphed into a stern taskmaster, throwing blockades into Miki's routine. He understood the Irish man's reasoning, but he didn't have to like it. The rambles he'd take every morning with Dude were now short peeks into an alleyway with barely enough time for the dog to go to the bathroom. The terrier didn't seem to mind, but the ache was growing in Miki's knee and thighs, a constant reminder he wasn't stretching out the old injury with his customary long walks.

And there was the incessant presence of someone near him every time he turned around.

If there was one thing Miki knew he failed at, it was being human. Not in the way that Quinn fought with. Or least he didn't think so. It was more that he really had no idea how to interact with anyone who didn't know him. He could wear a mask for short periods of time, a social construct that let him say hello or begin a conversation centered on the food choice or what kind of coffee he wanted that morning, but beyond that, he was often left adrift. Having a phalanx of dark-suited men shadowing his every move didn't just make him uneasy, it was slowly driving him insane with the need to interact every second of the day.

He must have missed yet another social cue, because the driver kept making eye contact with him in the rearview mirror, as if waiting for Miki to say something. A smile seemed to be all the man needed, because as soon as Miki stretched his lips back, the man nodded pleasantly and returned his gaze to the road.

The late afternoon sun gilded Chinatown's busy streets, turning dross into gold. He found something comforting about the chaos, a spangled, multicolored storm of signs and noise. He knew its streets like the back of his hand, and like his knife-scarred and guitar string–pocked skin, the streets were beaded with age and violence. The district's buildings wore a hard elegance, a spackle of Asian influence over sturdy New England bones. The Chinese influence over the area was draped on with its *hanzi* signs and pagoda streetlamps. The scent of dark teas flavored the air along with the coppery sting of boiled water and slightly off greens. It was a smell he'd missed when the band was out on the road, a nostalgic perfume he woke up to every morning alongside the hard, warm length of his lover. The driver gave him a warning look when he cracked open the car window, but Miki ignored him. He needed to drown out the new world he was living in with a wash of the familiar.

The tinted windows made it impossible for anyone to see into the car, but Miki felt everyone's eyes on him. Or that sensation could have just been the result of being handed off from person to person nearly every waking hour of the day.

"I am going to take a turn down here to the right," the driver said. "Maybe we can get clear of some of the crowd and I can get you home sooner."

This time, Miki remembered to nod and smile before the man looked away.

It was a road they'd taken too many times for Miki to count, but each slow cruise over the weather-beaten blacktop was a trip down memory lane. This time, Miki needed more than a glimpse. He was so lost, and something broken cried out inside of him.

"Stop the car." Miki slapped at the seat in front of him. "I need to get out over there."

"I can't do that, Mr. St. John," the driver replied with a shake of his head. "I have my orders."

He was tired of being pushed around and boxed in. Slamming the leather seat stung Miki's hand, but the hard slap woke something up inside of him.

"I swear to God, if you do not stop this car, I'm just going to jump out. And if you lock the doors, I am going to break the fucking window." The traffic was slow enough they were inching down the street, and a thin crowd wandered across the sidewalks, drawn to the beacon of a row of crimson and white signs advertising fine jewelry at low prices. The brick buildings never seemed to change, only slapped with another coat of bright, cheap paint that quickly dulled under San Francisco's relentless weather. "I'm serious. Stop the car. I need to get out. Over there by the noodle factory."

The driver—*Dan*, Miki remembered—visibly debated his options, his placid features twisted by the two sides of a silent argument going on in his head. He edged the sedan to the right side of the road, cutting off a minivan filled with children driven by a harassed-looking older Chinese woman. They were a few feet short of the alley, but luck was with them as a parking space opened up, and his security detail slid into the spot. Throwing the car into Park, Dan locked the doors quickly, then turned around to face a fuming Miki. The professional demeanor on the man's stoic face had been replaced by something more human, more raw, and he turned, looping his arm across the back of the bucket seat.

"Look, when I first got this job, I figured I was going to be babysitting some spoiled rock star who would spend most of his time drunk and passed out on the couch. You seem to be going through some shit, and while I don't know what it is fully, it seems to be more than just some random asshole trying to hurt you." Dan leaned across the seat, the fabric of his suit jacket catching on the leather, exposing the thick gold watch around his wrist. "Up until right now, you've been an easy job. So, I am going to ask you to be honest with me about getting out of this car. If it's something that you *have* to do, you're going to have to do it on my terms. I need to know where you're going to go, because I'm going to need to cover you. So what *exactly* are you going to do?"

The man was a stranger, asking Miki to bare his soul and rip open his secrets to be rifled through. He paused, wondering if the mewling want crying out inside of him truly needed to be succored or if he could just go home and pretend the emptiness inside of him didn't exist. He looked away, losing himself in the kaleidoscope patterns of people walking by. It was easier to talk to the translucent reflection of his face staring back at him from the darkened windows.

"That alleyway over there is where it all started. Where *I* started." Miki bit his lip, unsure how to unravel the Möbius strip of his confusion. "I need to be there for a moment. I've got to find where I began because, right now, I have no fucking clue where I'm going."

Dan studied him for a while; then, with a flick of his fingers, the doors were unlocked. Nodding toward the alley, he said, "Letting you go down there is risky. There's too many doors leading to places I can't secure, but if I don't let you do this, you're going to find a way to get down here without one of us to cover you. Am I right in that?"

Miki smirked, curling his lip as he answered. "Nobody *lets* me do anything. So yeah, you're right. One way or another, I'm going to be walking down that alleyway."

"That's what I thought." Dan sighed. "I'm going to stand at the mouth of the alley, and you go do your thing. But if there is any sign of trouble, I need you to promise that you'll listen to me when I yank you back to the car."

It was a compromise Miki could live with, and he nodded, reaching for the car door's handle.

"Don't make me regret this, St. John." Dan undid his seat belt, then opened the door to get out. "I've got a husband and kids to go home to tonight, and I really need this job. So if you fuck this up and I go down—"

"I'll take care of you," Miki vowed. "And if it's any consolation, Sionn knows how I am. I'd bet money he wouldn't fire you if something goes wrong. He'd just pat you on the back and buy you a bottle of whiskey to apologize."

THE SHADOWS were the same even though the colors were different. The wall he'd leaned against while eating his cobbled-together meals of customers' leftovers and slightly burnt castoffs was now a light blue, and the fire escape gleamed a glossy black, a far cry from the peeling cream paint he'd picked out of his palms every other night after his shift. His fingers ached with the memory of washing dishes and his shoulders twinged at the thought of busing tables, but there'd been a simplicity in his life then. Newly freed of Vega and Shing, Miki lived surreptitiously, always keeping one eye open in case his monsters came looking for him.

His sneakers squeaked over the damp cobblestones as he walked toward the restaurant's back door. It didn't take much for him—for his mind—to go back to the day when a British-accented voice jerked him out of the song he was belting out. The alley had been a secret paradise for him, and he'd been annoyed at Damien's intrusion.

"What if I'd never met him?" Miki wondered, turning around to drink in the alley around him. "How fucking lost would I be then?"

He could pinpoint the momentous moments in his life, shards of time piercing the ribbon the Fates wove for him. He didn't remember being found on St. John Street, but he knew the park at the corner and the run of houses on the short road. There'd been pictures he'd seen, taken on that day, but he'd never wondered how he'd gotten there. Not until a now-dead woman scraped open a scab he didn't know he had.

"I didn't want these questions," he muttered, scrubbing at the ache forming behind his eyes.

His knuckles dug in, scraping at his cheeks, and when he let his hands fall away from his face, he was left staring through a smear of stars and watery confusion. He didn't know who he was speaking to—maybe the ghost of himself sitting on the fire escape above him—but the alley was empty of people and it seemed like a safe place to rifle through the conflicts growing inside of him. With Dan standing guard by the sidewalk, it seemed as if Miki had the world to himself once again.

"Did you want to throw me away?" He stared up at the sky, caught up in the unknown of his life. "I never needed a mother. Hell, I always figured you would be worse than Vega—worse than Shing—but now I don't know. It was so much fucking easier to leave you in the goddamned box I put you in. Why the hell did you have to crawl back out?"

The tears stinging his eyes seemed to be made of molten razor blades. They sliced through his vision, ripping apart the alley, leaving Miki to stand in the ruins of the carefully constructed lies he'd wrapped around his birth. He didn't know what to do with the half truths unfolding before him. They were origami traps, glittering unicorns and cranes armed with sharp teeth, poised to sink into his flesh and soul if he got too close.

He didn't want to get any closer, but he didn't have any choice. The universe was going to unravel his life whether he wanted it to or not. Denying his mother had been so easy when she was nothing more than a shadow, but her name now lingered on the edges of his knowledge, and her face lay somewhere in a box, captured in photos and perhaps even a letter.

Pretty soon, everything he never wanted to know was going to come crashing down on him.

"I already have parents." Miki threw the words to the sky, whispering a protest to the fluffy river of clouds dotting the endless blue. "I have Donal, God fucking damn it. I found him. When Kane fell in love with me, I *found* Donal. He'll catch me when I fall. He fucking promised that and he has never let me down.

"And Brigid." He sniffed, blinking away the smear along his lashes. "I didn't want her. She fucking scares me because she is everything I am but turned inside out. She's stronger than I am. I can't fight for the people I love. Not like she does. I'm too fucking scared all the time and she's not. I wish I could be more like her. I could defend the fuck out of myself, but she's the first one to step up to defend me—to defend the rest of her kids. How the hell are you going to compete with Brigid? When you had me and you couldn't even hold on to me? Or did you even fucking try?"

"St. John? You doing okay?" Dan's voice broke through the darkness rising from Miki's thoughts, shattering the spiral that threatened to pull him in. "I've got to get you in the car soon. I can give you another five if you need it."

"No. I'm good." Miki wiped at his face, then took one last glimpse at the newly painted fire escape. He glanced up at the sky, the irony of a bright sunny day spreading over the city as he fought a maelstrom of despair. Dropping his voice to a whisper, Miki shoved back at the clouds in his head. "I'm not going to let your ghost take away everyone I love. I can't guess what knowing your name or seeing your face is going to do to my head, but Kane seems to think it's—*you*—are important. Maybe it's because everything he is connects to his family, connects to his blood and that green fucking rock he was born on, but I have to trust that he knows what's best for me in this.

"So yeah, I'll find out who you are, but that's not going to change who I am. I'm not letting you do that to me. If you'd wanted it to shape who I'd become, you should have been here from the beginning. And maybe I'm not being fair. Maybe you couldn't hold on to me, but I needed you to." He took another sniff, hating that he couldn't breathe through his pain and grief. "The things people have done to me, I can't even talk about. But I have to, because I feel so fucking small inside. And I'm scared to love. I'm scared to death of losing who I love because am I even worth it? Or is it all a lie like you are? I can't hope that you loved me. I can't risk that, because if I do, and you didn't, you are going to tear me apart and there's nothing Donal and Brigid would be able to do to stop you. God, I really wish you would have just stayed in that fucking box, Mom."

THE MUSIC hit nearly as soon as Miki came through the front door. It was elusive, a whistling thread of something he couldn't quite grab at, but when he did, it was a fiberglass froth, cutting open his mind and leaving him with minute bleeding wounds. He was going to lose it. It was already a whisper but for brief sparkling flashes, and he could feel the pain inside his heart.

He *welcomed* the pain.

Torn between needing to grab at what his mind spooled out and calling Kane, he reached for one of his notebooks and a pencil, only stopping long enough to snag a bottle of sparkling water and a treat for Dude. The dog was happy to see him, winding about his ankles and nearly tripping Miki when he crossed the living room to the couch.

The words poured out of him and onto the page, a tornado he couldn't hold in and could only snag the end of it before it whirled out of control, skipping away from his grasp. Too many thoughts crowding in on him, yet they whispered away as soon as he focused on one, a seductive tease of ideas and song hidden behind oblique stammers and notes.

Miki didn't hear Kane come in. The sun had fled before the night's hard grip, and he hadn't noticed the light easing from the room until a golden flare erupted next to him. His breath caught on a phrase lodged in his throat and Miki coughed, startled at the taste of his own tongue.

"You're going to go blind doing that in the dark, *a ghra*," Kane warned. His lips were forceful, demanding a deep kiss from Miki's mouth, and he leaned his head back, silently begging Kane to take more.

Kane gave him what he wanted—or maybe took what Miki needed to give. Either way, he was left breathless and needy, his cock heavy and aching. Kane tasted of coffee and something deliciously spicy, a tang of heat on his tongue.

Pulling back, Miki eyed Kane suspiciously. "Did you get kim chi wings? I can taste them on you."

"Yeah, and I'm not going to be apologizing for it." Kane's mischievous grin earned him a quick pinch of his left nipple. He gave a playful yelp and rubbed the injured spot but didn't pull away. "We had a meeting down there. Would've seemed rude not to eat something since I was on the clock and could only have coffee."

"Did you bring any home?" His stomach wasn't quite ready for food, but Miki was never one to turn down a meal.

"No. It wouldn't have kept. Besides, I had Connor and Kel with me, so we didn't go chasing down a rabbit hole, and you know they don't leave leftovers. Sionn should feel lucky there's still a pattern on the plates." Kane tapped the dog's rear leg, urging the canine off the couch. "Move, Dude."

Dude gave Kane a weary, beleaguered look but shuffled off the cushion in an exaggerated slither. Kane came around the front, shedding his jacket as he walked. His holster was already empty, the weapon stashed in the gun safe by the front door, but he hadn't unbuckled the leather straps crisscrossing his broad torso, so Miki reached up and hooked his finger into one, tugging Kane closer. His cop half kneeled on the sectional, his weight tipping Miki toward him, but it wasn't enough of an angle to topple Miki over.

"Well, even with no food, glad you're here. I didn't think you were going to be home just yet," Miki murmured, his fingers still wrapped around the rig's strap. "Not that I'm complaining. Are you still hungry? There might be something to eat in the fridge."

"No, Finnegan's wasn't that long ago," Kane refused. There was something in his storm-blue eyes, a fold of darkness Miki knew he should dig at, because that's what lovers did: ferreted out the shadows their other halves picked up along the day. "It really was about the shooting, for the most part. I told you we were going to try to see if the task force had anything for us, but we had punted over to the DEA. Luckily, Alex could hook up with us. He had a lot of good insight and some solid information. I've got a lot more to go on now. You remember Alex, right?"

"Your agent friend. The one who got hurt, no?" Miki cocked his head back, welcoming a gentle brush of Kane's mouth on his again. "How long do you have? If you didn't come home to eat, then I can think of other things we can do."

"Actually, I wanted to come home and talk to you about the case." Kane's serious words were a deluge of ice water on Miki's arousal. "I've got a little bit of news. Actually, I have a lot of news."

"Jesus, you were only gone a few hours. How much could've happened?" Miki protested, then remembered how his own life had been altered in quick slams of time barely a blink long. "Forget that. Probably the stupidest thing I've said in a long time. Shit happens fast sometimes. I get that. It is usually when you've got a case that seems to last forever."

"Sometimes they do," Kane admitted. "This one is moving slower than I'd like it to, but today I think a lot broke open for us. There's a few things you need to know, and I want to remind you that no matter what, I'm at your side. Okay?"

"I know." Despite his apprehension, a warmth spread through Miki's gut. "You love me. You've promised never to let go of me. I believe you. I do, you know? It's just hard sometimes because—"

"Being alone is a hard habit to break," he cut in. "But I'm willing to stick by you for a lifetime until you do."

Kane sat down next to him, angling his body to face Miki. He looked like he needed to have his hands on Miki as much as Miki needed to feel Kane's strength beneath his fingertips. He'd taken to running his palms along Kane's sides, tracing the muscles rippling over his lover's belly and down his hips. It was enough just to touch Kane, to know that he was there in front of him instead of a ghost of his memories. Still, Miki glanced back toward the double doors of their bedroom; he wouldn't have said no to dirtying the clean sheets he'd put on the mattress that morning.

"Get your mind out of the gutter. I just want to talk to you before I have to head back out." Kane's smile was in his tone as much as it was plastered over his handsome face. The somber returned, but the light in his gaze remained. "The captain just told me the DA is going to release copies of what was in the packet Chaiprasit gave Edie. There's enough evidence to prove it's connected to her murder, so I'll be formally including it in my case files, but the contents more than likely won't incriminate anyone, so it can be shared with you and Edie. Da and Book pulled in a few favors for this, but you might want to know the truth about your mother before you see that therapist you talked to."

"I don't know what I'm supposed to do with that. What good is that going to do?" The knots returned to Miki's stomach, churning up the sick he'd tamped down. "Fuck, I don't know if I'm ready to even see her face."

He wasn't ready for the truth. Miki actually couldn't find any reference point to hold on to besides an unsettling fear. It was curious to be terrorized by a photo or a name, but there he sat, trembling with the reality of knowing where he'd come from finally sinking in.

"When? I mean, when are we... fuck, Kane, I don't know what to even think." He leaned into Kane's chest, his rattled nerves calming when he felt his lover's breath on his face.

"You don't have to think anything, Mick. It's up to you when you open up that Pandora's box." Kane tangled their fingers together, squeezing lightly. "I am going to have to go through that packet and look at it as evidence. So I'm probably going to know about her— about your mother—before you do. But I'm not going to bring her up until you're ready. Okay?"

"Okay," Miki mumbled. He was grateful for Kane's touch, drawing on his lover's steady strength to shore himself up.

"Now here comes the hard part," Kane started.

"Jesus, these past couple of weeks almost killed me and you're only now getting to the hard part?" Miki scoffed. "What the fuck else can there be?"

"In the course of this investigation, we might… *hell*, we're going through a lot of information about people involved with Wong back when your mother worked for him." Kane took a breath, then clasped Miki's hands tightly. "There's a slim chance that we might find out who your father is. Alex suggested I don't bring that up to you because it could come to nothing, but I wanted to prepare you, just in case that happens. I want you prepared for that."

Kane might have said more, but Miki couldn't hear him. The noise of his mind crashing drowned out everything around him, and the numbness he'd fought off was back. It took him a moment to realize he'd stopped breathing, drawing in a sucking breath only when his lungs began to pound and ache.

Then the enormity of Kane's words struck him, and he stammered out, "But how? I mean, you don't know for sure about just how? The woman—Sandy— she was a whore for Wong, right? And she knew my mother—probably *worked* with my mother—how the hell would anyone know?"

"Babe, it's a possibility. I just wanted to let you know there was a possibility and that we'll cross that bridge together when we get there, okay?" Kane's phone buzzed, a harbinger song Miki knew all too well. Someone had died and hadn't died well. It was a chiming toll of a potential murder, the ringing of a bell that would pull Kane from him.

Kane didn't so much as glance at the phone he'd left on the chest in the middle of the room.

"You've got to go. Someone needs you now. A hell of a lot more than I do, because I'm still here and they're not," Miki murmured, jerking his chin toward the phone. "And before you ask, I'm going to be okay. Just… come home to me tonight. I'll be waiting up. I just need to hold you before I go to sleep."

There was a tenderness to Kane's kiss that Miki wasn't sure he'd ever felt. It was a bloom of affection, a delicate, tentative exploration of Miki's mouth. Everything that they'd been—that they'd done together— never, ever strayed into delicate, but in that moment, Kane's kiss was a stroke of a soft feather on his rattled soul.

He could have taken anything—survived anything—and had, but Kane's *fucking* kiss broke him.

"I'll be back home before you know it, *a ghra*," Kane promised, then pressed his mouth to the corners of Miki's closed eyes. "And if you should need me before then, *call*. You mean more to me than my badge and the dead. I love you. And if I have to, I would give up everything I've become—everything I've accomplished—just to hold you if you need me."

CHAPTER TWELVE

I see you scraping the black,
The black on your soul
When are you going to leave him
When are you going to let go?
I see you hiding the blue
The blue on your skin
Holding in all your tears
Not letting anyone else in
What is it going to take
For you to finally see
I'm not asking you to go
I'm begging you to leave
—Tight on Time

"THIS IS a message," Kel muttered under his breath. "Because this sure as fuck can't be a coincidence."

"It's an alleyway in Chinatown," Kane replied, picking carefully through the debris scattered about the alley's wide opening. "I'm not going to call it a message until we have enough evidence or something points us that way. Let's see what Horan has for us and then we can decide."

If the police department didn't sleep, the morgue was probably staffed by the undead. It was past normal business hours, but the slender blonde medical examiner was as bright-eyed and perky as ever. She looked up as they approached, gesturing with her gloved hand at a box of booties sitting outside of what Kane could only guess was the edge of their crime scene.

"Suit up, gentlemen," Horan ordered. "Avoid anything that looks sticky, because I can't tell yet what is blood and what is squid guts."

"You'd think she would be able to guess from the smell," Kel muttered.

"I dare you to say that to her face," Kane whispered back, pulling paper coverings over his shoes. "Or at least if you do, wait until after this case is over. I'd like to get my reports back to me before Connor's first kid graduates high school."

"Hold on. I'm losing my balance." Kel clamped a hand on Kane's shoulder before he fell over. "Speaking of Connor, did he and Forest ever tell your mom that they're married?"

"Shit, don't even remind me about that." He didn't have time to fold that bit of nonsense into his brain. Not with everything else going on. "It's bad enough I am tiptoeing around the others trying to figure out who knows besides me. Not like I can talk to Sionn about it, because if Damien doesn't know and he finds out, I might as well have put an ad in the paper announcing it. That one can't keep his mouth shut to save his life."

After taking a few latex gloves out of his jacket, Kel separated them into pairs, then handed Kane a set. "Well, Quinn knows."

"You sure about that?" Kane lifted an eyebrow.

"It's *Quinn*," Kel asserted, snapping on a glove. "I'm pretty sure he already knows the date you and Miki are going to get hitched."

"I don't know if Miki will ever be ready to wear my last name, much less a wedding ring," he admitted quietly. "But none of that really matters to me. I just want to wake up next to him every morning for the rest of my life. I don't need anything besides that. Okay, maybe I need a little bit of patience when dealing with Damien, but he comes with the package. That's something I signed up for the moment I fell in love."

Kane stopped short, caught with one hand gloved and the other only partially encased in latex. He stared down the alleyway where Miki had found his soul mate years before. He couldn't pass by the side street between the buildings without immediately thinking of Miki, and to some extent, Damien. It was one of the first places Miki opened up about, an elusive glimpse of the love kindled by a man they'd thought dead, one Kane used to wonder if he was going to have to compete with for the rest of his life. When Damien surfaced alive and well, the alleyway turned from a shrine to a tribute, no longer a memorial of a dead brotherhood but more a place of remembrance.

He'd walked through the alleyway with Miki before, strolling hand in hand toward one of the businesses at the far end. The unassuming cream-painted security door led to Dino's Bar and Grill, an old-school blues club the band played at every once in a while to get the feel of the stage beneath their feet.

The profanity of a murder played out beneath Miki's fire escape turned Kane's stomach.

Death was rarely pretty. Since the day he'd first pinned on his badge, Kane had a front row seat to humanity's depravity. He would've liked to have said Rodney Chin's murder shocked him, but sadly, he was one in a long line of corpses. Still, his death stung just like every other Kane had attended. It was a senseless ending of a life and extinguishing of a soul and consciousness gifted to a creature by God and the Universe. Murder sickened him, and Kane felt the anger tightening his gut at how little a person's life meant to some people.

"Are we sure that's Chin?" Kel asked Horan, letting one of the uniforms get past him. "And I'm not saying anything about—look, there's not much left of his face—I'm just asking."

"The body has distinctive markers that lead me to believe it is him, but we've made plans to take fingerprints to verify. One of the restaurant workers recognized the pair of tattoos on his arm and made a tentative ID." Horan consulted her notes. "He has Wong's sigil, and the task force sent over their file on him so I could compare the other tattoos to the photographs taken at his last booking. So unless he has a twin with identical tattoos and a missing pinky finger, I'm going to say this is Chin until proven otherwise."

Kane took the printouts Horan offered him. They were a bit pixelated, having been run off the thermal printer that was standard issue in most medical and patrol vehicles, but the photos were clear enough to match the body's markings to Chin's intake photos. It was a shock to see the tattoo he kissed nearly every night on Miki's arm displayed on someone else's body. The juxtaposition of his realities jarred Kane, and he took a step back, needing a moment to adjust his thoughts.

"Where's the restaurant worker now?" Kane glanced about. The alley was clear of anyone but uniforms and medical technicians.

"Inside the restaurant with one of the officers first on the scene. I was a few blocks away when I got the call, so that's why I beat you here." The examiner took back the papers. "I've got a set of these for you with my assistant. Nothing's been moved, so you can document for your report, but if you guys can double-team it, I'll be able to get him out of here quicker."

"How about if I work out here and you go inside to do the questioning?" Kel offered. The detective glanced over the carnage. "I'm on a diet anyway."

Whoever killed Chin meant business. There was a rage fueling his death, the evidence of its fury smeared all over the alley's walk and surrounding walls. At first glance, Chin's body looked more like a pile of rags than a human being, and Kane couldn't even begin to guess if the man had been dead or alive before what was done to him had begun.

For Chin's sake, he really hoped all of the damage was done postmortem, but from the blood spray arcing the wall, reaching up past the fire escape, Kane wasn't convinced.

It was obvious Chin was beaten, but there wasn't any evidence of a weapon, or at least not a visible one. A couple of open dumpsters next to the restaurant's back door were marked with yellow tape, cordoning them off to be rifled through. The lids were down, but they were made of heavy, thick plastic rather than the industrial metal found in the outer city. They were light enough that Chin's killers could've easily lifted the lid, disposed of any weapon, then lowered it back down without creating a clang loud enough to alert anyone.

Still, Kane studied the beating victim. There was no way in hell Chin died silently.

"With this much blood, they had to have done him here." Kel circled the kill scene, cautiously skirting its edge. A photographer worked inward around them, his camera whirring away. "Jesus, there are parts of his legs that are beaten almost flat."

"Whoever did this was angry," Kane surmised. "But notice we can still see Wong's mark. If I'm going to jump to conclusions, I'm good to say Chin's boss wasn't too happy he didn't kill Miki. Everything we've got on the guy says he likes to hand out lessons so people don't fail him. Chin was loyal but not that high up in the hierarchy. He'd be somebody Wong would be willing to sacrifice."

"See, I've got to wonder how many people Wong actually has if he's willing to lose one just to teach the rest a lesson about doing the job right." Kel's attention drifted to the crowd gathering near the street. "So far, he's only moved against Miki and Chaiprasit with— we're alleging—Chin being tapped for both jobs. Does that mean he has more people he can use, and if so, does he also have more targets?"

"I was wondering that myself." Kane turned his back to the people milling on the sidewalk. "My gut says Wong did this, but I cannot rule out that Chin may-be crossed the wrong person and the reason the tattoo was intact was to send a message to Wong himself. He wasn't even on the task force's radar because he lacks support."

"So you're saying that he might have stepped on a few toes and someone offed Chin to remind the old man of his place?" His partner chewed on the corner of his lip. "If that were the case, then why the alleyway? We connected it with Miki. How is it connected to Wong?"

"That is something I'm going to ask the restaurant guys inside." Kane grinned. "Have a good time with Horan. Be sure to take a lot of notes, and whatever you do, don't get in her way. She'll eat you for lunch and spit your bones out picked clean."

"HEY," DAMIEN called as he came through the front door. "You hungry? I got Sionn to stop by Finnegan's for some grub after I was done with the dentist. My teeth are all perfect, but my stomach is empty."

The aromas coming from the plastic bags Damien carried made Miki's belly rumble in anticipation. He nodded, setting his notebooks aside, and waited while his brother took his shoes off. Dude tried to crowd in closer, readying himself for any tidbits Miki and Damie might drop, but Damien nudged the dog off the couch before he sat down.

"That dog is such a beggar," Damien drawled. "Reminds me of you back before we made it big. We'd get the food all divvied up evenly and somehow you'd end up with at least half of everybody else's. Dave was the biggest sucker."

"Dave's mother made the best cookies." A wash of sadness overtook Miki. He'd never been close to the other band members' families, and after their deaths, the distance only grew between them with firm walls erected by teams of lawyers and official documents protecting everyone's already broken hearts. "I tried calling her the other day, but she never calls back."

"That's not on you, Sinjun," Damien said. "They don't respond to me either. But then, we're probably reminders of what they lost."

"Do you think they're pissed off at us because we went back on the road with Forest and Rafe?" He leaned his head against Damien's shoulder, debating how hungry he truly was. "That was hard for me to get my head around, you know?"

"Are you okay with it now?" Damien stroked Miki's hair.

"Yeah. Now when I turn around, it doesn't shock me to see them there." He shrugged, amending his words. "Most of the time, anyway. Some of the old songs Forest plays exactly like Dave, and it takes me a moment. But I'm okay."

The notebook at the end of the couch might as well have had a beacon over it because Damien's attention kept drifting to where it lay. Miki knew his brother would grab it before Damien's hand even moved. They had a tight intimacy, but for the first time in his life, Miki felt a territorial twinge about the notebook and Damien, probably sensing Miki's disquiet when he picked up the notebook, glanced back at Miki, then said something Miki never imagined Damien would say.

"Can I look?" his brother asked. "Will you let me?"

Miki nodded, and the moment was broken, a salt crust shattered beneath the thrust of trust and mutual love. The words he'd written on those pages weren't in any way, shape, or form malleable around a melody yet, but they were a start.

"I can see where you're going with this," Damien said softly, turning the page. "I never thought I would see this from you. It's good. Even as raw as it is right now, it's good."

"Do you think?" He didn't realize he was holding his breath until Damien spoke, and he had to pull in air in order to answer. "I don't know. I can't find the right words to say what I want to say."

"You'll find them," he murmured, kissing Miki on the corner of his mouth. "You always do. Get off of me so we can grab some food and I can tell you the good news."

"I need all the good news I can get. I'm not too sure what to do with the bits Kane gave me." Miki filled Damien in as they divided up the containers. He absorbed the information about Miki's mother and possible father with a slight frown.

"Do you want to talk about it?" Damien stopped dishing food out. "That's a lot of shit to dump on you in one day, dude."

The dog looked up, and Miki chuckled despite the heaviness weighing him down. "Nah, I've got to process, you know? Maybe I'll call Donal later. He can always screw my head back on straight."

"Yeah, your dad's good that way. I'm here if you need me, okay? Maybe we can talk about it after Donal and you connect." Scraping the contents out of one take-out tray into Miki's Styrofoam bowl of wings, Damien grinned at Miki's horrified grunt. "Too bad. Eat them."

Screwing his face up into a grimace, Miki complained, "I don't want any Brussels sprouts. You take them."

"Pretend you're an adult for five minutes." Damien stabbed one with a fork, then waved the offensive mini cabbage under Miki's nose. "Eat at least eight of them and I'll split the chocolate cake in the fridge with you."

"Fuck your cake," he grumbled back, but he bit into one of the sprouts, focusing on the bacon wrapped around its leafy body rather than the acrid taste of cabbage on his tongue. "What's your good news?"

"The contractor said Sionn and I can probably move into our side of the warehouses in a couple of days. We'll be out of your hair, so you and Kane can run around naked like the wild animals you are."

Of all of the things Damien could have said, he and Sionn moving out hit Miki like a ton of bricks. His world was already sliding from under him, and the idea of not being able to reach out—to find his own brother within the safe confines of the brick warehouse he'd made his home—pierced Miki, gutting him more than the possible discovery of his mother's name and a maybe father lurking out in the shadows.

"Okay, I like that look on your face even less than I liked the disgust you gave me about the Brussels sprouts." Damie nudged him, then took Miki's container away, setting everything on the chest. "Now I really do need you to talk to me, Sinjun. You've gone pale."

Miki tried to wrap his tongue around his thoughts, but nothing came out. It was all too much—and he didn't know how many times he could experience that feeling without breaking—but it was all just too *fucking* much. The back of his throat burned, and his teeth began to ache, his gums tightening and his saliva going thick. The burst of heat he tasted from a mouthful of chicken went to ash on the roof of his mouth, and it took him a moment to hear through the rush of blood pounding through his ears.

"I don't want you to go," he finally uttered. Damie's look of concern turned solemn, and he sat back to study him. The expectation stiffening Damien's expression goaded Miki on. "You want me to be honest with how I feel. I mean, that's the whole point of therapy and trying to get the shit out of my brain, right?"

"That's part of it," Damie concurred. "Mostly I just want you to stop being angry inside. Because you're hurting yourself, and I hate to see someone I love in as much pain as you are."

"I'm not gonna say that you're wrong." Miki stalled, unscrambling his thoughts and emotions until he could find what he needed to say. "I just—"

"What do you want from me, Sinjun?" The gap between them was slight, but it seemed like a chasm to Miki, and when Damie turned to face him, it grew into even more a veritable canyon Miki hated as soon as Damien's leg drew away from his thigh. "Are you upset about Sionn and I moving out? I thought you'd be kind of happy about it because you and Kane need your own space. We've talked about that."

"I know," he mumbled. "I just can't…."

To someone as fearless as Damie, Miki knew he would sound weak, but he didn't care. He needed something in his world to remain solid, something firm for him to stand on as everything else turned into chaos and unraveled. He had Kane. He would always have Kane. But some part of his brain—some part of his heart—needed more, and he couldn't explain why, but there had to be more than one anchor for him to hold on to until he could sort out the mess he'd created in his head.

"I don't want you to leave just yet," he confessed. "I mean, not that I want you to feel like you can't move into your own place with Sionn, but for right now—until all of the shit is done—I kinda wish you'd stay. No, I really need you to stay. I don't think I am going to be able to make it without you and Kane near me. And yeah, you're right next door, but in my head, you're not. In my head, you're just someplace I can't get to, and that takes me to places I've already been. Places I don't want to go again."

"Okay," Damie murmured, nodding slowly. "I understand—I *do*. But at the same time, I've got to ask you if you'll talk to Kane about it as well. Because he and I… we do this dance around you, and I can't step on his toes, Sinjun. We work really hard to share you and not push on you. If you're asking me to stay—asking Sionn and I to stay—then Kane has to be okay with it too."

"He loves me," Miki chuckled. "He'll understand. Probably more than I do. My gut just says I can't let you go right now, and I don't know why. It's not like you're going to be that far away, but I *can't* right now."

"Is it just too much to deal with? I mean, I know Edie getting shot kicked you in the balls, but is it this thing with your mom that's messing with your head too?"

"I don't know. I mean, Kane just dropped it on me that they're going to give over what that woman was going to give Edie, and suddenly I've got to deal with finding out something I thought I never would discover. I was okay not knowing because it meant that everything I am is what I made. Even as fucked-up as that is, it's still me… *I'm* still me." Miki stretched his leg, scratching Dude's back with his toes. The terrier crooned, a little contented growl, and Miki glanced up at Damien, worn out from the day pounding at him. "I feel like I've talked this thing to death and I still haven't come up with how I feel about her, about me. Now we're going to throw a father into it and that fucks me up more. It's like, couldn't he have done something for her? Or does he even know I happened? Or does he care? I didn't give a shit about any of those things when I woke up this morning, and now they dominate my brain."

"Maybe you should eat some dinner, then ring Donal up," Damien said gently, passing Miki's food back to him. "I can't give you any insight on what it is to be a son because, well, my own father, you know how that is. I kind of wish I had the relationship with Donal that you do, but I know me, I would fight him more than I would accept him. You, Sinjun, for as wild as you are, you just want to be loved. And as someone who loves you, I can tell you that you deserve it, even though you think you don't. So eat your fucking Brussels sprouts, then go call your dad. Your *real* dad."

DONAL'S VOICE over the phone was a rich roll of Ireland and paternal love. Miki could feel everything in the man's heart from the moment Donal said hello. He'd passed Damien off to Sionn, took a shower, then dragged Dude into the bedroom so he could swaddle himself in a heavy quilt. The lights were left on, washing the unpainted brick of the front wall with a golden stain and lifting the shadows around the bed to a soft dove gray. He'd put on sweatpants so he wouldn't pick at the corner of the Salonpas patch he'd stretched over his scarred knee, and one of Kane's T-shirts he'd dug out of the pile on the chair next to the bedroom door. His arm itched where he'd been shot, but the soft fabric soothed the faint sting, much like hearing Donal did his nerves.

"Hey," Miki replied, then winced at the odd informality he always seemed to toss out at Kane's father. "Sorry. Um, how are you doing?"

It was always the small social things that tripped Miki up, and that evening, even with a full belly and a troubled mind, he scolded himself for forgetting the simple patterns he'd learned. Donal's chuckle told him he didn't mind, and then his soft burr assured Miki he was well.

"Did Kane talk to you about what he found out today?" Miki was never sure how much each Morgan knew about what was going on in his life.

Information jumped through the family like a firestorm in high winds, and sometimes he assumed one of them knew his deepest secrets when, in fact, confidences had been kept. For the most part, Miki knew Brigid would only be told bits and pieces in passing, leaving Miki to forge that unpredictable river on his own. Even if she did find out from Donal, she would wait, respectful of the boundaries he'd put up now that she understood how much he needed them.

Donal, however, was a different story. Family knowledge flowed to him as if he were a lodestone, gathering power and strengthening the bonds between the people he'd claimed. Miki was one of Donal's chosen, protected and precious to a man he knew he didn't deserve to be loved by. Accepting that love was difficult during the easiest of times, but now, as Miki tangled himself in questions and doubts, he needed to fling himself onto Donal's mercy and wisdom, hoping to find a way out of the maze he'd stumbled into.

Explaining to Donal what happened only took a few minutes, and to Miki's ears, it seemed so cut and dried, hardly anything to even be bothered about, but the turmoil inside him churned and tossed, picking away at his resolve to stay untouched by the ghostly presence of a woman he'd never met. Donal listened, only the sounds of a sip at a glass and the occasional indistinct mew of a nearby cat carrying across the phone as Miki spoke.

Coming to the end of his thoughts, Miki took a breath, then asked, "What do you think I should do?"

"Do ye be wanting an answer or can I be asking ye a question first?" Donal ventured.

"I'm open. If you want to ask me to grab you a cup of coffee, I'll do it." Miki rubbed at his face, then gently pushed Dude aside when the dog climbed up the bed to lick at his cheek. "I've talked to Kane and Damie about it, but mostly I don't know how to feel. Like I think I'm so angry at her and I shouldn't be because she doesn't really matter to me. Then another part says I don't know what happened then, so I can't—sorry, what were you saying?"

"Do ye need me to tell ye that I love ye, Miki boy?" Donal rumbled, a granite mountain moving through Miki's uncertainties. "Do ye need me there? Because if ye do, I'll be there in a moment. I've always vowed to be there for my children, so if ye need me, I'm there."

Miki refused to cry, but his eyes didn't get the memo. Sniffling, he tried to keep the noise down, but between the dog wiggling against him and Donal's heavy sigh, Miki knew he'd failed.

Screwing up his courage and swallowing the emotion drowning him, Miki said, "Just talking to you like this reminds me. It's hard right now because I want to be mad at somebody and she—my mother—was easy because I didn't have to think, but now I have to think, and I guess what I—"

"Ye just needed to know, to remember, who ye are." Donal found the knot in the middle of Miki's thoughts, tugging at it and loosening the hold it had on everything dark he'd tried to keep back. "Are ye still scared of losing yourself if ye go to therapy? Or are ye more scared of losing yourself to someone else's past coming to hunt ye?"

"I think I asked myself that already, and I convinced myself that no matter what, I would still be me, but now I'm not so sure. I was doing okay until Kane said he could find my father, and fuck, I wanted to punch him and scream that I already had a dad because… you're *him*."

"Then maybe what ye need to hear from me is that no matter who comes into your life, I will not let them hurt ye, and I will always be there when ye call out for your da." Donal swallowing echoed in Miki's ear. "I'll be telling ye something, Miki boy, and I want ye to hold on to this. Do ye understand me?"

"Okay," Miki whispered. Cradling Dude against him, he pulled in on himself, unsure if he was ready for what Donal had to say. "What?"

"If Kane ever does find yer dad and he's not man enough, not good enough for ye, then I promise ye this, son." Donal's sigh was loud enough to make Dude cock his head. "He will never come near ye. I would sooner skin him alive and salt his bones than have him say even a sharp word to ye. I've tried to be a good man all of my life and raise good men in return. I may not have raised ye, but I would welcome God's condemnation and hellfire to keep ye safe and loved. So mark my words, Miki boy, ye should only know love from anyone claiming to be your da, including me. I would kill for ye, son. On all that is holy, I swear, I would kill for ye."

CHAPTER THIRTEEN

Stars on the black
Stretching out into the abyss
How could you leave me, baby?
Didn't you think you'd be missed?
A slash of metal on your arm
Stole my baby from my world
Spilled life on white tile
Death's cloak came unfurled
Sing a song for the Devil
Sing a song for a God
Take my baby's soul to Heaven
I'm sorry for its flaws
—Soul for the Taking

IT WAS ironic that so much of Miki's life was spent in the Chinatown restaurants' kitchens, because if there was one thing Kane knew about his lover, it was that Miki St. John could barely open a package of dried ramen noodles, much less cook them. So for him to be standing in the middle of a steam-filled back room where Miki probably once washed dishes for a living was a surreal experience.

From the stacks of cutely posed Asian women wearing barely anything pinned to the wall next to a rotary phone, to the huge industrial double sink, the restaurant didn't appear to throw a lot of money at aesthetics anywhere before the swinging door leading to the dining room. The walls were covered in a pebbled plastic siding, the kind Kane only encountered at rest stops where the bathrooms were hosed off rather than mopped. They'd probably once been an ivory but over the years had been stained by a variety of vegetables, and age yellowed their surface until it was easy to see when a piece of paper taped in place had finally fallen off, leaving a pale shadow behind. The drywall by the phone was covered with numbers, some of them suspiciously close to gambling spreads, the occasional indelible ink scrawl fighting off a sea of smeared pencil markings.

The tiny back room was an offshoot of the main kitchen, a table set up in the corner for employees to take a break at, or, as was the case now, to chop up bok choy for the evening's use. The greens had been relocated to bins half full of water, and a too skinny young boy struggled to carry them one by one into the kitchen. Kane offered to help, but the boy stiffened when he approached, scurrying away as quickly as he could, burdened down by at least thirty pounds of cabbage, plastic bin, and speckled water.

After the last of the bok choy had been removed, Kane waited for his witness to sit down and make himself comfortable. It didn't take years of being an SFPD inspector to deduce that the man was nervous. His anxiety practically crawled off his skin, tightening his jaw and furrowing the wrinkles across his forehead until he resembled a bulldog with its face pressed against a pane of glass.

It was difficult to tell the witness's age, mostly because the years hung on him hard, dragging down his face and shoulders. The Chinese man was skinny, nearly emaciated, but there was a wiry strength in his thin arms and pigeon chest. His nose was big, nostrils flaring when he glanced around the room as if he had never seen it before, and his hard brown gaze never settled on Kane. He was bald except for a thin ring of sparse hair stretched around the back of his skull, and his age-spotted pate glistened under the harsh fluorescent lights. The man wore a pair of blue work trousers Kane had come to identify with most kitchen workers in Chinatown, and his once-white tank top was splattered with a whirlwind of stains. The jeans had a fraying hole in the right knee, and his fingernails kept returning to it, plucking at the white threads, ghosting little dust motes into the damp, hot air. He dabbed his pale tongue against his thin lips, and his eyes made one more pass over Kane's face, then slid away, roaming about the room again.

Kane remained standing, his thumbs hooked into his front pockets, his hands lax at his waist. Normally he would've sat down next to his witness, hoping to establish some kind of empathy, but his gut told him that in this case, it would be a waste of time. The man was jittery, and the longer Kane stood there as silent as the one-eared ceramic cat sitting on a shelf near an old watercooler, the more jumpy his witness became. He was about to say something, a little push to begin the conversation.

There were times when being a Morgan had its benefits, and the size that came with it was certainly going to help Kane deal with the lies poised to roll off the man's slippery tongue.

"I've got your pertinent information from Officer Walters, so I won't go over that again with you. He has your name down as Paul Huang, and you've been working at this restaurant for about eight years. Is that correct?" Looming in front of the table, Kane pitched his voice down, nodding when the man grunted. "I can follow up with the rest of your personal details later. Let's get to the point here. We know you found the body and that you IDed him. There is very little chance that you will be called up as a witness to trial, so anything that you say to me beyond what you saw today will be kept in confidence. But I have a feeling you can tell me a few things that I need to know. So let's start with how do you know Rodney Chin?"

The man's eyes began to play pinball under his lids, shooting about and nearly tilting over when Kane's question sank into his brain. Shifting in his chair, he stammered, "I don't know him. I—"

"You told the responding officer that it was Chin." Kane stepped on the lie. "You were certain enough that the medical examiner had his records called up so they could verify the ID. Not *make* the ID, but verify it. So let's start with the truth. How did you know Rodney Chin?"

He was careful not to lead Huang or make any mention of Wong. If Chin was well-known in the area, more present in underground activity than what the task force pinned on him, Kane wanted to hear it direct from

Huang's lips. Killing Chin to send a message to Miki didn't make as much sense as delivering one to Wong. Either Chin overstepped boundaries by shooting up the farmers' market on his own or his killing had been retribution for Wong ordering him to do so. Either way, Huang's response would tell them which path of investigation they would take.

"I knew him from before." The man clamped his lips tight, as if unwilling to let his words go without a fight. "I don't do what I did back then. I have a job here. I do a *good* job. I work long hours, and I don't have anything to do with people like Rodney Chin anymore."

"Did you work for Danny Wong or someone else?" Kane prodded. "So far everything you're saying tells me you knew Rodney, but not how. I need to know *how*."

"I used to pick up packages for people." Huang's bony shoulders nudged up into his neck, his collarbone jumping about his chest. The loose skin on his arms flapped a bit and Kane spotted a gnarl of scar tissue under his exposed right pectoral. "I didn't work for anyone. People would just call me, and I would grab what they needed me to pick up and take it to where they wanted it to go. I didn't ask questions. I didn't look in the packages. Rodney was one of the guys who would call me for a pickup. That's how I know him."

"How many years did you do that job?"

"About twenty," Huang admitted slowly. "I used to help my uncle when I was about eight. I took over the deliveries after he died. Wong was the reason I got busted. His sister Susan called me to do a job, but when I went to do the delivery, the cops were there. They were looking for people to turn on Wong and I was right there."

"What were you left holding?" Kane crossed his arms. "And don't lie to me. All that's going to do is piss me off after I check you out. Which means I'd have to come down here again to talk to you. I'm pretty sure your boss is okay with me talking to you once, but twice? I don't think things will go well for you after that."

"No lie. I'm telling you, I'm clean now." Huang sighed heavily. "I was carrying two kilograms of heroin. Uncut. So the feds said if I talked to them, they'd make sure I didn't go to jail for very long."

"And did you talk to them?"

"No," he said, shaking his head. "By the time they got around to me, they'd already nailed Wong and everybody else in his organization. My sentence got reduced by the judge, so I was out before anybody else. Chin never went in. Neither did Wong's sister. Now her son's in charge and Rodney's dead. And I'm here, chopping up vegetables for less money a month than I would get in a day back then."

"Who do you think killed Chin?" Kane asked. "Because my guess is even if you aren't working the streets, you're surrounded by enough of what's going on that you know. Did Wong do it? Or is somebody trying to tell Wong to clean up his act? You know what happened down at the market, right?"

"Yeah, I know." His chin bobbed as he rattled about on the chair. "That's how things were done before. Really old-school. Back then, Rodney and his brother Mark would do runs like that. Didn't care who they hurt or killed, just so long as the people they were trying to scare got scared. We used to see them come in together, but a couple of months ago, Rodney started coming in by himself. Just every once in a while, but he was mad. Someone told me Mark died and Rodney was pissed off about it. Then Wong got out, and all of those guys went back to doing what they did before. Or close to it. I can see some people not liking that."

"Would those some people be Wong's nephew? Adam Lee, right?"

"I'm not saying names." Huang shook his head. "I don't want to end up like Rodney. I am staying out of those kind of things. They want to kill each other, let them. But I can tell you that if Wong doesn't watch what he and his boys are doing, Adam Lee is going to put him down. Things aren't done like that anymore. Those days are over. And if Wong thinks he can just kill anybody he wants, he's going to be the one ending up dead."

"So THAT'S all you could get out of the restaurant worker? That Adam Lee probably isn't too happy with his uncle? *I* could have told you that." Kel leaned against the sedan they'd gotten from the motor pool. It had been slow going back from the murder scene, and Kel had resentfully thrown it into Park as soon as they'd found an open spot at the station. "Maybe we should drive them around in this until somebody coughs up something useful?"

It was a khaki-colored monstrosity, one he'd grumbled about ever since they left the station, but Kane didn't mind it as much as his partner did. Considering some of the vehicles they'd been given in the past, most notably ones reeking of dog poop or vomit, the off-green sedan was a step up. Everything worked, and for once, it smelled as pleasant as a freshly squeezed lemon.

So Kane felt obligated to defend the maligned car. "It's not that bad."

"One of the back tires is flat, K," Kel pointed out. "I can see a piece of rusted metal sticking out of its side from here. I somehow don't think we picked it up along the way. That looks like somebody actually stabbed the tire. I don't know why you don't believe me when I tell you the guys down there have it in for me."

"Maybe because sometimes when I request a car, I get a shitty one too. It's not just you." Gathering up the rubber-banded folders Horan had given him, Kane chuckled at his partner's impotent fury. "We all get shitty cars sometimes. It's not just you."

"They give you crappy cars because you're my partner. Everybody knows that. If they gave you a good car every time you went down there, then it would be really obvious they were trying to piss me off. So if they give both of us the bottom of the barrel, it doesn't look like they're trying to burn me."

Kane gave Kel a skeptical look. "I think you're a little bit paranoid. And as conspiracy theories go, it's kind of weak."

"Look, I'm not saying that it's on the scale of cow abductions, I'm just saying I pissed somebody off down there, and now, for the rest of my life, the motor pool is going to screw me over." Kel shrugged, slamming the driver's door closed. "They talk to each other, you know? It won't even matter if I change departments or stations. Once you're marked by the motor pool—*any motor pool*—you're screwed for the rest of your career. So you might as well get used to being driven around in shitty cars until you promote your way out of a partnership with little old me."

"Somehow, Sanchez, I can't see myself going very far without you," Kane drawled, heading toward the elevator.

"Are you kidding? You're a fucking Morgan, K." Kel caught up with him. "I'm pretty sure SFPD forged a pair of captain's bars for you on the day you were born. That's so inevitable, they are probably sitting in a vault next to death and taxes."

"Keep that up and I'm going to ask them to partner me with someone who's sane," he scoffed. Tucking the folders under his arm, Kane stepped into elevator, holding the door open with his foot. "For right now, let's just get upstairs and see if we can't find out who killed Rodney Chin."

The bullpen was buzzing with activity when Kane and Kel walked through its doors, and it took them about three seconds to realize why. In the middle of the warren of desks and filing cabinets, DEA agent Alex Brandt sat in Kane's chair, rocking its seat back as he tapped the end of a pencil against one of the department's landline phones. If the tailored blue suit wasn't enough of a clue he was there on official business, the shiny badge on the lanyard around his neck sealed the deal. Glancing up as the partners approached, Brandt excused himself from a conversation he'd been having with one of the junior inspectors, a plump-faced young woman with a pleasant smile and a cunning mind.

"I hope you have more for me than the witness I just interviewed." Kane playfully kicked at the agent's foot. "And get out of my chair."

"You can always tell someone who's had an older brother," Alex said to Kel as he stood, rebuttoning his suit jacket. "They are always quite possessive of something they think is theirs."

"You think he's possessive about the chair? Try checking out St. John's ass. He goes from Lucky Charms to Giantsbane in the blink of an eye." Kel dragged over a spare office chair. "Here. Unless this conversation needs an office."

"No, it's actually going to be very short. The only reason I waited for you was because I knew that you were coming in. My boss wanted me to have a talk with your captain, who pretty much turned to me and said you were going to run with anything I gave you." Alex tapped at a slender folder lying on Kane's desk. "The department has decided to release information on the agents who worked the Wong case. Of the five who'd gone undercover, only a couple are still active, and one of those is currently in Washington heading up a research department. The rest of them are scattered about California, but two still live in the city, including the active agent.

"The other papers are lists of associates and informants, including what information that DEA used on the case. I don't know what good it's going to do you, but it might lead you to someone who knows where Wong is. Criminals like routine, even if the world changes while they are inside prison. A lot of them drift back to the exact same patterns they had before they went in." Brandt ignored the chair, perching on the edge of the desk. "With regards to the agents, the only thing the agency asks is that you approach them respectfully and understand most have hung up their badges a while ago, so they could run the gamut between fuck you and bend your ear off. If you run into any problems, you can certainly reach out to me, but I can't promise you anything."

"You have no idea how much this is going to break our case open for us." Kel grinned widely. "I had a feeling we were going to have to knock on every single damned door in Chinatown just to find the bastard. Somebody in here has to know where we can find Wong."

"I'm still going to bet that the nephew is looking for him too." Kane let Kel rifle through the folder first, peering over his partner's shoulder. "I think Chin was retaliation. Everything we have on Wong says he's impulsive, but he didn't like to waste resources. He's not one to kill Chin just because he fucked up the market shooting."

He had too much information to absorb all at once. The names were a blur, mostly Asian, and most of the women Wong had working for him were Thai. The DEA agents' file was smaller, barely thumbnail photos with sparse information, a few phone numbers and a couple of addresses for the former undercover operatives, but nothing else. Kane took a moment to stare at the scatter of squares across the pages, trying to see Miki's features in any of the men or women, but they were grainy black-and-white copies, obscuring the fine details of individual faces.

"These would be better if we could get them electronically." Kane glanced up at Alex, who shook his head at the cops. "Or I guess we can try to hunt down if SFPD has more on them."

"Chances are you're not going to get a lot on the DEA personnel, but your criminal records might be able to help you flesh things out. These were a long time ago, Kane," Alex reminded him. "You're lucky you even have this digitally. Some poor guy probably stood in front of a scanner for hours trying to upload past records, and it was just pure luck he did *these*. We've got decades of reports that are still sitting in boxes, waiting for somebody to go through them."

"Look at the dates on these things." Kel handed Kane one of the pages. "Half of these people have been dead since about the time Wong was incarcerated. Makes the list shorter, but if Adam Lee has his mother to draw information from, he'll know who to target to cut Wong's knees out from under him. Chin is pretty much decimated. Do you think Lee would have gone to that extreme? Or could it have been one of Wong's people taking Chin out to gain favor with the old man?"

"I don't think we can rule that out, but, to me, something that brutal was drawing a line in the sand for Wong to cross. There's also the matter of Rodney having a brother that's gone missing," Kane pointed out. "If both of them were working for Wong, I wonder if the guy who went after Miki in Vegas was Mark Chin. If it was, then Wong is down two people he could count on. We just have to find out who's left and try to get to them. They might lead us to Wong if Adam Lee is going after Wong's associates."

"Yeah, provided Lee leaves you anyone to find," Alex replied. "Still, it's hard to stay loyal to a guy who's been locked up for a few decades if teaming up with him gets you killed. That's not a good bet to take. Not if Wong is dying, because when he's gone, you're still going to have to deal with the nephew."

"See, that just opens a bigger can of worms." Kane looked up. "If Wong's associates are few and far between, and he doesn't have a lot of time left to him, he's going to want to hit the bigger targets. Have you told the agents who worked the case that Wong's gunning for people?"

CHAPTER FOURTEEN

Kane: (reading one of Miki's notebooks):
Cherry cola kiss? The things that go
through your head, a ghra. What the
hell does that even mean?
Miki: (takes a sip of soda, kissing Kane
and sliding a bit of liquid into
Kane's mouth with his tongue) That.
Kane: Why don't we go into the bedroom
and you can show me what else that
tongue of yours can do. And bring
the soda.
—Red notebook musings

CHINATOWN WAS asleep by the time Kane unlocked the warehouse's front door. It'd been an easy
ride through the district's streets. He'd hit the sweet
lull spot when the restaurants were closed and the early

morning crews hadn't quite filtered in to begin their shifts.

Red and gold banners were strung up between the buildings in preparation for the coming moon festival, high enough to allow trucks to pass through the streets without tangling on the wires. The verdigris pagoda streetlamps sparkled, recently cleaned by a collection of benevolent societies and a couple of church groups. Here and there storefronts gleamed with a slap of new paint, but the awesome garishness of the district's spangled and effusive imprint remained. Until he'd moved into the warehouse, Kane hadn't really appreciated Chinatown's chaos. It'd taken falling in love with a mercurial singer to show him the kaleidoscope of life whirling about him, a hectic dance of colors, languages, and cuisines he had only just begun exploring.

If he'd never met Miki, Kane didn't know when exactly in his lifetime he would have discovered the snacking deliciousness of whole deep-fried garlic cloves, especially when drenched in a shoyu-chili oil dredge.

A few doors down from the warehouse, the bakery Miki bought egg tarts at lit up, prepping for the morning rush due to hit in less than a handful of hours. Behind their main counter, a round-faced older man hefted large bags of flour onto a worktable while another sped through pallets of eggs, cracking them one by one into an enormous metal mixing bowl. Kane made a mental note to stop by and grab moon cakes early in the week before all that was left were the ones with an egg in them, an atrocity that would offend his lover on levels Kane hadn't realized even existed before he'd met Miki.

"For a guy who has the eating habits of a five-year-old, he can be pretty fucking picky." Kane let himself into their home.

Then stopped short when he realized someone was sitting on the peninsula counter between the dining area and the kitchen, a dark silhouette with its back to the front door. A rustling of something plastic carried over the long space. Only one of the recessed lights was on, keeping the kitchen area dim. The rest of the house was dark, illuminated sporadically by the electronic devices set up under the large-screen TV in the living space and the night-light left on in the bathroom.

Kane intimately knew that shape, having explored that delectable body with his mouth and fingers over the past few years. Dude hadn't so much as whispered a peep at Kane's entrance, long inured to the sound of the Hummer coming home. Whatever Miki was doing, he was lost in thought because he didn't so much as glance behind him when Kane put away his gun, then shut the front closet door. Kane shed his shoes and then his jacket, draping it over the back of the couch as he walked by. The dog gave a murmured woof but didn't stir from the mound of pillows he'd nested on.

"No, don't get up," Kane grumbled at the canine. "I wouldn't want you to wear yourself out greeting me hello when I come home at night. Let's go see what our Miki is up to in the kitchen."

Miki looked up when Kane entered the kitchen, his hazel gaze a bit unfocused and thoughtful. He had a half-unwrapped ramen packet in his hand and was fiddling with the dried noodles, breaking them apart. The smile Miki gave him washed away nearly all the darkness Kane'd rolled in that evening.

In that moment, under the dubious romantic lighting of a dimmed LED bulb, Kane was struck by how much he *loved* Miki St. John.

They hadn't started off on the best of footing, mostly due to Kane's Irish temper and Miki's aggressive detachment and inscrutability. Looking back, Miki, about fifty pounds short back then and too lean by far, should have been cowed by Kane's height and breadth. Fueled by his frustration, Kane had thrown everything he had at the tall, lanky, pretty man who'd opened the door, glanced down at the thieving canine who'd violated Kane's shop, then categorically denied owning the dog even as Dude trotted past him into the warehouse.

Miki hadn't so much as blinked.

Instead, he'd squared his shoulders and told Kane not only to go fuck himself but how to do it and what sex toys he could use to make sure it hurt. Kane hadn't wanted to respect the man he'd come to tear apart, but a glimmer of awe and admiration settled in then. He'd spent three decades herding younger brothers and sisters with little more than his voice and an ingrained sense of authority. His siblings listened to him more than they listened to Connor, probably because they knew Connor's tender heart lurked beneath his bluster. But Kane usually meant business and got results.

Until *that* day.

Back then Kane hadn't seen the pain in Miki's face or how he held himself. All he'd seen was the erotic pout of Miki's full mouth, the snarling defiance in his tumbled emerald-and-citrine eyes, and the punch of graceful sensuality in the way he draped himself against the doorframe.

He still saw all those things. He'd scraped back the prickly, aggravating nature the feral street rat used to defend himself and discovered the still-not-too-gentle soul underneath. Miki had fire in his soul, an eternal ember of something visceral and raw that drew Kane in every time. The wildness of Miki's spirit excited him, provoked him into living life with a fierce enthusiasm, something Kane hadn't really considered until he'd met the musician.

Falling in love with Miki had been frustrating, exasperating, and nearly killed him, but something shifted in Kane, making him finally understand why his older brother ran into dangerous situations with nothing more than a bulletproof vest and a heavy arsenal behind him. Living with and loving Miki was as close to being on a SWAT raid as Kane ever wanted to get.

And probably just as dangerous.

Not many men could say their lover eyed them suspiciously as they approached, but it was a look Kane knew well. Especially when Miki was huddled over food. Grinning despite the fatigue pulling at him, Kane stood in front of Miki and placed his hands on either side of his lover's hips, parting Miki's knees so he could press in between his legs.

If anything, the suspicious look grew even more feral and territorial.

Kane was man enough to admit it kind of turned him on.

"Do you have any idea how much I love you?" Kane murmured, pressing a kiss against the corner of Miki's mouth. He tasted of slightly salty doughiness and was still chewing when he returned Kane's kiss.

"Want some?" Miki tilted his hand, offering Kane access to the crumbled, uncooked ramen noodles.

Oddly enough, that tiny gesture spoke more of Miki's love for him than anything else he could have done. Kane was struck speechless, unsure how to speak around the swell of his heart in his chest. Cupping Miki's face, he stared into the beauty he found there, amused by the slight lift of Miki's upper lip and the confused frown narrowing his eyes.

Miki put another pinch of noodles into his mouth and chewed. "*What*? I took out the flavor packet. Not like you couldn't taste it was foil if you put it in your mouth."

"For the life of me, I do not know why you eat that shit." Kane grabbed a single ripple of uncooked noodle and popped it in his mouth. It tasted as disgusting as it had the first five times he'd tried one in a misguided attempt to understand its attraction to Miki's taste buds. "No, it still tastes like shite."

"I like how you get all Irish when something goes really bad." Miki chuckled, helping himself to more ramen. "This tastes like—I don't know—it's just something that makes me feel better when my head gets all noisy. Kind of like you do."

"I sure hope to God I taste better," Kane mumbled, sliding his hands up Miki's legs, feeling his warmth through the low-slung cotton pants he had on. His SFPD shirt hung on Miki's smaller frame, but the singer often wore his things to sleep in. "I can't tell you how much I love seeing you in my clothes when I come home. Makes it extra special taking them off of you. Where's your brother and my cousin?"

"Upstairs, asleep." The suspicion was back in Miki's eyes. "Why?"

"Because I want to do very naughty things with you on top of this counter, and if they've already gone to bed, there's less chance of them coming through the front door and catching us." Kane hooked his thumbs into the waistband of Miki's pants, tugging at them. "Actually, someone possibly catching us makes it even more naughty."

"Hold up. We have a no sex in the kitchen rule, remember?" Miki put the ramen packet down, then closed his fingers over Kane's wrists, stalling him. "If I recall you said: 'We have to cook on these counters. I'm not eating off of anything where somebody's ass has been.' You give me shit for just sitting here."

"Sometimes, Mick," Kane murmured, bending in to capture Miki's mouth, "rules are meant to be broken."

"I'm going to remember you said that when Sionn catches us doing this," he growled into Kane's kiss. "Because if I get thrown under the bus for this, I'm taking you with me."

"Living room couch, then?" Kane suggested, nibbling down Miki's neck. "We'll just have to kick the dog off."

"What's wrong with our fucking bed?" Miki grabbed at Kane's shoulders, hissing as he was picked up. "Dude, you're going to drop me. Fuck, why did I name the dog Dude? Kane!"

"When are you ever going to trust me not to hurt you, Mick?" Kane cupped Miki's ass and slid one hand up to the middle of his back, cradling his lover against his chest. Miki's legs were hooked around his waist, his thighs tight around Kane's middle. He trembled in Kane's arms, his throat working as he held himself tight, and sucked in a breath when Kane walked them out into the living room. "I'm not going to drop you, babe. I will never drop you."

"Shit happens," Miki reminded him. "I've got a couple of scars on my knee to prove that to you if you need it."

"Dude, move." Kane nudged the couch cushion with his knee, and Miki tightened his grip. The dog opened one eye, then slowly slithered off the sectional. "Mick, you've got to let go a bit. I'm going to put you down now. You know, most people would think this is romantic. Me carrying you over to the couch is pretty high up there on the romantic gesture scale."

"Most people are idiots." Miki released his grip on Kane's neck as he was lowered onto the sofa. He breathed a sigh of relief when cradled in the cushions, then glowered up at Kane. "How the hell was that romantic? Like I couldn't have walked over here by myself?"

"It means that I'm taking care of you." He tugged at the hem of the shirt Miki had borrowed from him, pulling it up over Miki's chest. "That I don't want you to do anything but relax and enjoy yourself."

"That's just fucking stupid." The sneer on Miki's face could've curdled fresh milk. "I don't need to be carried around. You forget, K, I'm not going to break. I don't expect you to treat me like I'm going to, either."

"You are about as romantic as that potato over there, but God help me if I don't love you for it." Kane stripped Miki slowly, taking his time to kiss and lick at nearly every inch of exposed skin.

Getting himself naked took a little bit more work, especially since Miki's hands were busy exploring everything from his belly button to the inside of Kane's thighs, but eventually he got free of his clothing. Chuckling, he returned to the task at hand, teasing Miki into a state of frenzied arousal. At some point the dog left the room, but Kane didn't see where Dude went, nor did he care. The thought of Damien and Sionn coming down the stairs fled his mind, and he was happily ensconced in a world that existed only as far as the ends of the sofa and containing only the man he loved.

Kane dwelled on the sensitive spots he knew would drive Miki crazy. He'd discovered several over the years. The rise of Miki's hip bones and the inside of his elbows where his skin was tender and soft. Taking a small bite of the skin under his left earlobe made Miki shiver, and Kane's fingertips running down the middle of his spine was always enough to harden Miki's cock.

He wasn't a musician by any stretch of the imagination, but he intimately knew Miki's body and could play a sensual dance across Miki's skin, drawing out every erotic reaction he could ever hope for. Kane reveled in the sighs and soft moans, grew arrogantly smug at Miki's irritated hisses when his fingers teased at the velvety skin of Miki's balls. His teeth always found the spots where a single bite could make Miki squirm, and he took pleasure in stretching over Miki's long, naked body, pushing his lover down into the couch.

Kane stared down into Miki's face, struck again by the simple beauty in his open expression and unguarded gaze. Naked underneath him, Miki was at his most vulnerable, yet also his fiercest. He could never find the words to express how awestruck he was that Miki loved him, that Miki *let* him love him. Knowing the horrors of Miki's childhood and the sacrifices he made, the battles he fought to get to adulthood, humbled Kane. Miki had a strength in his scarred, muscular form and unyielding spirit Kane envied. He didn't know if he could ever survive what Miki had gone through, and he was thankful to the marrow of his bones he'd never be tested that deeply.

He was about to tell Miki how much he admired him when his lover opened his mouth and murmured into the quiet they cradled between them, "*I love you.*"

Once again, Miki stole the words right out of his heart.

"Fricking beggar," Kane growled, lowering his mouth over Miki's. "What the hell would I do without you?"

"Nothing if you don't have any lube on you." Miki canted his head back, glancing at the bedroom just out of sight. "Another good reason we should be doing this on our bed. Everything's in there. I mean—"

Kane *saw* something in Miki's face, something edging on the ridge of fear and apprehension. Miki's lip trembled, something he didn't normally see, and his eyes were guarded, despite his flushed cheeks and definite arousal.

Stroking Miki's cheek with his thumb, Kane gently prodded, "Are you okay, *a ghra*?"

"Kind of," Miki whispered back. "I just want to go to our bedroom. I just *need* to feel… safe."

THE CUSTOM-MADE bedroom doors were closed, and their room was lit only by the ambient glow of the streetlamps shining through the narrow slit between the blackout curtains drawn over the space's arched windows. With the world shut away, Miki straddled Kane's bare hips, his palms pressing against his cop's chest and his knees barely complaining at being bent while he rested his weight on his shins.

And he felt *loved*.

God, he needed to feel Kane's love. Now more than ever.

Having sex in the living room was… wrong. Not because he didn't want Kane. God, his desire for Kane made his teeth ache most of the time. He never wanted anything more than the touch of Kane on his body and in his soul. Where music calmed the monsters dwelling in his head, it only muted their ravenous hungers, and their rage surfaced time and time again, always seeking out the cracks in his control to tear him down.

Kane silenced those demons long enough for Miki to catch his breath and see the world through wide-open eyes, stripped of terror and doubt. His cop grounded him and, at the same time, sheared the chains holding Miki captive in the prison he'd made from his own memories.

"Never imagined I'd love somebody touching me." Miki looked down at Kane, tracing his lover's chest muscles with the tip of his finger. "But fuck, I guess I never imagined I'd ever love someone either."

"See, that's a sad state of affairs," Kane replied in his low, Irish-accented rumble. "I can't imagine anyone not loving you, Mick. Especially me. Especially *now*. Are you sure you want to do this?"

"What? Make love to you?" He followed his finger with the tip of his tongue, licking at Kane's nipple until it tightened into a bud beneath his lips. Drawing out a hiss from his lover with a light bite, Miki chuckled. "Yeah, I can't think of anything I'd rather be doing right now. Especially since I need you so fucking much."

If ever someone had asked him in the past—before Sinner's Gin died—who Miki thought he would fall in love with, his answer never would've been an Irish cop. Kane and his protective, fierce, giving heart wasn't anyone Miki could have dreamed up. There'd been no affection for him, no hugs that led to foul things, and certainly no kisses meant to soothe away any hurts. Loving Damien had been training wheels and how to open up his heart—*fuck*, how to *find* his heart—so while Miki knew how love felt, he hadn't been prepared for how it would consume him.

God, how his love for Kane *consumed* him.

He reached for the lube first, stealing it out of Kane's reach. His body tightened with the expectation of being filled with the thick shaft he cradled against the curve of his ass. Lifting his hips, Miki mourned the loss of the heat of Kane between his thighs but knew that in a few moments, he would experience a heat he could only find with Kane. The oily salve poured between his fingers when he tilted the bottle, and Kane let go of a low laugh at the splatter of fragrant lotion on his leg and hips. A gasp soon followed when Miki's fingers closed over his cock, the long slow stroke of oil on his skin hardening Kane in Miki's loose grip.

"You keep that up, *a ghra*, and I am never going to get inside of you in time," he rasped. Miki shot him a mischievous smirk, slowly circling Kane's cock head with his thumb. Kane's hips twitched between Miki's legs and he growled, "There's only so much a man can stand, Mick. You're about reaching the end of my limit."

"We just got started," Miki reminded him, fluttering another touch around Kane's slit.

"It doesn't take much of you to drive me crazy," Kane responded, sliding his hands down Miki's back. Spreading his cheeks apart, he slid his cock into the crevice. "I could lose myself right now."

"That would suck pretty badly." Canting forward, Miki slid Kane's cock head against his entrance.

"Considering I kind of need you hard for what I want to do to you."

The anticipation of having Kane inside of him tightened his nerves and sent a shudder through him. If there was a way to prolong Kane pushing into him, Miki hadn't found it. He loved the initial press of length against his ring and then the sliding rush of Kane's shaft into an emptiness he'd never thought he'd want filled.

He used to fear being touched, being stroked. It'd taken all of his willpower and strength to hold still when Damien held him for the first time, a seemingly meaningless gesture after their first successful gig, but it had been enough to drive Miki to the bathroom sink to empty everything he'd eaten. That was how Damien found him, opening the door to a conversation Miki never wanted to have—never imagined having—where he told another living soul what had been done to him and someone finally believed him.

With Kane, it was even more of everything Miki had been taught to fear.

But with Kane, it was now everything he'd learned to love.

The scent of sweet almond lubricant made his mouth water. The brush of Kane's callused fingers along his cock or belly made him hard. When Kane's mouth closed over Miki's nipple, he let himself fall into the pleasure of feeling it all the way down to his toes. Nothing would ever take away how much joy he now found in the sensual exploration of a man he'd come to cherish—of a man he would give anything to—including himself.

That first push—*shit, that first push*—made Miki arch his back, opening himself to take Kane in. His cop went slow, easing past the tightness he found at

Miki's entrance. The theft of Miki's breath seemed inevitable, especially when, despite the countless hours they'd shared in each other's bodies, Kane was nearly too thick for Miki to handle.

Or maybe he was just too scared to admit how much he wanted Kane inside of him.

Not now. Not naked and mewling with need. Poised and breached by Kane's shaft, Miki had to fight not to sink himself in one swift move. That would hurt, his brain whispered. But it would feel so *fucking* good, his body reminded him.

Seating himself made Kane growl and hiss. His lover's fingers tightened on Miki's hips, dimpling his skin nearly hard enough to leave bruises. Or they might leave bruises, Miki didn't care. Nothing made him feel more alive than riding Kane's muscular, long body. The sinewy strength and give of his moving thighs under Miki's ass always seemed to match the rhythm of Miki's heartbeat. Sex with Kane was like finding music in the folds of a rainbow and a stormy sky. Bursts of color and sensation, hammered into the steel threads of craving more. The crinkle of Kane's hair at Miki's thighs tickled but then turned erotic when the heat of their bodies brought up the musk of their skin.

Kane struck that spark in Miki's body, and he reached out, pressing his palms into Kane's shoulders to let the lightning riding his spine loose. Chasing the sensation, Miki ground his hips, gyrating with long powerful strokes down Kane's cock. His cop's skin grew slippery, slick with sweat but still sweet from the faint traces of lube from Miki's fingers.

Another stroke of lightning and Miki was almost lost.

"Turn us over," Miki said, tugging at Kane's arm. "I want you on top of me."

"That I can do, *a ghra*," Kane said through gritted teeth. "Hold on to me."

Sex was never elegant. There were times of lazy, drifting pleasure, and sometimes they'd lost themselves in the pounding pleasures racing toward the climax. Elbows and knees never seemed to work properly—not that Miki's old scars were any help—and there'd been more than a few instances where one or both of them had ended up on the floor because they had misjudged the edge of the bed.

Not this time. Not this joining of who they were into what they'd become.

They moved easily, barely missing a stroke, and if Miki had any complaints it was that Kane needed to go harder, go faster. A few muttered words and Kane eagerly complied, pressing Miki back into the sheets and rocking his hips until the slap of their skin nearly stung with each thrust.

"Not going to last." Kane bit at the curve of Miki's neck and shoulder. There would be no hiding the bruise. "The things you do to me, Mick. God in heaven, I can't hold on."

The stretching grew intense and the thrusting of Kane's cock against the nerves inside of Miki's body broke his mind apart. He no longer fought the pleasure rising to drown him. He couldn't. He couldn't stop the wave of sharp threads cutting through his reason, slicing through his control. And when Kane's lips found his, his tongue plunging into Miki's mouth, licking and penetrating the depths there, Miki surrendered.

Giving Kane everything he had inside, then taking everything Kane had to give.

He held on as tight as he could, but Miki knew he'd be swept away. It hit him hard, stealing away every whisper of air in his lungs and then every drop in his release. The splash of his orgasm took him by surprise despite the vortex he'd climbed to reach his breaking point. The wind they'd built between them caught him, throwing them back into the storm, and for a brief moment—or maybe an eternity—Miki flew.

And as he began to spiral down, Kane was there to catch him.

"I love you above all others," Kane whispered—or maybe shouted—into Miki's ear. It was hard to hear amid the rush of blood through his veins and the final throes of his release, but Miki felt Kane's words, taking them into his heart. "I will *always* be yours. *Always*."

His lover filled him with a gush of hot liquid and ravaged his mouth with kisses. His lips were swollen from Kane's small bites and his hips ached, complaining that his thighs had been spread apart for so long. He was sticky with sweat and come, but Miki was reluctant to let Kane go.

"Stay here." Miki ignored the pangs resonating through his body. He tightened down on Kane's softening length, wanting to hold him there for a little bit more. "Don't go just yet."

"I'm going to be too heavy on you soon." Kane stroked at Miki's sweaty hair, pushing it back away from his face. "Are you okay? Are you good?"

"Yeah, I'm good. Better now that you and I…" He hated the burn of embarrassment across his cheeks nearly as much as he loathed the feeling of Kane sliding out of him. Sighing in resignation, Miki let himself get scrubbed off with the shirt he'd stolen from Kane's pile of clothes, then stretched out on the bed, watching his cop climb onto the mattress. "Give me five minutes. I might want you again."

Flopping on his back next to Miki, Kane tangled their fingers together. "I'm old, *a ghra*. You're going to have to give me more than five minutes."

"Okay," Miki conceded. "I'll give you ten."

They lay next to each other, shoulders touching for nearly all of Kane's five minutes. Then his cop said, "Are you sure you're okay? A little while ago—"

"I was scared." Acknowledging his monsters was easier when he was the only one who saw them, but Miki knew he was only fooling himself. Kane saw everything, knew everything, and would push if Miki tried to avoid talking about the shadows stalking him. "I don't know why. I just felt like I needed to be alone with you, and out there it was too open. *I* was too open. Or maybe I just didn't want to share *us*. I don't know. I just felt like I needed to be here with you. And not fucked on the counters, because that's a house rule."

"That's the first thing we're going to do when Damien and Sionn move next door." Kane reached over and tapped Miki's nose. "We're going to resanctify every flat surface in this place."

Miki tilted his chin up, meeting Kane's playful gaze. "Do you mind if they stay here for a little bit? I don't know if I'm ready. Not for a long time, but maybe just until all of this is done?"

Kane's kiss was gentle and too brief for Miki's liking. "Babe, I don't care if they never move out. I just want you to be happy. And for some reason, that means your brother, Damien."

"And the dog," Miki grumbled back.

"Well, most of the time, I *like* the dog." Kane grunted when Miki's elbow found his ribs. "Damie's okay. It's Sionn I can't wait to get rid of. I worked too hard to move out of my family's house, and here I am with my cousin right upstairs. And before you jab at me again, I'm joking. They can stay until whenever you or they feel like it's time to go. It's not like the two of you aren't going to be living in each other's pockets anyway. It's just going to be a matter of what side of the wall we're going to find you on."

"I need to find me," he admitted, whispering up into the dimness above them. It felt good to say, especially while holding Kane's hand. "When you called me to tell me about that guy's murder today, all I could think about was how maybe no one cared that he was gone. I mean, if that guy in Vegas was his brother, then I don't know. My brain is kind of like a salad today. There's just so much stuff going on inside of my head, and I think I expect you to help me find the edge of all of the noise."

"I will always be here, remember?" Kane pulled Miki closer. "I love you. I will always love you. No matter what happens, I will always be here for you."

"I've been thinking about that too," Miki confessed. What he longed to say was a risk, but it was one Miki knew he had to take. They'd been through too much, loved fiercely, and fit into each other in ways Miki still couldn't quite understand but would mourn the loss.

"You doubt I'd be here for you?" Kane gave him a confused look. "What do I have to do to convince you, *a ghra*? How many more times do you have to hear me tell you I love you before you believe me?"

"I do believe you." Miki pushed himself up, resting his weight on an elbow so he could see Kane's face.

"I know that you'd be here for me. But I also know that there are times you wonder if I'll be there for you."

"I've *never*—"

"Maybe not you, but the rest of the world," Miki murmured. "So, I'd like you to marry me, K. I want to make you my family, because no matter who you find—whatever fucking parent or anything I have out there—I want you to remember that I have you *first*. That I love you and I never ever want to lose you. I can't ever go back to how I was—when I was lost before—when I was so fucking alone. So, K, will you make me your family? For real?"

CHAPTER FIFTEEN

Connor: Babe, how do you feel about kids?
Forest: I'd use my hands, but people don't like when you pick up their kids.
Con: You know what I meant. Kiki and I had a conversation, and she kind of mentioned she'd be okay with us— well, you—she wants to give us a few eggs so we can get a surrogate. Told her I'd talk to you first.
Forest: Well, you'd kind of have to because you know, I'd have to do... the thing into a cup.
Con: So what do you think?
Forest: I'd love to have kids with you, but before we knock some strange woman up, we probably should tell your mom we're married.
—Cooking omelets for dinner

"So, I told him yes." Kane cradled his coffee cup, a double-walled, swirled paper creation meant to insulate his hand from the liquid's heat, but the molten temperature of Finnegan's morning brew seeped through. "Then I spent the next couple of hours making sure he didn't regret asking me."

"That last bit is something I didn't need to know, K." Connor rested his forearms against the pier's railing, joining his brother in contemplating the choppy gray waters of the Bay. "But I'll be the first one to tell you, I'm happy for you."

Tuesday mornings were usually spent working up a sweat with weights, followed by a long run to nowhere in particular so long as it got their hearts pounding and their legs aching from exertion. But today was different. Today, Kane began the morning with words he never thought he would ever say—Miki St. John proposed to him.

It still seemed surreal.

He was so far outside of where he thought he would be on Tuesday morning that instead of pounding his body into submission, Kane reached for comfort from the one person who'd been there with him from the very beginning—his older brother.

The morning was cold, a bite in the wind with the promise of rain on the horizon. Dawn slapped at the sky only a few minutes before they'd gotten the coffee, and its hint of gold brightened the gray clouds dotting the cerulean stretch above him. The foot traffic on the pier was slight, a few die-hard walkers accompanied by the occasional dog, and a riot of seagulls fought over the remains of a spilled dinner or two at the far end of the dock, their cries rising and falling amid a barrage of flapping wings.

Kane and Conner were mostly hidden by one of the many warehouses lining the pier, taking advantage of the windbreak it provided, but the chill crept in anyway, rising off the water to nibble at Kane's unshaven cheeks.

They'd been coming to that spot at the pier on and off for years, at least long enough for the railing to shrink down to the point the Morgan boys could finally lean on it. As noisy as it was, the pier and its chatter of chaos was still quieter than the home they'd grown up in, especially after the twins arrived. Back when they were kids, it'd been a fifty-cent bus ride to the pier as a lark, and the dockside spot became one of the few places he and Connor could stand and talk without worrying about someone coming out to find them or calling for them to do something. When they'd found a gym nearby, one they could both lift and box at, a dock run was rolled into their morning get-togethers when they could manage it, and it always ended with a cup of coffee stolen from Finnegan's morning setup crew's carafes or one of the diners nearby.

And while where they got their coffee changed, where they drank it rarely did.

"When are you going to tell Mom?" Connor broached. "Because she's going to lose her mind. Not that I'm doing any better. Of all of us, you two were the last ones I'd expect to be married."

"Agreeing with you there, Con," Kane conceded, saluting his brother with his cup. "But it's odd how right it feels and how much him saying that to me shifts everything about us. I'd never have given it much weight, but here I am sitting on the other side of that moment and thinking, God, it all feels *right* now."

Connor tapped his brother's cup with his. "I know how that is. And I noticed you haven't answered me about our mother."

"Maybe right after you tell her about the Las Vegas trip you took with Forest." He grinned at his brother's exasperated hiss. "The longer you wait, the harder it's going to be."

"I'm thinking we don't tell her at all and just say we're going to be married." Connor shot him a guarded look. "We just have to kill the people who do know so she doesn't find out otherwise. Sadly, that'll be you and Miki, by my last count."

"If you think the rest of Crossroads doesn't know, you're fooling yourself, brother mine," Kane pointed out. "And it's a toss-up about whether Quinn knew before Forest told Rafe. Our third brother is psychic. Oh, and Kel knows. Kiki might know, too, but I'm not sure."

"She knows," he replied with a shake of his head. "We told her because… well, let's deal with you and your Mick first. I'd love to say we want to have a wedding and just not mention that we've already done the deed, but that's gone out the window. Time's running out for me. I just need you to be my best man."

"Agreed. I'd kill anyone else you asked until I was the only one left." Kane grinned at his older brother, warmed at the asking. His eyes might have misted, but he wasn't going to own up to it. "If I have a wedding, then I'd like you to return the favor, right?"

"Whatever you have, I'll be next to you," Connor rumbled, hooking Kane into a swift one-armed hug.

"For the rest of mine, I've got Sionn, Quinn, and Rafe to stand up next to us."

"You sure you've got Rafe on your side of the aisle?" He shifted away from a wet spot on the railing, hoping he hadn't smeared bird poop over his arm. "You forget Andrade's in your husband's band?"

"I've been friends with Rafe since before the dawn of time. He was my brother before he became Forest's." Connor scowled. "Forest has other friends. He can find a couple more other than Damie and Miki. Rafe's *mine*."

"Still don't like to share," Kane teased. "You'd think you'd have learned to by now."

"All of us have come a hell of a long way with each other." Sipping at his coffee, Connor grunted. "I'm having Rafe standing up next to me. You worry about yours and I'll worry about mine."

"I can't see Miki wanting anything more than a piece of paper saying we're married, but that's up to him. You two going the full stretch?"

"Everything but the church," Connor replied. "But that's on them, not us. Spoke to Forest about it and he's of the same mind. We're marrying—again—in front of God and family. That's what binds us together, not the house we're standing in when we do it officially."

"When are you going to break this to Mom?"

"Why?" His brother glanced over at him. "You plan on piggybacking your announcement onto mine?"

"Probably," Kane admitted. "I want to give Miki as much of a buffer as he can get, and if I have to throw you and Forest under the bus to do it, well, I hope the tire marks on your back wash off."

"Nice. Soon. Probably this Sunday. Da's given us a window." Connor took another sip from his cup.

"So Da knows?" Exhaling a long breath, Kane shook his head. "You're fucked, Connor. How the hell did that happen? It wasn't me."

"No, it was someone he knows in HR. Came by and congratulated Da." His brother sighed. "Change of status forms did me in. Had to file them so they knew to contact Forest in case—well, the *job*. You know it. If something happens to me, the department needs to take care of him."

"If something happens to you, I'll kick your ass," Kane muttered at his older brother. "And you know we'll be there for him. He's a Morgan now. We never let go of one of our own, even when they try to fight tooth and nail to get out. Look at Rafe, the poor bastard."

"Aye, the poor bastard." Connor chuckled. "He never had a chance. Between Mom and Quinn, he should have just accepted his fate and came along willingly. Now look at him. He's having to show up every Sunday until she's satisfied he won't be slipping off into the shadows when she isn't looking. So it's a yes, then? You next to me?"

"Safe to say, Con." Kane grinned. "It's a yes. Just don't get married until I get Wong locked up."

"Shit, how is the case going? Last I heard you were trying to dig Wong out from wherever he's hiding, and the DA agreed to release the vic's property to you."

"Yeah, I don't know what the hell's up with that guy. Captain thinks he's trying to play politics, which doesn't make a fuckton of sense. What's to gain by holding back evidence I've got for an ongoing case? The official word was he needed to assess its value to the investigation and determine whether or not the package actually belonged to the vic or to Edie."

"Glad he finally got his head out of his ass and decided it was Edie's," Connor interjected. "Still, be good to know what changed his mind. In case one of us runs through this again."

"I think Book and Dad pulled it out for him. I hate having to use a gold shield to pry something loose from the DA's office, but fucking hell, there could be something in there that'll give me some information on who Wong ran with that wasn't in the damned sketchy files we got from the gang detail and the DEA," Kane growled over his coffee. "Kel and I are going to go over everything this morning and figure out who we're going to hit up first since Chin's dead. His nephew's running a few operations now. Everyone keeps telling me they don't get along but—"

"Family's hard to turn your back on," his brother finished Kane's thought.

"Yeah, Wong's sister is my next cold call, but I don't know how that's going to go. She gave up federal protection to come back to the city." Kane shrugged at Connor's raised eyebrows. "Husband retained joint custody of the kid, so either she walked away from her son—the guy now running Wong's old territory—or came back out into the open and split custody."

"Once again, family," Connor pointed out.

"Yeah, that's how I read it," he agreed. "Problem I have is Miki's in the middle of all of this. *Something* happened to his mother. Either she ended up on Wong's bad side and he killed her, or she was in the wrong place at the wrong time, which is what I think happened to Chin. I think he was murdered to tell Wong to stop muddying the waters with his shit."

"What does your partner think?"

"Kel? He's open to any and all suggestions," Kane snorted. "Including Wong offing Chin to show what happens to people who fuck things up."

"And you disagree?" Connor turned, giving Kane his full attention.

"Yeah, I don't see it that way," he replied. "Most of Wong's people aren't around anymore. Or at least the ones we could track down. The few that are around aren't going to suddenly chuck away the lives they've built while he's been locked up, just to stroke Wong's ego. He doesn't have enough people to waste. The man was brutal and bloodthirsty, but he wasn't stupid. I just don't see him losing IQ points simply because he was in prison."

"So why go after Miki? What's the point of that if his mother was one of Wong's?"

"Truth? My gut tells me this isn't about Mick's mother." Kane felt out the edges of his thoughts, returning to the same circle he'd found himself in time and time again. "Wong used to give his—best performers—a bonus of sorts, mainly women who worked his brothels or massage parlors."

"And Miki's mother was one of these women?" Connor whistled under his breath. "Are you sure it wasn't the woman who met Edie?"

"Yeah, coroner said the vic never gave birth. That's one of the first things I asked because, shit, who wouldn't wonder that, but that came back with a no. Chaiprasit's package allegedly holds personal effects from Miki's mom." Kane scoffed. "DA confirmed the articles *might* just be of some value, which is why they're releasing it to the department."

"It never should have been in their possession to begin with." His brother frowned. "Is that what we're getting to? That office stepping on top of us? Making it harder to do the job?"

"Da says politics muddies the air up there," Kane pointed out. "That's all this was. Someone in the place grabbed at the shooting, hoping to make it some endemic violence and ride out the drama storm they'd made, but it went deeper than they expected. Book's hoping whoever did the grab got their hands slapped for it, but—"

"None of us are going to hold our breath. There's lines that can't be crossed. Interfering with a case is one of them." Connor's frown deepened until he looked like their father did one Christmas morning when he'd come down to find his three oldest boys had stripped the tree of candy canes only to puke them all back up onto the mound of presents gathered in the corner of the living room. "So now what? You find out his mother's name and then what? How is knowing who she is going to help your case? Or is this just for Mick?"

"First and foremost, it's got to be for the case. Miki knows that, and besides, Edie's going to share what she's getting. Honestly, I want her name so I can chase down anyone who connected her and Wong. It might open up a few doors for the case or be nothing. Either way, it's some place I can dig through and maybe find *something*." Kane sighed, wishing he could dance around the elephant in the middle of the situation. "Miki's caught on deciding if he wants to find out more about his mother or just letting it go. Edie's dropping off her copies for him to look at today. I asked if he wants me to be there, but you know him."

"I do. He'll be wanting to stew over it for a while. That's one thing about him, he doesn't expect you to do anything but be there for him if he needs it." Connor pursed his mouth, obviously choosing his words. "Thing is, will he ask you if he does?"

"Yeah, he will," Kane said with a nod. "Finding out who his mother is—was—isn't the worst of what he's facing down. A couple of the guys working for Wong were DEA, and when Wong was handing out his favors, they were on the receiving end. Had to keep their covers intact, so…."

"You'll be opening up a whole different Pandora's box if his mother was tapped for one of those agents. Case could always be made that he didn't know she was pregnant." Connor exhaled hard. "But what if he did? Suppose the guy knew about Miki? And walked away anyway?"

A simmering rage ignited in Kane's gut, spreading through his soul. He'd seen photos of what'd been done to Miki by a man who should have taken care of him. Vega died at the hands of one of the young men he'd terrorized, his killer driven by anxieties and fear until he'd developed an obsession with being Vega's sole focus. Knowing what Miki had survived—was still struggling to survive—shook Kane to the core, and the idea ghosting through his thoughts that a man, his natural father, could have prevented the nightmares and terrors haunting his lover only fed the fire of Kane's anger.

"If that's the case, then I don't know what I'm going to do." Kane drained his coffee cup, then balled it up in his hand. "But I sure as hell know where I can get a shovel, because if I don't kill the guy, then Da will. There's no changing the past. I know that, Con, but someone put shadows into my Mick's eyes, into his heart. And I can't kill the man who put them there, but I sure as hell can beat the shit out of the man who could have stopped it."

"You'd lose your badge," Connor shot back. "And jail's no place for an ex-cop. Keep your head about you."

"I know. I will," he grumbled. "Miki needs a break, Con. He knows I love him. I've worked damned hard at making sure he feels it down in his bones, but if there is anyone who needs to know he's not trash, it's my Mick. And I hope to God in Heaven that the man we find at the end of this can be as much of a father to him as Da is. He deserves it. He does."

"Then I hope that's what's waiting for you both." Connor patted Kane's back. "Just don't you forget, just like you'll all be here for Forest, we're all right here for your Mick. No matter what happens, no matter who crawls out of the woodwork, he's a Morgan now, through and through."

FOR AS much death rode on its coattails, the manila envelope Edie handed over to Miki hardly seemed worth the effort of opening, much less killing for. It lay on the chest, a plump yellowish-beige rectangle with hidden fangs and sharp edges. Miki stared at it for a long minute, still unsure about how to handle the sudden thrust of his unknown past into his tumultuous present, but he was at a now-or-never point, with *now* biting him in the ass so he could move on with his life.

"Hardly seems worth the effort for all this fuss, yes?" Damie groaned, reaching for the envelope, but his hand stopped short, fingers a few inches above the package. "Shit, Sinjun. That's on me. Just reaching for the thing. Habit, I guess. It's been *what's yours is mine* for so long."

"It's okay." He scrubbed at his face, wishing he could rake away the odd, unsettled discomfort in his guts, but it lingered, poking at his sanity. He inched closer, scooting forward on the couch, but the envelope only got slightly bigger, hardly large enough to loom over him, no matter how he felt about it. "I keep telling myself I should just open it, but I can't fucking do it."

"Edie said all of it's just copies. The real thing's over with Kane." Damie poked at a corner of the package and Miki snorted. His brother was more curious than a kitten, and sometimes as destructive. "You going to wait for him? I mean to open it?"

"No. It's weird. *This* is weird." He shook his head, restarting the ache in his temples. "It's his case and this is… *fucked*. He's going to be opening up the real thing—probably today—and anything he finds out, he probably can't talk to me about. Or if he can, it's going to be all flashy red light crap where I can't tell anyone what he found out. This shit's connected to a murder—that woman's murder—and he's got to dig out why she got killed."

"Thought they found the guy who did it. Dead, but still, found."

"Head guy is still out there, remember? It's why I can't go take a piss without someone standing outside of the damned door," Miki grumbled. He was growing tired of the constraints on his life. It wasn't as if he had a daily routine, but he liked the freedom he'd had, even if that meant he spent days without actually leaving the house. It was frustrating to know he couldn't simply get up and leave. "Dan's okay, but I don't like that Richie guy. He's an asshole."

"Don't think he's going to be coming back," Damie reassured him. "Sionn said he tapped out because it wasn't exciting enough for him. Me? I like the boring. Means no one's trying to kill you, and I've grown kind of fond of having you around."

"You just want company onstage." Miki sneered.

"You know me, Sinjun. I've got ego for days. Do you really think I'd want to share the stage with someone prettier and hotter than me?" He nudged his shoulder against Miki's. "Besides, knowing you were here kept me going, right? Let's not forget that."

Damie leaned against him, a nearly too-warm, too-heavy weight Miki never, ever wanted to lose again. They'd forged a brotherhood between them, and a couple of bands, but underneath all the words and sentiment, they were *easy*. Even in the throes of an irrational anger at Damien for allegedly dying on him, Miki'd held on tight. Something in each other completed a connection, knitting their psyches together. It was easy to put into musical terms—a melody and harmony— but it went deeper than that, a twinship of sorts, thriving without question and as inseparable as the stars and the night sky.

Miki hitched back the torturous memory of the time he spent mourning Damien's death, layering it with the moment he'd seen his brother amble into the Morgans' kitchen as if he'd simply gone out for a walk instead of disappearing for nearly two years. Clearing his throat, Miki said, "I missed you so damned—"

"Oh no, Sin," Damie countered quickly, sliding his fingers across Miki's trembling mouth. "We don't look back, you and I. We can celebrate Dave and Johnny, but we're not to have regrets. *I* am not your regret. I came back. You've got me back, and we look forward."

"Some days—*shit*." Miki couldn't finish his thought, not and hold back the tears already threatening to wash away his shaky world. "*Fuck*. I can't stop thinking about the what-ifs, you know?"

"That's why you're going to go see Penny, and she'll teach you how to do that. I'm not saying we don't look at our past and feel sad, but you and I both know you keep coming back to it, picking at it like a scab. And I can't help you stop that. She *can*." Damien swung his arm around Miki's waist, dragging him over. "Someday, we're not going to be together, but it'll be only for an instant. Just like you and Kane or me and Sionn. Death just holds us long enough for the others to catch up, and then we're back into the stars. Some part of you knew I was lost back then, because you were waiting for me. Even when Kane came into your life, you still held something of me in you. Like the seed I needed to get my head back to where it needed to be. I really believe that. We've got a lifetime of music and love ahead of us, and I'm going to need you to be sane and healthy while we live through it."

"D, I've never been sane and healthy." Miki tapped his head. "Suppose all she does is take away what makes me tick?"

"You're too fucking stubborn for that, Sin. Trust me, no one can dig their heels in like you." He laughed at Miki's elbow jabbing into his ribs. "You're going to be fine. And if she isn't the one to help you out of that bramble you got yourself into, then we'll find someone else. No matter how long it takes, we'll find you someone who will show you it's okay to be happy and that no one's going to take that from you. That's what I've got to get you to believe, brother. That all of us, our love for you, won't go away and that you fucking deserve every bit of it. So you work on that and let us hold on to you until you do."

"It's hard. I'm just so damned tired of being scared all the time." His admission was a soft one, but its roots ran deep, a weed gripping at Miki's core foundation. "It's just like a low hum, like an old tube amp."

"Yeah, that I get." Damien stretched his arm out and snagged the package off the crate. Shaking it at Miki, he asked, "So, Sinjun, the question is, are you going to open it? And it's okay not to."

"I kind of have to open it. Kane's going to have to dig through it for what he's doing, and I can't have him looking at me knowing who I am when I don't know what he's seeing." He made a face, disliking the push at his guts. "I have to open it."

"You want me around for that?" Damie laid the package on Miki's lap. "Because this is big for you. I don't know if—"

"I want you here." This time, it was Miki who reached out to pinch Damie's mouth closed. "Just fucking hold on there for a bit. Because I think I know who else needs to be here with me… with *us*. Let me just make a call."

CHAPTER SIXTEEN

She walks through dreams
Childhood wishes on stars
A faint echo of a woman
Look for her in dives and bars
Familiar stranger
To fill a hole in my heart
Never been together
Never been apart
—Hole in My Heart

"DAMNED SHAME about the timing of this," Kel grunted from the driver's seat of their most recent police-issued car. "But Chang said Wong's sister is heading back over the pond, so it's either we talk to her now or wait for her to come back after whatever festival's going on in China."

"Moon festival," Kane supplied, trying to work his seat belt buckle. It fought him, almost as if the two ends were from two different cars rather than together in the late model sedan. "Sanchez, I swear to God, you pissing off the motor pool is going to get me killed. I can't even work this damned seat belt."

"You've got to lick it first," his partner shot back, easing the car around a corner. He slowed as a pack of teenagers skipped and jumped their way across the street. "Don't give me that look. I'm serious. It needs a bit of lube to get it in there."

"Kel, I grew up with brothers. I'm not licking this fucking seat belt," Kane retorted. "And how the hell would you even find that out? Who licked the damned thing first? And what's wrong with WD-40?"

"Marsha in Motor Pool told me to do it," Kel mumbled, his voice nearly lost in the car's sudden backfire. "Shit, she told me they fixed that."

"Swear to God, one day they're going to sell you a handful of magic beans." Kane felt a small surge of triumph when the belt finally clicked shut. "Here we go."

"Yeah, too late. We're almost there." Kel glanced down at the map display. "A few more blocks anyway. How weird is it that you know Miki's mother's name and he probably doesn't yet?"

"I don't like it," Kane admitted. "I think we need more time with what was in that packet, but our window with Wong-Lee this morning is really short, so we are going to have to take what we do have and try to play it. The thing is, we can connect Chaiprasit's murder to Wong through Chin. Even with the preliminary evidence we have of Chin's gun being used in her murder, you and I both know we need to cut the head off of the snake. Wong has a list of people he wants dead and Miki is on it. Chin probably wasn't, so we have a secondary player trying to level the field."

"Which is why we're talking to Susan, but is she going to be willing to let the cops handle it? Or is that secondary player her kid?" A bus cut in front of their car and Kel sighed in frustration. "The problem I see is if Chin was a message to Wong, that means our secondary isn't willing to spill Wong's blood. It could be the nephew, but it could just as easily be the woman we're going to go see in a few minutes. Any idea on how you want to play this?"

"Like you said, our secondary is as much of a worry as Wong. If it is somebody who is close to him but estranged, it wouldn't take much for things to flip and our secondary decides to do Wong a favor and pick up his people-who-need-murdering list." Kane estimated their arrival to be another fifteen minutes, considering the traffic around Union Square. "I just wish we had a better idea of how she feels about her brother now that he's terminal and out of prison. We know that she is going to protect her son, first and foremost. She stepped out of protection for him, so that is a hard point on the board."

"Yeah, when someone is staring down the big C, family tends to forgive everything and anything from the past." Kel worried at the steering wheel with his thumbnail, scraping off the remnants of a sticker left near the horn. "The reports we got from Chang said there had been bad blood between her ex-husband and Wong—"

"I think her relationship with Wong is a lot better than people realized. That's the same ex who ended up dead a couple of years after she got her kid back from him. Wong was in prison by then, but it was all fresh. He still had power."

"So you're thinking that Wong did his sister a solid by killing her ex-husband?" Kel mused. "Are we sure it's her son running things and not her? She sounds cold. The kind of cold you need to be when running drugs or slinging people on beds to make a buck."

"Nobody said she didn't have a hand in what her son has going on now." Kane stared out the window, watching a group of businesspeople in sneakers walking while chatting. "You and I both know it's harder for women to gain respect in some organizations. It could be that she has a lot more influence and power than what everyone attributes to her. For all we know, she was the brains behind Wong's business."

"Well, one of the bonuses of being the puppet master is that you don't have a target on your back. Wong was lined up to take the shot in case things fell apart, and when they did, it does seem like she stepped in to fill the vacuum." Kel swore under his breath in Spanish, shaking his head. "I don't like going into this interview not having a clue about where she stands. Maybe it's because Miki is involved, but this case has got me on edge."

"I wish we had enough time to go through the stuff Alex left for us and get a good look at what the DA had been holding. I'm not sure I believe she's headed anywhere. It just seems too convenient." Kane understood Kel's frustration. They were going in blind and nobody seemed to have any answers other than to feel out Wong's sister. "What doesn't fit here is if Susan Wong-Lee came back out for her son, I would think she would leave another woman's son alone. And maybe I am just speculating here, but if a woman feels that strongly about her children, they normally assume other people do as well. I know my mother does."

"Shit, Morgan. Your mother feels strongly about the children you guys drag home like stray cats. If anybody was going to head up a criminal organization, it would be Brigid. Thank God she hooked up with a cop." Kel flinched dramatically at Kane's playful backhand on his thigh. "I just feel like we are missing a really big piece of something, and it's probably staring us in the face, if only we were back in the station digging through a mountain of information instead of chasing after Wong's sister. I would love for her to take one look at us and cough up where her brother is, but we both know that's not what's going to happen. So we're back to how do we want to play this?"

"Let's see if we can get a read on how she feels about her brother and whether or not she benefited from him going to jail. She might give us a few leads. She called back and is making an effort to see us. Hell, that says something," Kane pointed out. "Wong could be destabilizing her son's territory. Even if he's not tons of influence, he still bringing in a lot of chaos. She might want to minimize that and, let's face it, like you said, Wong is terminal. If she has to choose between her brother and her son, she's going to choose the future and not the past. You don't need to know her to understand that."

"We've got two dead bodies, a primary influencer as well as a possible secondary who probably has more resources but less motivation to kill." Kel's eyes narrowed and he said, "I say we don't use any other name but Chaiprasit's and Chin's. Let's see where she takes us. If she drops the DEA guys into the mix, then we'll know she has a line in on Miki."

"Agreed. We can definitely lead her around that. I would want to start a discussion about how Wong is only hurting himself and the family in the long run by targeting people from the past. Anything that he does is going to have a ripple effect on her son. She might know exactly who Wong wants to target based on who he feels betrayed him the most, and even if she doesn't know where he is, it'll give us a very clean idea about who is on his hit list." Kane whistled under his breath at the building they were pulling up to. "Looks like she hasn't done too bad for herself. If I were her, I would want to make sure nothing threatened my livelihood. She's got to know if Wong gets his way, it could open up a whole lot of interest about things she and her son do. That's something else we need to drive home. As long as Wong is out there trying to take people out, the SFPD is going to be her family's very best friend— probably not what she or her son wants."

"So then, we're going to go with the friends and family plan?" Kel grinned. "I like how you think, Morgan."

THEY COOLED their heels in the penthouse's foyer for five minutes before the grim-faced Chinese man who let them in returned. The outer walls were glass from top to bottom, giving the space an incredible view, but the elevator bank on the one side of the six-by-six-foot room and the black lacquer double doors on the far wall hemmed everything in. Someone had gone to great effort to make the space seem welcoming, with a broad, colorful frieze spanning the remaining empty wall, but upon closer inspection, Kane discovered the images were of hunters and their prey.

"Interesting choice," he said to his partner, studying a particularly gruesome square. "Do you think this is a warning to solicitors or just an indication of who lives here?"

"You're the one with the minor in art," Kel reminded him. "To me it looks like a bunch of tiles with people killing rabbits and shit."

"You're not far from wrong." Kane turned when the doors to the apartment finally reopened. The gaunt, hollow-cheeked man who'd greeted them at the elevator looked, if possible, even less happy to see them there.

"The lady will see you now." He shuffled back, his limbs stiff and graceless as he let them in.

The black suit Wong-Lee's majordomo wore was slightly oversized, as if he needed room for a musculature he didn't have. His appearance was at odds with the sleek elegance of the apartment he guarded from unwelcome guests. The door opened immediately to what had to be the penthouse's great room, a long, wide area wrapped in windows and furnished with a sparse collection of Asian-influenced furniture. There were more pieces of art on the walls and on pedestals than places to sit, and Kane felt like they'd walked into a museum rather than someone's house.

A hallway jogged off to the right, blocking any line of sight to the rest of the high-rise apartment, leaving only the great room accessible to whomever came through the front door. Kel hovered a few feet behind him, leisurely studying a statue, then a painting, but Kane knew his partner was using the tour he was taking to assess the place. Dark hardwood floors provided some relief from the light gray walls and pale upholstered furniture. Most of the art ran to stonework, with only a few paintings adding spots of vivid color to the area. It was a space washed with the gloom of a rainy day and little hope for sunshine, easily fighting off the blue skies and panoramic view of the apartment's glass outer walls.

Kane couldn't imagine anything looking more like the lair of a supervillain, and he leaned over to mutter at Kel, "All this place is missing is a bunch of sharks with lasers on their heads."

"If you would please wait here, she will join you shortly. The lady prefers the divans by the fireplace should you want to sit down," the majordomo droned flatly, his expression curled into the edge of the sneer. "I will return with coffee and tea."

"Oh, we don't need—" Kel stopped himself short, an amused grin on his face as the marionette of a man step-jerked his way quickly out of the room and down the hallway before either of them could say anything else. "I guess we're having coffee and tea."

"I guess so," Kane agreed with a chuckle. "Fireplace looks nice. Lots of marble, have you noticed?"

"Yeah, last time I saw this much veined stone, I was inside of my uncle Fernando's mausoleum trying to get my aunt to stop beating his crypt with her shoe because his five girlfriends showed up for his funeral." Kel strolled over to the circle of low couches near a gas fireplace set into the far wall. "I like how this place is set up to show you she's very rich but doesn't really want you to stay and visit. Nothing here looks comfortable, everything is too short or too stiff. What do you think?"

Kane cocked his head, catching the echo of heels on a hard floor. "I think we're about to have company."

They'd taken a bit of time back at the station to look at a few photos of Susan Wong-Lee before driving over to interview her. *Do yer homework on anyone ye're going to meet*, Donal taught Kane long before he'd earned the badge his father pinned on him. *Know how they look, know where and how they live, and most importantly, find out what kind of person they are,* he'd said. *That way yer not surprised in any way, because I will bet my last penny, son, that the person ye need to be the most wary of is the one who is going to do their homework on ye.*

Susan Wong-Lee was definitely someone who'd done her homework on Kane and Kel long before she ever agreed to an interview.

She probably came up to Kane's shoulder, but her stiletto heels added a couple of inches to her height. She was older than Kane expected, having achieved the pearlescent beauty of a middle-aged Asian woman. Her sleek black hair was cut into a long bob, curving along the line of her strong jaw. Her dark brown eyes were sparsely made up, a few strokes of black eyeliner and a coating of mascara done only strong enough to emphasize their shape and color. Her flawless skin was dewy, but the beginnings of faint lines were forming on her brow. There was an imperfection next to her right eye, a small divot of a scar winging back toward her temple, and its hollow played with the shadows, dancing in and out of focus as she moved. She'd gone with a strong plum lipstick, a hint of wine in its tint to go with the merlot shell top she'd paired with black pants, and she wore very little jewelry, only a slender white jade bangle and matching earrings.

But mostly, Susan Wong-Lee wore her power.

There was something about how a powerful woman entered a room. Having had a ringside seat to his sister Kiki's transition from childhood to inspector in the SFPD, Kane had seen the shedding of pigtails and hula hoops happen nearly overnight, replaced by a psycho-logical strapping-on of armor and sharpening a cunning wit into a lethal weapon. If there was any sibling Kane felt in his gut would one day wear the captain's bars, it was his baby sister. He planned to wear them first—he was older—but there was no way he could match Ki-ki's determination and drive. She wore her competence firmly on her squared shoulders and her intelligence in her hard gaze. She'd never spend years proving she was just as good as any boy because she'd grown up know-ing she was better than most. She had an unmistakable, unshakable confidence in her core, and Kiki led with it, a life-forged lance she used to fight her daily battles.

Susan Wong-Lee carried herself the exact same way as Kiki Morgan, leaving Kane with no doubt as to her place in the world and the influence she wielded.

"Your mother could take her," Kel whispered be-hind Kane. "It would be ugly, but Brigid could take her down."

Kane pretended not to hear his friend and instead took a few steps toward the woman and held his hand out. "I'm Senior Inspector Kane Morgan and this is my partner, Inspector Kel Sanchez. We are very happy you could take the time out to meet with us."

"Let me be perfectly clear before we get started. I wasn't going to bother until there was a warrant or court order, but my lawyer advised me to be coopera-tive if contacted." She glanced down at Kane's hand, then back up at his face. "He believes that since I have nothing to hide, I should try to minimize my involve-ment with the police and assist in any way I can, on the assumption that once I've told you everything I know about the situation with my brother, that you will go away and leave my family alone."

"Ma'am, I cannot promise you that we will go away," Kane countered. "But I can promise you that if you are up front with us, this will go easier and smoother than if you are not. At this time we do not suspect you of being involved with the recent incidents your brother appears to have orchestrated, but we do have a few questions. We hope not to take up too much of your time."

"I hope not. I am a very busy woman, and there is still a lot for me to do today." Wong-Lee paused as her majordomo returned to the room carrying a tray with coffee cups and a carafe. Turning to her servant, she motioned toward the coffee table next to Kel. "You could put that down there, but I don't imagine these gentlemen will be here long enough to drink an entire cup. We will make this quick so I can go back to my life and they can go back to doing whatever it is they need to do. Inspectors, please make yourself comfortable."

The look Kel gave him was a telling one, and Kane didn't need to say anything to know his partner felt the same visceral response to Susan Wong-Lee as he did. Kel's eyebrows flicked up, a silent question if he and Kane were going to follow the game plan they'd set in the car, so Kane nodded, assuring him they should continue.

Kel sat, then thanked the servant for his coffee, refusing cream and sugar, then waited patiently as Kane was served. Wong-Lee took her coffee the same as Kel, cradling her cup as she dismissed her majordomo. She took a deliberate sip, her control over the situation in conversation firmly in her grasp. Kane let his cup rest on the table, leaning forward to minimize the space between them.

He wasn't doing it to establish intimacy or build a connection. While useful behaviors to have for interviewing, they wouldn't work on Wong-Lee. She'd been studying their body language probably from the moment they'd gotten off the elevator, more than likely hearing their exchange in the foyer. She was combative in her attitude. Kane knew they wouldn't be able to get around it, so instead he was going to have to dig for the slender threads of vulnerability hidden behind the hard carapace she'd built up over the years.

"When was the last time you spoke with your brother?" Kane asked as Kel began to take notes. "Either in person or on the phone? Perhaps even email?"

"My brother has been incarcerated for over twenty-five years." Her laugh was bitter and short. "Technology is beyond him. He wouldn't know how to send email. And to answer your question, the last time I spoke with him was when he contacted me after being released. He told me he was dying of cancer and that he had a few things he wanted to clear up before he passed."

Kane studied her briefly, then asked, "Can you elaborate?"

"He wanted to apologize for trying to have me killed." Her reply was tight and terse, her lips flattening. "I am assuming that the DEA is like most federal agencies and has not shared everything about my brother or what he had done."

"We do know that you were placed into federal protection and then you refused to stay in," Kel said. "You are not bound by any agreement with the feds, so if there is anything you would like to share with us, we would be more than happy to listen."

"Inspector Sanchez and I suspect that you were unwilling to let your son become a target." Kane shifted back on the cushion, opening up the space between them. "You knew that if your brother tried to kill you, he would go after Adam next. Just like he is going after the son of a woman who used to work for him. What we are trying to figure out is what is driving this murder spree he is on and what we can do to stop it. We're not going to play games with you. We all know you are aware of what is happening in Chinatown, and while we can only speculate about how involved your brother is, you probably are very much attuned to how he fits into this. Our sole focus is to prevent him from killing any more innocent people."

She leaned back in her chair, and for the first time Kane saw a glimmer of humanity in her cold, hard eyes. Cocking her head, she studied them, her gaze flicking back and forth, and something must have convinced her of their sincerity, because when she leaned forward, the brittle mask she'd worn fell off. Her face changed, a subtle peeling away of ice and draconian haughtiness. What remained was a woman who wore a few hard years on her body and battled to shape her world.

"I knew he went after one of the prostitutes who used to work for him," she admitted softly. "It didn't make sense until one of my employees decided working for my brother was more preferable than working for me. Danny still has a few men who are loyal to him, but they are older and not as sharp as they used to be."

"Was one of those men Rodney Chin?" Kane asked.

"Yes. Rodney abandoned his position to fall in with Danny. And look at what happened to him." She tilted her chin, the angles of her face sharpening as the light played across her features. "Danny is like a spoiled child, and instead of taking the time he has left to him and living well, he is rolling in hatred and revenge. I left federal protection because of my son. I knew if I did not raise out of myself, he would turn out exactly like my brother. As it is, I have to keep a very tight control over how our family does business so we do not fall into the same trap as Danny, thinking we are invincible and above the law."

"What revenge is he looking for?" Kane had a feeling he knew the answer, but he needed to hear Wong-Lee confirm it. "And why would he—or anyone else—kill Rodney Chin?"

"It is very simple if you know all the pieces of the game." Her smile was nearly reptilian, but with a glimmer of warmth. "Danny wants to get to the man who put him in jail. There is someone who got away with what he did back then, and now that Danny is out and causing trouble, it threatens him. Rodney Chin was killed to tell Danny to back off, but there are a couple of men from back then who would go that far. Danny doesn't care, but I do, because if he does not stop and these men feel as if what he's doing will bring them down, they could turn their attention to me and my son. That is something I cannot have. I have not come this far only to have my idiotic brother get me killed."

Kane took a second, then asked, "Who is the man Danny feels is responsible for him going to prison?"

"It was one of the DEA agents on the case, the one Danny gave one of the Thai whores to. He was the one closest to Danny, and my brother knew that is who betrayed him. I have no quarrel with that man. My brother is a monster and he likes nothing better than to play with people before he kills them. He needed to be stopped. But there were quite a few people on the police force who made a lot of money covering for Danny." Her fingernails clicked against her cup as she reached for it, a nervous chittering across the painted porcelain curve. "I don't know which one it would be, but I'm guessing the man who killed Rodney Chin was a cop who used to work for Danny. That's who is afraid Danny will get to the agent and expose him."

"We have a few details of the case, but I'd like to hear who you think it is Danny is trying to kill. There were several men who Danny paid special attention to. I cannot rule out any of them as being his target." Kane handed her a napkin, not commenting on the dribble of liquid she'd gotten on her fingers when she picked up her cup. "It will go a long way toward knowing who we have to focus on. And the sooner we can get your brother contained, the safer your family will be."

"That is the only reason I agreed to speak with you," she admitted, her voice breaking, and she looked away, her mask sliding back into place. "There was a man Danny admired. He was hard and controlled, everything Danny wanted to be. Said he reminded him of an assassin or an international spy, that is how Danny saw him. We should've known he was a DEA agent, but he was too rough around the edges, too much of everything a man should be. He refused to say that he worked for Danny, calling himself a partner. He challenged Danny at nearly every turn, but everything always went how he said it would go, so Danny began to trust him more and more. Of course, now we know the DEA was manipulating things so he would gain Danny's trust."

"You give a man that kind of trust and he betrays you, that would anger most men," Kel said. "So your brother nursed this anger for over two and a half decades, and now that he is out, he wants to hurt this man as much as he was hurt."

CHAPTER SEVENTEEN

Miki, whispering: So I just light the fu—candle?

Kane, chuckling: Yes. And I appreciate you not swearing. I'd have to answer to that priest over there. He's eyeing us.

Miki: Of course I'm not going to swear. It's a da—church.

Kane: And now he's heading over here.

Miki: Jesus, why? They're like the fucking cops. It's like a goddamned soultrap in this place.

Kane, with a heavy sigh: Well, at least you tried. Light the candle and, if you want to, say a prayer for your mom. In your head. And just so you know, Father Ignacio told me a long

time ago that God doesn't care if
you swear in your prayers.
Miki: God gets what He fucking gets. I
just want those bastards up there to
take care of my mom.
—St. Patrick's, San Francisco

MIKI OPENED the door before the knock. It
wasn't that he knew instinctively she'd arrived. No, he
knew she'd come because he heard her heels on the
cement sidewalk outside, a full circle of percussion
raps he'd first experienced years ago. This time he was
ready for her. This time he knew her fiery personality
and brash attitude were weapons she would use to defend him rather than hurt him. Miki now saw the bits
of her she gave Kane, just like he recognized Donal in
him. So this time, when a pair of red stilettos beat on
the floor like the drums of war, they were summoning
the heavens to come protect him—a son she found rather than a son she'd borne.

She'd come cloaked in motherhood and strength,
a few years on her face, lines earned from laughter and
worry, but her dark green eyes, so much like Quinn's,
were crystal clear and bright. Despite her diminutive
stature, there was no denying she'd descended from
warriors. It was a warm day, so she'd dressed casually, a pair of worn blue jeans and a beat-up Crossroads
Gin shirt he'd given her from the first package Edie
sent them, but with her shoulders thrown back and her
chin tilted up to meet his gaze, she might as well have
been wearing a full set of armor and carrying a flaming
sword.

He didn't know what to say. *Thank you* seemed
too meek, an insipid mewl whispered over a bowl of

porridge handed across a table. There had to be stronger words, but he couldn't find them. Instead Miki stood there, staring down at Brigid Morgan with his tongue tied by complicated emotions and simple confusion.

She took care of anything he might have fucked up saying by wrapping her arms around him and pulling him into a hug so tight he could feel it envelop the broken child he sheltered inside of himself.

His arms always seemed like they were a second too late to respond, but eventually he slung them around her, cradling the small birdlike woman into his chest. There was power in her grip, but her body was so tiny, so delicate, that he was almost afraid to hold her too tightly.

She took care of that too.

Threading her fingers through the hair at the back of his head, Brigid pulled him even closer, until his face was buried into the curve of her neck and his shoulders ached with the strain of bowing forward. Miki didn't care if the pain in his spine crippled him, because nothing felt as wonderful as a hug from his *mother*.

"I've got you, Miki boy," she murmured. "No matter what you find in that package today, you will always find me here. Because you're one of my boys."

Tears shouldn't choke a man. It made no sense for a strong emotion to close off his air supply, but Miki struggled to breathe around the expanding thickness in his chest and throat. He couldn't tell if it was sorrow or joy or if it never mattered what was stealing away his reason. All he knew was that Brigid holding him in front of the home he'd made with Kane, Damien, and Dude transformed something—no, *healed* something—he'd struggled to hold together for way too long.

"I wanted to wait for you," Miki mumbled into the shelter of her hug. Her riot of flame-hued hair smelled of berries and some kind of tea, and the earring poking into his cheek felt like a knot, its edges scratching at his skin, but he was reluctant to pull away. "Damien's inside. So is Dude, but I don't think he gives a shit."

"I'm sure the dog cares, just in his own way," she said with a laugh. "How about if I make us a pot of tea, and you can decide if you want to open that today."

"It's going to have to be today. It's already been a lifetime," Miki murmured, finally letting her go. He let his hands run down her arms until he found her fingers, squeezing lightly before releasing them. "I know she's dead. Kane doesn't want to say it, but she is. He thinks my father is still out there, but I don't know if that really matters either. I've got you and Donal. What more do I need?"

"Miki love, *you* don't need anything more," Brigid replied, her arm around his waist. "But perhaps he needs you. Let's cross that bridge when we get to it, yes? For right now, let us go meet the woman who gave you to me. I would like to know her."

"Suppose she's like Forest's mom or worse?" The words were easier to say because she was touching him, but the reality of his childhood lingered, a spreading stain on his every thought. "I'm scared to find out stuff I can't handle."

There were too many possibilities—too many realities—and most of them were nightmares and tragedies embroidered by his own experiences. He wanted to romanticize the woman who'd given him life, but from what he knew about her situation and the circumstances surrounding her, there was little chance for a happy beginning. Especially since there hadn't been a happy ending.

"I can't *not* think the worst of her," he admitted. "The asshole who is trying to kill me now, the fucker who put this tattoo on me, probably killed her just like he killed the woman who was trying to get this package to Edie. I could have talked to her friend instead of finding out about her through a bunch of papers and photographs, but I can't because of one fucking asshole with a small dick and a tiny brain. But there's always the part of me that wonders if she even cared about me."

"Let's see what we find, and if it is the worst you imagined, then we'll deal with it." Brigid rested her head against his arm as they walked through the front door. "If she was a saint, we will deal with that too. But I think you will find she was a woman who did the best that she could do, and that is all we can ask of her now."

"And my father?" He held back, not wanting to drag the conversation with them to the living space where Damien sat slung across the couch. "What if he knew and didn't give a fu—"

She stopped him before he could go any further, tightening her grip on his arm. Miki looked away, catching Damien's attention, and his brother frowned, about to get up off the couch when Miki shook his head *no* to stop him. They were close enough for D to hear them, but there was nothing he wouldn't share with the young man who'd given him his life back.

Still, Brigid dropped her voice to a low whisper as she cupped Miki's face and said, "You will need to stop borrowing trouble. If any man has the gift of being your father and is not proud to be so, then he is not truly a man. Donal thanks God and the stars for Kane bringing you into our lives. You are a treasure, and I'll not have you worry about someone who may or may not be smart enough to realize that. We'll find what we find and go from there."

"Okay," Miki murmured through the press of her hands against his cheeks. "But if he was an asshole, I'm not going to go begging after him."

"You wouldn't be my Miki if you did," Brigid said, then arched up to leave a kiss on the tip of his nose. "Now let's go meet your mother."

An open bottle of Jack Daniel's was waiting for him on the crate in front of the couch. The package he'd gotten from Edie lay next to the whiskey bottle's cap, and Miki glanced at Brigid, unsure about what she'd say about either the alcohol or Damien putting it there.

"Figured if there was ever a time you'd want a bottle of Jack next to you, it would be now." Damien grabbed the neck of the bottle, then held it out for Miki. "Unless you want some of that fancy Irish shit our guys keep bringing into the house."

"No, Jack's fine." He snuck another look at Brigid and caught her amused expression. "What? Too early? Am I supposed to be a fucking adult and not—I don't have any rules here. I don't know what I'm supposed to be doing."

"Well, I think your brother is right. If ever there was a time for a draught of whiskey, it is now." She patted Damien's shoulder before she sat down. "Of course, I'm Irish, and I think having oatmeal for breakfast is a good reason to have a shot of whiskey. Quit driving yourself crazy and settle in."

The first time he'd gotten drunk was on Jack Daniel's. It'd been after their first gig together, and Damien scraped together a few dollars so they could each have a shot to celebrate. He'd been way too young to drink, much less be in the place, but no one seemed to even notice. The bar had been three deep with people, and the guy behind the counter winked at Damien as he passed a small black-labeled bottle over, refusing Damien's handful of bills.

"You guys put on a hell of a fucking good show," the man shouted over the bar's clamor. "This one is on me."

The bottle hadn't come with glasses, so they'd taken turns swigging mouthfuls down. Like all things, the band shared equally, and while the other three were older and much more seasoned drinkers, Miki'd kept up with them, shot for shot. His first gulp was like sipping from an out-of-control fire, its flames eating up his skin and then his bones until nothing was left of his body but the warmth of the Jack's kiss. Surprisingly enough, he didn't get sick the next morning, and eventually he learned to love its taste as well as the brief, skittering numbness it settled over his pain.

They'd been drinking Jack the night of his greatest heartache, and its smoky bite would forever remind him of rain and screeching tires. But like many things in Miki's life, it was complicated with fond memories as well, so it seemed fitting he would have a shot of the same whiskey on the day he would probably see his mother's face for the first time.

And oh God, did it *burn*.

His fingers trembled, but only enough to make opening the plump package difficult. He braced himself for grainy copies, out of focus photos and hard to read notes about daily things his mother had shoved into a box and given to her friend to hold. He'd refused to learn her name from Edie, information the attorney's office had given her about the contents of the original package she'd meant to intercept.

He wished he'd heard her name before he read it as a subject line of a printed report.

"Achara Sangsom," Miki whispered, his throat catching his breath, turning his words into a staccato beat. His mother's name was at the top of the page, followed by a cornucopia of information he couldn't see past the tears in his eyes. "Her name was Achara Sangsom."

The second shot of Jack went down a hell of a lot smoother than the first.

He felt Damien's arm around his shoulders and Brigid's hand on his thigh, but Miki couldn't do much more than stare at the open package and wonder how his life started without him knowing the name of the woman who'd given birth to him. And whether he could live knowing what she'd done to survive and how she'd died.

"I need Kane," he sobbed—God, he couldn't stop crying—and despite the two people he loved sitting next to him, he needed the one who filled his soul, who'd found his heart and healed it—he needed *Kane*.

Dude whined, pawing at Miki's leg to get his attention. His hands were still shaking badly as he stroked his dog's head, smoothing back the terrier's ears. Brigid picked up the package from where it fell, gathering up contents from where they landed on the floor. Damien was on his phone, but Miki couldn't hear what he was saying past the rush of blood pounding in his ears; then suddenly he heard Kane's voice call his name.

"Hold the phone, Sinjun," Damien ordered, wrapping Miki's nerveless fingers around the device. "Talk to your man here. Kane's on the line."

Miki wanted to crawl into bed and wrap his lover—his soul mate—around him, burying the struggles he'd fought through and the trauma he was living now underneath a blanket of love and warmth, but the truth was, it would be hours before he felt Kane's touch.

"Mick?" Kane's voice was as much a hit of lightning as the Jack in his belly. "Talk to me, *a ghra*. Tell me what's happening. Damie said you're having a hard time of it."

"I thought I could do this without you. I mean I know I can, but it's hard," Miki confessed without shame or guilt. It was hard to admit he needed anyone, and he still argued with himself about sharing what he'd always thought was his greatest weakness, a deep-seated longing to be considered special in somebody else's heart. Hearing Kane's voice and feeling the joy it brought him, Miki finally understood admitting someone was in *his* heart was his greatest strength. "I know her name, and I don't even know if I'm pronouncing it right. I wish to fucking God I'd let them tell me it before I opened up this damned envelope. I'm not even sure if this is her."

"It's her. There's things in there—let's just say that we know for sure she's your mother. And for the record, I pronounced it *Ah-cha-rah Sang-sum* when I read it, but I don't know if I got that right either." Kane chuckled. "How far did you get? Have you seen her photo? You look like her."

"No. I dropped the whole damned thing and your mom had to pick it up. Everything's probably out of order or even if there was an order. I just saw the report and it became so *fucking* real." He scrambled for the package, and Brigid passed over the bundle she had in her hands. "There's smaller envelopes inside the big one and a few pieces of paper from the DA's office. I don't even know what I'm looking at."

"I don't know how they copied the photos, if they did them individually or if they did several on one page." Someone nearby called Kane's name, and he told them to wait in his rumbling Irish accent.

"Do you have to go?" Miki asked.

"I don't care if the sun is burning up in the sky right now, you are much more important," Kane told him. "Do you want me to tell you what you're going to find?"

"*No*," he grumbled back. "It's stupid, but I wanted to hear your voice. I needed to have a part of you with me right now. I've got your mom and Damien here, but I think I just needed to hear you."

There was a brief bit of silence that Miki guessed was Kane absorbing the fact that Brigid was in their home while Miki was tearing open his past. Then he heard a resigned sigh, and Kane cleared his throat.

"How about if you put me on speakerphone and go through the rest of it?" his cop suggested. "Or you can wait for me to come home and I'll do it with you, but I don't know how long that's going to be. I've got an interview coming up with an ex-cop who IA suspected of working with Wong back then. With any luck, Wong contacted him. I'm hoping once we find Wong, we can end all of this."

"I want to go through the rest of it," Miki admitted softly. "It's going to eat at me, knowing that it is sitting here, and eventually Brigid and Damien are going to lose interest in watching me stare at it, and leave. If I don't do this now, I don't know if I'm going to be strong enough to do it later."

"You be as strong as you need to be, Miki boy," Brigid said, rubbing his cold fingers between her hands. "And you have the two of us here for as long as it takes."

"Yeah," Damien agreed. "Besides, I've been watching you stare at things for years now. It's become like a hobby, almost."

"K, hold on. I'm going to put the phone down." He fumbled with the device, fighting with the screen to find the button, then just handing it over to Damien, who managed with a few flicks of his finger to turn it to speaker mode. Miki was trying to decide what he needed more, a steadying breath or another shot of whiskey, when he heard Kane call his name through the phone. "I'm here. Just deciding whiskey first, then breathing. I think I need booze more than air right now."

"Are the three of you getting drunk in the living room?" Kane said over the speaker. "I'm stuck here at work with bad coffee and Kel."

"Just your Miki, and I'm sure Damien will be joining him in a little bit." Brigid tsked. "None for me. I'm driving."

"I'm not getting drunk. Just a little... Irish," Miki muttered back, then took a short swig of Jack. The numbness remained, the fire was a bit dimmer, but his hands finally stopped shaking. Sucking in that steadying breath helped, but not as much as Kane's laughter, a soft roll of heady pleasure brushed with affection and amusement. Leaning over the phone, he whispered, "I'm glad you're here with me. Even if you probably already know all of this shit, I'm just really happy."

"I love you, *a ghra*." Kane's words seemed a little thick with emotion, and they lightened the weight in Miki's chest. "Go as far as you need to, and if you find that it's too hard, put it aside and wait until I come home. Okay, Mick?"

"Yeah, okay. Honestly, I kind of have to do this, and I know it." Miki let go of the breath searing his lungs. "You needed to go through all of this because it's for your case against Wong, so you couldn't wait on me. And we're doing the one thing that we promised we wouldn't do, and that's talk to each other before we both knew what was in this thing."

"Like I've already told you, Mick," Kane laughed. "Some rules are made to be broken."

"It's not that I don't love you, Sinjun, but either you decide to open this thing now, or I drag you up to the rooftop and we get drunk." Damien scratched at the dog's shoulders. "It's just like going onstage for the first time. At some point you have to commit or decide to come back to it."

"You shoved me onstage the first time," Miki accused him. "I was standing there under the lights all alone, remember?"

"Not for long," his brother reminded him. "And just like now, I'm right here with the promise of Jack when we're done."

"Take your time, Miki." Brigid sounded cool and calm, but she had a hint of steel in her voice for Damien. "Don't rush things if you don't want to."

"No, this is stupid. Let's do this so I can get on with my damned life." Miki fretted, working off a rubber band holding a sheaf of papers together. "But I'm not going to say no to the Jack later. Hell, not like I'm saying no to it now."

Someone at the DA's office had taken great care with his mother's memories. The photos were so clean and crisp, Miki wasn't totally convinced they weren't the originals. The paper cutouts were thinner, odd lines here and there around the edges of the images leaving a white frame around the copied photos. But suddenly there was no doubt in Miki's mind that he was staring at the woman who'd been taken from him.

"Fuck, you look so much like her," Damien whispered. "She's so damned beautiful, she makes my teeth hurt. And it's kind of weird seeing your mouth on a woman's face."

She was Asian, but Miki wouldn't have been able to tell anyone what kind just by a glance, with something else in there, too, or maybe a genetic oddity cropped up once in a while, because her eyes were so much like his, a tumble of citrine and peridot hammered into a coppery brown. Her gaze was sad, a recurring theme in every single image taken of her, even the ones where she stood with a group of people, a smile plastered on her face.

A smile that never *ever* seemed to reach her hazel eyes.

Judging by the images, she led a life of parties filled with men and alcohol. Her hair was dark, nearly black, but dyed blonde or auburn in some of the images. He definitely hadn't gotten his height from her, because she barely came up to most men's shoulders, but she held herself like a queen, regal and charismatic with her spectacular face and stunning figure. And while Achara's stunning beauty was captured flawlessly in the top stack of images, so were the bruises on her wrists and arms and the occasional swelling around her haunted eyes.

"She was so young," Brigid remarked, taking the photos as Miki handed them over. "Barely more than a baby herself. Ah, look at this one. I think she's pregnant here. You can't see much of it, but right *there*." She pointed to the rounded line along his mother's abdomen. "I suppose that's you."

A photo at the bottom of the stack was so different from the others it stole Miki's reason. It had been taken down by the wharf at a spot Miki recognized so quickly it made his head spin. Finnegan's sign was visible over her right shoulder, and a crowd of people gathered around a fire swallower performing for tips. Her face was bare of makeup, but her eyes were lit up, a genuine grin on her full mouth. From what he could see, she wore a tank top, exposing an all-too-familiar tattoo on her shoulder, and a strong breeze caught at her chin-length hair, whipping it away from her face. Achara was turned toward the camera, caught in midmotion as she was saying something to the chubby-cheeked wide-eyed toddler she held in her arms.

The smile missing in the other photos now shone as bright as the sun in her eyes as she cradled what was obviously her child.

As she cradled *Miki*.

It could have been the only moment she ever held him tenderly, but it was enough for Miki's heart to break for a woman he didn't remember. The tears came again, and he dug the heels of his hands into his eyes to push his sorrow back, but they flowed too hard and too quickly for him to catch. Bending over, he held on to his knees and prayed he could breathe again, could stop the pain in his heart from tearing him into tiny pieces, but the tears still wouldn't stop coming.

"*Fuck.*" Miki swore into the shadows he created, into the small dark space he'd made by curling up onto himself. "This hurts so fucking much. Why does it hurt so goddamned *much*?"

"I think she loved you a lot, Mick," Kane said gently. The noise of the bullpen was absent, replaced by an echoing silence Miki guessed belonged to one of the interview rooms nearby. "Kel and I are going through everything with a fine-tooth comb right now, but from what I can see, she loved you. And I think she loved your father too."

Miki sat up, passing over everything in his hands to Damien and Brigid before he soaked the papers with his tears. Sniffling, he asked, "Is his name in here too?"

"No, but Wong's sister told us who she suspected got your mother pregnant." Kane cleared his throat. "I can't confirm or deny his involvement with her just yet, but as soon as I know, we can figure out what to do with that information. I can tell you *one* thing. Her name is not the only one in there."

"What other name do I have to know besides hers?" Miki bit at his lip, his thoughts running crazily through the possibilities. "Her family? Did anybody give a shit about her being with Wong? About him using her? Do you think I should give a shit about their names if they didn't stop him?"

"I don't have any information about any of her family except you," his cop replied with a sweet tenderness as poignant as when Miki saw his mother's face for the first time. "I want to say something."

"Say what?" Miki bent forward and growled into the phone. "I'm so pissed off right now about Wong, I'd kill him if he was right in front of me. He fucking took her from me. Just because he *could*. It's not fair, Kane. And I know life isn't fair, but the son of a bitch needs to die."

"I know, and if it wasn't my job to make sure that that didn't happen, I'd let you, but you and I both know

CHAPTER EIGHTEEN

A word from you opened a window
A window in my soul
It showed me a way out
Of the prison I had made
I couldn't let go of my past
Forged the bars myself
Carrying every blow
Coloring in every bruise
Gripping my wounds tight
Until I bled out inside
Then you found a window
A window in my soul
Painted over, hammered shut
This window in my soul
A word from you opened it
A hug from you gave me the sky
And your love gave me wings
—Talking to Dad

"SO LET me get this straight: you're Thai, Irish, and Scottish? That's wild. I mean, there was definitely Asian in there because, well, you look it, but the rest of it is kind of a surprise. Like a Kinder Surprise." Rafe nudged at Miki's shin with his bare foot. "And Kane knows who your father is?"

"Maybe," Miki countered. "He says he has a name and it jives with some of the case notes, but it isn't enough to say for sure. I don't even know what to think about knowing who my mother was right now, so I can't deal with the maybe-this-is-your-dad thing. But he did say he suspects something and needs to chase it down first before he talks to me about it. I don't even know if they're going to let him talk to me about it, but, shit, there's a lot I don't know."

He'd taken an hour to go through the photos and a few of the papers, but most of it was indecipherable to him, either in Thai or receipts for things his mother'd purchased, including a white wooden crib, a couple of pieces of jewelry, a gold band, and some slender jade bracelets, much like the kind sold in Chinatown's storefronts. Except for his birth certificate and a couple of birthday cards addressed to his mother, there was nothing personal in the package, nothing to connect Miki with a woman whose name he wasn't even sure he was pronouncing right.

In the movies and the occasional book, the deceased left touching letters proclaiming their undying love and exposing their great sacrifices. Miki didn't get any of that. Instead, he got a name—his own as well as hers—and a face so much like his own it broke his heart.

It was hard to discover Achara wasn't much younger than he was now when she died, and she'd given birth to him when she was little more than a child herself. Her friend had included a clipping of her obituary, but it said nothing about a son or any of the family, merely a terse announcement of the violent murder of a woman living in Chinatown. He had a brief tickle to know how she died, but Kane quickly threw a bucket of cold water on that hot idea.

"It will only piss you off more, Miki," he said over the phone. "Let's just say that everyone knew Wong had a hand in it, but no one did anything. Think on it, and if you're still interested in knowing, when I get home we can talk through that."

In the five minutes it took Miki to tell Kane he loved him and his cop assuring him he'd be home before it got too late, Miki's curiosity was satisfied with every dark thought his imagination could throw at it.

He no longer wanted to find out how his mother died.

Brigid was a comfort, one he was grateful for, but there was an itch forming under his skin Miki knew could only be scratched by calling in his band. The Irish matriarch hugged him hard enough to rattle his eyeballs, then left in the clatter of noise and kisses. Damien hadn't escaped her affection, and Miki didn't point out the lipstick prints she left on his cheek until Forest and Rafe arrived. A bit of laughter happened, some light shoving, but it eventually led to the studio built next to the garages. Miki was struck senseless by the tight embraces from brothers bound to him through music and friendship.

Then they played.

For hours his bandmates held him up, refusing to let him fall and stringing a net of music he could rest on. It felt good to lean against that wall of sound and rasp words he'd written for his own pain into a microphone connected only to a recording studio. And when it felt like they'd played everything he knew, one of the others would find a chord or two to a song he hadn't touched yet.

Miki called it quits before any of the others did, his fingertips aching and tender from picking at merciless guitar strings. His throat felt raw, and fatigue settled into his bones, a thick and heavy slumber he didn't have the energy to fight. Collapsing onto the wrap-around couch sitting in the corner of the room, Miki sat panting as Damien and Rafe put down their instruments before joining him. Forest eventually found his way to the couch after sluicing most of the sweat from his body and changing into some of the clothes he'd left behind after their tour.

"You guys probably need to get home soon." Miki swallowed at the dryness in his throat. They'd brought the whiskey with them from the warehouse, but nobody seemed inclined to open the liquor bottle. "I know you guys all have lives. Well, except for Damien, because Sionn's working."

"I told Connor I would be here." Forest gingerly got up from the couch, wincing when he stretched out his legs. "I feel like I've run five marathons. Anybody else want water?"

"Maybe get one for each of us, and you might want to bring the whiskey over. We're all going to be cramping up after what we just played out," Damie suggested. His lanky brother stretched his arms over his head, then mirrored Forest's wince. "I think my fingers are bleeding. Or at least blistered. But it was a good run."

"Tightest it's ever been," Rafe agreed. "So now what? You've got a name—which is kind of close to the one you have now, and a mom—"

"He already had a mom. We both do. Her name is Brigid." Forest tossed Rafe a bottle of water from the small fridge next to the door. Their bassist got ahold of it, but it slithered out of his grasp, rolling across the couch to land against Damien's side. "Guess that one's going to be D's. I'll bring you another one."

Miki lay in between Damien and Rafe, his legs stretched out over the short side of the U-shaped couch, tucked behind Rafe's back. His toes were growing cold from the blasting air conditioner, a necessity when playing a long, hard set, but uncomfortable once they were done. Damien must've noticed the ripple of goose bumps over his arms, because the guitarist reached for the remote and turned the temperature up, veering it away from arctic. A second later, Forest returned to where he'd been sitting, and Miki's toes were warmed by his drummer's torso leaning against his bare feet.

"See, I would've guessed you were Japanese," Damien remarked. His fingers were in Miki's hair, giving an occasional stroke along the back of his head. "I wouldn't have ever guessed Scottish. Do you want to find out where her parents are?"

"Do you think they're still alive?" Lifting his head up, Rafe quirked an eyebrow at Miki. "If they are, you should definitely get ahold of them. They might not know you were born."

"I bet your father didn't know either." Forest had an odd look on his face, and Miki gently dug his toes into his friend's ribs to get his attention. Grinning back at Miki, he shrugged. "I don't know how I would feel about finding out who my dad was, you know? I always knew my mom, which definitely wasn't giving me a step up, but I don't know, Sinjun. I guess for me it would feel like I was opening up a can of worms and hoping it's not snakes."

"Oh, I have a feeling it's going to be snakes." Miki chuckled. "It's *always* snakes."

Damien opened Miki's bottle of water for him, then passed it back. "You knew who your dad was, right, Andrade?"

"Yeah, but he walked off before I knew him, and then by the time I decided he was dead to me, he really was." Rafe quirked his lips into a brief grimace. "I guess in the back of my head I always figured dads should be like Donal, so maybe I'm hoping Miki's dad just didn't know about him."

"But you're still on house arrest, right?" Forest asked. "I don't think I could do that."

"It's better having you guys with me, but yeah, I'm about done with it," Miki confessed. "But I guess no matter what, this has been kind of a good thing to happen."

He'd been open with his bandmates about therapy, and thankfully none of them pressed any further than asking if he was okay. The anger inside of him was still there, bubbling away and searing off some of the confidence he'd built up, but he could feel it easing back.

"Penny—the therapist I am talking to—says— no, *suggests*—I talk to you guys about how my music makes me feel—*our* music—and how hard it's been for me to...." Miki stopped, drowning in the words and thoughts flying at him from the anxiety crippling his mind. Damien's hand in his hair stilled, but the press of his palm against Miki's head comforted him. "Fuck, this is hard."

"Dude—no, not you, dog," Rafe told the terrier who'd been asleep next to the couch but lifted his ears as soon as he heard his name. "Sinjun, if you need us to be your group for therapy, we're here for you, man. God knows, it's not like any of us here are normal, and some of us could use more than a few hours on the couch too; not that I'm looking at you, Mitchell."

"Don't take this wrong, but I spent more than enough time wearing a straitjacket to feel comfortable about a therapist right now, but Miki seems to like this one, so, there you go." Damien's caress turned into a hug that never seemed to end, and Miki let himself be cradled against his brother's side. "Nothing that's said in here goes outside, agreed? Not even with our Morgans, or in my case, Murphy."

"Never has been," Forest swore. "Never will be."

"I don't know about you guys, but I sleep with Quinn," Rafe protested with a laugh. "Pretty sure he can read my mind."

"I talked to Quinn about this kind of stuff, so he'll probably know before you do," Miki scoffed. "Mostly Penny thinks that if I am more open with you guys about how I feel trapped sometimes, it'll help me get through some of the harder moments."

"Why do you feel trapped?" Forest raked through his blond hair, working out some of the tangles he'd gotten during their set. "Okay, other than being locked inside of the warehouse waiting for the cops to get this crazy guy."

"Was it touring?" Rafe posed. "I used to feel like that when I was on the road, but this last time with you guys, it was a lot easier. It was like the pressure was off and all I had to do was enjoy playing."

"I think a lot of it was… and don't take this wrong, okay?" Miki paused, unsure despite getting nods from his band. "I talked a little bit to Damien about this, but

I guess I really didn't know how much it was affecting me. I love you guys, but it's still hard not to hear Johnny and Dave behind me when I'm onstage. And I don't know why it's okay when we're in the studio, but as soon as the lights are on and I hear the crowd, I guess… they were with me for so long and I'm not used to you guys. This is coming out *really* shitty."

"No, it's okay," Rafe assured him. "It still shocks the hell out of me not to see Jack on the other side of the stage."

"You guys were all together for a really long time, even before you hit it big." Forest rubbed at Miki's foot, apparently careful to avoid the ticklish spot he knew damn well was there. "You guys were close and it all happened so fast. I'd be pissed off at life for a really long time if I were you."

"I was kind of born pissed off at life," he muttered. "Mostly I was angry at Damien for dying. Which sounds stupid as fuck, but I guess these things don't always make sense. When your head kind of falls off the edge of the world, the dumbest things make sense to you. So I guess what I needed to say was: I'm sorry if I've been an asshole—*when* I've been an asshole—and I'm going to work really hard to be better about talking to you guys instead of just letting it get to me."

"It's going to take time," Rafe told him. "And take it from me, it's hard to train yourself out of behaviors, even if you know it would be better for you. Just remember not to kick the shit out of yourself if you fuck up."

"And I'm shit at saying I'm sorry," Damien added, his melodic voice a soft grumble in Miki's ear. "Never meant to hurt you, Sinjun. I fought like hell to get back to you."

Squeezing Damien's thigh hurt his already injured fingers, but with his back angled against Damien's side, it was the best he could do. "I know that. It's why I'm so fucked-up over being angry and sad about it. I don't understand how I got from being happy to see you to being pissed off you're with me. But it's kind of better now—a *lot* better. This afternoon when I felt so fucking lost even though I know more about myself than I did when I woke up this morning, after I spoke to Kane, all I wanted to do was be with you guys, play with the band, so you could heal me.

"It's like today broke me, but it made all of these tiny little lines instead of shattering me apart," Miki whispered, staring at his hands. It was easier to speak about the craquelure fracturing his identity and breaking off minute pieces of his heart if he wasn't searching for rejection in his brothers' faces. "Kane and I were watching this weird show about pottery because—he likes bowls—and one of the guys said there was this thing about how something is more beautiful *when* it's repaired. It's this philosophy of embracing the flawed. In the show, the artist filled the cracks in with gold lacquer so you could still see the vase had been broken, but it became more than it was before. So I was watching the show and Kane said, 'That's you. That's how I see you.'"

Miki blinked, refusing to let himself cry, but the words were caltrops being dragged up his throat and his emotions were raw, as abused as his fingers from the strings. He risked a glance up, and even through the watery veil across his vision, he saw his bandmates reaching for him right before their touch on his bare skin washed away the sorrow choking him.

"That's how all of us see you, Sinjun," Damie murmured. "You've taken a worse tumble than any of us in life, and you might see yourself as broken, but all we see is how beautiful you are, even when you're being a shit."

"Fuck you, D." Miki let out a short laugh, then wiped his nose. "What I'm trying to tell you is the gold inside of my fractures is the three of you. Kane picked up the pieces and held me together, but you guys went a long way in laying the gold down to heal me. So I guess what I really need to say is thank you for being my brothers, and if I haven't told you this before, I'm sorry, because it's crappy of me not to let you know how much I fucking love you guys, and I can't wait to share a stage with you again."

NO MATTER how Kane dissected the information from the report he read, he didn't like the conclusions he was drawing about the man they were soon to meet. With bits cobbled together from what he'd learned from Miki over the years and the stark reality of a police report buried in dusty archives, Kane knew it was time to talk to Kel about his suspicions. Opening his mouth, Kane found himself cut short by one of Kel's infamous complaints.

"Jesus, are we still in the city?" Kel grumbled from the passenger seat. "Where does this guy live? Half Moon Bay?"

"Fuck, Sanchez. How long have you lived here? That's the total opposite direction of where I'm driving." Kane spared his partner a glance as he maneuvered through the marina's parking lot. "You've been to Berkeley. Shit, Quinn teaches right up the way from here."

"Look, as far as I'm concerned, it's all the Wild West once you get past Oakland and the Raiders." Kel scoffed, rattling the ice in his soft-drink cup. "And the times I was visiting Quinn, I wasn't thinking about how fucking far out this place is. I was more focused on the scenery."

"You, my friend, are a sick, perverted man. Really? College kids?" Kane shook his head. "Aren't you a little too old for that kind of thing?"

"What makes you think I was there to visit Quinn's students?" *That* really earned Kel a scathing look, and the bastard had the nerve to laugh in Kane's face. "I like both sides of the field, brother, just like you used to. Before you hooked up with a rock star."

"I thought you said you didn't lust after my baby brother?"

"Well, it seems kinda safe to admit it now that he's with Rafe so you're less likely to rearrange my face. Mostly, I was his friend," Kel replied with a shrug. "Now, if he hadn't been your baby brother, I might have had a chance."

"As long as Rafe Andrade drew breath, you *never* had a chance, Kel." Kane checked the pier markings against what he'd written down back at the station. "There's the mooring. Let's see what Sergeant Hall has to say for himself. With any luck, he will have had an attack of conscience and tell us where Wong is hiding."

"Do you really think he knows where Wong is?" Kel asked as he climbed out of the sedan. Leaning on the roof, his partner studied the boats bobbing in the Bay. "Internal Affairs couldn't nail him, remember? And even though they let him pension out, he rode a desk for years after he was pulled from that assignment."

Kane shut the car door, but instead of heading for the boats, he turned toward his partner. Now was as good a time as any, especially since they were about to knock on Hall's front door. "I should probably tell you something that I did a few years back and again a couple of days ago to refresh my memory."

"Tell me this isn't about Vega or Shing and I'll let you talk," Kel interrupted.

"This isn't about Vega or Shing."

"Good, because if you tell me you'd killed them, I would have to then admit that you were drinking on the job and could not be held responsible for what you said." He nodded at Kane, tapping at the roof of the sedan. "Continue."

"I might have opened up Miki's files from when he was a teenager. Actually, I did a little digging back then when I suspected him of murdering Shing. Do you remember me making that request from records?"

"Yeah, and if *you* remember, I told you it seemed kind of lean." Kel went back to studying the Bay. "His foster records were spotty until Vega got him, but that was kind of par for the course back then. Why did you go back into them? And I'm not even going to ask you to let me look at them again. I know how you Morgans work. Sometimes the less I know, the better."

"You make it sound like we're a mafia family." Kane chuckled.

"You guys are not far from it. I'm just glad you're on this side of the badge. What did you find that you're bringing up now?"

"I knew I'd seen Hall's name before. And don't give me that look," Kane warned as Kel's attention flicked back to him. "I know it's a common last name, but his first name isn't. How many guys do you know are named Pattrias?"

"Weird, but what does that have to do with anything?" Kel turned to face him. A nearby gull squawked defiantly, guarding a spill of French fries near a dumpster, but Kel ignored the bird's warning cries. "Does he have to do with Miki?"

"Do you remember me telling you the story about how Miki found out what his name was?"

"Yeah, something about a cop reading his name from that tattoo on his arm, which we now know was bullshit." Kel's eyes narrowed. "Wasn't Hall stationed in Japan when he was a Marine? Was he the guy who translated the tattoo?"

"He was not only the guy who translated it," Kane replied, "he was the one who *found* Miki. I don't think there was any other cop. Everything Miki knows about what happened that day was told to him, so there was a telephone game of information, but the police report Hall filed says the little boy knew his name was something that sounded like Mieko. There's a drawing of the tattoo with the word Mieko underneath it. At that time, I wasn't involved with Miki, so I really wasn't paying a lot of attention. But now it's different."

"Micah. Mieko." Kel ran the sounds through a couple of times. "He was what? Two-ish? Three? You and I know kids that young have a hard time speaking sometimes. Hell, most of the time it just sounds like a babble of noise. Are you thinking that Hall didn't just find Miki? You thinking he had a hand in killing Miki's mother but didn't want to kill a kid?"

"I'm thinking it's more than a possibility. And I hate to say that about a fellow cop, but considering IA already had him in their crosshairs, there had to be something going on. I've got a retired military guy with some knowledge of Japanese who puts down on a report that a badly scribbled tattoo matches the name a two-year-old responds with when asked. Nobody questioned Hall about it, and by the time Miki was old enough to look up the kanji, it didn't matter anymore. Not to him anyway," Kane said. "I should've told you sooner, but I wasn't sure until right before we left the station."

"And you're still not really sure now," Kel replied softly. "This thing's got your head tangled up, Kane. A couple of weeks ago we would've had this conversation on the way over. Instead, we're having it in the parking lot right before we go interview an ex-cop who may or may not be responsible for murdering your lover's mom. I have a real problem with your timing."

"Fair enough. I just needed to slow down and work it out in my head before I put it out in front of you." He laid his hands flat on the roof, his fingers playing in the grit on the sedan's paint. "We know we caught this case because I was on scene at the first shooting and Book's gone to the mat for us—for me—so it doesn't get taken away. Thing is, I don't know if there's someone in the DA's office that is trying to protect Hall or Wong, but that package should've been admitted into evidence from the moment they picked it up.

"My dad said it was politics that held it up, but at this point in the game, we've got DEA, a Gang Task Force, and an ex-cop all on the board as players. Wong's sister says she hasn't spoken to him, but it seems like he sure as hell knows a lot about what's going on for someone who's been inside for over two decades," Kane pointed out. "I feel like we are playing chess, but I can't see half of the pieces and I don't know what my next move is going to be. All I know is I can trust you, and my gut says we're about to go see someone who could blow this case wide-open for us if we can just get him to talk."

Kel didn't answer, at least not right away. The setting sun turned Kel's face into a somber, striking profile, his golden skin burnished with the dying light. Around in the parking lots, streetlamps were flaring to life, dingy yellow glows warming up the encroaching dusk. His eyes were hooded, his expression unreadable, but Kane knew he was gambling on their friendship to keep their partnership intact.

"I get that you needed time. Especially after that phone call with Miki, but when did you know?" Kel took his time, inhaling a long breath, then letting it go slowly. "Did you find out about Hall right before we left, or did you know earlier and didn't tell me?"

"I actually read the file when we stopped at that burger place so you could get a soda," Kane informed him. The ramifications of Hall's presence in Miki's life had taken some time to filter through his thoughts. "I really didn't put things together until we got out of the car. And even now I'm not sure if I added two plus two correctly. I'm just going with what my gut tells me."

"Your gut hasn't steered us wrong before. One thing I can always count on a Morgan for is that their gut instincts make them better cops than some guys with years on the force." Kel grunted. "Do you want to know what my gut tells me? It's whispering, *Sanchez, someone is going to shoot at you before the week is out, so you better get your affairs in order*. Now with what you tell me about Hall, I'm not so sure he won't be the guy shooting at us."

Kane worked through Kel's words. "Okay, so you think he's going to shoot at us? Because I've had to spend years trying to figure out what Quinn is saying to me, and I'm going to tell you, there are times when you are just as confusing."

"What I'm saying is, this is going to get really ugly and we need to watch our step. I've got your back in this, but you've got to tell me which way you're veering so I can adjust the course." Kel grinned. "Did you get the boat reference in that, because there was a boat reference. You know, because we're at the marina?"

"Yeah, I got it," Kane groaned. "And if your gut is as good as mine, it should be telling you I'm going to be the one to shoot you, not Hall. Let's just do this safe, and if anything even smells wrong, act on it. He knows that we're here to talk about Wong, but he probably also knows we could tighten the noose around his neck too. Just watch your step, and if push comes to shove, we shove first."

CHAPTER NINETEEN

Brigid: A ghra, he called me today.

Donal (looking up from his book): Who?
We be having a lot of hes in our
clan. If ye'd said she, I'd have had a
50-50 chance of it.

Brigid: Mick. Kane's Mick. He called me
just to talk.

Donal: The question is, love, did ye talk
to him?

Brigid, smiling as she climbs into bed
next to her husband: For a little bit.
Then after that, I shut up and just
listened to our sweet boy ramble.
It was the best phone call a mother
could ever ask for.

—Answering a mother's prayers at the
   oddest times

"WHAT STATION are you from?" a gruff voice called out from the houseboat's shadowy interior. The man it belonged to emerged slowly, a skeletal remnant of a bull-bodied powerhouse. "And don't bother denying you're cops. You both smell like a badge and I'm guessing the dark-haired one is related to that Irish son of a bitch over at Central."

"There are a lot of us Irish son of bitches over at Central," Kane shot back, his long legs eating up the dock's length. He stopped at the fishing boat's mooring, shoving his hands into his jeans' pockets, the manila envelope tucked under his arm crinkling slightly against his side. Kel was a few steps behind him, a lean elegant shadow with wary eyes. "And I would be telling you not to speak of my mother that way, but knowing her, she'd take it as a point of pride. Am I speaking to Pattrias Hall?"

"Sergeant Pattrias Hall," the old man corrected. "Earned my rank. Not going to let some puppy take it away. Now, are you the two that called me, or is SFPD so bored they're sending cops out to investigate me dumping fish guts over the side of my boat?"

Little remained of the massive man Kane had seen in Hall's identification photos. Folds of flesh hung from his face, flapping jowls where there were once fat cheeks. His neck skin draped down from his jawline, gray-tinged crêpe curtains pocked with red lesions, and his bulbous nose was thick with swollen tissue, a virulent crimson splotch on his sickly face. A pair of heavy white eyebrows seemed to take up most of his forehead, looming over his small, narrowed brown eyes, their snowy coarseness almost an exact match for the uneven crewcut covering most of his square skull.

His clothes were obviously purchased when he had more weight on him, because his skeletal body swam in a Hawaiian shirt dotted with palm trees and flamingos and a pair of khaki cargo shorts that looked about five sizes too big. A pair of thick formerly white socks probably helped keep his Crocs on, but they slid under his feet as he stepped farther out onto the deck.

"Is dumping fish guts illegal?" Kel drawled. "I'd think it would be something people wouldn't mind, considering they're living on a boat."

"If that is supposed to make me feel like we're buddies, you can save it. They taught those tricks even back when I was in the Academy." Hall creaked his way across the boat's deck, grabbing at the railing to steady himself. Stopping at the bow, he glared down at Kane. "I thought I told you I said everything I was going to on the phone."

"And I thought maybe I would give you some time to change your mind," Kane replied as he opened the envelope's clasp. "Do you mind if we come aboard?"

"I mind like shit. Anything you've got to say to me can be said from over there," the ex-cop growled. "Last thing I want is a couple of baby-faced assholes poking around my boat."

"We just want to ask you a couple questions about Danny Wong and the time you spent assigned to the task force that took him down." Kel came up behind Kane, his shoes scraping the grit on the pier. "I believe my partner informed you that we're looking for Wong. If there's anything you know about his whereabouts, we would appreciate if you shared with us."

"I don't know where the fuck Wong—" Hall stopped talking when Kane held up a photo of Achara Sangsom holding her son.

It was hard not to climb over the boat's railing and pound of the shit out of Hall until he confessed to every crime he'd ever committed, but Kane knew he had to step carefully. He and Kel were on thin ice, chasing after ghosts and thin leads, so there was no room for error. He had to force Hall in any way possible, even as he buried the knowledge of what happened to the smiling little boy cradled in a beautiful woman's arms.

"We suspect you were acquainted with this woman. Her name was Achara Sangsom, and she worked for Danny Wong. She had a little boy who you allegedly found on St. John Street following her murder." After handing the first photo to Kel, Kane pulled out another, then held it up for Hall to see. "I don't know if anybody showed you this, but I don't think they needed to."

It was a part of Miki's past Kane never wanted to share with him. The crime scene photos of Achara's murder were brutal in the stark savagery of her remains. Horan spent half a day going through the evidence and then breaking down the events as she saw them. Miki's mother hadn't died cleanly, and more than a few times, Horan had to stop to give Kane and Kel a break from their briefing. If anything, her remains resembled Rodney Chin's, slaughtered and then beaten down nearly to a pulp.

But what broke Kane's heart was the sight of a chewed-on teddy bear, sticky from soaking up the blood from Achara's battered body.

"They found her body two days later, and Forensics had a hard time determining time of death because her killer sealed up the apartment and turned the heater on to muddy the evidence, but I had our medical examiner look at everything, because science evolves." Kane forced his expression to go flat. "Based on what the doctor found, it looks like you found Achara's little boy about half an hour or so after she'd been killed. Now, I understand you might not have known she had a kid, and Forensics back then didn't seem to think it was important to tell the investigating officer that she had given birth, but you were around Wong when you worked undercover. You were aware he liked to get his people inked with his symbol, but you didn't say anything about the tattoo on the kid's arm. You *knew* that mark, and you buried it. Why?"

"Look, I don't know what the fuck you're talking about, and I want you off of my dock," Hall spat. "Who gives a shit about what happened to a whore twenty years ago? It's not going to change anything now."

"We know you're dying, but so is Wong," Kel added, his voice soft but edged with the finality of what Hall was facing. "No, you can't change what happened that night, but as my partner pointed out, science evolves. The little boy right now is a young man Wong wants dead for one reason or another. So as we see it, you got a choice: tell us where Wong is and we walk away, or you spend the last few months you've got left to you inside of a jail cell, charged with Achara Sangsom's murder. No matter how long you've been off the force, you'll still be going in as a cop, and even as sick as you are now, they're not going to show you any mercy inside."

Kane had never really seen the life leave a person. Not until he watched Hall fold in on himself. The old man staggered, grabbing at the rail, but it didn't seem as if he could hold himself up any longer. Kane crossed over the dock to get to the boat, but the ex-cop barked at him, forcefully forbidding them from boarding his boat.

"You don't understand. I tell you where Wong is, and he'll do to me what he did to her, what he does to anyone who crosses him." Hall shook his head, the sweat beading at his temples and running down his florid cheeks. "There's still a guy who would fucking suck Wong off if he wanted it. That's who you're looking for. That's who killed the whore. I was just there that night to be his lookout. I thought he was just going to talk to her, find out who double-crossed Wong. He wasn't supposed to murder her. There wasn't supposed to be a kid."

"So what? You stood by and watched someone murder Achara Sangsom?" Kel prodded. "And did nothing?"

"I did something." The cop sneered at them, using the back of his hand to mop away the moisture on his forehead. "I grabbed the kid and ran. She was already dead when I came through the door. I didn't say anything about the tattoo because I figured if I did, someone would connect him with Wong and that asshole I was with would kill him, if he could be found."

It was difficult to hear. Kane could almost see the genesis of Miki's pain and sorrow. He'd been set on the path, seemingly destined for a life of violence and abuse he'd finally clawed his way out of. Kane would be damned if Miki stumbled back into it again.

Studying the ex-cop, Kane asked, "Why was it so important to kill Achara Sangsom just to get a name?"

"Because she'd been hooked up with the DEA guy who popped Wong. They buried him so deep nobody could find him, but Wong figured if anybody knew where he was, it would be her. Wong's guard dog worked her over way before I got there, but he told me he got the guy's name out of her—his real name, not the one he gave Wong." Hall rubbed at his chest, his bony fingers making tight circles over his heart. "I hid that boy so Wong couldn't find him. Then I walked away from all of it. I don't give a shit about what happens to Wong or that DEA guy, Stewart. They can kill each other for all I care. I've got about six weeks left to me, and I sure as hell am not going to spend that in a fucking hole."

"We can take you in for accessory, based on what you told us today," Kane said as he walked toward the bow of the boat. Passing the envelope and the photos to Kel, he reached into his jacket pocket, closing his fingers over the zip tie loops he'd tucked there earlier. "What's the name of the guy who killed her? Give us something to go on, and we can try to convince the DA to leave you on house arrest instead of taking you in."

"The view from your boat is a hell of a lot better than the one you're going to get in jail," Kel remarked. "We just need to make sure you don't give Wong a heads-up, and then you'll be back here before you know it."

"I told you already, I don't know where the fuck Wong is, and it's been years since I've seen his pet dog, Zhou." Hall stumbled a few feet forward, resting against the V of the front railing. "You got pictures from back then? Just find any of Wong and you'll see Zhou lurking behind him someplace. That ugly scarecrow was pissed off because Wong gave Achara to Stewart. Zhou had a thing for her, but Wong wasn't going to waste something as sweet as her on a piece of shit like him. Kind of ironic Wong gave his best whore to his own personal Judas."

Hall spat and his face lost all of its color. He leaned forward and something on the boat rattled loudly, like a latch being thrown open. Hall's hands dropped out of sight and Kane's instincts set off every warning bell he had.

"Let me see your hands," Kane ordered, drawing his weapon. Kel's was up and steadied a second later, his partner grabbing at a heavy barrel with one hand to pull it in front of them. "Hall, I'm only going to tell you once."

"Go ahead. I already told you I'm not going to let you take me in." The ex-cop coughed, spittle forming a froth over his lower lip. "There isn't a day that goes by that I don't think about that fucking kid. I knew who he ended up with. I thought I was doing the right thing, but Vega was as much of a monster as Wong ever could be. How the fuck was I supposed to know? You see Zhou and you tell him I'll be waiting for him in fucking hell. He didn't need to kill that woman. And I don't even want to know what he did with her before that, but I did my best by that kid. You tell him I'm sorry."

The gun was an old one but still deadly. Hall's face was blank, his eyes pinned to the horizon, and his chin lifted defiantly as he raised the weapon to his temple. Kane shouted the ex-cop's name, but Hall didn't so much as flinch. The boom shattered the marina's lazy serenity, and Hall began to topple even before Kane could reach the side of the boat. He heard Kel shouting for backup and an ambulance, but as soon as he reached the deck, Kane knew it was already too late. Shaking his head, he rubbed at his face, then sighed at the hula girl pinup inked on Hall's bare shin.

He'd seen his share of cover-ups, some good and some bad. The hula girl was a flirtatious nod to an innocent era, but the artist hadn't been good enough to hide the tattoo he meant to obscure. Maybe it was because

Kane intimately knew the shape, or the color saturation hadn't been deep enough, but Sergeant Pattrias Hall died with Wong's symbol still on his flesh, as if nothing he did would ever erase his sins.

KANE WAS sick of coming home in the dark.

He knew it was a part of the job, but every day the badge got heavier and heavier. He was tired of cold dinners and empty living rooms, of stale coffee warmed up in a microwave and fast food hastily shoved into his mouth in between coordinating a murder scene.

It was never easy when it was a cop. And it sure as hell wasn't a walk in the park when it was a cop who ate his own gun.

It was well into the next day by the time he pushed open the warehouse's heavy front door, a few steps ahead of the sun, with the cold night still biting at his back. They'd shut down the marina, clearing out any bystanders and residents to make way for the coroner and brass from a variety of departments. His father showed up, accompanying their captain in a black sedan that screamed authority and disapproval.

Kane had been willing to take the hit. There should have been a hit, but the bars outweighed the badges, and politics muddied the waters before the coroner had a chance to load Hall's body into the van. They'd been given absolution like Catholics lined up at a confessional, a wave of the hand and a demand of a full report in lieu of a rosary. Kel said a brief thanks to God and climbed back into their police issue, but Kane hadn't been satisfied.

"I fucked this up," he'd muttered, shoulder pressed against Donal's. "I should've taken him off that boat. He was a cop. We both knew going in there was probably a gun somewhere, but I thought I had him talking. We had him *talking*."

"Go home, son," Donal ordered. "Wrap this thing up and look at it again in the morning. But for right now, you've got to remember we are sitting on somebody else's watch. Berkeley is going to have to take lead on this because it's in their corner. After the shit they pulled with Quinn, the captain is going to want to bury this because he doesn't want any more ripples. This wasn't on you. Hall was going to do himself in no matter what. So go home."

The drive back to the station to pick up his Hummer had been mostly silent. Kel made a few halfhearted attempts at conversation, then lapsed into a numbed shock neither of them felt like breaking. After handing the keys over to the motor pool's late-night attendant, Kane turned to find Kel behind him, his arms out for an embrace.

It felt good to hug his friend, a solid warm body to remind him they weren't the ones being scraped off a boat's deck, and Kane held on to Kel long enough for his partner to let go of a short laugh. Then Kane turned and fixed a steely eye on the kid who stood slack-jawed with the sedan's keys still dangling from his fingers, daring him to say anything.

"Go home," Kel repeated Donal's order. "Go home and kiss your rock star until he wakes up and makes you smile."

It seemed like a good idea, except Kane's rock star was still awake.

He'd grown used to Miki's habit of stealing his clothes and leaving guitars in odd places around the house. He'd adapted to running a lint roller over his jeans before going to work every morning, although some days he simply gave up and got knowing looks from other dog owners when they spotted the stray beige hair on his jeans. Coming home to find the refrigerator packed full with barely nibbled-on take-out Chinese no longer fazed him any more than being woken up by a video call from a musician or two who'd provided the soundtrack for his sexual exploration during puberty.

But Kane didn't think he would ever get used to the sight of Miki St. John wearing nothing more than a pair of low-slung cotton pants and a sexy smile, sprawled out over the sheets he'd gotten on sale one Black Friday.

It wasn't the first time Kane had been thankful for his lover's vampiric sleep schedule, and it probably wouldn't be the last.

The contributor of beige hair was asleep at the foot of the bed, curled up over a pillow Miki had donated from the nest he hoarded against the headboard. Dude lay on his back, looking more like an overturned furry soup tureen than a vicious defender of the household. The dog's feet twitched as Kane passed by. Then he stretched out, opening one eye to watch as Kane stripped off his clothes.

"He probably thinks I'm going to kick him off the bed," Kane muttered at Miki, then swore when he caught his chin on his shirt collar. After tugging himself free, he balled up the sweaty garment and tossed it into the open hamper. "You gonna be up in five minutes? I need to take a shower, but I'd really like to spend some time with you."

"I'm not tired. Spent the day a little drunk and a lot weepy, so I guess I'm embracing my Irish." Miki's kissable mouth curled into a smirk. "Go take your shower, and if you feel like kicking the dog off the bed when you get back, I'm good with it."

"I don't know if I have the energy," Kane grumbled. "The spirit is very willing, Mick my love, but the body is very weak. I'm up for cuddle and a talk."

"I'm good with that too," he replied with a laugh. "I'm sure Dude would approve. I think he just got settled."

The hot water on his skin felt good, but the soap and a scrub did nothing to wash away the unsettled feeling Kane had in his gut. On his way back to the bedroom, Kane did one final check of the door locks and turned off the lights, then joined Miki on their bed.

"Dad called me and told me what happened," Miki said as Kane stretched out on top of him. Parting his legs so Kane could settle his weight between his knees, Miki stroked at the scruff on Kane's jaw. "It's been a pretty fucked day."

"I don't think there is a word strong enough to describe how fucked a day this was," Kane murmured. "But damn, it's good to be here with you now."

Whatever he did to deserve Miki, Kane was grateful for it. They fit each other in ways he hadn't understood when they first met, but eventually he saw they moved in similar ways, thought along the same paths, and often laughed at the stupidest things. They argued over small, senseless bits but stood shoulder to shoulder when it mattered. Kane always thought that the greatest gift he could give Miki was his family—his own family—and now as he stared at the ashes of Miki's past, he understood that he'd been fooling himself. Miki fit into the Morgans of his own volition, carving out his space and defiantly daring them to love him.

Kane had missed that the most precious treasure between them was Miki opening up his heart to let Kane in. Lying against Miki's warm body, with an odd-looking terrier licking his big toe, Kane gave thanks to the God who'd thrown Miki into his path.

"You make my heart hurt, I love you so much," he whispered into Miki's ear. A lock of hair tickled Kane's nose and he fought off a sneeze. His body adjusted around Miki's, and he rolled over onto his side, taking his lover with him. Miki, as usual, fought him a little bit. "Can't you just let me hold you? Sometimes you're like trying to give a wet, angry cat a nail clipping."

"My knee." The bed gave a little bit as Miki adjusted his leg. "Was twisted funny."

"Better now?" Kane rubbed at the gnarled scar tissue stretching over Miki's knee. He knew where to massage, having worked out muscle spasms and cramps after Miki spent a long day of playing. "How are you doing?"

"Are we just not going to talk about the fact that a cop blew his head off in front of you?" He tilted his head back, his hazel eyes skeptical and doubting. "I thought I was the only one who thought denial was healthy."

"Right now, I'd rather talk through how you feel about your mom and maybe come up with what we're going to do about your dad."

"What am I supposed to do about Donal? Bake him cookies?" He scoffed. "I can't even make ramen right for you."

"Since you consider making ramen opening the package and just eating the noodles, then no."

"You act like I make the flavor packet into Kool-Aid." Miki laughed as Kane gagged dramatically. "I just saw my mom for the first time today, and I don't know if I can handle any more family right now. Why?"

"Because today a man died because... actually, I can't tell you why he killed himself, but I need to tell you he was sorry." Kane took a deep breath and continued. "I talked to Book about what I can share with you and what I can't. There's some things I'm not going to tell you because I don't think you need to hear them. And that's on me, because I'm not going to give you that kind of pain. I want to ask you to trust me on that, okay?"

"Is this about how my mom died?" Miki's whisper was like the chiming of the church bell in the dark of the storm, caught by the wind and slightly out of control. The emotion in his trembling voice struck Kane hard, and he reached up to run his fingers through Miki's hair. "If you're telling me that I don't want to know, then I'm going to trust you. But if in the future, I ask you, will you tell me?"

"I promise to get you drunk first," Kane vowed. "Because of the two of us, I think you've carried enough. It's time for me to shoulder that burden. Okay?"

A few years ago, Miki would've told him to fuck off and pushed him away. Kane half expected him to do that now, but instead Miki nodded and snuggled closer. They lay together for a few moments, serenaded by the snoring dog, and Miki sighed.

His rock star lay against him, mute and attentive as Kane told him of Hall's apology. His eyes shimmered a bit, but his mouth was set into a firm line, a stern expression Kane quickly kissed away. The taste of mint on Miki's tongue soothed Kane's rattled nerves, and he deepened their kiss, wishing he had enough breath to make it last forever. Sighing, Miki broke off first, breathing hard.

"Still okay?" Kane asked.

"Yeah, I am. I just wish I had the chance to kick the guy in the balls. That's some kind of fucked-up crap he had going."

"I'm not going to argue with you about that." Kane rubbed Miki's nose with his thumb, pleased to get a hiss out of his lover. "Cancer was eating him up alive, just like his guilt. I got the feeling he really meant to save you. For everything that he did, he wanted to do one good thing and you were it."

"What do they say? The road to hell is paved with good intentions? The guy pretty much put down his own yellow bricks. Okay, tell me about my fucking father," he grumbled. "What did Book say you could tell me?"

"It's not necessarily what Book approved of but rather what the DEA shared with us this evening." Kane ran his thumb down the ridge of Miki's spine, glad to feel the muscles there rather than the rough terrain of his bones from lack of eating. "The undercover operative—former DEA Agent Liam Stewart—is in San Francisco and has been for the past six months. It seems he's the reason Wong has targeted you because the son of a bitch can't reach Stewart, so he's going to try to kill his son."

"And Wong thinks that's me?" Miki's upper lip lifted. "How the hell—"

"It is you, *a ghra*," Kane broke in gently. "And he wants to meet you tomorrow… if you're willing."

CHAPTER TWENTY

Fortunes left on paper
Iron grate at my back
Handful of songs in my pockets
You pulled me up from the black
Dragons on the streets
Fireworks in the sky
We've gone and come full circle
A curl of time gone by
Sinners at the Crossroads
An X in the road
Sipping gin, counting time
Getting ready to explode
—'Nother Sip of Gin

MIKI DIDN'T spend a lot of time at the police station Kane worked at. It held bittersweet memories, long hours spent being interviewed first by Kel, then again by Kane, about his abusers' murders. The clatter of cop talk grated at his nerves, waves of authoritative voices bound together by a certain mind-set and a macabre sense of humor he didn't share. He didn't understand why it was so different around the Morgans, because they were as much of a cop as anyone could get, but it was. Maybe it was due to the sense of safety he had around them, but Miki didn't intend to ever pick at the why of things. He'd learned at an early age it was better to adapt and adjust than question.

That philosophy went out the window as soon as he discovered he had a mother who, at least on the surface, seemed to have cared for him, and a father who'd disappeared into the shadows only to reemerge at the worst of times.

"Not that there is really any good time for somebody you didn't know existed to come shoving his way into your life," Miki muttered.

Meeting his father at a cop house seemed like a good idea when Kane suggested it, but being surrounded by badges and guns was never a comfortable situation. He'd spent too much time in his teenage years looking over his shoulder, wondering when someone was going to drag him back to Vega, or worse, and despite it all, Miki hadn't outgrown his edginess.

"Fuck this." He scrubbed at his face, then ran his hands through his hair, wishing he could loosen some of the tightness along his scalp. "I've already got a mom and dad. I've got Kane, Damien, a band, and even a damned dog. How many fucking people am I supposed to care about?"

"There usually isn't a limit, Miki boy," a deep Irish voice rumbled behind him. "That's the best part about the heart. It's as big as ye need it to be."

For as large of a man as Donal was, he sure as hell was silent. Miki figured it was a ninja skill the man developed over the years of raising eight headstrong, independent personalities who seemed to view childhood restrictions as bendable so long as no one was hurt and it wasn't against the law. If anyone needed to be able to sneak up on a plotting horde bent on death and destruction, it was Donal Morgan.

Even knowing that, it still scared the crap out of Miki when Donal appeared out of nowhere.

The Donal he knew existed in old jeans and comfortable T-shirts. His feet were either bare or he wore sneakers. His slightly silvered black hair was usually tousled, and the only bit of shine he wore was the battered gold wedding ring he'd put on once and apparently never taken off since. So it was always a surprise when Miki's dad appeared in front of him wearing a crisp set of formal blues and a badge shiny enough to blind the sun.

"I always forget you're a cop," Miki said, shaking his head. "I know Kane is one because it's like a jacket he wears sometimes, and, well, Connor stinks like one, but I never think of you as a cop first. Seeing you like this kind of freaks me out."

Miki didn't know what he expected from Donal, but it sure as hell wasn't a hug.

As good as it felt, Miki was very aware they were standing in the middle of a police station, and he was being hugged by one of the top cops. Squirming a little bit didn't help. All that did was dig Donal's badge into his chest, and he might have heard Donal chuckle. It lasted only for another second, then he was let go, off-balance but reassured he was loved.

"How are ye doing?" Donal asked, tugging at Miki's leather jacket to straighten it. "Who brought ye in?"

"Dan, one of Sionn's security guys. Damien came with me, but I think he got hung up going to the bathroom. There were a couple of guys there who wanted to talk guitars, and I didn't want to stay. Too jumpy." He let Donal push his hair from his face, smirking when the Irish man grumbled good-naturedly about having a hippie for a son. "Kane said he'd meet me here when the guy got in, but I haven't seen him yet."

"Yer man's already inside the room." The cop was back in Donal's eyes, a glacial frost over his smoky blue gaze. "I have a lot of questions and I know it's not my place to ask them of him, but… damned if I don't feel like I need to stand in front of ye."

The shift from gentle counselor to fierce protector shouldn't have been a surprise, but it was. It felt good in a way Miki couldn't put his finger on, but right then and there, for the first time in his life, he understood what it might have felt like growing up with a father. He didn't need anyone to fight his battles for him. He'd learned that particular viciousness at an early age. But standing shoulder to shoulder with a man who could shatter a mountain between his hands—it felt damned good knowing Donal Morgan would have his back in any fight.

Once again, he was reminded of how perfectly suited Donal and Brigid were. They seemed to fit each other in ways Miki could never see working, but it did. He supposed people wouldn't say that about him and Kane because, on the surface, they just didn't make sense. But they didn't see the silences Kane shared with him or the laughter Kane could bring up out of him. Sionn and Damien made sense. So did Quinn and Rafe, and there was no denying Connor and Forest were married from the moment they met each other. Seeing Donal in warrior mode illuminated how he and Brigid were meant for a lifetime together. Pound for pound, Miki would always put his money on Donal's wife, even if he was the one with the gun, but they definitely knew when one had to brandish their sword while the other lifted their shield.

No one ever looked to Miki for comfort. His idea of consoling usually included an awkward pat on the back and a nervous look for someone who knew what they were doing. This time, oddly enough, it seemed like words Donal might need to hear were right on his tongue. And even if they weren't, he was going to say them anyway.

"You told me to call you Dad. To think about you as my dad. And I do. I don't know the guy who's in there and I don't know *why* he's in there. Shit, I don't even know where *there* is." Miki stared down the line of interrogation room doors. "I don't know if I'm ready for all of this yet. Should I have everybody with me or be by myself? I keep going round and round about what the hell I'm supposed to do here and what I'm supposed to feel. It's all just shit, you know?

"But I know you're here for me, and I'd be stupid not to stand behind you if you want to go through that door first because… you're a fucking hell of a lot bigger than me and you'd clear the way, even if I know it's shitty of me to want you to do that." Sighing, Miki threw a glance down the hall toward the bullpen. He really wanted Damien with him. Kane and Donal were a given, but there was an emptiness at his side he knew only D could fill. Shit, if they'd let him bring Dude, he would have. "Shit, where's Brigid? She's not here, right? I mean, I love her, but I don't know if I can deal right now."

"Ye told her ye were afraid she'd gut him if she saw him, right?" Donal huffed indignantly. "I'm ashamed ye'd think that of her. She'd at least punch the man first, *then* gut him. I love my bride, but she's short. She'd have to bring a man down to his knees so she could get a knife to his throat. And she's in Book's office, pacing. In case ye'd be needing her."

"After. If it goes wrong." Miki grimaced. "No, I'll need her anyway. It's going to go wrong. And even if it goes right, it's not going to be *right*-right. I'm going to get D and then head in. If you go in first, just—"

"I'll not be killing the man, if that's what yer saying," Donal intoned, putting his hand on Miki's shoulder. Turning him toward the bullpen's door, he gave Miki a slight push. "Go on with ye. I'll go find Kane, and then, well, we'll see. Just go get yer brother and let's see where this is going to take all of us."

LIAM STEWART had Miki's height and, oddly enough, more than a little bit of his standard cynical expression. If Achara Sangsom gifted Miki with her beauty, the tall, street-savvy man pacing about the interview room poured his world-weary skepticism into Miki's soul. Even if Kane didn't know who Stewart was, if he passed him on the street, he would take a second look.

Stewart's face was a blend of the Highlands and the Emerald Hills, a strong jaw and sharp cheekbones with very little softness to them. His hair was unkempt, messy from the wind and the color of a good lager with a hint of mink hidden within the strands. Stewart wore a pair of black jeans and a blue polo snug enough to follow the lines of his lean, muscular torso, an artless grace to his body as he moved, a wiry strength bristling with unspent energy, and even his smirk when Kane opened the door held a hint of charisma Kane had seen flow through Miki when he was onstage with his band.

"If you're looking for your suspect, I'm not him," Stewart drawled. Even his flat edge of sarcasm mirrored Miki's, and Kane couldn't help but smile. "I'm supposed to meet someone here, and I'm going to go out on a limb and say you're not him."

"No, I'm not. I'm the fiancé," he replied, holding out his hand. "Senior Inspector Kane Morgan, SFPD. Miki and I have been together for a couple of years now. I sent one of the watch guys to go get him. They just told me you were here."

The assessing look in Stuart's green-flecked brown eyes only held a mild curiosity, erasing the slight challenge there a moment before. He studied Kane for a moment, then said, "Nobody told me he was gay."

"Is that going to be a problem?" Kane tucked his hands into his jeans pockets, widening his stance and squaring off his shoulders. "Because if it is…."

"I didn't say it was going to be," Stewart shot back. "Just that nobody told me. But then, DEA tends to hold their cards close to their chest even if their own players need to know what's in their hand. All I was told was that he's a musician and they're pretty sure he's Achara's son. Since I am fairly certain I was the only one with her about that time, more than likely he's mine. Beyond that, I've got nothing."

"So you've never heard about Sinner's Gin?" Kane pressed. "The rock band? That accident after the Grammys? Only the lead singer survived and then the guitarist resurfaced and now they formed a new band called Crossroads Gin? None of that sounds familiar?"

"Look, I listen to two types of music, blues and jazz. And you probably thought I was going to say country *and* western, but are you even old enough to know that movie?" Stewart turned at the sound of the door opening, and the wariness returned to his expression. It quickly changed to a brief flicker of surprise when Donal walked in. He glanced between the two men, then crossed his arms over his chest. "I'm going to guess that by the looks of both of you, you're related. Also, the name tag on the brass was a dead giveaway. So, is there even really a son, or was this put together by Wong so the two of you can work me over?"

"And here I was thinking that Miki was a pain in the ass in his own right," Donal rumbled as he closed the door behind him. "I didn't think it was hereditary, but that is what life is about, learning new things every day. Yer Miki went to grab Damien out of the bullpen. He'll be by in a bit, just long enough for me to have a talk here with this one."

The look on his father's face was familiar. Kane'd seen it quite a few times before, usually when he was caught trying to sneak into the house at three in the morning before he was eighteen. It was concern mingled with authority with a hint of unrelenting righteousness. More than a few times when Kane stepped in to take a scolding for Quinn because he dragged his younger brother in much too late for his father's liking, and for a moment, he had a wild suspicion he would have to do the same for Stewart, but Donal merely nodded and introduced himself.

"So I wasn't wrong," the former DEA agent said. "You're related? Brother, nephew, or son?"

"He's my son. Just like Miki," Donal said quietly. The Irish rolled from his father's tongue, a thickening of emotion and family covering his every word. "I'll not be lying to ye by telling ye I hadn't planned on coming in here to tell ye not to hurt my boy. Because I'd meant to. I'd meant to come in here and scare the living shite out of ye, because our Mick doesn't need any more pain."

"For a nonthreat, you're pretty close to telling me you'd be okay ripping my legs off and feeding them to the dogs." Stewart let out a soft scoff. "You sure you're not here for Wong?"

"Actually, that's what I wanted to talk to you about before Miki got here," Kane interjected, resting his hip on the edge of the table in the middle of the room. "I'm guessing you know that Hall took his own life yesterday."

"That was a part of the briefing I got when I was dragged in to get my head yelled at last night." He pulled out one of the four industrial-steel chairs tucked under the table, then straddled it, resting his arms on its back. "Let me catch you up with what I know. Or at least tell you what I can. When I was taken off of the assignment, it was because they suspected Wong knew I was a plant. They buried me for two years so no one could touch me until I testified in court. It took that long to put Danny Wong behind bars, and by the time I finally shook free of the lockdown, Achara was dead. Nobody said anything about her having a kid, so I moved on. Wong was supposed to die in jail. Honestly, I never thought he would last longer than six months, because he made a lot of enemies. Now he allegedly is out and orchestrating hits? Who the hell is working for him? And how the hell do we stop them?"

"Hall gave us a name before he…." Kane trailed off. He didn't need to spell things out for Stewart or his father. At least, not about a dirty cop with a heavy, guilty conscience. "Do you remember a man named Mark Zhou? Hall said he was Wong's go-to when he didn't want to get his own hands bloodied."

"Yeah, I remember him. He's the one who was going to pop me for Wong. He wanted me out of the organization because he thought he could step in, but he didn't realize everything I got was because it was fed from the DEA. He also had a thing for Achara, but there was no way she was going to let him near her." Stewart's attention was still on Donal, standing sentinel by the door. "I haven't been in the city for a long time, but I still have some connections. Give me a couple of days and I can find out where Zhou is."

"I don't know if we have a couple of days," Kane remarked, looking over his shoulder as his father walked toward the table and chairs set into the middle of the room. He could see Donal reflected in the one-way mirror set into the long side of the wall. "A good guess says Wong knows you're in town, so I expect the attacks to escalate. Someone took out one of Wong's guys, and I don't know if it is someone protecting their territory or it was to show Wong still has power."

"Are you talking about Rodney Chin? Because if you are, I can pretty much guarantee that was Zhou. I read the reports. It looked like something he would do. The guy liked to cause pain, preferably with something heavy, so even with twenty years on him, I could see him doing it." A knock on the door brought Stewart's head up and his expression shifted, an indiscernible something flickering in his gaze. "We're going to have to shelve this for now. I think I've got a son to meet.

"And just so you know, Morgan," Stewart said to Donal, rising from his chair. "I don't know anything about being a father, and from what I'm guessing, everything he's learned about being a son, he's learned from you. I don't know where we are going to end up—he and I—but I don't have any illusion that I'm going to be as good of a dad to him as you are. Micah and I are going to have to work things out—however we work things out—so I'd appreciate a little bit of breathing room, and if you feel the need to punch me out, I understand. Especially since I'm asking you to share your son."

"Fair enough, Stewart," Donal conceded, moving aside so Kane could open the door. "But just so ye know, I'm not the one yer going to have to worry about if ye hurt him. That'll be my wife. And fair warning, I've got a whole clan who is more than willing to help her dig a hole in the garden about yer size. Just remember that every time ye look at Miki."

THERE SEEMED to be an unspoken conspiracy among the people Miki brought with him, because he went through the door of the interview room, and much like falling through a looking glass, he tumbled in alone. He had a vague impression of a deep kiss left on his mouth by Kane and a Donal-scented hug, but no memory of Damien leaving him behind in a square box painted in industrial blah, containing a man who moved like he did. The lights were on in the observation space behind the faux-mirrored wall, showing the normally hidden room was empty. Miki wasn't sure if the privacy the Morgans and Damien gave him was something he actually wanted, but it was too late to protest, especially since when next he blinked, the only one left in the room was a man who had his eyes.

And possibly even a little bit of his pain.

"Dear fucking God, you look just like her." The man—*his father*—breathed out his words, a whispery, almost prayerlike tone Miki heard people say over rosaries from his spot in the back of the Morgans' church. He took a few steps closer to Miki, his hands stretched out with trembling fingers that almost brushed Miki's face, but Miki backpedaled before they touched him. The sardonic laugh Liam Stewart let go echoed in the tiny room. "And then, there's the me in you."

"There's only me in here. Not any of you. Not any of her." Miki shook his head, lengthening the distance between them with a few short steps. Staring at Stewart across the table, he knew what he'd just said was a lie. The man sounded exactly like him, battered and coppery with more than a full helping of acerbic vitriol and burgeoning doubt. "Kane said you didn't know about me. That true?"

Stewart blankly stared at him for a few seconds, then rolled his shoulders back. Letting go a long sigh, he gripped the top of one of the chairs and leaned on it, meeting Miki's gaze. "No, I didn't know about you. They yanked me out before I could even do something for her. I kept telling myself she'd be safe because Wong liked her, but—"

"Yeah, I guess he liked her long enough to keep her alive until he went to prison." Miki grimaced, shutting his mind off before it wandered down an all-too-familiar dark path. "And Wong hates you enough to try to kill me. It all started with her friend. The cop who killed himself knew I was hers, knew I'm yours. I never thought about why she reached out now, but it makes sense if they were looking for you the entire time."

"I remember Sandy. She really was a good friend to your mom." Stewart threw the word *mom* out so casually, as if it was how Miki'd thought of Achara Sangsom his entire life. It struck him as much of a shock as seeing his face on hers or hearing himself in Stewart's voice. "She was very sweet but not bright. Someone had to have put her up to contact you."

"She went through my record company and my manager, Edie." Miki caught himself before he leaned on the chair, mirroring his father. "Kane and Kel haven't talked to me much about the case, just enough to tell me to keep my head down and stay indoors until they figure out where Wong is and who he has working for him."

"That's not bad advice," Stewart muttered, and then he glanced over Miki's shoulder at the observation room, still lit up and empty. "SFPD seems to take protecting you very seriously. I got patted down and gone over with a wand before I was let in here. Your boyfriend probably would have asked for a cavity search if he thought he could get away with it."

"There's enough of his family at the station that if Kane wanted it to happen, they would've held you down and just did it." He matched Stewart's sneer, and the older man laughed. "I don't know what I was expecting. I guess I wanted to see the guy who walked away from my mother. Who let her die."

"You're not saying anything to me that I haven't said to myself over the past twentysomething years, kid." His tone softened and his knuckles relaxed their grip on the chair's back. "I get you're angry at me—"

"I don't even get why I'm angry at you. I walked in here without any expectations for you, but my brain keeps coming back to one thing." This time Miki laid his hands on the table and leaned forward. "You were a cop, or as good as one. Why the fuck didn't you get her out? Even if you didn't love her, she was a fucking kid and you left her there."

"Because they had me locked down. Because the damned DEA pulled me out and threw me into a hole. As far as my superiors were concerned back then, she was just one of Wong's assets, no matter how much I fucking begged," Stewart spat back, his eyes going green with anger. "And by the time I got someone to finally listen to me—to finally let me out—she was dead. After that, I spent my time working and trying to find the bottom of every whiskey bottle I could get ahold of until a couple of days ago when a DEA agent assigned here to the San Francisco office hunted me down and told me I had a son, Achara's son.

"And if you walk out of here knowing one fucking thing today—" His voice broke, as fractured as shattering glass, and Stewart swallowed before continuing. "You're fucking wrong. I loved her. As much as I could love anybody. And walking in here—seeing your face—makes me want to crawl right back into that bottle, because looking at you hurts. And knowing that I could've saved you from what sounds like a really fucked-up, shitty life, that I could have had a part of her with me, helps me understand why that dirty cop ate his gun because he couldn't handle the guilt."

CHAPTER TWENTY-ONE

I slide into the crack of midnight
Forgotten, broken, bitten and torn
Just need to survive what you do to me
Just need to see the morn
I lit all the candles
Given to me by a man
Who told me to pray
God has me in his hand
You came anyway
Walking through the flame and smoke
I'll never get back my innocence
I'll never get back what you took
—Innocence Lost

"LOOK, LET'S take a walk or—at least—get out of here. You and I aren't the kind of people who do well in boxes, and this is the worst possible box." Stewart pulled himself up, inhaling sharply. "This would be a lot easier if we were sitting down with a bottle of whiskey between us. Except I'm trying to cut down on the whiskey part, so it'll have to be coffee."

"Why?" Miki rocked back on his heels, his thumbs hooked into his pockets.

It was hard to get a read on the guy, especially since his emotions were a maelstrom of confusion, doubt, and resentment. He hated wanting to like Stewart. It seemed as if he was being disloyal to Donal somehow, and Miki had to take a step away from the conversation. Even if it was just for a moment, he needed some space to work through the tangle in his head.

Still, as much as he wanted to go back out through the door to find someone familiar, that need felt like he was running away, and Miki refused to tuck his tail and bolt.

"Why what?" Stewart cocked his head and frowned a little. "Why the coffee? Or why not the whiskey?"

"Why do you think this would be a lot easier?" The resentment was ebbing, replaced by a burr of curiosity. He kind of hated wanting to know more about Stewart and maybe hearing a story or two about his mother. Miki didn't know if his heart could take it. The what-ifs were too heavy and looming, but also so damn tantalizing. "Also, if you've forgotten, someone is trying to fucking kill us. Or maybe just me. I don't know. Maybe Wong thinks you knew about me the entire time, unless you're lying and you did."

"My mother cursed me with having a kid just like me, and fuck me if she didn't get her wish." Stuart rubbed at his face, then let out an exasperated sigh. "Why would I leave you to Wong? If I'd known about you, I could've told the agency, and then they would've gotten off their ass to get Achara out. That was why they kept pushing back, because she and I didn't have any connection, but you would've been enough to tip the scales my way. What kind of asshole would leave a kid someplace Wong could get to them?"

"The cop that blew his own head off yesterday?" Miki reminded him. "He didn't have any problem dumping me in the lap of the guy who didn't seem to understand there are things you don't do with little kids. So don't talk to me about assholes, I've had to live through enough of them. So yeah, you're going to have to excuse me if that's my first default setting when you ask me that question."

Stewart seemed shaken, and Miki shoved down the flicker of remorse he felt trying to flare up. His father looked away, his attention fixed to a corner of the room, and when he finally looked up at Miki, his eyes shimmered with unshed tears.

"I don't know anything about you," Stewart confessed. "I found out about half an hour ago you're apparently a musician I should've heard about and that your childhood was shitty, but I don't know anything else. I don't know what happened to you and I can tell just by how wary you are that there's a lot I'm going to be sorry for."

"You want to know the truth?" Miki pushed forward, unable to hold back his emotions anymore. "Right now, I'm pissed off about *everything*. In the last couple of weeks, my whole fucking life has been turned upside down, and it isn't that I had an idea in my head about who you were going to be. I never *once* thought about you. I never *ever* thought about my mother—Achara—because I figured I wasn't good enough for her to hold on to—"

"I may not have known about you, but your mom wanted kids so badly. But she knew if she had one then, Wong would just use it against her," his father cut in. "She'd have done everything she could to keep you safe. We used to talk about having kids one day, but I couldn't even tell her I was undercover. If Wong found out she knew, she'd have been dead before—well, I guess none of that really matters because either he had her killed or Zhou murdered her because he couldn't have her. But I know without even being there, without even knowing you existed, she would've loved you so fucking much and probably died protecting you. I don't doubt that for a moment."

If the photos hadn't made his mother real, then Stewart's words *did*. What he'd lost when Achara died became all too real in that moment, and Miki staggered back, unable to keep the grip on the chair he'd clenched as if he would drown if he let go.

And God did he drown.

He didn't need to feel like he'd missed knowing the most important person he ever should've held in his heart. Miki couldn't hold back any of the raging sensations of loss and regret pouring from where he'd walled them up years before. The little boy he'd been remained in the dark, shivering as a cold blanket wrapped around him from years of neglect, woven by every intrusive touch on his body. Long nights of physical hunger and emotional thirst slammed back into him, and as hard as he tried, he couldn't stop the seething memories from engulfing him.

There'd been nights when he no longer felt his own body, cast out of his flesh because of what was being done to him, and he'd run toward dreams he knew were made of nothing but wishes and tinsel. In his young mind, there'd been a family who'd somehow lost him and mourned the absence of their son in their lives. He'd never been able to see the faces of the man and woman he'd created from the shadows, but now he knew how they looked, knew their smiles, and the dramatic scenes of their reconciliation would never come true because *she* was gone.

And the other face was of someone who'd never known he existed.

He missed a woman he never knew—would never know—and to hear that she'd loved him from the lips of someone who'd known her intimately finally broke Miki's heart.

Gulping for air, he tried to keep Stewart back with a shove, but the man came at him in a rush. Panicked, he swung, connecting with a hard thump, but his mind was too scattered to follow up with another hit. Something crunched under his fist, then he heard Stewart swear. Chest heaving, Miki reached for the chair, but Stewart's fingers were around his wrist before he could pick it up.

"*Stop.* I didn't mean to scare you," Stewart gasped, holding his nose. There were speckles of blood down the front of his shirt, the blue darkening as the fabric soaked in the tiny drops. "Jesus, you've got an unreal left hook."

"I can't take this. It's too fucking much right now and I fucking hate that you know her—knew her—and I don't get to." Miki was so damned tired of crying— nearly as much as he hated trying not to—so he gave in, letting his tears go. They ran unchecked as he struggled to suck in a breath to calm his shattered nerves, but nothing seemed to help. "What the hell did you want from me? Because I don't know what to do with you.

I kind of want to go out of the door and just leave you here, but if I do, I'm never going to know about her, and I want to. But that gives you power over me, and I'll be fucking damned if I get played. So what the fuck do you want?"

Stewart's hands settled on Miki's shoulders, their bodies close enough to feel each other's warmth, but Stewart didn't pull him in for a hug. Instead he squeezed lightly and murmured, "I came here today because I needed to see my son. If it makes you feel any better, you scare the fuck out of me. I don't know what I want. I never imagined I'd have a kid, and here you are, pretty and broken and loved by what looks like a large Irish rugby team.

"I don't know if you'll ever let me into your life, and I don't know if you'll ever like me, much less love me," he continued, his expression as leery as Miki felt. "I want to get to know you, and more importantly, I want to get to love you. Because I'm your dad, and just like your mom, I never would have thrown you away, and I will fucking die rather than let Wong have you."

IT WAS interesting to sit at a table in their lieutenant's office with an order of Mexican food with a man who'd just brought Miki to tears and *not* punch his face in. Judging by the speckles of blood on Stewart's shirt and his swollen nose, it looked like Miki'd beat Kane to it. Kel didn't seem to have an issue with Stewart, but Kane was definitely conflicted. He'd gotten a quick kiss and a fierce hug from a rattled Miki, then a mumbled insistence about getting to his therapist on time. A second later, Miki and Damien were both ghosts, leaving nothing behind but the impression that they'd been there and a shell-shocked Stewart standing in their wake. Kel, a bottomless pit, suggested they hit up a taco shop a few yards away from the station to discuss the case over nachos, and Stewart threw in a mumbled agreement, providing the shop delivered tequila.

They didn't have the tequila, but the shop more than made up for it by packing at least a pound of meat on Kane's carne asada fries. Stewart eyed Kane's lunch, then dug a chip through the toppings of his nachos, ignoring Kel's rambling dialogue about salsas and a preference for the shop's green tomatillo sauce over his mother's.

"Do the two of you want me to give you some space to talk? Because if you guys want to brawl it out, I suggest you take it down to the gym. Can't see Casey being happy about his office getting fucked-up." Kel stopped rifling through the take-out bag and met Kane's glare with an exaggerated mockery of a grimace. "We need to talk about Zhou. We all agreed that Stewart and Miki need to meet, so we got that out of the way, but there's business to be done and none of us have time for a pissing match. Or did someone find Wong while we were all waiting for the family reunion to be over?"

"Is your partner always this much of an asshole?" Stewart asked softly. "Or is he playing the bad cop so you look good?"

"We like to switch things up." Kane pushed the Styrofoam container away from the edge of the table, leaning back in his chair. "I don't think in this case anyone is going to be the good cop. Whatever you said to Miki back there screwed with his head a little bit, so I'm kind of on the fence about you, Stewart."

The office was large enough for Casey to have a meeting table set up in one corner, and the lieutenant had suggested they discuss the case behind closed doors. He'd agreed to it solely so he didn't have to deal with his siblings and father hovering nearby, but having Miki's father only a few feet away meant the man was within strangling distance. Stymied by Miki's hasty exit, Kane wondered if he would be throttling Stewart before the end of the day.

"I don't know Micah—Miki—well enough to tell you how he's doing right now, but mostly I think he's dealing with losing his mom. Shit, I thought I had dealt with losing her years ago, but seeing him brought everything back." Stewart bit off his words, throwing them out at Kane like they were poker chips and he needed to lay them down before a roulette wheel was spun. He had a frenetic energy to him, a wound-up-tight vibe Kane knew all too well. If it was Miki, he would know what to do, but Stewart was a whole different kettle of fish. The man stood, pacing off a few feet. Turning back around, he said, "I fucked up his life. And I pretty much got her killed. I don't expect I'll be invited to the Christmas dinner anytime soon, but I really wanted—*want*—to know my son. I woke up this morning knowing I wasn't going to be able to apologize for what happened, but I sure as hell didn't think I'd break him."

"He was broken the moment Hall picked him up and threw him into the system," Kane growled. "I'm not going to tell you what was done to him because those are his secrets, his pain. I can tell you there's room in his life for another father, but you're going to have to earn it."

"Shit, with Miki you have to earn every single fucking inch." Kel snorted. "I like him, but he's hard, and knowing everything that I do about him, I don't blame him. Still, *every fucking inch*."

"And he's worth it." Kane rocked back in his chair, lifting its front legs off the floor as he watched Stewart make a circuit around the room. "He and my da are close. I wouldn't have expected it because Miki doesn't have much space in his life for cops and authority—despite loving me—and my family bleeds blue. But there is something about their relationship that humbles me, because it's not like the one I have with my da. Miki is his son, so he knows what it's like to have a father, but that father is Donal. You're going to have to show him that there's other ways of being a dad, because you're not the man my father is and you never will be. That's nothing against you but everything for him, and that's how Miki sees him."

"So it doesn't sound like I've got much of a chance," Stewart sneered. "Why the hell should I bother, then?"

"How's that saying go?" Kel chuckled. "Apple doesn't fall far from the tree? Looks like Miki just rolled off the branch and laid there."

"Aye, they're very disagreeable," Kane muttered, rolling his eyes. "What I'm saying is you have to tell him what you're about and show him that you'll be there if he needs you. And right now, the best thing you can do is help us get Wong and Zhou off the streets, because Miki isn't safe until we do. Just go slowly with him, and if he tells you to back off, step away. Give him some room, because he needs it and we've just gotten him to the point where he tells us."

"What did he do before? Knife you?" Stewart stopped his pacing. "Because the bastard punched me in the nose. I didn't even see it coming. It was that fast."

"You should be glad he didn't pick up the chair and hit you with it," Kel added. "That's a thing with him.

Don't get into a fight with Miki and expect to come out with all of your teeth. He'll grab whatever is nearby and fuck you up. Most guys get into a fight to prove their point. Miki gets into a fight to kill you."

"Lovely. My son is a rabid ferret," the former agent growled. "Well, lucky for me, ferrets are legal in this city. They are, aren't they?"

"They are. So how about if we table our boxing match until later and get down to work?" Kane gestured at the chair next to him. "If you're smart, get my da on your side. It'll go a long way in smoothing out your relationship. I'd say try to sweet-talk my mom into helping you, but she's a harder nut to crack than Miki."

Kane didn't think he was ever going to get used to seeing Miki's expressions on another man's face. Stewart sat down and picked at the nachos in front of him. He looked weary, his shoulders slumped forward, and the silver shot through his hair gleamed under the fluorescent lights. He was a handsome man in a lot of ways, someone Kane might have given a second look to a few years ago, but now he only saw a package of trouble landing on his front porch.

Stewart began to talk. "Wong was big on family, probably still is. His sister ran a lot of things, but her ex-husband was a piece of shit. We got her to flip because she'd wanted the ex killed, but Wong refused because the guy was running a lot of books for him and doing a good job.

"He didn't hurt her, but he was definitely holding her back, because while he was good at numbers, he wasn't really good at being faithful. Danny didn't see that as a problem, but Susan did. About a few years into Danny's prison term, Susan's ex-husband ended up dead and she got sole custody. She keeps saying the reason she dropped out of protection was because of her kid, but truth is, she probably missed the power. Susan likes being rich, and from what I hear, her kid is more like her than her ex. Have you guys talked to her son?"

"We've got Chang down at Gang Task Force trying to get us a meeting, but the guy is slippery and we can't nail him down. We did a meet and greet with Susan Wong-Lee before she headed to China, but the biggest thing she dropped on us was your name." Kel resumed eating, passing Kane a napkin as he dug into his fries. "We got Zhou from Hall."

"What we have on Zhou is a bit spotty. A lot from the days when you were on that case, but not much afterwards." Kane reached for the pile of folders he'd brought in with him. Finding the one on Zhou, he opened it up, careful not to drip food on the pages. "Don't have good photos and nobody by that name appears to have a driver's license in the database, so we don't have anything to go on there. Who else would he have gone to after Wong went in?"

Stewart rattled off a few names, but Kel shook his head when he heard them and said, "All of those guys are dead or incarcerated. We were hoping for a hit with Adam Lee's known associates, but it doesn't seem like he picked up any of his uncle's lackeys."

"What we're going to need you to do is look through the current photos that we have of Wong's people and tell us who you think can give us a lead." Kane slid over a pack of mug shots. "Chang's been great for active players, but we're looking at people we may be able to dig into because they don't want Wong in their lives. And since Hall took himself off the playing board, you're all I've got now. Find me somebody so I don't have to keep Miki in a box anymore."

"So I guess you were pissed off at him?" Damien stretched out as much as he could in the back of the black sedan, slinging his long legs over Miki's thighs. "Enough that you needed to see your therapist?"

"Shut up. You know I had an appointment with her this morning and it just lined up with meeting him," Miki replied with a scowl, giving his brother a fierce look. "Are you mocking the whole therapy thing?"

"Sinjun, I am for anything that makes you feel better inside." He smiled, warm and affectionate. It was comforting to have Damien's weight on his legs and the touch of his fingers on Miki's arm to leech away the bristling aggravation he'd nursed since they left the police station together. "I thought I would ask you about it now because you didn't seem much like talking on the way over to Penny's office."

Miki glanced up at the back of Dan's head, conscious of how much the security guard could overhear between them. He must've felt Miki's eyes on him because the man looked up into the rearview mirror, then smirked. Reaching out, he touched a button on the sedan's cockpit-like dashboard and a smoked window rose from a crevice in the front bench seat's hard plastic backing. Miki mouthed *sorry* but didn't know if Dan could see it through the tinted glass.

"Never thought I would see the day when you cared about how somebody else felt… that didn't come out how I meant it to," Damien objected when Miki balled up his fist. "Don't be a pain in the ass. I know you're not going to hit me."

"I hit *him*." Miki's confession pulled out a small laugh from Damien. "It's not funny. I've got anger issues, remember? That's the whole point of going to see her."

"Did you hit him because you were angry?" he asked, not bothering to hide his mirth. "Or because you got scared? Because from what you told me, he came around the table and tried to put his hands on you. I know and love you, Sinjun, but you're not someone who welcomes the random cuddle and hug."

"People should warn you or at least warn *me*," Miki grumbled under his breath. "You just don't go around grabbing people. So I punched him. Like I meant to. It just happened."

"Well, at least you didn't hit him with a chair."

"I think I was going to, but it was too heavy. Cops should really rethink their furniture. You could kill somebody with those things if you really wanted to."

"Pretty sure anyone else sitting in that room with an intent to kill," Damien reminded him, "usually are wearing handcuffs and there's cops with guns right next to them."

Miki leaned against Damien, needing to touch something—*someone*—warm and solid in his life. He'd wanted to throw himself at Kane when he left the interview room, but it would've looked weak. And he wasn't ready to be that vulnerable in front of his father. He got a quick one-armed hug from Donal, and then he'd given them a flurry of excuses, reminding everyone of his therapist appointment.

Penny had been shocked to see him two hours early, but she'd taken him in and he'd stalked into her counseling room, grateful she'd been willing to see him during the time she'd set aside for paperwork. He'd poured his heart and soul out to her, unable to sit down, and the room seemed too small—too hemmed in—for him to work off the anxiety crinkling beneath his skin. An hour and a half later, she finally got a word in edgewise, or at least it took him that long to hear her. What she asked him struck Miki hard, and he reeled back, wishing he had an answer for the question she threw at him.

He still didn't have an answer, but Damien's presence made it easier to think.

"Penny asked me if I was mad that he was alive," Miki whispered. "Or if I wished he was dead because it would be easier to deal with him that way. Because of all the people who hurt me, the only one left alive to ask for my forgiveness is someone who never meant to hurt me. So she thinks I'm—I could be—pouring all of the shitty things I feel inside of me about Vega, Shing, and even that asshole Hall into how I feel about my real father."

"It's not a bad way to look at things," Damien agreed. "Especially since you know your mom pretty much loved the hell out of you. Seems like the only one you have left to be mad at is him, especially since you're no longer pissed off at Brigid."

"I was never pissed off at Brigid," Miki corrected.

"I think—and this is coming from knowing you for years—a lot of how you felt about Brigid had to do with how you felt about your mom before she became real to you and you found out about how she was." Damien's voice dropped, a gentle, soothing tone softening his words. "Up until a few weeks ago, your mother was somebody you avoided talking about, hell, even thinking about, because there was always a part of you wondering if she wanted you. So you took that and put it on Brigid, even though you knew she wanted to love you as much as she loves Forest and any of her other boys. So that leaves your dad, someone safe for you to be angry at."

Miki wanted to tell Damien to fuck off, but the words lodged in his throat, unable to crawl past the bitterness he had nursed inside of him. He'd hated the idea of his mother for so long, to be faced with the truth of who she was knocked the wind out of him, and then Stewart stepped into the place Miki'd made for her years before. He wanted to deny the anger burning in his chest, and Miki opened his mouth, ready to argue, ready to find some way out of where Penny's words put him, but as he was about to speak, Dan's voice boomed through the speakers built into the sedan's sound system.

"Get down!" Dan's voice was sharp, harsh with panic and worry.

Then Miki's world turned over.

Again.

CHAPTER TWENTY-TWO

Stealing our money
Diluting our minds
Taking from the forgotten
Beaten for no crime
You tell me to watch my mouth
Spit on me and tell me to drown
I'm telling you Jack
To watch your own ass
Always getting back up
Just so I can take you down
—My Life, Not Yours

IT WAS Miki's worst nightmare.

One he'd been in and relived for years.

And again, one of the most precious people in his life was with him when his world began spinning.

The horrific crunch of metal on metal was a sound guaranteed to pull in his muscles until he folded, fetal and trembling. He couldn't tell if there was blood in his mouth or the echoing taste of past horrors rising from his mind, slapping him back in time when death tore his world away from him, tore his band of brothers away from him.

They were only a block away from the police station when the large SUV blasted out of an alley and slammed into the sedan. The brazen hit happened too quickly for Dan to do anything other than shout a warning before the car was lifted off its tires and rolled.

And God did it roll.

They'd been on a side street, a lane and a half of one-way traffic tucked in between squat buildings decorated with flashing red banners celebrating the upcoming moon festival, vivid splashes of color against the drab, fading baby blue and pink hues dominating the area. The hit was quick and violent, flipping the car over, and Miki's view filled with a Neapolitan swirl of pastel ice cream colors and blacktop. The stink of rubber burning overwhelmed him. Then, as abruptly as it began, the sedan stopped turning, skidding across the sidewalk and slamming into something hard and unyielding.

It was incredible how silent the world got when it held its breath.

So much of that night came rushing back to Miki, much like it had when the truck struck the band's limo during their tour. This time it seemed easier. This time when the sedan tumbled, he grabbed Damien and held on tight. He was still holding him when the car came to a rest. He ached, and his knee protested when he moved, but the warmth of Damien's body in his arms gave Miki hope.

The car lay on its passenger side, tiny bits of broken glass scattered all over the back seat and both windshields were spiderwebbed, their tint film holding the panes together, but the rear was beginning to buckle, falling into the cab. A trickle of blood ran down Miki's forehead, but even through the throbbing pound along his skull, he only had one concern—making sure his brother was still alive.

"Damien!" Miki cried out to his brother, needing to see his crystal blue eyes. Shaking Damien, Miki swallowed the vomit rising up from his stomach, driven by fear he couldn't wish away. "Oh God, *please*. Don't leave me again! Fucker! Don't you fucking leave me again!"

"Sinjun…." Damien groaned. "Fuck, hurts. My ribs. Stop."

"Are you two okay?" Dan grunted from the front seat, his body caught up in the belt. He hung over the dashboard, his weight on the buckle. Miki heard him moving around, then a small boom followed when Dan kicked open the driver's side door. "Hang on. Stay down. I'm going to get you guys out."

Dan didn't get farther than hoisting himself up out of the open door.

The shots were a storm of noise and blood. Damien curled an arm around Miki, trying to pull him down into the well between the seats, but moving must have caused him so much pain his face turned white and he went limp, passing out in Miki's embrace. Dan went slack, falling back into the seat belt's webbing. Blood dripped from holes puncturing the back of his suit, and his face was turned away from Miki, making it hard to see if he was still alive. The car rocked when a bullet hit it, but nothing seemed to be penetrating its steel shell.

Damien was still breathing, and he moaned when Miki slapped his face. The color returned to his skin and his eyes fluttered open, but when Miki reached for Dan, he got no response from the security guard. Shifting his weight, Miki dug his heels into the back seat's headrest, trying to leverage himself up. Damien coughed, and his fingers were cold when they brushed on Miki's exposed stomach where his T-shirt rode up.

Damien ground out, "Where are you going? Someone is shooting at us. You've got to stay—"

"I can't tell how hurt Dan is, and I'm not going to sit here and wait for someone to kill me. Or to kill you." Miki knew Dan had a weapon on him, and he fumbled at the man's side, pulling back his jacket, trying to ignore the gush of warm blood on his hand. He found the gun and drew it, steeling himself for what he knew was waiting for him outside of the car. "D, find your phone or mine and call 911. Dan needs help now."

"Sinjun!" was all Miki heard as he shouldered open the back door, then launched himself out of the car.

What he knew about guns was pretty slim. Kane had tried to show him a few things, and the two times they'd gone to a shooting range he'd done well enough for Connor to make a joke about Miki becoming a cop. That remark reaped Connor a filthy look and put the rest of the Morgans into a laughing fit Miki hadn't thought they would ever recover from.

Guns—any kind of real weapon, really—were not his thing. Going into a fight terrified him, and he always went in fueled by rage and fear to end the conflict quickly. There was no way he was ever going to go back into the cage Vega built for him, and he sure as hell wasn't going to let anyone take Damien away from him again.

Even if he had to die doing it.

The adrenaline pouring through him softened his rough landing on the uneven road. Trusting the car to protect Damien and Dan, Miki kept himself tucked and took in what he could of the street's uproar. Someone was screaming at the top of their lungs from an open window nearby, and an SUV's driver's side door hung open, its front end smashed into the sedan's undercarriage. In the chaos of broken glass and torn metal, Miki heard footsteps through the debris, and then a haggard, skinny Asian man walked out from around the totaled SUV.

Miki didn't need to know anything more about the older man, especially when he spotted the lethal-looking black gun held to his side. And if he needed any further incentive, Miki got it when the man's hangdog face curdled into a sick smile when he spotted Miki and raised his gun, aiming it at Miki's head.

"Fuck you, asshole." Miki returned the man's smile and fired.

"WE'VE GOT an active shooter not more than a block away from here!" A uniformed young woman popped her head into Casey's office, her cheeks flushed and her eyes bright with excitement. "They're calling for all hands on deck."

"Stay here. Don't move until we come back," Kane ordered Stewart. "I want you someplace we can put our hands on you."

It took them less than five minutes before Kel and Kane were on the street, but fighting a stream of cops while pulling on a bulletproof vest was never easy. Tugging on the last of his vest's straps, Kel fell into step behind him, shouting directions at Kane's back. The choppy burr of a police helicopter grew closer and its loudspeaker buzzed with indistinct instructions, but Kane knew from experience they were warnings for civilians to stay inside.

"Which way? Where do they want us to cover?" Kane yelled at his partner, who finally caught up with him.

"Half block over, side street. Cut in and across." Kel's directions echoed the dispatcher droning through Kane's earpiece. "Just run. Shooter's gone, but there's victims on the street. Uniforms are doing sweeps."

If there was ever a time that Kane was thankful for Miki's seemingly endless energy and need for long rambling walks, it was now when he needed stamina more than speed. Sirens drowned out everything, making it hard for Kane to hear the dispatcher or Kel, but the wail of an ambulance cutting through the singsong screams of police cars was never a good sign.

Neither was the sea of uniforms surrounding an all-too-familiar black sedan and a long-limbed, hazel-eyed rock star who made kitten noises during sex and liked to eat raw ramen noodles.

"Miki!" His throat went raw with his scream, and when Miki turned to give him a wavering smile, Kane's world dropped out from under him. He couldn't remember crossing the distance between them, but a heartbeat later Miki was in his arms, and he was shaking off a uniform insisting Kane step back.

"You're bleeding, Mick. What the fuck happened?" Kane cupped Miki's face, tenderly pressing his thumb against the gash on Miki's temple. "Did anyone look at you?"

"Sir, I'm going to have to ask you to let him go." The thick-necked officer wrapped his meaty hand around Kane's upper arm. They were of similar heights, but the cop had nothing on Kane's rage, and he reeled back when their eyes met. The cop's gaze flicked down to Kane's vest, POLICE emblazoned in white across his chest, and then to the badge hanging from a lanyard around his neck. "I'm sorry. I just need to secure the scene, and he's got residue on him. I need to keep him—"

"Kane, I'm fine. Quit eating this guy's face and let me go so the Forensics guys can do whatever they need to do," Miki murmured, breaking Kane's anger at being shoved back. "Damie's hurt and Dan—our guy—was shot so much. They won't let me get Damien out—"

"I'll see about Damien," Kel said, patting Kane on the back as he went by. "Ambulance is pulling up, but there's some guys already on scene. I'll see if they've got the driver stabilized and check in on your boy's brother."

"Where's the shooter?" Kane said to the cop, and then turned toward Miki. "Miki, stay here and I'll go help hunt the guy down. He couldn't have gone far."

"The guy split as soon as I shot him. He got into an old beater. I don't know what kind, but the thing looked like it was about to fall apart. I didn't see who was driving it, but I did get a look at the old guy who shot at us." Miki glanced over his shoulder at where EMTs were climbing onto the car to assess their patients. He chewed his lip and his hands began to tremble. "Kane, I've got to get to Damie. I... he can't go to the hospital without me."

"You shot at somebody? With what?" If Kane already didn't have a glacier of worry in his guts, hearing Miki had exchanged fire with his attacker would have sent him into a frenzy. "Where was the man Sionn gave you guys?"

"I told you, Dan got shot—"

"Sir, I've got to get someone to take care of his hands first. There's no way." The officer stopped short when Kane's gaze found his face. "Look, I'm just trying to do my job. I'd appreciate it if you backed me up. I don't need to lock horns with you, sir, because I know I'm going to lose every time, but I was the first on scene and I've got to follow protocol."

"I know. Sorry. It's an active case, and this is the second time someone's gone after him," Kane grumbled. "Mick, let me find someone to take care of testing you. We just need to exclude you from being the shooter. It's procedure. Officer Kendricks, you got the gun secured, yes?"

"Everything's locked down. I just need to get a kit going on him, then he's good to go. I've got a witness saying he saw Mr. St. John climb out of the struck vehicle, but I want to cross everything off the list. I don't want anyone at the DA's office coming back at me saying I didn't catch everything." Kendricks nodded at another cop heading toward them. "That's my partner with the kit. Just give us ten minutes and we can release you, sir. We've got an APB out on an early eighties Volvo painted primer red. One of the other responding officers saw it turning the corner, but we didn't know it was connected to the case until we caught up here. There's a bank across the street by the intersection. Someone's already gone there to ask for any surveillance footage."

"Good job. Okay, Mick, you stay here and do the damned test. I'll go check on Damien and Dan for you, okay?" Kane sucked in a long breath. He didn't like the shivers running through Miki's body any more than he did the worried fret of Miki's teeth on his lower lip. "*A ghra*, stop that. You're going to bite through your lip if you keep doing that. It'll be okay."

"You can't promise me that, Kane." Miki's eyes went flat, accusatory and firm. "You didn't see Dan. You didn't see what that fucker did to him. Or to Damie."

"I can promise you the EMTs will do their best. And we'll get you there." One gurney, then another joined the circus around the upturned sedan, and Kane watched as one of the EMTs climbed down into the car. Miki paced, turning around in a small circle as he kept his attention on the medical techs. "Go with Officer Kendricks and get this done. We've got a handful of head shots you can go through and see if one of them was the guy you saw today."

He hated leaving Miki, hated turning his back on the best man who'd ever walked into his life, but Kane pushed himself to take the first step toward the car, then another one, reaching the vehicle as the medics were pulling a limp man strapped to a bodyboard out of the front seat.

If Kane had a choice, he would never leave Miki again.

As he drew nearer to the car, Kane heard possibly the sweetest thing he could ever encounter in the middle of such widespread carnage—a husky, aggravated British voice loudly complaining, "I'm telling you, I'm fine. Just get me out of—*ouch*—that's my arm. *Fuck*."

It appeared that the Mitchell part of the Mitchell-St. John brotherhood was still intact and running on all cylinders.

By the time Kane picked carefully through the debris from the damaged cars, the EMTs had gotten Dan clear of the front seat and were working on pulling Damien out of the rear. The gurney holding the security guard moved quickly, a paramedic working on Dan's chest; his chin dipped and his mouth worked fast, spitting out instructions and his patient's current state into a mouthpiece fixed to his shirt.

"Where are they taking them?" Kane asked one of the attending techs. "I've got to follow with the other passenger of the car. I want him looked at too."

The tech rattled off the name of a nearby hospital, then grimaced as another streak of blue cut-glass profanities filled the air. "St. John's already refused medical, and the other one is about a step behind that right now. If you can get him to change his mind and cooperate, I'd appreciate it."

"Let me see what I can do, because Miki won't get looked at unless someone is poking at Damien." Kane stepped over more debris, trying like hell to ignore the blood pooling near the sedan's front tire. It was difficult to get enough height to see into the wide sedan, but standing on the sidewalk helped, and when he put his hand on the door to steady himself, it creaked, then fell to the ground. Peering in, he muttered, "Great, now even the car's trying to kill me. Damien, quit being an ass and let these guys get you to the hospital. Miki's bleeding across his head and if you don't go, he won't go. I don't give a shit if you bleed out, but I swear to God, if he's got a concussion and—"

"Stop your threatening, you overgrown leprechaun," Damie complained, his shoulders wedged against the back seat as he lay half on a bodyboard the EMTs were trying to work under him. "I'm going. Is Sinjun okay? He took Dan's gun, and that was the last time I saw him. None of these fuckers will tell me what's going on."

"He's okay, but I want him to get looked at. Dan looks like he's in bad shape, and Miki's going to chew through his lip soon." Kane moved aside as one of the technicians slid down into the car. "I'm going to follow you with him unless I can get him into the bus with you—"

"They're putting me in a bus?" Damien snarled when the EMT's fingers touched the spot on his side. "Bloody hell that *fucking* hurts."

"Just it's what they call an ambulance. Just get on the damned thing and stop complaining. I'm going to have silver hair by the time you two are done causing trouble today." Kane sighed as he heard Miki swear loudly at one of the cops. "And if I have to kill one of you in order to get the other to behave, it's going to be you, because I can always beg forgiveness from Sionn, but I can't live without Miki."

"I DON'T know why they're keeping Damien if he's okay. Dan, I get. Son of a bitch took three shots and had surgery, but Damie said he was fine. They should have let him come home." Miki's bitching followed Kane into the kitchen, but his cop didn't look back. Instead, Kane got out a couple of short glasses from a cabinet, then dropped an ice cube into each. After setting the glasses on the counter, he reached for one of the whiskey bottles left on the bar. Holding up the amber-liquid–filled bottle, Kane lifted his eyebrows, silently asking Miki if he wanted some. Nodding, Miki snorted. "Why don't you just bring the bottle with you? We can sit on the couch and get drunk."

"Because, Miki mine, I have to work tomorrow, and it is one in the morning. If I am going to lose sleep tonight, it's not going to be because I fell into a bottle," Kane said, pouring out about a finger of whiskey into each glass. He stalked back into the living room, where Miki leaned against the couch arm, to hand over one of the shots. Clinking his glass against Miki's, Kane said, "If I am going to wake up tomorrow bleary-eyed and sore, it's going to be from me having my way with you until you're too tired to leave the bed for at least a week. Maybe that way, I'll know where you are and I won't worry so much."

With that, Kane drained his glass.

Shaking his head, Miki took a sip of his whiskey, then sighed. "It's not like we went out looking for trouble. This time he came and found us."

"It always comes and finds you. This Sunday, I'm going to go into Saint Anthony's, light a candle, and ask God to give you your own guardian angel because I really need the help," he muttered as he took the glass out of Miki's hand.

"Hey! That's mine." The whiskey went down Kane's throat; then he handed Miki back the empty glass. Staring mournfully at the few drops left pooling around the crackling ice cube, Miki said, "Dude—"

"They're keeping Damie because they want to make sure he's not done anything to his guts. And as for the whiskey, I forgot, you have a concussion. So none for you."

"Maybe. I *might* have a concussion. Doc said he wasn't sure," Miki corrected. "And I deserve something after today. I even looked at all the damned photos you gave me. Not my fault the guy wasn't there. Or if he was, I didn't recognize him."

Kane's face changed. Under the scant light, he looked older and more tired than Miki'd seen before. He reached up to touch Kane's mouth when Kane cupped Miki's jaw, pulling his chin up and staring down into his eyes.

Emotions played about in the smoky blue depths of Kane's gaze, flickers of awareness Miki couldn't begin to pin down. His cop was often hard to read, masked behind a veil of authority when working, and sometimes, despite Kane's best efforts, the blood and gore followed him home, deepening the shadows in his eyes.

And sometimes, Miki was the reason Kane shouldered a darkness he'd never asked for and couldn't quite seem to shake.

"I love you, *a ghra*," Kane murmured. Pressing his mouth to the taped-over slice on Miki's temple, he hooked his arm around Miki's waist, pulling him closer. "God, I can't take many more days like this. I want to put you in a room until this is all over so I know you're safe."

"Dude, I'm already stuck in the warehouse. Anything smaller and I'm going to chew my own leg off." He kissed Kane's thumb, then bit at its swell. Hissing, Kane jerked his finger out of Miki's mouth and let go of his face, shaking his hand. "Today was… *fuck*, that guy pissed me off."

"I still can't believe you shot him," Kane whispered. "And you don't know if you hit?"

"No idea. I just pointed and pulled the trigger. Dan shouldn't drive with the safety off, but hell if I'm complaining about that. I just wanted that guy gone. I wasn't going to go all Duck Hunt on him." Miki shrugged. "I just wanted him to know I wasn't going to go down easy. And I'd be fucked if he got to Damie or Dan."

He let himself be cuddled, sliding his legs in between Kane's. His knee hurt, and he was pretty sure he still had bits of glass in his hair, but it felt good to be home.

It felt like heaven being in Kane's arms.

"How about if you and I take a shower and I wash every inch of that gorgeous, bruised body of yours." Kane bent his head, stealing a brief kiss. "Then, if you're up to it, let me show you how damned glad I am you got to come home with me."

CHAPTER TWENTY-THREE

Rock a bye, baby, don't say a word
Your cradle is broken, childhood's all
    blurred
In the house you once lived, all the win-
    dows are black
Not who they wanted, can never go back
Come play in the sunshine, We've all
    gathered here
Laugh at the rainbows, learn to grin ear
    to ear
So come find this family,
Painting their roses bright bright red
Come to us, Alice, And be loved instead
—Roses for Alice

THE ONLY thing Miki hated more than waking up alone was waking up alone with a note telling him it was okay he fell asleep on Kane.

Still, his body ached in so many places, and the car tumbling about on a Chinatown street fucked up his knee something fierce. He hadn't felt any pain in the joint when it happened, but as soon as the adrenaline and then relief at Damien's well-being drained away, Miki found himself reaching for the bottle of painkillers he hadn't touched in months.

Dude gave him a reproachful look when he heard the rattle of pills.

"Look, I fucking hurt and the stuff is supposed to take the swelling down," he informed the dog. "Not like I'm going to take a handful. *Just one.*"

Cradling the bottle in his hand, Miki realized it had been years since he'd had the urge to empty an entire bottle into his palm, toss the whole thing into his mouth, and wash it down with a fifth of Jack.

"You were the start of pulling me away from that shit. You know that, Dude?" Miki scratched the dog's ear, and Dude's leg thumped against the bed in appreciation. "And Kane was the rest of it. But you man, if it weren't for you, I wouldn't have hung on. So, just one so I can get out of bed without screaming like a smoky jungle frog."

It took five minutes for Miki to get out of bed. Most of it was spent cuddling the dog, but he was very much aware of every twinge in his knee when he stretched out his leg. Huffing short breaths, he gingerly swung his legs off the edge of the bed, then stood, sucking air in between clenched teeth until he could handle the sharp jabs along the joint.

The dog, however, jumped off easily and trotted out of the bedroom.

By the time Miki got to the front of the warehouse, he was breathing hard and disgusted to find another note from Kane taped to the bathroom door.

"*Call Liam when you get up. Damien is fine but Sionn is going to check them into a hotel so he doesn't have to climb the stairs. There is probably a message on your phone—which I plugged in for you since it was dead—from Damien telling you which hotel. Mom probably will check on you later and Da sends his love. I love you too. Eat something*," Miki read the note to Dude after he was done with the bathroom. "The p.s. says you've already been fed and outside. But you probably need to potty."

Kane was right. A message from Damien was waiting, telling him that they'd not ended up in a hotel, choosing instead to take up Rafe's offer of his penthouse, considering he and Quinn had moved into Quinn's home near the Morgans. Frowning, he texted his brother, then tossed his phone onto the couch, intending to grab Dude's leash from the hook by the front door.

"Shit, I used to call Dan to cover me. Who the hell do I contact now?" Miki looked at the dog doing his potty dance across the living room floor. "I'll text Sionn. He's got to have somebody outside there. Hold on, Dude. I'm just going to take you out in the back."

It was a quick, furtive trip, and Dude seemed to understand Miki's urgency, hastily doing his business, then bolting back in through the open door.

Still… it wasn't quick enough.

Crouching at the back door to undo the latch on Dude's leash, Miki didn't see the man creeping up behind him until he felt hands on his shoulders. Startled, he swung his left arm back, his elbow connecting with something hard, but his knee—*his damned knee*—gave out.

The pain was incredible. Nothing like he'd ever felt before, and it overwhelmed him, digging sickening shards into his stomach. His guts churned and he tried to swallow the bile coursing up his throat, but Miki couldn't keep it down. Spitting out a mouthful of sticky green saliva, he fumbled to reach the doorknob, screaming at Dude to get back. Instead, the dog let loose a furious barking storm, his teeth gleaming white before disappearing into the fleshy mound of the hand on Miki's right arm.

It was enough of a distraction for the clawlike hand to jerk back, pulling Dude with it. Turning over, Miki kicked out with his good leg, hoping to hit any part of the man's body, but his insides turned to ice when he caught a peek of a gun drawn out of the man's loose jacket.

He knew that face. He'd seen it before it had a bandage plastered across the cheek. Up close, it looked even more haggard than it had yesterday. Deep lines gouged into long brackets on either side of the man's thin mouth, and his greased-back thinning dark hair gave in to gravity, flopping over his gaunt face. Folds of skin nearly obscured his eyes, pleats of crêpe-thin curtains caught up on his stubby lashes, but his glittering black gaze shone with malevolence Miki could almost taste. He was skinny to the point of almost being skeletal, and Miki's mind fought with the memories of Shing crawling over him. They looked enough alike—smelled enough alike—for Miki's body to react violently to the echoes of repulsion gathered in the corners of his mind.

Dude refused to let go, and Miki screamed as the older man brought his gun up to the dog's head, shouting at Miki with a spittle-flecked rage, "Lie face down or I will kill it. Just like your mother."

"Answer's still fuck you, asshole!" Miki kicked, catching the man's hip. He flung back, stumbling down the short stoop, and landed in a puddle. The gun was still in his hand, but Dude was loose and Miki called him, "Dude! *Home!*"

The terrier had very few tricks in his bag, but the one thing he knew was *home*. Kane worked diligently to get Dude to respond to normal commands, but the dog, in true owned-by-Miki fashion, marched to the beat of his own drum. There were very few people he respected enough to follow and barely a handful of words he acknowledged understanding, but he always listened when Miki told him to go home.

The dog raced into the warehouse, and Miki twisted to reach the knob, slamming the door shut as soon as Dude was clear. It was a struggle for him to get on his feet, but he forced himself through the pain. He only needed to stand long enough to do one thing: launch himself at the man lying in the middle of the alleyway.

"ARE YOU the inspector looking for my uncle?" A slender, pretty-faced Chinese man intercepted Kane as he exited the coffee shop.

The street was full of people much like Kane, whose hands were loaded down with two coffee cups—one for him and one for Kel—and he debated tossing the lattes aside and reaching for his weapon. Something in his face must have given his thoughts away because the young man shook his head, then held his hands up.

"I'm not here to cause problems, but rather provide solutions." He cocked his head, drawing Kane's attention to a café table on the coffee shop's outside patio, its two empty chairs guarded by a pair of enormous, placid-faced men dressed in jeans and oversized leather jackets. The table had been separated from the rest of the patio, occupying a far corner of the gated area, giving them enough privacy to have a talk without attracting too much notice. "If we could just sit and talk for a moment, I think I can help you."

"I don't know. My partner's coffee will probably be cold by the time I get back if I do." Kane matched the man's professional smile with a scowl. "He really hates being kept waiting. Especially if I'm the one doing the coffee run."

"I can make it worth your while," he replied. "And I can get An Chan to get you a couple of lattes before you leave. Please. It is imperative that you and I talk."

"You first." Kane nodded at the table. "I'll follow."

The other tables were occupied by tourists and people with late enough of a morning start to be able to sit and have a leisurely cup of coffee. A small cloud of harmless chatter followed them, mostly people making plans to take advantage of the relatively nice day, but he did hear a murmur of appreciation from a woman eyeing the young man's ass as he walked by.

His companion must have heard the comment, because a small smile was on his face when he sat down. The men standing near the table made way for Kane, distancing themselves with a few short strides to lean on the wrought iron fence enclosing the patio.

"I take it you are Adam Lee. The last photo I have of you must be from a few years ago. You look *different*." Kane eased himself into the open chair, setting the coffee cups down. "Unless there is somebody else's uncle that I am looking for."

"My apologies. I should've introduced myself. I have recently lost a lot of weight, so my face was round." Adam puffed out his cheeks. "And well, it has been a while since I have had the police take my picture. I was *maybe* nineteen?"

"We've left messages for you and heard nothing, so I'm a little bit curious as to why you are here right now." Kane gave a slight shrug, giving Lee a thin smile. "Other than the fact that they make really good coffee. I met your mother. Nice woman. Said she didn't know anything about where your uncle was."

Kane kept an eye on the men behind Lee, not seeing any bulges beneath their jackets, but it was harder to tell if someone was armed under thick leather. One of them met Kane's gaze and smiled, warm enough that Kane almost viewed it as flirtatious. Lee glanced behind him, smirking when he saw his employee's expression go blank.

"They act like I beat them, but mostly the guys like pretending they're hard-core." Lee chuckled. "Since we are going to be getting your partner a new coffee, do you mind if I have his?"

"Help yourself," Kane replied, moving Kel's latte over. "You said something about your uncle?"

"And you said something about my mother," he murmured, picking up the coffee but not bringing it to his mouth. "My uncle is causing problems. Small ones, but violent ones."

"I don't consider Sandy Chaiprasit and Rodney Chin being killed a small problem." Kane shoved his hands into his pockets, feeling for his phone. The men by the fence stiffened, and the one who hadn't smiled at him reached for the edge of his jacket, stopping only when Kane fixed a glare on him. "You might want to tell your friends that if I see them reaching one more time, we'll be having this discussion someplace you would not like."

"None of my men are armed, Inspector. Well, not with a gun. Sammy probably has a baton, which he is going to leave in his pocket. You have to understand, with my uncle running around loose, it has made us all very jumpy." Lee slouched back in his chair. He looked more like a game developer than a crime lord, especially with his artfully tousled black hair framing his narrow face and the nervous energy pouring off his slender frame. "I've never known my uncle. I was a few years old when he was put away. But I've heard enough stories from my mother. He is a… disruption. Not just to business but to my family."

"My family too," Kane pointed out.

"It is your family I do not want harmed or pissed off at me," he said with a rueful expression on his face. "I inherited a business that sometimes operates in gray areas. A lot of businesses in Chinatown do, but I work very hard to keep things legal, even sometimes if it is at a disadvantage to me. Unfortunately, I still have people who feel a familial connection to my uncle Danny. I need to show them that following those connections— adhering to that misplaced loyalty—will serve them badly in the end. My mother handed me a dynasty, and if there is one thing that I know, one does not get into a war with another powerful family when the law is on their side. And you, Inspector Morgan, belong to a dynasty I do not want to battle."

"And here I thought you hadn't met my father," Kane drawled.

"Your father is just the beginning of your family. You, your brothers—even your sister—are building blocks laid down in a very fertile field. I find it interesting that all of you seem to find a different section of the city and the department to work in, as if you intentionally leave room for the other to take over an area." Lee finally took a sip of his coffee, making a face when Kel's preference for quadruple shots in his latte hit his tongue. "Your partner must be very hairy to drink this all the time."

"I've never actually looked. So, you don't want to get into a fight with the Morgans, but you've got to be careful of your relationship with your mother, even though Danny Wong killed your father?" Kane knew he'd made a hit when Lee's eyes narrowed. "Funny coincidence, your uncle killed my fiancé's mother. Now Wong's trying to kill him and his father, and I don't really have time to stop and have coffee with you unless you can help me get my hands on your uncle."

"That is exactly why I'm here today," Lee remarked. "You see, my mother lied to you when you came to her apartment. She told you that she did not know where my uncle was hiding. The truth was Danny Wong was only a few rooms away from where you were. And the man who served you tea and coffee? That was Mark Zhou, the man who right now would kill me if he knew I had my uncle's body in the back seat of my car."

MIKI DIDN'T give a shit that the man was at least thirty years older than him. Guns had a way of equalizing things. Maybe in some small part of his mind he knew his weak knee would give the other man an advantage. One kick. One good shot. And Miki would be down for the count.

Truth was, none of those things mattered. None of those things entered his mind.

It dawned on him he was staring at a man with a gun who'd come close to murdering him—nearly killed his brother—and worst of all, slaughtered his mother.

"You're a hard one to kill," the man shouted at him, a wide sneer tugging at his thin lips. "You're a cockroach, just like your mother. But even roaches die when stomped on enough."

Achara's faded, smiling face filled Miki's mind, and suddenly his fingers itched to close around the man's neck. The stoop gave him enough height, enough anchor to propel himself forward and onto his mother's killer. There wasn't anything in reach for him to grab. Not really. And that didn't matter. This time he needed to feel the fight against his knuckles and let the blows rattle his shoulders. He was going to hurt. Hell, he already hurt.

One more bruise wasn't going to make a difference, not since he was going to die if he lost the fight.

This time he was going to cause as much pain as was done to him his entire life, because he'd found the man who put him into Vega's hands and tore him away from a woman who may not have been able to give him much but had given him her entire heart and soul. As much as he loved Kane and didn't want to die, deep in his bones Miki knew it was time for someone to care about Achara Sangsom, and that someone would be her son.

His knee found the killer's crotch first. It wasn't going to be a fair fight. Not if Miki could help it. The man grabbed at Miki's hair, yanking to the side as he tried to bring his weapon up, but Miki smashed his fist into the man's cheekbone, slamming his head back. The blow opened up the gunshot crease along his cheek and loosened the bandage over the wound. Blood poured out from under the gauze, and a rivulet caught in the wrinkles around the man's mouth, diverting over his chin and jaw.

Another punch to the man's temple and Miki found himself flying, shoved off by a fierce push. The gun went wide, cast off by the man's frantic flailing to get Miki off him. It landed a few feet away, its muzzle pointed toward Damien's warehouse, its grip submerged in the water running down the middle of the alleyway's length. Miki rolled, scrambling to get to the gun, but his footing gave out from under him, his sneakers unable to get a purchase on the painted concrete's slick surface.

His attacker was already on his feet by the time Miki was halfway up. His jeans were wet from where he'd fallen into the puddles left over from the morning rain. Despite the shadows draped over the alley, the sticky afternoon heat grew and a sudden rush of hot air stole the breath from his lungs. The damp, stiffening fabric wrapped tighter around his swollen knee with each bend of his leg, cutting into his flesh, but Miki couldn't stop.

"I kill you and Danny is free. You should have died back then. You're a mistake I need to fix." The man turned, screaming into Miki's face. His breath was rotten, nearly as hot as the bursts of wind driven down the alley's length. Up close, his skin was patterned with runnels of broken capillaries and sickly yellowing spots. "I told him you were dead. You have to stay dead."

"You're fucking crazy, old man," Miki spat. "And I'm going to show you just how not dead I am."

The first few steps he took toward the gun were good, but the alleyway and its slick ground had other plans. His Converse slid out from under him again, and the killer tumbled past Miki, his outstretched hands reaching for the gun. It hurt to feint, but Miki knew he didn't have a choice. If he didn't get the weapon before the man did, he was as good as dead. Shoving to the right as hard as he could, he caught the man's ribs with his shoulder, throwing him off-balance.

Behind them, Dude continued to rage, tearing the air up with his barks. Miki could only hope he would live and be able to calm the dog down. At this point, he just wanted to be able to survive.

They both landed hard. The man rolled over onto his side, and Miki landed on his back, jarring his spine. Miki twisted around, grinding his hip into the ground, but it gave him enough leverage to shove his fist into the man's open mouth. Throwing one leg across the man's torso, Miki scissored his knees together, trapping the wiry man's limbs between his thighs. Holding tight, he dug his thumb into the hollow of the man's throat, punching again and again until his attacker was gasping for breath.

It was either a lucky shot or the man had seen Miki favor his knee, because in his wild flailing, he struck Miki's aching joint with a mind-staggering blow. Miki couldn't hold on, and he jerked back instinctively, releasing the man and pulling away to protect his injured body. The man didn't follow. Instead, he lunged again for the gun, his nails scrabbling over the drainage grate, ripping them from his fingers.

Unable to catch his breath through the pain, Miki bit down on his lip and climbed over the man, yelping when he felt teeth sink into the tender skin of his underarm. They tangled and rolled, and Miki got a few digs into the man's eyes, shoving his fingertips into any bits of soft flesh he could find.

And then his free hand brushed against the gun.

Grabbing at the weapon, Miki rolled, knowing he needed some distance between him and his attacker in order to get a clean shot. He hit the brick wall of Damien's warehouse, his shoulder lodged into the wooden stair frame they'd built between the buildings for Kane. He tasted blood and his tongue felt like it was shredded, but nothing hurt more than his leg, a pounding throb that seemed to run up his body and straight into his temples. He couldn't see straight, and every time he blinked, the man's silhouette shimmered.

His attacker had already gotten to his feet, and the gun in Miki's hand didn't seem to be slowing him down.

Miki pulled the trigger.

For a brief hiccup of eternity, nothing happened. Miki pulled it again and heard the click, and then he looked up to see the man standing over him, wild-eyed and insane. Lurching forward, he reached, rushing at Miki—then a boom broke over the sound of their heaving breaths.

The man's face was gone. Fuck, his whole head was gone. So was a bit of the brick wall above Miki's head, and then his mother's killer crumpled in on himself, falling forward to land at Miki's side. There was blood everywhere. Bits of bone and brain scattered around Miki's hips, a speckled spray of gore covering his shirt and splattering his cheek. The man's arms flopped and twisted before finally stilling, and his legs gave a final twitch, making a small splash in the runoff from the gutter's spout.

At the end of the alley stood a woman holding a smoking gun.

The click of her heels on the solid ground oddly reminded Miki of Brigid. As she approached, Miki raised the weapon he'd fought so hard to get ahold of. She was beautiful in the way a praying mantis was, her triangular face canting to the side in a robotic tilt and her delicate Chinese features nearly luminescent despite the alleyway's dim light. Her business suit was black—or at least that's what it looked like in the shadows—her pencil skirt ending just above her knees and her porcelain complexion contrasting against the dark color. The red shirt she wore under her jacket was nearly the color of the man's blood, and the strings of pearls hanging around her neck looked too much like bone for Miki's liking.

The older woman was still holding the gun loosely in her hand as she approached the man's sprawled body.

Motioning with her fingers at the weapon he kept trained on her, she said haughtily, "You can put that down. If I was going to shoot you, it would have been from back there."

She gave the man's leg a slight kick, and Miki couldn't tell if it was to check to see if he was really dead or out of spite. He would've guessed spite if her pretty but cold features showed any emotion. When she turned her dark eyes to stare at Miki, he finally saw an expression flicker over her face, and it hung there, a hint of regret and familiarity. She stepped over Miki's feet, then perched on the partially finished stairs, setting her gun down on the deck.

"I was not prepared for how much you look like your mother." She tilted her head to the left as if to get a different view of Miki's face. "I knew her, you know?

She was like a butterfly caught in the same cage as rabid dogs, beating her wings against the bars, but we all knew she would never be free of my brother. At least not until…well, no, even after Danny went to jail, she wasn't free of him."

"I don't know what you want, but—" Miki started to say, keeping the gun turned up despite the nearly unmanageable ache of pain running through him.

"I don't want anything." She sagged a little bit, sighing as she put her hands in her lap, and she began to fidget with a jade band on one of her fingers. "I regret that my brother couldn't see reason. I am sorry he had to force our family into a corner. You see, your inspector said something to me that struck me deep. I am a mother—nothing I *ever* forget, mind you—but he reminded me that you are a son without a mother. One we took from you. In Danny's rantings about murdering you, I'd forgotten that. Your mother was very sweet, but she wasn't smart. If she'd been intelligent, she wouldn't have made a living on her back. Still, she never would've abandoned you. A mother doesn't abandon her son."

"So you came to kill him because you remembered my mom was sweet?" Miki hitched himself up against the wall, hoping to steady his aim. He wasn't going to drop the weapon, especially since he heard sirens echoing through the streets. "Lady, there's something really fucking wrong with your family."

"No, I killed him because I was reminded I was in debt to your mother for protecting my son from his uncle when I stupidly allowed the federal government to hide me away, or I would've shot you to protect myself." She lifted her chin as if to study the clouds she could see in the stretch of sky showing between the buildings. "Really, you can put the gun down. You look like you are about to faint, and I do not want to get shot just because you cannot handle the weapon. I'm the one who called the police. If I hadn't, I would've been able to shoot him and walk away because you don't know who I am."

"Then why didn't you?" Miki asked. It was surreal, having a conversation with a porcelain dragon with the dead man lying a few feet away, but Miki had long given up trying to make sense of his world. "Not like I would've said anything. Asshole's been trying to kill me for the past couple of weeks."

"You see, my son has done something stupid. As something he thought he had to do in order to protect the family. I can't allow him to take the blame for it." She kept her composure as a cop car pulled up in front of the warehouse, its tires screeching as it came to a stop. "You see, Micah, a mother would do anything for their child, even confessing to her brother's murder. Because there is nothing a mother wouldn't sacrifice for her child, including her freedom. Now smile, and be sure the policeman knows which one of us is a killer."

CHAPTER TWENTY-FOUR

Gypsy roses, and a white daisy crown
Waltzing in circles, We all fall down
Spin a thread, make it of gold
Weave us a family, brash, loud and bold
Let me sing to them in the darkness
Let me sing to them in the light
Let us sing together under the moon
Let us sing to keep back the night
When the road comes a'calling
Let me remember where I've been
'Cause once our song is over
We'll want to come back again
Don't sell your soul to the Devil
Take a nickel for every sin
Lift your voices so we can hear you
And dance with Crossroads Gin
—Shouting Down the Moon

MIKI'S HEAD hurt.

Not from being slammed against the filthy alleyway ground. No, it ached from the amount of noise generated by a family room full of Morgans and one Damien Mitchell.

Dude barking his ass off wasn't helping either.

"Hush, dog," Brigid admonished the terrier. "The cat's not going to hurt you. You outweigh her by at least ten pounds."

"To be fair, love," Donal interjected, "yer cat's mean. There's dragons that wouldn't be taking that one on."

"You hush as well," she said, picking up the tiny orange feline curled up next to Miki's hip. "She is just a tiny little thing."

"Funny. That's what everyone says about *Brigid*," Damien muttered into Miki's ear, resting his arms on the back of the couch and leaning forward. "And look how much havoc that woman can wreak."

"I can hear you, Damien Mitchell," Brigid remarked as she stroked the cat's head before putting it down on the floor. "And shouldn't you be taking up a corner of that couch? Your head is probably still rattled about."

"I figured Sinjun needed it for his leg. I'm good leaning here." His brother moved, shifting the cushions behind Miki's back. "My ribs feel better if I'm standing, and I've got one of the ottomans back here to rest my knees on."

Much of the family and all of Crossroads Gin were settled around the room, nearly bursting at the seams, but no one seemed to mind being elbow to knee with one another. A footstool had been found somewhere in the house, the perfect height for Miki to rest his heel on and extend his braced leg out in front of him. It wasn't the most comfortable of positions—either the footstool or caught in a crowd of Morgans—but it was better than being dead.

Kane sat on an ottoman near Miki's good knee, his hand on Miki's thigh and his thumb rubbing along the inner seam of Miki's jeans, a potent reminder of how a simple touch from Kane could arouse him. Forest and Connor took up an entire love seat, but Rafe paced about, periodically brushing his fingers over Quinn, who was sprawled on one of the recliners. Sionn had taken one look at the assembly and appointed himself in charge of coffee, grinning when Donal suggested a bit of Irish in the brew for those not on pain medication, pulling a rumble from Damien at being excluded.

Dude jumped up on the couch, squeezing in between Miki and Donal. The older man adjusted the dog so his weight wasn't on Miki's hip, but Dude refused to be moved, curving back into the spot he'd already claimed. Sighing contentedly, the terrier twisted over, offering his belly for Miki to scratch.

Miki obliged.

"So, Susan Wong-Lee killed her brother and Zhou, who she hired to be her butler? He used to murder people for her brother and she hired him to serve people tea and cookies? That's so Borgia." Quinn hooked his fingers into Rafe's waistband, then pulled him down to sit on the recliner's wide arm. "Okay, how did Danny Wong get into his nephew's car?"

"See, that is the problem, magpie," Donal replied. "We've got two people confessing to a single murder. We know who killed Zhou because Miki is the witness, but there's a good argument for self-defense there. Or at least, she can claim she was trying to protect him. It is stickier where her brother is concerned."

"Wong-Lee is claiming she'd put Wong in the car, intending to dispose of his body later, but her son, Adam Lee, found it in the parking garage and is trying to take the blame. He denies this." Kane glanced over at Miki, the worry in his eyes fading away when he realized Miki was only adjusting the pillow under his left thigh. "One of Lee's men says he was the one who shot Wong because the uncle had become violent, going after Adam as they fought about him hiding in Wong-Lee's apartment."

"Because that's always the way you end an argument," Connor drawled sarcastically. "You just shoot who you are arguing with. No one is going to buy that."

"I don't know," Damie cut in. "There's times when I'm arguing with Miki when I would love to shoot him."

"You are not needing to add to this conversation, Mitchell." Sionn came in from the kitchen, carrying a loaded-down tray of mugs. "The ones with spoons in them have a nip. Pass them around, and then I'll make some more."

The family room's couches were long, a relic of times when Brigid had more than a handful of growing boys to accommodate. Over the years other furniture crept in: a couple of recliners and the love seat sturdy enough to hold up under continuous roughhousing. It was one of the rooms Miki loved the most in the Morgan house. The thick rug under his feet was soft enough to lie on and covered nearly the entire open space not taken up by seating. A river stone fireplace at the other end of the room would eventually find its mantel weighed down by a sea of stockings with names embroidered on their white, fluffy cuffs. He'd had to leave the room when he spotted his name among the Christmas offerings, overcome by the elaborate cursive scrawl picked out in a bat-black metallic thread with a red-sequin skull dotting the first *I*.

His head did hurt—his knee hurt like fucking hell—but cradled between Donal, Dude, and Kane, with Damien pressed into his shoulder, Miki realized he was okay. For the first time in his life, he felt *okay*. Maybe even better than okay. The smile he got from Kane when their eyes met and the feeling of something warm and precious forming in his soul definitely edged things into fantastic.

"I'm glad she shot him and not me," Miki added. "I can't believe she shot her brother. She's cold. Dead-eyed like a dragon. But man, her son's trying to take the blame, so that says something about her. I think Adam put Wong in the car so he can say one of them did it, but I don't think she'll let him go to jail, right?"

"So far it looks like the same gun that shot Wong was the one she used on Zhou, but we're not going to know until the lab is done." Kane shook his head at Connor's derisive snort. "I agree with Miki. But luckily all I have to do is arrest everybody, charge them with something, and let the district attorney figure it out."

"That office has its own problems." The Morgan patriarch moved his arm, meaning to make room for his wife to sit down, but Brigid had other plans, perching herself on the edge of the couch with one leg flung over her husband's thigh. "Internal Affairs is meeting with the DA this week. It seems like one of their people had some connection to Wong, and that's who was mud-dying up your investigation. Between him and Hall's connections in the police department, they were able to throw up obstacles to slow you down."

"Having Chang and the DEA was a godsend," Kane said. "We just couldn't get any traction, and Wong-Lee covering for her brother and Zhou being right under our noses just pissed me off. If Wong-Lee hadn't had an attack of conscience, who the hell knows what would've happened."

"Sinjun would've kept pulling the trigger until the damned thing fired and took care of Zhou himself." Damien snorted. "And if that didn't work, you probably would have sensed something was wrong and headed home. The two of you are too *destined* to be together. And if anyone deserves a happy ending, it's Sinjun."

"No more getting shot at," his cop declared, squeezing Miki's thigh. "And no more hospital trips until after we get married, so I don't have to fight with the nurse to let me in the doors."

"Hey, I'm the one who proposed, so that means the wedding arrangements are on you," Miki shot back. "Isn't that how it works? One of us asks the question and the other one has to decide what color flowers there's going to be? You're the one that said yes, so I'm off the hook for everything else."

"Wait." Brigid's voice was remarkably low but stretched tight with emotion. "You two are engaged? When did this happen? Why wasn't I told?"

Most of the time Miki knew he didn't understand how families worked, especially when the siblings began to argue what they thought of as good-naturedly and he took as all-out acts of war. There were a few snickers from around the room and a few smug looks as the family braced themselves for what was probably going to be a storm of epic proportions. Miki caught Donal's flinch, and then the older man squared his shoulders, more than likely ready to wade into the tide of Gaelic about to come out of his wife. Kane opened his mouth, leaning forward to head off his mother's questions when Miki stepped in.

"Hey, we're just engaged. At least you'll be able to see *us* get hitched." Forest made eye contact with him, and for a brief second, Miki almost considered giving in to the silent plea his drummer gave him, but if he'd learned one thing from the Morgan clan, it was how to deflect an incoming barrage. Turning back to Brigid, he pointed toward the love seat where a very silent Forest and Connor sat. "*Those* two got married in Vegas a while back, and they were just waiting for the right moment to tell you. So, here's the right moment."

Then Miki sat back, glad that his Gaelic wasn't as good as his Cantonese, and returned Kane's shit-eating grin with a smirk.

"Well done, Sinjun," Damien whispered into his ear, his words nearly lost under Brigid's tearful congratulations and the torrent of apologies from Forest and Connor. "It seems like you finally learned how to be a baby brother."

"What do you mean *finally*?" he asked, leaning his head back to stare up at Damien's handsome face. "I've been your baby brother for years."

Two Months Later...

MORNINGS WERE hard. About an hour before, Kane had heard Miki get up to use the bathroom, a trail of aromatic mint following his lover back into their bed. Forty minutes later, Dude scratched at Kane's foot, demanding to be let outside. He lay flat on his back, wondering if Miki would respond to the terrier's demands, but all he heard coming out of the mound of pillows was a muffled snort.

"Okay, how about if you go out and I brush my teeth too," Kane mumbled, edging the excited dog out of the way with his foot. "Just let me get out of bed, *boyo*."

The back door now opened to a fenced-in lawn of sorts with his new woodworking shop tucked in between the warehouses' outer walls. It was cold, unsurprising for the first week of October, but the shiver running down Kane's spine had nothing to do with the weather and everything to do with the day.

He finished washing his face, then opened the back door, clicking his tongue at the dog to get Dude's attention. Following the terrier in, Kane scooped out half a cup of dry kibble into Dude's dish and left the dog to his breakfast. It seemed strangely quiet with Damien and Sionn not sleeping upstairs, even though the thick interior walls were fairly soundproofed and he'd never heard them before. The new windows cut into the kitchen's outer wall gave him a good view of the warehouse next door, but none of the lights were on.

"Jesus, what was I thinking? It's not even seven o'clock in the morning yet," Kane reminded himself after checking the time. "Neither one of those slackers are going to be awake until it's well into the double digits. Seems like going back to bed isn't a bad idea. Wouldn't you say, dog?"

Dude didn't give Kane a bit of notice, instead focusing his attention on reaching the bottom of his dish. Chuckling to himself, Kane headed to the bedroom, where he was surprised to find Miki awake and propped up against the nest of pillows filling the upper right corner of their bed.

Tradition dictated a couple didn't see each other the morning of their wedding, but Miki wasn't one for tradition and Kane wasn't willing to spend one morning without waking up next to his mercurial lover. Standing on the threshold of their bedroom, Kane was struck dumb by the beauty of the man willing to spend the rest of his life at Kane's side.

The Miki lying in bed was so very different from the man who'd opened his front door and stood toe-to-toe with Kane to defend a thieving dog.

They'd half argued a bit the night before, a good-natured teasing about Miki getting a haircut and Kane letting his hair grow out. Their dinner had been *carne asada* tacos, beef chow fun dry style, and eggrolls, the result of Kane losing a round of *jan-ken-po* and Miki's voracious appetite being in charge of the menu.

Taking in Miki's pretty face with his kissable mouth and enormous hazel eyes, a disheveled wealth of caramel-shot strands curving around his face and brushing his shoulders, Kane was glad he'd lost the haircut argument. He liked the look of Miki's shoulders and arms, a healthier blend of muscle and sinew than the first time they'd met. Kane also had an overwhelming fondness for Miki's chest and tight stomach, the wink of gold from the ring Miki threaded through his belly button occasionally.

There were scars, and Kane knew every single one of them. With Miki's life as it was, there were marks and keloids left from careless handling and tragic circumstances. There was a tangle of knotted skin across Miki's knee, a troublesome spot he nursed from time to time, and more than a few thin crisscross lines on his back. Plastic surgery could soften the scars or even eliminate some of them, a proposal Kane had pitched more than a few times before. He'd argued for erasing those symbols of cruelty, if only to release Miki from those memories, but Miki didn't see the marks like Kane did. And in the end, Miki's opinion was the only one that mattered.

Miki wore them as badges of the war he'd fought and the ground he'd gained, something Kane not only understood but celebrated. Still, there was one mark Miki refused to carry: Wong's hateful symbol.

It still was strange to see the brilliantly colored Thai-influenced cat curled up over Miki's arm and around his shoulder, but it'd been good to see the light in Miki's eyes shift when Ivo from 415 Ink packed in the final shading, then washed away the gritty ink debris, revealing the elaborately embellished cover-up on Miki's skin. They'd been determined to do it in one shot, something Kane wasn't too keen on, but Miki insisted that if it could be done, he would sit for it. They'd taken an hour's break, but by the time Kane got off shift and to the tattoo shop, Ivo was finishing up the inking.

And Miki's life was changed once again.

He grumbled about how much it smarted for a few days, but Kane knew he was happy.

And he intended for Miki to be even happier later on that day.

"Hello, Mister Micah Liam Morgan St. John," Kane said from his spot by the door. "Do you want some coffee? I can make you some."

"I would rather you come over here and make me forget that we have to go to a party tonight, Lieutenant Kane Aodh Sinjun Morgan." Miki wrinkled his nose. "It's weird we have new names but you kept the one that sounds like a bunch of Es and took what D calls me. It's weird you have a new rank. Okay, it's all just fucking weird. No, I don't want coffee. I want you to come back to bed and maybe we can pretend we don't have anywhere else to go today."

"My mother would gut both of us." Kane walked across the bedroom floor, his toes chilled from the cold wooden planks, and he was grateful for the warm blankets and an even warmer Miki when he climbed on top of the mattress. "Didn't I leave off somewhere last night? Maybe it was here."

He found Miki's belly button ring with his mouth, looping his tongue into the hoop. Miki's fingers dug into his hair and tugged, trying to loosen Kane's grip, but he had no intention of letting Miki go. Instead, he let his hands wander, stroking at the powder-soft skin on the inside of Miki's thighs, then reveling in the tickle of down on Miki's balls.

Miki's hardening cock was enough of a welcome for Kane to continue his exploration.

"Do you like that, *a ghra*?" Kane kissed up Miki's stomach, his fingers wrapping around the base of Miki's cock as his mouth teased a hard brown nipple into a peak. "Because we have a few hours and I'm aching to see what I can do to you this fine, blustery morning."

Miki's eyes were dark with desire, and he licked the corner of his mouth in a quick dab. Capturing Kane's mouth in a savage kiss, Miki took every bit of Kane's self-control, stealing it cleanly away before Kane could offer up even the smallest of protests.

He broke off their connection only to sink his teeth into Kane's lower lip, then whispered, "Take your time. We've got the rest of our lives."

MIKI DIDN'T need a ring to know he belonged to Kane.

He didn't need the piece of paper they'd picked up yesterday or the words a priest would speak over them later that afternoon.

All he needed was to have Kane's arms around him, to feel Kane pushing into him, and Miki's heart knew it'd found its home.

His soul sang when Kane was near, sometimes a low murmur of chords and the occasional bits of laughter adding a hint of brass to the melody, but he lived for the symphonies they created between them when they fell into bed and played.

There were times Miki truly believed the greatest thing Kane had ever given him was teaching him how to play. Right up until the moment when Kane stripped naked, baring his glorious, powerful body, and spread himself over Miki to remind him he could hold the stars in his hand if he tried hard enough.

For Kane had hung stars in Miki's darkness, lighting them up every time they kissed, tangled their bodies together, or more importantly, when Kane reminded Miki he was loved.

He licked at Kane's shoulder as his cop spread oil into the dip of his body, biting at Kane's sun-bronzed skin when his thumb pad pressed against Miki's entrance. Kane hissed when Miki worried at the spot, retaliating by sliding a couple of his fingers around the tight, muscled ring, then pushing in. Even as prepared as he was for Kane's intrusion, Miki gasped, letting go of the flesh he'd trapped between his teeth, then growling playfully when Kane's mocking laughter echoed in his ear.

"Last chance you're ever going to get to live in sin, Miki love," Kane reminded him, returning Miki's bite with a nip at his earlobe. "Because after today, you'll be stuck with me for all eternity."

The morning light stretched through the slender windows set high on the outer wall, catching at the few silvery strands in Kane's thick black hair. It played over the planes of his shoulders, gilding the spots Miki loved to lave with the flat of his tongue, sometimes to Kane's faux-disgusted delight. Running his hands through the beams, Miki played with the shape of the shadows he could cast over Kane's arms, letting his fingers dip and dive into the lines of Kane's muscles. His cop's weight pressed him into the mattress, and Miki shifted, resting his legs on Kane's hips and thighs. Kane's cock head was already damp, leaving a trail of wet anticipation on Miki's skin.

He shivered, unable to hold back the want gripping him. An eternity wasn't going to be long enough, he was sure of that, but if that's all the universe would give him, he'd take it.

Just as he intended to take Kane.

"Can't wait," Miki murmured, arching up to bite Kane's chin. "Now would be a damned good time to start, K."

They shared a laugh the moment Kane dropped the lube on Miki's belly, trying to toss it onto the nightstand; then Miki lost track of his heartbeat when Kane's cock pushed against Miki's slickened entrance. It was always hard to remember to breathe, and it wasn't until his lungs ached from being held in, did Miki finally hitch in air nearly in time with his racing pulse.

He was always afraid of breathing when Kane pushed into him, not wanting to feel anything other than his body being filled and his flesh tightening around Kane's heft, the slight burn of his muscles giving in to

Kane's gentle thrust. There was a glory to the slide of Kane's body on his, how their stomachs touched for a brief instant, followed by the press of Kane's hips against his.

Kane's cock went deep, hitting every single one of Miki's needs and raking its length over the core of his pleasure. Something drove Kane on, and Miki could only hold tight when Kane's hands slid under his ass and squeezed, lifting him from the bed so Kane could seat himself fully into Miki's heat.

The storm broke in Kane's gaze, and Miki fell into its fury, working hard to meet Kane's thrusts. The beat of their bodies meeting echoed in the vastness of their bedroom, and the shadows curled away from the brightening day, driven back by the encroaching light. It didn't take long before their bodies were beaded with sweat from the effort of chasing their climax. Then Kane slowed down, roiling his hips and catching Miki off guard.

"Fucking killing me here, K," Miki ground out. His stomach clenched, his balls aching for release, but the slow, steady pace Kane fell into carved the rising edge of his climax. Another long glide and Kane's cock head teased at his nerves, a tickle of sensations running down Miki's thighs and back up to grab at his dick. "Damn—"

"I love you, *a ghra*. And I cannot wait to make you mine." Kane panted over him, resting his hands on either side of Miki's shoulders. They were cocooned in the musk of their joining, a sweet earthiness Miki eagerly pulled into his lungs right before Kane lowered his mouth on Miki's, angling for a kiss.

Miki took as much as he gave, surrendering to Kane only long enough to pull him in, then licked and bit at Kane's mouth, teasing his lips open so he could have more. Their lovemaking continued at its slow pace, their arms moving in languid strokes over their torsos until Miki raked his nails down Kane's back, and he grinned into Kane's shoulder when he felt Kane's asscheeks clench.

"Already yours, right?" He was leaving a trail of tiny purpling marks down Kane's neck, dappling his cop's tanned throat, but Miki had gone past the point of caring. With Kane stretching him wide-open, the heat of his length piercing Miki's core, he wanted to leave something of himself behind on the man who'd taken him apart and then put him back together. "We're just doing this for the cake, remember?"

He got the laugh he wanted, then the soaring race to the peak Miki ached for. Kane's cock drove into him, each thrust slamming Miki deeper into the pillows at the head of the bed. He reached for his own dick when the first arcs of lightning curled up his spine, but Kane's hand was already there, wrapping around the base in a tight grip. Squeezing down on Kane's shaft, Miki pushed up to seal his lover's mouth in a fierce kiss, then let the storm Kane brewed between them hit—

And rode it with the fury Kane unleashed from inside of him, pulling his cop along for the ride.

They lay panting on the bed a few strokes later, sticky with come and sweat, but when Kane pushed himself to the side, Miki grumbled at the separation, then crawled on top of his cop once Kane lay on his back. Easily taking Miki's weight, Kane wrapped his arms around Miki and kissed away a drop of sweat Miki could feel rolling down his temple.

Their world remained a dull roar of heavy breathing and rushing blood for a long stretch of minutes.

Then Kane shifted Miki to the bed, so they could lay on their sides to face each other. Miki used the space between them to tweak Kane's sensitive nipples, his left peak slightly dimpled by Miki's sharp teeth. His cop tsked sharply, grabbing at Miki's fingers to stop his lazy exploration.

"You're stronger than you think, Mick," Kane whispered, breaking the silence they'd nursed. "With all the hell you've been through, I couldn't have done it. It would have broken me, but you…."

"See, here's the thing about hell, you've got to just keep pushing through." He pressed his fingers against Kane's kiss-swollen mouth, tucking his thumb under his lower lip. "Because the moment you decide to stop, you aren't going through hell anymore, you're living in it. I had to keep going. I had you and Damien waiting for me on the other side. No way I was going to live my life without you."

A bark from the other side of the bedroom door brought a smile to Kane's lips and he murmured, "Don't forget your dog."

Miki snorted, rolling over onto his back so Kane could climb over him to open the bedroom door. "Yeah, that's not my dog. He just lives here."

EPILOGUE

Miki: Dearly Beloved? Why does it always start like that?

Damie: It's tradition. People like tradition. It's... a ritual of sorts. Like making tea and when someone adds milk beforehand, you know they're one of Satan's demons.

Miki: Traditions are stupid. You're just saying things to say things. It should mean something, you know?

Damie: The words do mean something. It's like when someone says a eulogy at a funeral. Those aren't just words, but you, my brother, didn't even give me a funeral.

Miki: I didn't need to. Those are just for the living to say goodbye so they can move on. I wasn't ever going to

let you go, so why the fuck would I
throw you a funeral?
—Taking a break from Katamari Damacy

FINNEGAN'S WAS packed with Irish cops, the occasional redhead, and a handful of musicians. A sign on the front door proclaimed the pub was closed for a private event, but Miki could have sworn its doors were busier opening and closing more than if it was St. Paddy's Day. It seemed anyone he'd ever met in his entire life had come in to celebrate his marriage to the cop he'd fallen in love with, and it was all he could do not to fling himself into the Bay to get away.

Mostly because he couldn't find an open window big enough to crawl out of, and he didn't want to see the disappointment on Kane's face when he failed to take the stage.

The weight of the simple gold band Kane had slid onto his finger anchored him into the here and now, a much-welcome reminder his cop loved him and wanted to share their joined lives with the rest of the world. But Miki's nerves got the best of him, and he'd given Kane a brief kiss, then whispered he'd be back. Everything was pressing in on Miki, and he needed some time to think and some quiet to do it in.

The pub's staff lounge seemed like a good place to start, but Damien, Rafe, and Forest had taken it over to double as a greenroom to fret over the set and to make last-minute changes to things they'd talked to death weeks before. One look at Miki's face and Damien pointed him to the pub's office, promising to stand guard at the front door so Miki could begin breathing again.

"Don't be nervous," his brother said, patting him on the back. "It's just another gig. Pretend you're playing to one single person. That'll help."

"I am playing to a single person. *Kane*," he snarled. "That's not fucking helping."

"Well, I'd say imagine him naked, but the last thing we want tonight is for the two of you to tear each other's clothes off and begin humping onstage." Damien snickered. "Okay, maybe we do. I'll put a tip jar out and that'll probably pay off our tab before the two of you even get started."

"Dick," Miki muttered. "Lucky it's my wedding day or I'd punch you."

"Lucky it's your wedding day or I'd punch you right back," Damie replied. "I'll try to keep most of the rabble out, but looks like Liam wants a word with you. Should I let him in?"

"Yeah, might as well." He cast a look down the long hall, seeing his father work past the short line of people standing in front of the bathroom doors. "Who knows? He might have a barf bag on him. Never know."

"Miki!" Liam called out, nodding when Damien motioned him in. "Thanks. It's insane out there. Thought this was supposed to be a small thing."

"This is a *small* thing." Damien snorted as he ducked back into the greenroom. "We sell arenas out. Think we can't fill a pub?"

"That one's got an ego on him." Liam chuckled. "You two balance each other out."

"Most of the time, when we don't want to kill each other," Miki admitted, hitching himself up onto the old wooden desk dominating the room.

Finnegan's office had been carved out of a storeroom, but someone'd taken it upon themselves to install a window, letting in light and, when open, the ripe fishy odor of the Bay and its nearby mammalian residents. Sionn'd probably cracked open the shuttered panes to start airflow between the office and the lounge, so Miki and Liam were graced with a serenade of raucous gulls and the occasional bellow of a disgruntled sea lion.

Still, Miki figured it was better than the high-level headache-inducing rumble of the pub's main room, and despite the smell, he needed the relative quiet more than anything else.

"Here, I got you something," Liam said, digging into his pants pockets. "Well, not really got you, but it's something I got for your mom before... then. I'd bought it before they pulled me out, and I thought I'd give it to her when I saw her again, but now I guess I should give it to you."

The box was small and flat, its edges grimy from being handled and its once-blue fabric faded across the flat surfaces, bleached to a pale turquoise. Its hinge creaked when Miki opened it, complaining at being forced to share its treasure, but it gave in and Miki found himself looking at a small pair of thick gold hoops, their flat surfaces carved with a pair of elaborately filigreed elephants.

"She liked elephants," Liam muttered, almost apologetically. "It was a Thai thing, I think. At least that's what she told me. Or maybe she just liked them. But I'd gotten them for her birthday. I figured you're fairly open-minded about stuff. You wouldn't think they were too feminine."

"Nah, they're great. They match my cat ink." Miki grinned, plucking one out of its nest, then setting the box down on the desk. Taking the stud out from his left ear, he worked the hoop in, closing its catch. "You should take the other one. Because she might have been my mom, but she was someone special to you too."

He'd meant to say more, something about them matching or maybe even keeping a part of Achara between them, but Liam nodded before Miki could open his mouth, then said, "It'll be nice. We can share them. I just don't have a hole in my ear."

"Shit, that's easy." Miki rested on his palms on the desk, leaning his weight back. "You're at a musician's wedding in an Irish pub with a bunch of cops and artists. All we need is a needle, an ice cube, and a piece of cork. You'll have it in before the sun comes back up."

"Or I could have it done by someone who's licensed to do it," his father drolly pointed out.

"Pretty sure we can find that someone out there. We know a lot of people who like to do things with needles," he replied, matching Liam's drawl.

"Can I be cutting in when ye're done?" Donal called out from the door. "Thought I'd say a few words to the boy before he goes out there."

"Yeah, come in." Liam edged toward the hall. "I'll see you outside, Mick. And maybe drink some water—you're looking kind of pale."

Liam was gone before Miki could say anything, and the room was suddenly filled with an Irish cop Miki loved nearly as much as the one who'd put a ring on his finger. Perching on the desk, Donal nudged his shoulder into Miki, then slung his arm around him, giving him a fierce hug.

"You okay, Miki boy?" Donal prodded gently. "Ye seem a bit overwhelmed, and I know ye've had bigger crowds than this in front of you. What's on yer mind?"

"This. Today. Tomorrow." Miki exhaled sharply. "He's going to hate it."

In a way, talking to Donal was like folding a bit of Kane into a healthy dose of common sense and wisdom, giving Miki a sneak peek of what his husband would be like in twenty-odd years. Donal didn't pull any punches, cloaking his hit in velvet but smacking Miki with a bit of truth he always tried to avoid.

"Ye're better than that, Mick. Ye know my boy. Do ye think he'd be that way?" Donal's arm was a slack embrace around Miki's back, a warm support against the chilled air creeping through the open window. "Try again."

"Kane's going to like it," Miki offered up with a half grin, grimacing when Donal fixed him with a stern look. "Fuck, okay. Kane's going to love it. He'll worship the ground I walk on forever even if I screw everything up when I get onstage."

"Well, it's a start and more than I thought I'd get out of ye," Donal admitted. "And speaking of our Kane, he sent me to come looking for you. Seems his heart's after a kiss before ye climb up onto those boards. Tell him ye love him and go do what ye were put on this earth to do. And that's *not* giving me any more gray hairs. Despite what ye think."

The band was ready for him when Miki emerged from the office, his belly warmed by the shot of whiskey he'd shared with Donal before his father gave him another hug fierce enough to crack his spine. The walk down the hall toward the pub's stage seemed to last forever and a day, then a burst of light broke open the room and Miki searched the crowd for the one face— the one person—he'd be singing to that night.

Kane met him at the edge of the raised platform, shoving Connor and Sionn aside to get to Miki while Quinn tapped at Forest's drums as he waited for Rafe onstage. Squeezing Kane's fingers, Miki leaned into his cop, kissing him deep enough to fold quiet over them, closing their world off from everyone around them.

"I love you, *a ghra*," Kane murmured after their kiss, their foreheads touching lightly, and their hands clasped by their sides. "Thanks for asking me to marry you."

"Shit, thanks for saying yes," Miki whispered. "I wouldn't know what to do if you'd said no. I love you too damned much to let you go, and, well, I'm already Dad's favorite. He'd have to give you up."

"Really?" Kane's eyes glittered silver. "Just— God, I love you, but your idea of romance—"

"I'll show you my idea of romance, just give me a chance," Miki promised, then turned when Damie tugged on his shirt. "Wait here. I need you some place I can see you while I do this set, okay? Don't fucking go anywhere."

"Hey, I'm not," his husband said, holding up his hand so Miki could see the gold band on his finger. "Didn't I just make you that promise this afternoon? Not going anywhere, Mick. *Promise*."

The stage wasn't fancy, but it would do. If anything, the intimacy of the tiny venue was exactly what Miki needed, what he wanted as he turned toward the crowd, seeing faces he loved surrounded by friends he'd found over the years. Edie saluted him from her place at the bar, her martini glass loaded with olives, while Brigid, Donal, and Liam sat nearby, his fierce redheaded mother laughing at something one of his fathers must have said. Kane'd kept his promise, sharing a table with Quinn, Sionn, and Connor, their cousin Cassie dropping off a bottle of whiskey and four glasses in front of them before she disappeared into the crowd.

It was time to dance again, to scream into the relative darkness and hope someone screamed back. But this time, Miki knew the voices he would hear and couldn't wait to see the light they'd bring with them.

His guitar hissed when he plugged it in, and the mike bounced the sound around the room a bit until he got settled. Taking a deep breath, Miki gave Damie a quick hug, running his fingers down his strings before he pulled away, and laughing when D swore a black streak at him for the echoing thrum he'd caused. Turning to the audience, Miki leaned into the mike and spoke into the poignant silence the pub offered.

"Today's the anniversary of the first gig Damie and I played together. It was a day that changed my life, and when I asked Kane to marry me, I wanted it to be today because, well, it's like the best fucking day ever, and I wanted him to be a part of it too because he's changed my life too." Miki cleared his throat, unable to find Kane through the tears in his eyes. "See, I was in a living hell before I met Kane, and he found me, held my hand as he showed me the way out. And the best way I can thank him is to promise to love him for the rest of my life because, well, I was going to do that anyway.

"A while back, my brother Damie asked me why I've never written a love song about Kane. I told him I wasn't ready to share Kane yet. See, I wanted Kane to myself, because I'd never had someone love me like he loves me." He swallowed, blinking away the sting along his lashes, and Kane's face rose out of the mist covering his eyes. His heart began to stumble, excited at the sight of his strong, fierce cop with an off-kilter smile and the large loving family he'd brought with him, and Miki forced himself to continue before he lost himself in Kane's blue eyes. "But today, it's time for me to share. This one's for you, K. Because you're going to be my forever."

> *You found me in the shadows*
> *And held me when I cried*
> *If you hadn't found me*
> *Pretty sure I'd have died*
> *See, I was already gone and buried*
> *By the time you knocked on my door*
> *Death and sorrow filled me up*
> *And I just couldn't take any more*
>
> *I'd shed my very last tear*
> *Holding the remains of my soul*
> *Clinging to the bleak 'round me*
> *Making sure it swallowed me whole*
> *With the light you have inside you*
> *A light burning bright and strong*
> *You pushed back my darkness*
> *Then dragged me right along*
>
> *So throw back the gates of Hell*
> *Pull me down the path I'd walked*
> *Find me in the darkness*
> *No matter if I balk*
> *Sing me a song of redemption*
> *Sing me a ballad of love and bliss*
> *Remind me of the Heaven*
> *I found in our first kiss*
>
> *I can't give you anything*
> *Other than the love that you've taught*
> *There's nothing bright inside of me*
> *Except for what you've wrought*

Love me for an eternity
Love me for forever and beyond
I can promise you a Heaven
With the love for you I've found

So throw back the gates of Hell
Pull me down the path I'd walked
Find me in the darkness
No matter if I balk
Sing me a song of redemption
Sing me a ballad of love and bliss
Remind me of the Heaven
I found in our first kiss
—A Song for Kane

AUTHOR'S NOTE

I'VE BEEN asked more than a few times to include the lyrics written for the books in one place, so I've included all of them here because, well, we're at the end. I've also been asked about the type of music Sinner's Gin and Crossroads Gin plays. My answer to that is... whatever you need it to be. This band... these characters... are yours. How they sound should touch a part of you, so they play whatever touches you. Except perhaps polka. I don't think that'll work, but you know, I can always be proven wrong. My last wish for you, the reader, is that you walk away from this series knowing I am so grateful you've been here with me. It's been a long tour, and while we're striking down the last and final stage, I cherish every last one of you. So... thanks again.

See, I was already gone and buried
By the time you knocked on my door
Death and sorrow filled me up
And I just couldn't take any more

I'd shed my very last tear
Holding the remains of my soul
Clinging to the bleak 'round me
Making sure it swallowed me whole
With the light you have inside you
A light burning bright and strong
You pushed back my darkness
Then dragged me right along

So throw back the gates of Hell
Pull me down the path I'd walked
Find me in the darkness
No matter if I balk
Sing me a song of redemption
Sing me a ballad of love and bliss
Remind me of the Heaven
I found in our first kiss

I can't give you anything
Other than the love that you've taught
There's nothing bright inside of me
Except for what you've wrought
Love me for an eternity
Love me for forever and beyond
I can promise you a Heaven
With the love for you I've found

So throw back the gates of Hell
Pull me down the path I'd walked

Find me in the darkness
No matter if I balk
Sing me a song of redemption
Sing me a ballad of love and bliss
Remind me of the Heaven
I found in our first kiss
—A Song for Kane

The poison inside of me kills what I touch,
So why should I love, when I know it'll die?
—Arsenic Kiss

Brick covered in blood
Face painted with spit
Skin the wrong colour
Want cock, called unfit

So many ways to kill us
So many ways to make us less
When's it all going to stop
That's just anyone's guess

Don't pick up that stone
Just unclench your fist
Turn the other cheek
We're all better than this
—Bathing in Hate

I've come a long way
Cried in the dark
There's been times when I've screamed
Times when my soul's barely a spark

You touched me then
Kissed my bleeding heart
Showed me the sunshine
Promised never to part
Wake up in the morning
You are still near
The world's only beautiful
When you're right here
—Beautiful Day

You cracked me open
Sucked out my filthy core
Held my heart in your hands
And gave in when I begged for more
—Begging Again

Hands on my skin, their filth working in.
I can't feel anything but pain.
Why won't this ever end?
Too hard to breathe.
Too worn to care.
Pushing sharp knives in my soul.
Bleeding inside, still too tired to cry.
—Bleeding Inside

Took a blind man to tell me I was some-
thing to see.
Took a man crossing his heart
to tell me where to begin.
And the kiss in the rain you last gave to me,

*Was the holy water I needed to erase all
    my sin.*
—Blind Man Crossing

*Drowning in tears,
Soaked too long in my salt.
This is what I am.
This is I should be.
Something that never ends.
But I want to be more than me*
—Blue Notebook 3/8

*Devil by my side, a devil I know
Riding the Crossroads, heading to the
    next show
Hearing my name on the crowd, never
    thought I'd be back
House lights going down, time to dance
    in the black*
—Breathing Again

*I hate you for teaching me how to fly
And then you burnt my wings
There's nothing left of me
But wax, feathers and grief
I can't put myself together
And I can't see the fucking sky*
—Burning Sky

World's gone too dark, too dark for me to see

I turn and reach out but there's no one there
        for me
Every time I hear a heart break, I die a bit
        inside
I cry for every child, I cry for every bride
Atlas carries the world on his shoulders,
Jesus hangs for our sins on a tree
White doves for peace are in the air
But something whispers we'll never be free
Light a candle for the darkness
Light a candle for our sin
Hug your nearest neighbour
Don't forget to let love in
—Candles Burning

Cherry pop lipstick
Black leather jacket dreams
Seeing my baby next Sunday
Good times, know what I mean?
She better stop her cheating
Better put that man to the side
Shotgun loaded, double barrels
Bastard better run and hide
—Cheating Woman, Cold Heart

Juniper wine and long shots of gin
That's where this damned hell all begins
Blood on a mirror, taint of a sin
He'll break my heart
And get under my skin
Can't help myself.
Butterfly on a pin.

Lord help stop this damned madness
'Cause he's done pulled me in.
—Crazed and Moonshined

I am only home in the dark.
The shadows are my only friend.
When a spark of light comes on,
I know my peace is about to end.
—Cursing the Candle

I was bleeding when I met you,
Blood running red over my skin.
You want me to love you,
I'm telling you I don't know where to
     begin.
You've got your hooks in deep,
Pulling at parts of me I can't see.
How can I believe I hate you,
When I don't want to be free?
—Cut Open to Heal

Fingers on my skin
Sin in my bones
Blood in my veins
Telling me there's no home
Finding solace above
From iron in the sky
Love's what you make it
Never let it walk by
—Dead of Night

*Butterflies and whiskey, catching fire to the
    moon.*
*Death's calling to me but I tell him it's too
    soon.*
Songs to sing, places to see.
I don't want to go but Death sure wants me.
—Death Calling

Reaper came for all of us
Jerked us up from the brine
Slipped out from his bony fingers
Landed on our feet just fine
Took four steps to Freedom
Took four souls to the line
Spat at the Devil at the Crossroads
Drank our sins with sweet wine
—Death, Devil and Sin

*I walked onto the Delta, hoping to make
    myself a man,*
Cocky as shit, with my guitar in my hand.
*Walked past the Crossroads, paid the
    Devil no mind.*
*He didn't reach for me, saying I was al-
    ready his kind.*
—Delta Spawn Blues

Tearing down the road, Devil on my tail
Told you not to love me, Told you I'd bail

Kittens and daisies, Picnics and wine
Loving me, baby, is all very good
Till the day I walk, and you're no longer
        mine
—Devil on My Tail

There's a door in the back
At the back of this bar
Death waits there
Even leaves it ajar
Don't wander there, boy
Don't dance too close, son
Else the Devil'll come take you
'Fore the night's even done

The Devil's waiting for me behind that door.
She's got my heart, lay waste to my soul.
Nothing I do can make her let me go.
Hard to touch a heart as black as coal.
—Devil's Waiting

Her tears are long gone, stained with ice
        and despair,
And no one knows why. 'Cause they sure
        don't care.
A rose on her stone gave me grace from
        above.
The dirt on my hands is as cold as her love.
—Dirt and Stone

Sucking on a razor's edge

The blood in my mouth isn't mine
Why does my heartache taste of you?
When you walked away just fine.
—Dislocated

Make mine a double,
And keep them coming, baby girl
Leave out the ice,
And drop off the bottle too
I'm drinking to forget
I'll drink 'till I bleed
Tonight's going to be long
That bottle's all I need
—Double Shot Dance

My blood has whispers of you
Stars caught in the red
I've held on to every memory of us
Held onto everything you've ever said
I can't live without you
I breathe, I eat but it is all grey
Baby, can't you see that without you
I'm dying a little every day
—Dying Without You

You act like I'm the only sinner you know.
And say I'm someone who sets your skin
    on fire.
But I know different, little girl.
I know other men who'd call you a liar.
—Empty Promises

Every day
I am one step closer to the box
Every moment
I am one step further away from you
Every breath
Is one we will never share again
Every night
There's a darkness of one instead of two
—Every Darkness Follows

We held on to each other
In the rain and at the dawn
People told us we wouldn't make it
Said we'd die off and be gone
I'm here for every step
Every inch of every mile
Down to our very last breath
Till it hurts too much to smile
—Every Mile

Wings under my skin,
Fighting to break free.
I need a razor to cut them out,
So I can live to as I'm meant to be.
A drop of music, A sip of wine.
Watch the sky when I fall
I'm sure I'll be fine.
—Falling

Splash of wine, sip of gin
Twisted metal 'round my heart
And nobody wins
Fire coming down hard
Coming hard from above
Skin torched clean off my bones
And my soul's done scarred.
—Fire and Bones

You say you're done with me
But every time I turn around
I see your shadow
Keeping us forever bound
I can feel you near
Haunting a few steps behind
A ghost I cannot shake
A nightmare I cannot find
—Forever Bound

They say I'm nobody to fear
And no one to love,
Soul blacker than ink.
Sin fits like a glove.
And the soft damning whispers,
Follow me where ever I go.
They can't hear me crying.
Even as they kill me real slow.
—Forgotten Son

Four damned sinners went into the rain
Strings bleeding red, soaking up their pain.
Sky fell apart, piercing their souls,
Night closed down, shadows filling the
*   holes.*
One woke up, And then there were two
Sun came back out, the sky black and blue
Too bright to be warm, too sharp to be kind,
Missing twin shadows, by the two left
*   behind.*
—Four Sinners Gone Walking

Don't talk to me about your God
I don't need your broken bread
Not for my soul
Not for my heart
Not for my countless sins
You want to give me something?
Something to save my wicked soul?
Give me the same as you've got
Loving who I want, and leaving me alone.
—Freedom Torn

He found me on a staircase of steel.
Nowhere near Heaven, a Devil making a
*   deal.*
Come on down, son, my Satan said with a
*   grin.*
Come with me and we'll make Sinner's Gin.
—Gin and Demonic

Picked up a piece of silver from the ground,
Used it to end a bit of my strife.
If I'd known I'd need it to get into Heaven,
I'd have carried it with me all of my life.
—Going Over The River

She walks through dreams
Childhood wishes on stars
A faint echo of a woman
Look for her in dives and bars
Familiar stranger
To fill a hole in my heart
Never been together
Never been apart
—Hole in My Heart

Shaking your ass down Broadway
Walking tight down the ole street line
Got a wink for the boys
Nasty smile that's just fine
Boy you've got some balls
Teasing cock as you go by
Better get some man to love you
Before you lose that sexy shine
—Hustle and Wink

The stars are crying
It's like the world knows you're gone.
Slipping away and sliding on,

The shadows hold your voice
I keep hearing you on the wind
Either come back to my side
Or leave me the hell alone
—In blue notebook margins, Page 82

Sliding around in my dreams
Your inky black kiss
Staining my life
With something I'll never miss
You pushed yourself into me
Down deep into my soul
Wish I could dig you out
Burn you till I'm whole
—Ink Black Kiss

I slide into the crack of midnight
Forgotten, broken, Bitten and torn
Just need to survive what you do to me
Just need to see the morn
I lit all the candles
Given to me by a man
Who told me to pray
God has me in his hand
You came anyway
Walking through the flame and smoke
I'll never get back my innocence
I'll never get back what you took
—Innocence Lost

When you said you loved me, I believed you.

*Then when you needed to be free, I deceived
     you.*
—Junie's Lies

Hey baby girl, smiling at me so wide.
*Much too young for what you have in
     mind.*
*Come see me in a few years, and then we
     can talk.*
*I'll show you how to scream, scream
     yourself blind.*
—Keep Walking

I found a letter you left me
Words written when we were in love
Every pen stroke a forgotten dream
All of your promises were broken
Shattered as clean as my heart
I don't know why hurt me
I don't know why the thought of you still does
If I could have one thing in the world
It would be to forget what you looked like
It would be to forget how we loved
—Letter from Nowhere

When Death took you, I didn't notice.
You left me behind you.
In the rain.
Tossed aside without looking back.
*Now you're back in my dreams, telling
     me you're sorry.*

*I need Death to come and take you back
    again.*
—Letter to My Mother

I promised to take you, take you to the stars.
Way past Pluto, once we clear Mars.
We'll dance in the black,
and I will right all my wrongs,
And before our fall from Heaven,
we'll sing our old songs.
*So long that we've danced, we'll forget how
    they go,*
Mumble a few words, then bask in our glow.
*I'll teach you to fly, And you'll teach me to
    win.*
Made me survive, and taught me to sin.
—Letters D and S

Locking down my heart
After I'm done with you
I've run the course of our love
There's nothing left to do
Can't listen to your lies
Won't let you into my life
Gave you everything I had
Your love's like a knife
—Lock and Stab

The road holds no life
Nothing to keep me warm
Hotel rooms bleached and fallow

Strings leaving my tips all torn
Just one more day without you
Another day gone in time
I'm another step away from you, baby
Please don't forget that you're mine
—Love Letter to the Lost

Metal on my fingers
Whiskey on my mind
Singing a tune to my baby
Wasting none of my time
Flip the record on that turntable
Pull the rug from the middle of the floor
Gonna spend the night with my baby
Send my blues out through that door
—Keeping Back The Blues

A marble bowl was my coffin
Woke up to find my life dead
Thought I'd stopped my breathing
But it was our love that died instead
God I wish every other waking hour
I could spare a minute or two
Sometimes I think it should be me
Sleeping that final death, not you
—Marble Coffins

Moonshine and ice
Bathtub swill and broken dreams
Climbing up on a stairway
Made of nightmares and pain

A slip of my hand
Wet blood on a rung
Hitting the stone down beneath me
Made me think 'bout what I've done
Thought about how I've hurt you
How deep and how long
Can't ask to forgive me
Since I've done you so wrong
—Moonshine and Ice

Stealing our money
Diluting our minds
Taking from the forgotten
Beaten for no crime
You tell me to watch my mouth
Spit on me and tell me to drown
I'm telling you Jack
To watch your own ass
Always getting back up
Just so I can take you down
—My Life, Not Yours

Shove me into a corner
Strip me of my pride
Lay me down on a bed of nails
Pry me open up wide
Show me the way to Hell
Keep me from Heaven's Gate
Break my heart so I can't love
Leave me alone in your black hate
—Nail Me In

You've danced around us for far too long
Hooked your fingers into my soul
You flirt and wink, pulling me along
What you want us to be
Just ain't going to last
I'll take a sip of your mouth
Then I'll be walking out fast
—No Good Johnny

Fortunes left on paper
Iron grate at my back
Handful of songs in my pockets
You pulled me up from the black
Dragons on the streets
Fireworks in the sky
We've gone and come full circle
A curl of time gone by
Sinners at the Crossroads
An X in the road
Sipping gin, counting time
Getting ready to explode
—'Nother Sip of Gin

One moon, a thousand stars
Crack open the sky for me
Point me towards Mars
Leaving you a bit of my soul
Hold on to it tight
'Cause nothing's forever, baby,
Not even tonight.
—One Thousand Stars

I came into this world, not knowing
where I've been
You came into my life, working down
into my skin
I fell in love once, with a man who loves
me still
You've been loving him since birth,
And probably always will
We dance around each other
A mongoose and a snake
You grab and hold and cherish
So tight that I might break
Can't you see your love, is as poisonous
as your bite?
You tell me to let you love me,
And I'm afraid I one day might.
—Orange notebook #3, Page #5

Rain on the glass, reminds me of you
A sip of hot chocolate, a song played in blue
Lyrics written on a postcard
Melody slick, deep and charred
Anyone not loving you
Ain't trying that hard
Shout at the moon, dance in the rain
Give me your heart, I'll keep back the pain
—Rain and the Blues

Red light, torn jeans
Filthy sheets by the hour

Aching feet, dirty greens
All of the work, none of the power
A skip along a white line
A snip of ice in my vein
Opens up the sky for a bit
Helps me forget all of my pain
—Reality Mirrored

People talk about tears
About the agony they've cried
They made you salted ground,
Left to fallow, dead inside
Made you wear their pain
Right on your broken skin
Covering in ink and blood
Doesn't hide them from within
—Reclaiming of D

Got shadows on my ass
Time's not on my side
Life came to give me a kiss
Then Death took me for a ride
—Riding A Pale Horse

Sour mash and cheap wine
Smokestack lightning, bathtub gin
Took me for a slow ride
Damn woman 'most done me in
Popping corks in long black limos
Champagne giggles and lots of skin
Breaking hearts more than a million times

Just like my own has been
—Riding Low

Standing in a river of stones
Drowning in sorrow
Water knee deep but cold
Even though my mouth is clear
I just can't breathe anymore
—River of Stones

Mouthful of whiskey
Sweat running down my back
Strings under my fingers
Amp cord hanging down slack
We gather here together
On stage for one more day
Stomp your feet and sing along
Rock and Blues are here to stay
—Roadshow Blues

Rock a bye, baby, don't say a word
Your cradle is broken, childhoods all
          blurred
In the house you once lived, all the win-
          dows are black
Not who they wanted, can never go back
Come play in the sunshine, We've all
          gathered here
Laugh at the rainbows, learn to grin ear
          to ear
So come find this family,

Painting their roses bright bright red
Come to us, Alice, And be loved instead
—Roses for Alice

Death kissed me low
Left me on the road so black
Took my brothers up with him
They ain't never coming back
Heaven saw me cryin'
Tearing up my soul inside
Reached down into its golden grace
To bring a Sinner to my side
—Saving a Sinner

Restless itch
Need to scratch my sin
Fingers in deep
Don't let it end
Confused and alone
Someone's puppet again
—Scratch My Sin

I can feel you breaking my skin.
My bones shatter when you walk by.
The blood I taste is from my tongue.
You say you love me but I know it's a lie.
—Shattered Lies

Gypsy roses, and a white daisy crown
Waltzing in circles, We all fall down

Spin a thread, make it of gold
Weave us a family, brash, loud and bold
Let me sing to them in the darkness
Let me sing to them in the light
Let us sing together under the moon
Let us sing to keep back the night
When the road comes a'calling
Let me remember where I've been
'Cause once our song is over
We'll want to come back again
Don't sell your soul to the Devil
Take a nickel for every sin
Lift your voices so we can hear you
And dance with Crossroads Gin
—Shouting Down the Moon

Bled onto my hand,
Shoved his fist into mine
Stood tall against anyone
Who'd break through our line

No matter what they do
No matter what they say
Death's already tried to part us
And we've already made him pay

So lift a glass to the Sinners
Lift a glass of cheap ass gin
Put your lips on the Gates of Heaven
'Cause we're taking you to sin.
—Sinners' Calling

An ounce of rotgut whiskey
A shot of bathtub gin
Teach one boy how to dance
Teach another boy how to sin
Laugh under a cold, pale moon
Cry in the pouring cold rain
Sing a song of sixpence
Fill your pockets full of pain
—Sixpence

Wrap me in leather
Buckle me down in hard lace
Drape me in white
Slap a mask on my face
Tie me down to your cross
Thorn ribbons in my hair
Blood down on my face
Kill me if you dare
—Skywood

Stars on the black
Stretching out into the abyss
How could you leave me, baby?
Didn't you think you'd be missed?
A slash of metal on your arm
Stole my baby from my world
Spilled life on white tile
Death's cloak 'came unfurled
Sing a song for the Devil
Sing a song for a God

Take my baby's soul to Heaven
I'm sorry for its flaws
—Soul for the Taking

Pretty pretty baby, legs so damned long
Stop for a little bit, hear some of my song.
You've got a twitch in your hips
Something sparkly in your hair
A twinkle in your eye
And not a damned care
Watch who you tease
Watch who you break
'Cause maybe one day
Gonna be your heart that aches
—Sweet Little Tease

Hey there pretty boy
Whatcha doing over there
Come on over now
Don't just sit and stare
Show you a right good time
Show you everything I got
Blowing town in an hour
But I've got time to hit the spot
—Talk is Cheap

A word from you opened a window
A window in my soul
It showed me a way out
Of the prison I had made
I couldn't let go of my past

Forged the bars myself
Carrying every blow
Coloring in every bruise
Gripping my wounds tight
Until I bled out inside
Then you found a window
A window in my soul
Painted over, hammered shut
This window in my soul
A word from you opened it
A hug from you gave me the sky
And your love gave me wings
—Talking to Dad

The prophets and the wicked both wear
      black.
How do I tell one from the other?
When both want to kiss me,
And ask for my soul.
—The Consuming of Me

Stronger than sour mash
Harder than liquid steel
Your hands on my skin,
Pouring fire into my veins
—The Devil's Brew

I see you scraping the black,
The black on your soul
When are you going to leave him
When are you going to let go?

I see you hiding the blue
The blue on your skin
Holding in all your tears
Not letting anyone else in
What is it going to take
For you to finally see
I'm not asking you to go
I'm begging you to leave
—Tight on Time

Time's come to take me away
Leave a coin on my eye for the toll
'Cause the river man needs his pay
Don't cry 'bout the way I've gone
Or the mud I've got on my soul
I've lived the way I needed to live
No way was I making it out whole
—Toll for the River

Don't care what you look like
Don't care who you know
Don't want to see you 'round
Don't come down to my show
You're always bringing Trouble
Trouble knocking at my door
Don't fuck with the guys I play with
I don't want you here no more.
—Trouble in Spades

The sweet smell of you stayed when the
    sun came up.

I needed you there, in the flesh not in
　　dreams.
And on the nights when I cry, so deep
　　from inside.
The sheets are cold and filled with my
　　screams.
—Untitled song, Hidden Track 34

Little boy, smile oh so sweet
Swinging your ass on C-town's dirty street
Pick up your heels, move that sweet ass
　　along
Stay here much longer
Someone's gonna do you wrong
—Virgin Kiss Blues

A bit of silver for a lady
Slice of gold for a guy
Giving out my soul in pieces
Got to give it all away 'fore I die
Need to leave this world better
Better than when I found it that first day
Dance my way on through to Heaven
Hoping Hell's devils and demons
Don't hunt me down to pay
—Working Off the Red

Miles of black
Whiskey and rye
Keeps the band warm
And our damned souls dry

A million miles to go
A million miles to get right here
We've drank from every bottle
And more than our share of beer

At every single show
On yet another stage
We find you in the dark
Ready to rock and rage
—Whiskey and Rye

Long roads, bad food, no sleep in sight
Screaming our lungs out for one or a
    hundred
Strutting on stage every night
Do it for love
Do it for money
Do it for fame
Just stay in the fight
One more show to go, Sin
And everything'll be all right
—Whore's Prayer

Working in deep
End of the line
Black river at my feet
Red fire down my spine
Getting harder every day
To hold onto what is mine
—Working In Deep

415 ☆ INK • BOOK ONE

Rebel

RHYS FORD

415 Ink: Book One

The hardest thing a rebel can do isn't standing up for something—it's standing up for himself.

Life takes delight in stabbing Gus Scott in the back when he least expects it. After Gus spends years running from his past, present, and the dismal future every social worker predicted for him, karma delivers the one thing Gus could never—would never—turn his back on: a son from a one-night stand he'd had after a devastating breakup a few years ago.

Returning to San Francisco and to 415 Ink, his family's tattoo shop, gave him the perfect shelter to battle his personal demons and get himself together… until the firefighter who'd broken him walked back into Gus's life.

For Rey Montenegro, tattoo artist Gus Scott was an elusive brass ring, a glittering prize he hadn't the strength or flexibility to hold on to. Severing his relationship with the mercurial tattoo artist hurt, but Gus hadn't wanted the kind of domestic life Rey craved, leaving Rey with an aching chasm in his soul.

When Gus's life and world starts to unravel, Rey helps him pick up the pieces, and Gus wonders if that forever Rey wants is more than just a dream.

www.dreamspinnerpress.com

ONE

SCREAMS SPLINTERED the night, pulling Rey from his sleep.

He was sleepy, and the last thing he wanted was to deal with his dad, especially since there was school to go to in the morning, a high school nightmare of numbers and words jumbled into a mess he struggled to make sense out of. But the screams, they were... unsettling... different... a high-pitched whine, then a rough, raw malevolent crinkle.

So very different from how his mother usually sounded.

Then he began to cough.

He couldn't stop, not long enough to catch a full breath. Then Rey caught the smell of charred something in his lungs and worked to clear what felt like sandpaper in his throat and nose. There were more screeches, loud, horrific shrieks coming from somewhere, and the noise sent him trembling beneath his blankets. His chest hurt where his father struck it that evening, a lash of anger he didn't see coming, but it was a day like any other, a tightrope walk between time dripping slowly in anticipation of his dad's temper flaring and the tick-tick-tick of the seconds hurriedly falling off of the clock toward his bedtime.

Tonight had been bad, and he'd stepped in between the terrifying hail of fists and his mother, taking the brunt of his father's rage. His eye was tight, lashes gummy and sticking, and he'd played with the cut on his lip long enough to make it taste like silver whenever he ran his tongue over it. Now he'd begun coughing again, massive wretched spasms long and hard enough to make his ribs hurt even more than they already did.

The burning smell had to be coming from the kitchen, probably his mother leaving a plastic dish in the oven and turning it on to heat up food for his father's breakfast. It was something thoughtless she'd done a lot, stumbling from her bedroom down the hall, tired from working a double shift but awake enough to preheat the oven.

His eye wouldn't open enough to see the clock, so all Rey could make out was a thin slice of red light, a blur of numbers through the dark. He'd lived in the room for ten years, and even after all that time, the space was hard to maneuver at night. Without an outside window, the only ambient light he had was from under the door, a sliver of orange-gold leaking out around the ill-fitting wood.

The hacking hit again, and he thumped his chest to stop it. He rattled on, caught in a vicious cycle of trying to breathe around the soreness in his nose and the need to relieve the heaviness under his sternum. His tongue felt swollen, and he couldn't seem to pull up any moisture, no matter how hard he tried to hawk through the thickness in his mouth. His throat was raw, a scraped-open tenderness he wasn't able to clear with what little spit he could get out.

Blinking with his one eye, he hunted around for his glasses, knocking over everything on his nightstand, but they weren't where he could find them. The smell from the oven clung to the inside of his nose, and Rey stumbled off of his bed and straight into hell.

The light was stronger now, uneven and thick, clotted with gray puffs. Horror edged into Rey's growing concern when the switch he'd hit didn't turn on the lamp hanging in a corner of his bedroom. Rubbing at his face, he winced at the pain in his swollen eye.

It was hard to miss the roaring crackle now, and there was smoke pouring under his door, or at least he thought it was smoke. It was hard to tell... too hard to see, but the smell of it—the putrid rankness he'd come to associate with his mother's forgetfulness—permeated his closed-in room, stealing the air from his lungs. It was difficult to breathe, and Rey struggled to catch a whiff of fresh air, trying to remember what he'd been taught in school, but nothing was coming to him. His brain was shutting down into a ripe panic, and he shuffled along the wall, trying to find the door.

The knob was hot, and he screamed when it seared his palm. His cry came out weak, a watery croak of flecked spit and sand; then the wall behind him crumbled, falling forward to strike his back.

Rey didn't know how long he lay under the heavy debris. Time wasn't something he could count anymore, and what little he saw was filled with stinging ash, followed by the flash of flames eating through the rest of the room. There was a voice—somewhere—and he tried to call out, screaming at the top of his lungs, but the fetid air in his chest choked out any sound he could make, and he ended up coughing, sucking in more smoke.

"Oh...." Grandma always told him to pray, but he couldn't find the words... the faith... not with the heaviness pressing down on his legs and back. His throat hurt too much, and it felt like he'd swallowed his tongue, because he couldn't get any air past it. Shifting didn't help, and something gouged into his back, slicing his skin. Hiccupping, he fought his tears, refusing to give in to the helplessness swaddling him.

"Hey, I've got you now." A voice filtered through the crash of the fire and the walls falling. "Stay still. Got to get you out, dude. Let me know if something hurts too bad."

There were hands on his arms. Rey could feel them, even with the pressure on his back and legs, he could *feel* those hands, and he started crying, a snotty, ugly sobbing he'd have been ashamed of if he hadn't been buried beneath the wall. The hands stroked at his shoulders, and the voice, rough and dipping deep with every other word, reassured him things would be okay... *he* would be okay.

He was too scared to be okay, his lungs too full of razor blades and glass, and when he caught enough air in his chest, he wanted to cry out for his mother, ashamed at the terror the flames brought out in him.

"Hold on, need to do this. Bear told me I had to cover your nose and mouth if I could. Just stay calm," the guy half yelled at Rey. After a dig under Rey's chin, he pulled Rey's shirt up over his nose, blocking out some of the air, and Rey panicked, struggling to clear his mouth of the fabric. His rescuer patted him on the shoulders, then said, "It'll keep the smoke out. I'm going to do the same thing. Just… breathe through your shirt. Okay, kid?"

The fire was getting nearer, catching on the pieces of wood sticking out of the remaining walls. His door crumbled, blackening at the edges. Then the frame burst into a line of red, angry flames, but the shadow at his side continued to work, his hands digging into the mess pinning Rey down. The heat was getting to be unbearable, and he turned his head, the collar of his T-shirt cutting across his face. Staring at the guy's red Converses, Rey coughed, and his body took up the spasm, tightening down on his breathing.

"Almost there," the owner of the Converses said. "Give me… a second."

The weight was gone, a sudden heave of boards and sticky, crumbling drywall, and then Rey was free. The young man's arms were under him, turning him over, then carefully lifting him up from the cheap rug Rey's mom laid down in his room, but the pain, the agony of his bruised muscles was too much, and Rey screamed, louder than the sirens wailing in the distance. Bits of the rug stuck to Rey's hands and arms, melted fibers clinging to his skin where the slag touched him, and he sobbed, scared he'd pissed himself or worse when he'd been yanked out from under the house's remains.

They went a few yards or maybe even miles, he couldn't tell which, but it seemed like forever before they stopped. Everything hurt. His chest ached, and his already swollen eye was sticky with grit. A streetlamp threw down some light, and he tried to move in his rescuer's arms, twisting around to see his engulfed house topple inward.

"My mom!" Rey caught a hint of fresh air. A cold rush hit his lungs when his shirt fell from his face as the young man carefully laid him down on Mrs. Brockington's plush green lawn. He doubled over in pain when his body knotted up around his spine. "I've got to get…."

"My brother got her out on the other side of the house. He got her. I know he did. He can't…. Bear had to have gotten her out." He moved to where Rey could see him. "I need you to stay still, okay? Someone's coming to look at you—"

Rey wasn't listening anymore. He let the young man's rumbling voice roll over him, and he stretched out as much as he could on a lawn he'd never dared put a foot on at any other time in his life. He tried to speak, find the words to say thank you, but he couldn't find them any more than he could the prayers he'd needed a few moments ago.

Blinking his one good eye, Rey couldn't hold on to his focus. The night was fracturing around the edges, turning everything into prisms, and when he turned over, his legs refused to work. He could hear his mom crying—he *knew* the sound of his mother's crying—and he wanted to reassure her, to stroke her hair and tell her everything would be okay, just like he'd been told he would be okay, but he couldn't get his tongue to work either.

"Mason! You got the kid, yeah?" Another voice, this one husky and rough, carried over the roaring fire. "I got his mom out. It's just the two of them."

Rey lifted his head, straining his neck, and the blond man got up from the lawn, wiping his dirty hands on his torn jeans. Smoke pouring from the burning house swept an acrid veil over the street, and the ash carried over on the breeze stung Rey's eye. He was massive, blocking out the orange glow, and it took a second before Rey saw his mother clinging to the man's side, his arm tucked around her waist to lift her up onto the curb.

"Dad... he...." Rey pushed himself up, then collapsed back into the grass, his hands smarting too much to hold his weight. There were stinging welts along his arms, sprays of red streaks rising along his filthy skin. His lungs were still too tight, and each shuddering breath left him wanting more. The neighbors were starting to pour out of their homes, taking to the streets in an alarmed shuffle, but he couldn't see his father in the thickening crowd. "I don't know where Dad is."

"Stay here. You're hurt." The blond who'd pulled him out—Mason—spoke with a hint of authority, firm and unyielding. "Just breathe in slow. Bear's got your mom. She said it was only two of you inside. Maybe he left for something, okay?"

There was a third guy, a kid about his age, running ahead of the older man half carrying his mother. Coltish, his young man's long legs ate up the distance between the street and Mrs. Brockington's lush front lawn. The white streetlights did funny things to the teen's hair, turning it nearly opaque gray, but there were flashes of gold and russet tucked into the strands, and when he turned to look at Rey, his eyes were a rich silver, a shimmering color he'd only seen in the moon.

If Rey hadn't already had problems pulling air in, the starlight-eyed lanky teen would have stolen his breath away.

Cocky—his brain whispered—the kind of too-fucking-gorgeous guy he hated in school, but damn if he didn't want to lose his first kiss to that smirking mouth. A dimple played coy on his cheek, a flash of a smile nearly as bright as his eyes, and Rey's hand curled into a fist, tightening at the tickle of something he couldn't understand forming in his belly. The fist didn't last long, unable to hold when the burned skin on his palm stretched and cracked open, leaving his flesh raw and weeping. Gasping, he fell into another hacking spasm, and the teen frowned.

"Gus, go tell the ambulance to come around." If Mason carried a thread of authority in his voice, the wide-shouldered man who gently set Rey's mother down wore his strength and confidence like a suit of battle-tested armor. Up close the guy went from massive to alarming, his dark hair pulled back from a harsh, strong face with a scar cutting through his right eyebrow. "*Now*, kid. Not later."

"Okay." Moving out of the way for the large man, the kid dropped an unopened bottle of water on the ground next to Rey's side. Then he was gone, swallowed up by the cloud of flecked smoke and the milling crowd.

The sirens were louder this time, but he could still hear his mother when she sobbed as she grabbed at his shirt, knotting her fingers into the fabric, then the murmur of the saviors someone—a saint or God—sent to pull him free from the inferno eating through his life. There were reassurances, different phrases than he would have used, but they seemed to quiet her, and she lay on the grass next to him, curling around him as if they were on the couch, watching an old movie she'd found on one of the free cable stations.

"Thank God. You're okay. Thank God they… oh God," his mother finally whispered, her face as wet as Rey's, but she let her tears fall, creating odd lines through the soot on her cheeks. "I don't even know how they... I don't know their names."

"It's Gus, Mom," Rey mumbled around the ash in his mouth. "Mason, Bear, and Gus."

"JESUS CHRIST, that hurts," Rey playfully bitched at the purple-haired younger man bent over his side. "You sure you know how to use that thing?"

No one threw a withering stare like Ivo, Mason's youngest blood brother, and Rey was amused when the inker's dark blue eyes narrowed. A chuckle from the next stall broke through the stinging silence, and Rey joined in, no longer trying to keep still under the stylus of vibrating needles held a few inches above his bared hip.

"He can take it, Ivo," Tokugawa called out from his spot in 415 Ink's guest stall, a midshop spot usually reserved for masters in the industry and directly across from a stall Rey refused to even glance at. "I've given him worse."

"Challenge accepted," the maligned artist mumbled, rolling his shoulders back, then resting his elbow on the massage table Rey'd stretched out on nearly half an hour before. "Remember, Montenegro, just because you're Mace's best friend, doesn't mean you're mine."

The first time Rey Montenegro went under the machine, it was to sublimate one of the scars on his side. He'd worn the smeared tangle of flesh for nearly ten years before he decided he was done carrying around his father's handiwork. It'd been Bear who'd taken the keloid and buried it beneath a Japanese-style tiger leaping up from his thigh to his hip, blending away white-gray streaks and pale pink patches until Rey no longer saw the marks of his father's abandonment on his skin.

There were other tats after that, but the first one—that tiger—pushed him in ways he hadn't even understood at the time.

And now it was time to finish the dragon on his other hip, to put himself under the vibrating needles again and own a little bit more of his own body.

He'd found a spot for his convertible in the parking structure a few blocks down from the shop, a monstrous cement thing meant to suck up the congestion on Jefferson Street, but nothing could stop the traffic along the piers' main thoroughfare. After dropping a couple of bucks into the tip cup belonging to a cowboy-hat-wearing guitarist slung against a pub's post, Rey dashed across the busy street, dodging bodies in the stream of tourists hustling to hit Fisherman's Wharf before the rain clouds broke open. A light drizzle ghosted over him, catching on his lashes, and he had a brief flash of regret in leaving the top of his car up when he left, since he was sick of being cooped up. After having spent the past few days either in the firehouse or on one of the trucks, heading into the flames or leaving covered in doubt and soot, the water-kissed San Francisco wind was nice to feel on his skin, even if he'd last about a second under its icy bite.

415 Ink shouldered itself into a spot between a souvenir shop bristling with T-shirts and cups bearing witty slogans and poorly drawn San Francisco landmarks and a fairly tame champagne lounge chasing after naughty-minded Midwestern tourists looking for a semi-risqué time amid the shirtless waiters, nacho fries, and two-dollar tacos. The tattoo shop was in a sweet location across the pier, the result of some deal Bear made with the owner of the building nearly ten years before. There'd been some mutterings from the owner

of the champagne lounge, sour-grapes rumors spread when Bear first opened, but they quieted down after Bear had a talk with him.

Now the man avoided Bear and the rest of the staff like the plague, something that seemed to suit everyone just fine.

Rey didn't know the details or even want to know what was said. Very few people crossed Barrett "Bear" Jackson, and those that had usually were nowhere to be found afterward. In the years since he'd known Bear and his oddball family, Rey had only heard the man raise his voice once, and that was one time too many. Still, when he'd walked into the shop earlier that afternoon, Rey only had a wide grin for the broad-shouldered man standing behind 415 Ink's front counter and bit back a pained grunt when Bear reached over and slapped him on the arm in a hearty hello. His arm still stung from the slap after half an hour, but he wasn't going to mention it, especially not to Ivo.

One didn't show weakness to any of the 415 Ink blood brothers, not unless a guy was willing to hear about it for the rest of his life.

He hadn't been in the shop in a while, but not much had changed. There was a new artist in the space next to Missy, one of the shop's full-timers, and at some point, the poured concrete floor got a coat of something shiny on it, but the long shotgun-style space still sported a high ceiling painted black and creamy walls covered in various sketches, colored-in drawings, and the occasional photo. The shop's eight half-wall stalls with their tied-back opaque-white curtains reminded Rey of a stable, but he was thankful for the privacy, especially since he was lying on his side with his ass half out while Ivo worked on him. The stalls were large, giving an inker space to not only maneuver around a broad massage table and worktable but left enough room for a couple of chairs or one massive, shaggy mutt named Earl, who'd only wander out from behind the reception area to visit people he liked.

Rey took a secret delight at Earl, sprawled out close enough to him to scratch at the dog's ears.

"Okay, love," Tokugawa murmured from the next stall. "We're done here. Let me clean you off and you can take a look at it in the mirror."

The familiar scent of astringent cleaner drifted over to Rey, and he lifted his head, catching a glimpse of the watercolor lotus tattoo, a spray of rich, soothing pinks, purples, and greens over a traditional Asian outline on an expanse of pale skin. The newly inked young woman met Rey's eyes around the partially open curtain and smiled, twisting around while holding the strap of her tank top under her arm. The piece covered a broad section on her chest near her right collarbone, draping tendrils of color and connective black lines up over her shoulder.

Holding a mirror up in front of her, Tokugawa asked, "What do you think, Steph? It's a blend, no? Henna-like outline but watercolor effect."

She stood breathless, a curvaceous blonde with sweet face, then exhaled slowly, her voice a rough, awed whisper, "Oh man, Ichi, it's… perfect."

"Good, let me wrap you up and you can get dressed." He cocked his head, a quirky smile lightening the seriousness of his Japanese features. "Well, not that you're naked, but it is cold outside, and you don't want any of this on your leather jacket."

"Down, Montenegro." Ivo tapped the back of Rey's head, a light rap of knuckles only softened by Rey's thick hair. "You're fucking with my canvas."

"Where's the dog?" Bear called out from the front, and Earl lifted his head, sniffing at the air. "Earl!"

"Better go, dude," Ivo murmured, scritching the dog with the toe of his red heels. His pleated black kilt shifted, exposing more of his lean, muscled shin. "Don't want Bear to come looking for you."

Heaving to his feet, Earl sighed, then shuffled off to the front of the shop. His toenails clicked on the floor, an echoing castanet chorus, before ending in a groaning thump of seventy-five pounds of dog slumping down on a covered piece of memory foam. Ivo's bark of laughter was subdued but sharp enough to hook Rey's curiosity.

Then the needles hit and Rey forgot all about the dog, Ivo's knees, or his fuck-me red pumps.

"Shit, a little warning, bitch," he grumbled around the pain.

"Oh, by the way, Montenegro"—Ivo's gleeful mutter tickled Rey's spine—"you're going to get a tattoo now. In this tattoo shop. You know, that place that does tattoos."

"Fuck you, kid," Rey shot back, then gasped when Ivo did something that felt like a lick of fire along his hip bone. "Fuck you for that too."

"Yeah, I'm not the brother you want to fuck," the younger man replied softly. "And speaking of the prodigal son, he's back, you know?"

Playing dumb with Ivo never worked, but Rey tried it anyway. "What the hell are you talking about?"

RHYS FORD is an award-winning author with several long-running LGBT+ mystery, thriller, paranormal, and urban fantasy series and is a two-time LAMBDA finalist with her *Murder and Mayhem* novels. She is also a 2017 Gold and Silver Medal winner in the Florida Authors and Publishers President's Book Awards for her novels *Ink and Shadows* and *Hanging the Stars*. She is published by Dreamspinner Press and DSP Publications.

She shares the house with Harley, a gray tuxedo with a flower on her face, Badger, a disgruntled alley cat who isn't sure living inside is a step up the social ladder, as well as a ginger cairn terrorist named Gus. Rhys is also enslaved to the upkeep of a 1979 Pontiac Firebird and enjoys murdering make-believe people.

Rhys can be found at the following locations:

Blog: www.rhysford.com

Facebook: www.facebook.com/rhys.ford.author

Twitter: @Rhys_Ford

RHYS FORD

SINNER'S GIN

"A raw, sexy read..." — *USA Today*

Sinners Series: Book One

There's a dead body in Miki St. John's vintage Pontiac GTO, and he has no idea how it got there.

After Miki survives the tragic accident that killed his best friend and the other members of their band, Sinner's Gin, all he wants is to hide from the world in the refurbished warehouse he bought before their last tour. But when the man who sexually abused him as a boy is killed and his remains are dumped in Miki's car, Miki fears Death isn't done with him yet.

Kane Morgan, the SFPD inspector renting space in the art co-op next door, initially suspects Miki had a hand in the man's murder, but Kane soon realizes Miki is as much a victim as the man splattered inside the GTO. As the murderer's body count rises, the attraction between Miki and Kane heats up. Neither man knows if they can make a relationship work, but despite Miki's emotional damage, Kane is determined to teach him how to love and be loved — provided, of course, Kane can catch the killer before Miki becomes the murderer's final victim.

www.dreamspinnerpress.com

BOOK TWO OF THE SINNERS SERIES
RHYS FORD

WHISKEY
AND WRY

*"This story is such a rollercoaster ride and Ford
just keeps the excitement coming"* — Joyfully Jay

BOOK THREE OF THE SINNERS SERIES

RHYS FORD

TEQUILA
MOCKINGBIRD

Sequel to *Whiskey and Wry*
Sinners Series: Book Three

Lieutenant Connor Morgan of SFPD's SWAT division wasn't looking for love. Especially not in a man. His life plan didn't include one Forest Ackerman, a brown-eyed, blond drummer who's as sexy as he is trouble. His family depends on him to be like his father, a solid pillar of strength who'll one day lead the Morgan clan.

No, Connor has everything worked out—a career in law enforcement, a nice house, and a family. Instead, he finds a murdered man while on a drug raid and loses his heart comforting the man's adopted son. It wasn't like he'd never thought about men — it's just loving one doesn't fit into his plans.

Forest Ackerman certainly doesn't need to be lusting after a straight cop, even if Connor Morgan is everywhere he looks, especially after Frank's death. He's just talked himself out of lusting for the brawny cop when his coffee shop becomes a war zone and Connor Morgan steps in to save him.

Whoever killed his father seems intent on Forest joining him in the afterlife. As the killer moves closer to achieving his goal, Forest tangles with Connor Morgan and is left wondering what he'll lose first—his life or his heart.

www.dreamspinnerpress.com

BOOK FOUR OF THE SINNERS SERIES

RHYS FORD

SLOE RIDE

"Rife with mystery and intrigue." — *Fresh Fiction*

Sequel to *Tequila Mockingbird*
Sinners Series: Book Four

It isn't easy being a Morgan. Especially when dead bodies start piling up and there's not a damned thing you can do about it.

Quinn Morgan never quite fit into the family mold. He dreamed of a life with books instead of badges and knowledge instead of law—and a life with Rafe Andrade, his older brothers' bad boy friend and the man who broke his very young heart.

Rafe Andrade returned home to lick his wounds following his ejection from the band he helped form. A recovering drug addict, Rafe spends his time wallowing in guilt, until he finds himself faced with his original addiction, Quinn Morgan—the reason he fled the city in the first place.

When Rafe hears the Sinners are looking for a bassist, it's a chance to redeem himself, but as a crazed murderer draws closer to Quinn, Rafe's willing to sacrifice everything—including himself—to keep his quixotic Morgan safe and sound.

www.dreamspinnerpress.com

RHYS FORD

ABSINTHE OF MALICE

Sequel to *Sloe Ride*
Sinners Series: Book Five

We're getting the band back together.

Those six words send a chill down Miki St. John's spine, especially when they're spoken with a nearly religious fervor by his brother-in-all-but-blood, Damien Mitchell. However, those words were nothing compared to what Damien says next.

And we're going on tour.

When Crossroads Gin hits the road, Damien hopes it will draw them closer together. There's something magical about being on tour, especially when traveling in a van with no roadies, managers, or lovers to act as a buffer. The band is already close, but Damien knows they can be more—brothers of sorts, bound not only by familial ties but by their intense love for music.

As they travel from gig to gig, the band is haunted by past mistakes and personal demons, but they forge on. For Miki, Damie, Forest, and Rafe, the stage is where they all truly come alive, and the music they play is as important to them as the air they breathe.

But those demons and troubles won't leave them alone, and with every mile under their belts, the band faces its greatest challenge—overcoming their deepest flaws and not killing one another along the way.

www.dreamspinnerpress.com